Moses

A Lost Egyptian Account of the Legend of Moses

Book One of the Moses Trilogy

by

Mechiel Pentz

A historical novel informed by the Biblical Lunar-Solar Chronology

Confirmation

What if Moses wasn't just raised in Pharaoh's court… but once ruled it?

This is the first book in a bold historical fiction trilogy that reopens one of the oldest mysteries of the ancient world. An Egyptologist, driven by a deep conviction shaped by years of personal study, has always believed what few dare to suggest—that Moses was, in fact, Pharaoh Thutmose II.

His search for confirmation leads him to a hidden chamber in ancient Thebes, the final resting place of an obscure prince named Menkheperre, son of Thutmose III. Inside, he uncovers inscriptions that appear to support his theory—that the final twelve years of Thutmose III's reign were not his alone.

Moses: A Lost Egyptian Account of the Legend of Moses is a powerful narrative told through the Egyptologist's own voice as he pieces together the lives of Kamose, Ahmose I, Amenhotep I, Thutmose I, Hatshepsut, Thutmose II, and the events that led to the exile of Moses.

Where historical records grow silent, faith and discovery fill the gaps— and a buried legacy begins to rise.

Moses – A Lost Egyptian Account of the Legend of Moses

(A historical novel informed by the Biblical Lunar-Solar Chronology)

First Edition

ISBN (Paperback): 978-1-7641625-5-5

Cover design by Mechiel Pentz

To contact the author or learn more, email:
mapenprojects@gmail.com

Table of Content

To the silent scribes of history,

who left behind echoes for us to uncover.

— M.P.

"And Moses was learned in all the wisdom of the Egyptians, and was mighty in words and in deeds."

— Acts 7:22

Preface

Every historian walks a lonely road when their theory contradicts consensus.

Mine began not with certainty, but with a troubling clue—a fragment here, a name scratched where it did not belong. A pattern emerged, overlooked by some and outright rejected by others.

People know Moses was adopted. A Hebrew child, raised in privilege but never truly belonging. But what if everything we assumed was wrong?

What if Moses didn't just grow up in Pharaoh's palace—what if he ruled from it?

For years, I followed that dangerous question through libraries, tombs, and temples. Most dismissed it. Heresy, they called it. Fiction. But then I found the chamber in Thebes. The name carved there—Menkheperre—wasn't just a forgotten prince. It was a key. A voice from a time when two histories overlapped: one buried in sand, the other buried in scripture.

This trilogy tells that story. Not just of ancient Egypt, but of a conviction slowly unfolding into a revelation.

Arthur Maddison

Chapter 1 - The Secret of the Monastery

January 2011 St. Mark Cathedral, Alexandria, Egypt

The January sun beat down mercilessly on Alexandria's ancient streets, baking the stone and sending heat waves shimmering across the polished marble floors of St Mark's Cathedral. Bishop Farouk Ahmani moved with the silent caution of a man hunted, his sandaled feet barely making a sound despite his considerable frame. The coarse fabric of his borrowed civilian clothing chafed against his skin, so different from the smooth comfort of his clerical vestments, but anonymity was worth the discomfort.

The vast cathedral around him held memories of centuries, its walls bearing silent witness to the persecution of Copts through the ages. Farouk's gaze swept across the ancient mosaics depicting St. Mark bringing Christianity to Egypt's shores in the first century AD. These images had survived conquests, fires, and the relentless march of time— just as his people had survived.

Outside, the modern city of Alexandria pulsed with life—car horns, vendors' cries, and the constant hum of five million souls navigating their daily existence. Yet beneath the surface, tensions simmered like water before the boil. Political unrest stirred in coffee houses and university halls, whispered conversations about change and revolution. The grip of decades-old power structures was beginning to loosen, and everyone could sense the tremor of coming upheaval.

But within these sacred walls, time seemed to slow, creating a pocket of stillness in which history and present coexisted in fragile harmony.

He paused, nostrils flaring slightly as he detected the faint scent of incense that still clung to the heavy curtain before him. With practiced hands, he drew it aside to reveal the ancient panel that generations of persecuted Copts had used for survival. The carved stone moved reluctantly under his powerful push, groaning like a wounded beast.

The darkness beyond gaped like the mouth of some primordial creature. Farouk's mind flashed with unbidden images—the massacre weeks earlier, blood pooling on these very cathedral steps, the screams of the faithful cut short by gunfire. He clenched his jaw until his teeth ached, forcing the memories back into their box.

The church bombing had claimed twenty-three lives. He had administered last rites to the dying, their blood staining his vestments as he murmured ancient prayers. After the funerals, he had wept alone in his chambers, questioning God's plan. But now he understood—the massacre had been what drove him to seek solace in the ancient texts, which had led to his discovery. God's ways were indeed mysterious.

"Control yourself," he growled, his voice a rumble in the emptiness. "The discovery is all that matters now."

The passageway engulfed him, cold and dank, smelling of centuries of dust and secrets. Farouk moved with the confidence of a lion in familiar territory, his fingers trailing along rough-hewn walls that had witnessed the passage of frightened Christians for nearly two millennia. Each intersection was a decision made without hesitation, each turn taking him closer to the street and the vital mission that consumed him.

The stones beneath his fingers told stories of their own—of Roman persecutions, of Arab conquests, of Ottoman rule. How many frightened souls had passed through these tunnels, their hearts hammering with the desperate desire to survive? Farouk felt their presence like whispers against his skin, the communion of saints made tangible in this sacred darkness.

When his foot found the ancient step—worn smooth by generations of desperate flights—he knew he had reached his exit point. The wall before him yielded reluctantly to his shoulder, the stone scraping against stone with the reluctance of age. Sunlight lanced through the narrow opening like a spear thrust, momentarily blinding him.

Alexandria stretched before him in all its chaotic glory—a city where past and present collided in a cacophony of car horns, shouting vendors, and the distant cry of muezzins. The Mediterranean sparkled beyond the jumble of buildings, blue and vast as it had been when Alexander himself had stood upon these shores and dreamed of empire.

The ancient city had been reborn countless times—Greek, Roman, Byzantine, Islamic, modern. Each iteration built upon the bones of the previous, creating a palimpsest of human ambition and faith. And now, Farouk held a secret that could illuminate one of history's shadowed corners, revealing truths hidden for millennia.

A group of Coptic faithfuls approached, candles clutched in work-worn hands, faces etched with the quiet determination of the persecuted. The men wore their crosses openly despite the risk, while the women's headscarves covered hair but not conviction. Before they could recognize their spiritual leader in his common garb, Farouk melted around the corner like a leopard avoiding hunters.

The yellow taxi gleamed like a nugget of gold in the merciless sun. Farouk raised his arm decisively.

"Taxi!" The word exploded from his chest.

The vehicle screeched to a halt with typical Egyptian disregard for physics, stopping mere inches from Farouk's knees. He yanked the door open and threw himself inside, the smell of cheap cigarettes and cheaper cologne assaulting his nostrils.

A small plastic figurine of President Mubarak dangled from the rearview mirror, swinging wildly with the taxi's abrupt stop. The irony wasn't lost on Farouk—a symbol of secular authority in a country where religious tensions simmered beneath the surface of uneasy coexistence, and political change lurked just beyond the horizon. Egypt was a pressure cooker, and the recent church bombings had only turned up the heat.

"Maritime Jolie Ville Hotel. Quickly!" Farouk commanded, his eyes constantly scanning the rearview mirror for the telltale signs of pursuit. The driver—a scarred man with the hawkish nose of his Bedouin ancestors—merely grunted and hurled the taxi into Alexandria's chaotic traffic flow with suicidal abandon.

The taxi plunged into the stream of vehicles with reckless determination, weaving between buses belching diesel fumes and ancient

Fiats held together with hope and baling wire. The driver leaned on his horn continuously, the sound blending with the thousand other horns to create Alexandria's urban symphony.

"You're in a hurry, father?" the driver asked, his eyes meeting Farouk's in the rearview mirror. Despite the borrowed clothing, something about Farouk's bearing had revealed his calling.

"A matter of great importance," Farouk replied, unwilling to say more.

The driver nodded, accepting the cryptic answer with the fatalism so characteristic of Egyptians. "Allah's will is mysterious," he offered philosophically, swerving around a donkey cart laden with vegetables.

The journey was an eternity compressed into moments. Farouk's broad hands kneaded his thighs restlessly as the taxi weaved through the congested arteries of the ancient city. His mind raced with possibilities—what if Professor Maddison had already departed? What if his enemies had reached the Englishman first?

They passed the great Biblioteca Alexandrina, its vast circular form a modern echo of the ancient library that had housed the world's knowledge before flames had claimed it centuries ago. Knowledge was fragile, Farouk reflected—inscriptions could be erased, history could be twisted to serve the needs of the powerful. But sometimes, rarely, truth survived buried beneath the weight of millennia, waiting for the right hands to unearth it.

Maritime Jolie Ville Hotel

When the ornate facade of the Maritime Jolie Ville finally appeared ahead like a mirage, Farouk thrust a handful of notes at the driver—far more than the fare demanded—and launched himself from the vehicle before it had fully stopped.

"Istanna!" The driver's curse followed him, but Farouk was already pushing through the hotel's glass doors, his eyes rapidly scanning the elegant lobby with the practiced vigilance of the perpetually hunted.

The hotel lobby was awash in colonial elegance—marble floors polished to a mirror shine, potted palms creating islands of greenery, uniformed staff moving with practiced efficiency. Western tourists lounged in plush chairs, their pale skin and casual attire marking them as clearly as tribal scarification might mark members of a distant culture.

His heart plummeted like a stone dropped into the Nile's depths. The lobby was devoid of any figure resembling the distinguished Professor Arthur Maddison—the one man in Egypt who could give meaning to his discovery. A discovery that could change history itself.

Farouk's shoulders sagged beneath the weight of divine timing missed, his feet suddenly leaden as he moved aimlessly across the polished marble. The bishop's normally sharp senses, dulled by disappointment, failed to register the commotion until an aristocratic English voice sliced through his despair like a scimitar through silk.

"This is utterly unacceptable!" The voice carried the unmistakable gravity of Cambridge education and gentlemen's clubs. "How could you possibly leave my laptop unattended?"

Farouk's head snapped up with the speed of a cobra striking. There, not twenty paces away, stood Professor Arthur Maddison himself—tall, imperious, his aquiline features flushed with rage as he berated the cowering receptionist. The sight sent a surge of primal hope through Farouk's powerful frame.

The Englishman embodied the archetypal Western academic— tweed jacket despite the heat, wire-rimmed spectacles perched on an aristocratic nose, silver hair precisely trimmed. His posture spoke of privilege and authority, a man accustomed to moving through the world with the confidence born of centuries of imperial dominance.

Farouk approached cautiously, his eyes scanning for watchers with the wariness of a gazelle at a water hole. This moment—this single, precious moment—could change everything.

"Professor Maddison," Farouk ventured, his accent rolling the name like smooth stones in a riverbed.

The Englishman turned, his eyes flashing with the irritation of interrupted fury. "What? Can't you see I'm occupied? Unless you know the whereabouts of my laptop, I have no interest in conversation!" The words shot forth like bullets, each one precisely aimed.

Farouk watched helplessly as Maddison snatched up his luggage and stormed toward the waiting taxi outside, moving with the determined stride of a man pursued by deadlines rather than zealots.

"Please, Professor—" Farouk broke into a trot, his heart hammering against his ribs like a prisoner demanding release.

Maddison slammed his luggage into the taxi's boot with unnecessary force before turning to face the bishop. His features were set in the dismissive mask common to academics interrupted in their righteous indignation.

"Look here, I'm dreadfully late. If you have questions, my website provides contact information. Good day to you." The finality in his tone was that of a door being bolted.

"Just one moment, please." Desperation lent Farouk's fingers unusual dexterity as he extracted the folded photograph from his pocket. "I have something you might wish to see."

"Good day, sir." The boot slammed with the finality of a coffin lid.

Panic surged through Farouk's veins like wildfire. In that moment of desperation, instinct took command of reason.

"Menkheperre is the incarnate son of Thutmose III!" The words burst from him like a prayer, ancient and powerful.

The effect was immediate. Maddison's hand froze on the taxi door, his body tensing like a leopard scenting prey. When he turned, the irritation in his eyes had been replaced by something far more potent—academic curiosity, the most powerful force in an Egyptologist's universe.

Farouk thrust the photograph forward. "I took a picture of this hieroglyphic inscription at Luxor. Look at the encircled area!"

The professor took the photograph with the reverence of a priest accepting a sacred relic. As his eyes fixed upon the image, Farouk watched the transformation—from annoyance to disbelief to the hungry gleam of discovery.

Chapter 2 - The Journey to Secrets

Ride to the Airport

"Will you ride with me to the airport? We can talk on the way." Farouk hesitated but then accepted the invitation. He could arrange with the driver to bring him back.

As they settled into the taxi's worn leather seats, tension sparked between them—intellectual, urgent, alive. The driver pulled away from the curb, inserting the vehicle into Alexandria's chaotic traffic flow with the practiced ease of a surgeon wielding a scalpel.

"This is... extraordinary," Maddison whispered, his voice suddenly dry as the desert winds. "How did you come by this?" His fingers trembled slightly as they ran over the photograph's inked symbols. "This appears to be some manner of king's list, but Menkheperre is prominently featured as Thutmose III's successor, claiming to be his incarnation." His eyes, sharp as a falcon's, fixed on Farouk. "Where precisely did you discover this?"

The photograph showed a section of wall covered in pristine hieroglyphs, the colors still vibrant despite the passage of millennia. The encircled section depicted a royal figure wearing the double crown of Upper and Lower Egypt, with cartouches naming him as both Menkheperre and, impossibly, as Thutmose III reborn.

"Beneath a Coptic church in Luxor," Farouk replied, sensing the shift in power between them. He deliberately avoided naming the specific location. "There's an entire chamber, Professor—walls covered with inscriptions that tell Menkheperre's version of how his great-grandfather defeated the Hyksos and established the 18th Dynasty."

Outside the taxi window, Alexandria's varied architecture flashed by—Ottoman-era apartments with wooden balconies weathered by Mediterranean breezes, Soviet-style concrete blocks built during Nasser's time, gleaming glass towers representing Egypt's uncertain future. The city was a physical manifestation of the layered histories that had shaped this ancient land.

"If authentic, this is..." Maddison's voice trailed off as he studied the photograph with the focus of a man glimpsing the undoing of everything, he thought he knew.

Silence stretched between them, filled only by the ambient noise of the city and the taxi drivers tuneless humming. Maddison's mind was clearly racing, calculating the implications of such a discovery for established chronologies, for accepted wisdom, for his own career.

"Professor," Farouk pressed, sensing victory within his grasp, "this could fundamentally alter our understanding of the 18th Dynasty. These inscriptions have remained hidden for thousands of years."

The 18th Dynasty had been Egypt's golden age—the era of Hatshepsut, the female pharaoh who ruled as king; of Thutmose III, the Napoleon of ancient Egypt; of Akhenaten, the heretic king who had abandoned traditional gods for the worship of the sun disk; of Tutankhamun, whose golden tomb had captivated the modern world. To discover new information about this period was the dream of every Egyptologist.

"Tell me more about where you found this," Maddison pressed, leaning closer. "How deep beneath the church? What condition were the inscriptions?"

Farouk's eyes glinted with the satisfaction of a fisherman who feels the tug on his line. "The chamber lies beneath a monastery guest house— a structure built about a hundred and fifty years ago, but standing on foundations far more ancient. The inscriptions are in remarkable condition—protected from light, moisture, and human interference."

Before Farouk could elaborate further, there was a sudden loud bang and the taxi jolted violently. Both men were thrown forward as the driver slammed on the brakes.

"What was that?" Maddison cried, clutching his precious photograph.

The taxi veered onto a side street and slowed to a stop. Farouk gripped the door handle tightly, his body tense. When the driver exited to examine the vehicle, Farouk's eyes darted nervously around the street, searching for any sign of pursuit.

They had stopped in a narrow alley lined with shops selling everything from copper pots to cell phone accessories. Merchants stood in doorways, watching with mild interest as the taxi driver circled his vehicle, cursing fluently in Arabic. Above them, laundry fluttered from balconies like colorful flags, and satellite dishes pointed skyward like modern prayer wheels.

"We have a blown tire!" the driver announced after knocking on Professor Maddison's window.

They climbed out to see the driver already removing luggage from the trunk to access the spare tire. The tire lay in ruins, rubber shredded like confetti around a metal carcass. Alexandria's streets were notorious for debris—broken glass, metal scraps, the detritus of urban life that claimed countless tires daily.

Maddison pulled out his mobile phone and made a call that Farouk quickly understood was to his travel agent.

"My agent said it's impossible to delay the plane any longer," Professor Maddison reported after ending the call. "He'll phone back about rescheduling."

The Mediterranean sun beat down on them mercilessly as they waited, heat rising from the pavement in visible waves. Sweat beaded on Maddison's forehead, his tweed jacket now an instrument of torture in the Egyptian climate. Farouk remained impassive, his body accustomed to the heat, his mind focused on the prize within reach.

"The British have been excavating Egypt for centuries," Farouk observed casually. "Carter found Tutankhamun, Petrie established scientific methodology, Belzoni carried away colossal statues. But this— this could eclipse them all."

Maddison's eyes never left the photograph. "Carter had Carnarvon's backing. Petrie had the Palestine Exploration Fund. Who supports your work, Bishop?"

"I have only the Church," Farouk replied with quiet dignity. "And now, perhaps, you."

As the driver worked on changing the tire, Maddison's phone rang again. His expression fell as he listened.

"The next available flight to London is in three days," he announced, then added with reluctant pragmatism, "It seems I'm returning to the hotel for an extended stay."

"You can stay at my place tonight," Farouk offered quickly, delighted when Professor Maddison accepted. The prospect of three days in Alexandria clearly troubled the Professor, but the lure of the discovery was proving stronger than his discomfort.

He turned to the driver, his voice suddenly firm with purpose. "There's been a change of plans." He turned back to Farouk with the hungry look of a man who had just glimpsed a world-altering truth.

"This had better justify missing my flight," he said, though the excitement dancing in his eyes belied his stern tone. "When can we depart for Luxor?"

"We can arrange transportation tomorrow," Farouk replied, relief flooding through him like cool water.

When the tire was changed, Farouk directed the driver to return to the Coptic church. As they settled into the backseat, Professor Maddison could barely keep his eyes off the hieroglyphic fragment.

"You must understand the significance of what you've found," he said, voice hushed. "If genuine, this contradicts established chronology. Menkheperre as Thutmose III's spiritual vessel? It's revolutionary."

Beyond the city's edge, the desert stretched vast and timeless. Egypt was a ribbon of green hugging the life-giving Nile, surrounded by sand that had devoured countless civilizations. Yet somehow, miraculously, the ancient voices survived—in tombs, in temples, and now in a hidden chamber beneath a humble monastery.

Farouk nodded solemnly. "That's precisely why I sought you out, Professor. Your expertise on the Thutmosid succession is unparalleled."

Residence of Farouk Ahmani

They arrived to find the rear of the church deserted, though they could hear angry demonstrators at the front. After paying the driver generously, they entered through a side entrance.

The church interior offered cool refuge after the harsh sunlight outside. Icons of saints gazed down from the walls with solemn, almond-shaped eyes—St. Mark, St. Anthony, St. Catherine of Alexandria—their golden haloes catching what little light filtered through the narrow windows. Heavy air hung with the lingering scent of incense from the morning's liturgy.

Farouk led Maddison through a series of corridors, past small chapels where votive candles flickered beneath images of the Virgin Mary, past storerooms filled with ecclesiastical supplies, to a heavy wooden door set in a stone archway. A simple iron key unlocked it, revealing modest living quarters beyond.

"Please take a seat," he said, gesturing to a small table with chairs.

The room was austere—a narrow bed, a wooden desk with a chair, bookshelves laden with theological texts in Arabic, Coptic, and Greek. A simple wooden cross hung on the whitewashed wall above the bed. The only concession to modern life was a small electric kettle and a stack of papers next to a worn laptop.

As they settled, Farouk explained, "We're in the old section of the church, estimated to be over three hundred years old. These rooms belonged to Bishop Christos, who raised me after my parents died when I was seven. He promised them he wouldn't let me go to an orphanage." Farouk's voice softened. "He became like a father to me. He died about three months ago, and the church made me the regional auxiliary bishop, which is why I live here now."

The setting sun cast long shadows across the stone floor, bathing the simple room in amber light. Outside, the calls of street vendors gradually gave way to the evening adhan, the muezzin's melodious call to prayer floating across the city from a hundred minarets.

"What does a regional auxiliary bishop do?" Maddison inquired.

"I visit Coptic churches to check on building conditions," Farouk explained. "Two weeks ago, I visited a monastery in Luxor. It's about two hundred years old and was being renovated with proper permits, but Islamic extremists violently objected to the restoration work—the presence of crosses, bells, and domes. They even prevented Coptic Christians from leaving their homes for several days."

Egypt's Coptic community had endured persecution across centuries—from Roman times through Arab conquests, from Ottoman neglect to modern sectarian tensions. Yet they had survived, preserving their ancient language in liturgy, their faith in private, their identity against all odds.

Farouk leaned forward, his voice dropping. "I stayed in the oldest guest house on the property. During my inspection, I found a door that had been sealed and forgotten. Using my keys, I managed to open it." His eyes took on a distant look, as if seeing again that moment of discovery. "Behind it was a shaft leading down into darkness—far older than the monastery above. I descended carefully with a torch and found myself in a narrow passage that opened into the chamber."

"The chamber was untouched—as pristine as the day it was sealed. Hieroglyphs still bearing traces of original pigment. The air so ancient it felt like breathing in history itself."

Maddison interrupted eagerly, "Can I see this room?"

"It's over thirteen hours by road," Farouk replied, "impossible within your current timeframe."

"We can fly there!" Professor Maddison declared immediately, pulling out his phone to call his travel agent.

Night had fallen, turning the windows into black mirrors that trapped the lamplight inside. The sounds of the city had diminished to a distant murmur, like waves breaking on a faraway shore. In the quiet of the ancient church, two men from different worlds conspired to unearth secrets that had lain hidden for millennia.

After a brief conversation, he announced triumphantly, "We have flights booked to Luxor for tomorrow morning." He looked pleased, like a schoolboy who had successfully solved a difficult equation.

A chapel boy silently entered with a bowl of fruit, placing it before Professor Maddison before disappearing. The boy's eyes had widened briefly at the sight of the foreign visitor, but training and respect had kept him from showing obvious curiosity.

"Please excuse me," Farouk said, rising. "I need to make arrangements before we leave tomorrow. Make yourself comfortable in my room and rest—tomorrow will be a long day."

As Farouk left, he glanced back to see Professor Maddison still studying the photograph, eyes alight with academic fervor, fingers tracing the ancient symbols as if they might yield their secrets through touch alone.

In the privacy of an adjoining chamber, Farouk knelt before a small icon of the Virgin and Child. His prayers were silent but urgent—for guidance, for protection, for wisdom. The modern world and ancient Egypt were about to collide, and he stood at the intersection, a gatekeeper to forgotten knowledge. The responsibility weighed heavily on his shoulders.

Travel to Luxor

The ancient words of morning prayer were still on Farouk's lips when he knocked on the door with a tray of tea and biscuits. "It's time to go," he announced, leaving Professor Maddison to prepare.

Five minutes later, Professor Maddison emerged freshly shaven and in clean clothes. Outside in the pre-dawn darkness, a taxi awaited them.

The road to Borg El Arab Airport was quiet, though their taxi, moving at 130 km/h, was still overtaken by even faster vehicles. The eastern horizon was just beginning to lighten; the first tentative brushstrokes of dawn painting the sky in pale gold and rose. Egypt was waking to another day that would unfold beneath the same sun that had witnessed the rise and fall of pharaohs.

They arrived with time to spare for their flight to Cairo and onward connection to Luxor. Less than four hours after departing Alexandria, they landed in Luxor International Airport.

The ancient city of Thebes—modern Luxor—sprawled along the Nile's eastern bank, dominated by the massive temple complexes of Karnak and Luxor. Across the river lay the Theban Necropolis, the Valley of the Kings, and the mortuary temples of pharaohs long turned to dust. Here the veil between past and present seemed thinner than elsewhere, where ancient gods still seemed to whisper on the desert wind.

Maddison was somewhat surprised when the taxi dropped him off at a modest hotel in the city center rather than one of the luxury resorts along the Nile.

"I will pick you up tonight, just after nightfall to avoid unwelcome attention," said Farouk as he prepared to leave for the monastery. "Rest well, Professor. Tonight, you will see wonders that have been hidden for three millennia."

Left alone in the modest hotel room, Maddison spread the photograph on the small desk and examined it again with his pocket magnifying glass. Each hieroglyph seemed to shimmer with meaning, every symbol a fragment of a cosmic puzzle. Outside his window, modern Egypt carried on its business, unaware that its ancient past was about to be reimagined.

The Monastery at Luxor

That evening, Maddison was collected by a driver named Ahmed in an old but well-maintained car. Maddison realized they were driving toward the Valley of the Kings when they suddenly turned left onto a gravel road. After a short distance, someone who clearly expected them opened a gate, and they drove to the front of a house in the back corner of a monastery complex.

The monastery was a cluster of whitewashed buildings surrounded by a high wall—a Christian island in the Islamic Sea of Upper Egypt. Inside, the compound was surprisingly verdant, with date palms and jacaranda trees offering shade to the modest structures. In one corner stood a small church, its dome painted blue to represent heaven, its simple cross silhouetted against the star-filled sky.

Farouk approached Bishop Makarios, who stood waiting in front of the house, and received a set of keys from him.

Bishop Makarios was a gaunt man with a flowing white beard and eyes that had witnessed decades of struggle. He greeted Maddison with the formal courtesy of one educated man to another, but wariness flickered in his gaze—the instinctive caution of one who had learned that foreign visitors often brought complications in their wake.

"Welcome, Professor," Bishop Makarios said in accented but precise English. "Bishop Farouk has told me of your expertise. We pray that what you see tonight will serve both truth and wisdom."

"We can go in now," Farouk announced to Professor Maddison after a brief exchange in Arabic with the older bishop.

Professor Maddison followed Farouk alongside the fence and the house behind it, entering through a back door. Farouk showed him to a small room with a bed and shelf for his luggage before leading him deeper into the building.

"Are you ready, Professor?" Farouk asked, pausing before another heavy door. "What you're about to see will change everything you thought you knew about the Thutmosid succession."

Maddison nodded, his heart racing with anticipation. Behind that door lay either the greatest archaeological discovery of the century or the most elaborate hoax ever perpetrated. Either way, his life was about to change forever.

Chapter 3 - The Secrets Beneath

Chamber under the house

Maddison put his luggage down and let his eyes adjust to the dim candlelight, searching for the door. Farouk pointed toward a passage and offered the keys to Maddison as if he were the one destined to unlock history, but then reconsidered.

Farouk twisted the iron ring embedded in the stone, his weathered hands moving with practiced familiarity rather than ceremony. The door—a simple interior passage of plain oak with minimal adornment—opened with a grinding sigh that spoke more of neglected hinges than ancient mysteries. As it swung outward, it immediately revealed what lay beyond: not a hidden chamber requiring further exploration, but a vertical shaft carved straight down into darkness, with an elevator platform directly before them.

Professor Maddison stepped forward, his broad shoulders silhouetted against the doorframe as he blinked to adjust his vision. The archaeologist's sun-weathered face betrayed momentary surprise. "Wait... is that—?" His voice trailed off as light from Farouk's lamp flickered over the metallic structure bolted securely to the shaft's edge.

A small platform hung suspended by thick, time-darkened cables stretching upward to a pulley fixed in a stone crossbeam. The elevator looked unmistakably Victorian—not an ancient construct but rather the product of nineteenth-century British engineering. Its iron framework was sturdy though oxidized in places, clearly installed during the great archaeological fever that had gripped Egypt during the late 1800s, when men like Howard Carter and Flinders Petrie were systematically exploring the Valley of the Kings.

"Lord Carnarvon's expedition," Maddison murmured, stroking his salt-and-pepper beard thoughtfully as he examined the construction. "Or perhaps Belzoni's work. This has all the hallmarks of British engineering from that era."

Farouk stepped onto the platform with a quiet smile, entirely comfortable with the arrangement. "Come—it still works." There was no ceremony in his invitation, just the practical confidence of a man who had made this journey before.

Maddison hesitated only a moment before stepping beside him, his considerable weight causing the metal to creak under their combined burden. The professor's tall frame made him stoop slightly beneath the low ceiling of the elevator cage. Farouk gripped the winch handle and slowly began turning it, lowering them with ease into the depths.

The shaft swallowed them in silence, the circle of daylight above shrinking as stone walls slid past. These walls bore the unmistakable marks of nineteenth-century excavation—regular chisel patterns different from ancient Egyptian techniques, occasional drill holes where dynamite charges might once have been placed, and even faded pencil markings in English noting depth measurements.

Ten meters down, with a gentle jolt, the platform stopped. Maddison instinctively reached for the wall as his boots touched solid ground, his large hand splaying against the cool limestone. The air was noticeably cooler here—still and heavy with dust, but carrying the subtle scents of coal oil, nineteenth-century preservatives, and the lingering ghost of British tobacco.

Farouk raised the lamp, its golden light stretching across rough stone and catching something carved just beyond the flicker. A rounded opening emerged from the shadow, barely wide enough for a man to pass through—clearly not part of the Victorian excavation but a doorway cut much earlier, perhaps by the ancients themselves.

"This is where Carter's team stopped," Farouk explained quietly. "They believed this section had been thoroughly explored and documented. They never realized what lay just beyond."

Without a word, Farouk slung the lamp through the hole and crouched, pressing his shoulder against the smooth edges. With effort, he pushed himself inside, his slender frame navigating the narrow space with practiced ease.

Maddison remained at the threshold, assessing the tight passage with the calculating eye of a man who had squeezed through countless archaeological bottlenecks. His broad shoulders would make this challenging. "Farouk?" he called softly, his words resonating against the stone.

A few seconds passed. Then Farouk's voice echoed from within. "It's safe. Bring the light."

The professor followed, turning sideways to accommodate his larger frame, crawling through the narrow entrance until his foot found stone floor again. As he stood, his breath caught in his throat, the scholar's trained skepticism momentarily abandoned.

Lamps now lit on either side of the chamber, and their glow revealed what words could not capture. Every wall—every surface—was covered in precise, flowing hieroglyphs, untouched by time. Gold-leaf inlays shimmered in the grooves, and carved gods looked back at him with timeless, knowing eyes. This chamber had somehow escaped the frenzied excavations of the nineteenth century, perhaps protected by its unremarkable entrance or simply overlooked in the rush to find more spectacular tombs.

Maddison whispered, his voice barely audible even in the perfect acoustics of the chamber, "This... this wasn't on any map." His hands, calloused from years of fieldwork, reached instinctively for the notebook in his pocket, though his eyes remained fixed on the spectacular preservation before him. "Not in Carter's journals, nor Belzoni's accounts. Nothing in the British Museum archives mentioned this."

Farouk smiled faintly, his eyes reflecting the dancing light. "No. Some places aren't meant to be found easily. But they remember who's willing to look." He ran his fingers reverently along the wall. "The Europeans were always in such a hurry—breaking through walls, carting away treasures. Some chambers require patience to reveal themselves."

Before them stretched walls alive with hieroglyphics—not the faded, weather-worn scratchings so common in exposed ruins, but vivid, pristine inscriptions, their colors still singing across the millennia. The small chamber—perhaps twelve square meters—seemed to pulse with ancient power, every surface covered in the sacred language of pharaohs and gods.

Maddison's flashlight beam danced across figures of gods and kings, priests and warriors, captured in eternal procession around the chamber. Anubis with his jackal head stood in judgment, Amun-Ra with his double-plumed crown bestowed divine favor. And there, dominating one wall, stood the figure of a pharaoh, his cartouche identifying him as the younger Menkheperre, son of the great Thutmose III, yet wearing regalia that seemed to bridge the gap between father and son, between past glory and present rule.

The red of ochre, the deep blue of lapis lazuli, the green of malachite, and the brilliant yellow of orpiment—all the colors still vibrant, preserved in this airless tomb of knowledge. These weren't the faded ghosts of color that survived in most tombs and temples, but the full glory of Egyptian artistic expression, as bold and confident as the day the artisans had completed their work.

"Dear God," Maddison finally managed, approaching the nearest wall with steps as careful as if he were treading on the surface of a frozen lake. "This is... this is beyond anything I could have imagined."

The air in the chamber felt charged, electric with the presence of something ancient and powerful. Dust motes danced in the beam of his flashlight; golden specks suspended in time just as this chamber had been suspended from the normal flow of history. The temperature was remarkably constant—cool but not cold, the perfect condition for preservation.

Farouk smiled, the expression transforming his severe features. "Take what time you require, Professor. These walls have waited millennia for the right eyes to behold them."

Maddison moved around the chamber as if in a trance, his flashlight dancing across hieroglyphs carved by hands dead for thousands of years. He paused before what appeared to be the beginning of the narrative sequence, his trained eye automatically seeking the start of the story.

"This first panel," he said, his voice gaining strength as scholarly passion overcame emotion, "appears to be the younger Menkheperre's account of how Ahmose I drove the Hyksos from Egypt." His finger hovered reverently above the carved symbols. "But the perspective is unusually personal, intimate. And here—" He indicated the royal figure adorned with distinctive regalia. "This appears to be Menkheperre—the son—yet he's depicted wearing attributes that belonged exclusively to his father, the great Thutmose III."

The scene depicted a battle—chariots and infantry engaged in violent conflict, the Egyptian forces driving foreign soldiers before them like chaff before the wind. The foreigners were depicted in the traditional Egyptian manner for showing enemies—disheveled, cowering, begging for mercy as the might of pharaoh descended upon them. But the text accompanying the scene was unusual in its detail, describing specific maneuvers, naming individual officers, recording the exact count of enemies slain and captured.

"Can you decipher it?" Farouk asked, though he already knew the answer.

"Parts of it, certainly," Maddison replied, already photographing and making notes with feverish intensity. "A complete translation will require time, but the narrative clearly tracks the rise of the 18th Dynasty, with peculiar emphasis on the younger Menkheperre's claim to his father's divine legacy."

His fingers traced the cartouches with reverent care—the oval shapes containing the royal names, protected by the endless loop of rope that symbolized eternity. Here was Ahmose, founder of the dynasty, wielding his khopesh sword against the Hyksos invaders. Here was Amenhotep I, consolidating the gains of his father. And here was the great Thutmose III himself, extending Egypt's empire into the heart of the Near East.

Moving to another section of wall, Maddison's excitement grew visibly. "This passage here describes the younger Menkheperre as the spiritual vessel of his father's military genius, divinely appointed to shield Egypt from another invasion like the Hyksos incursion."

The central figure on this wall was a pharaoh depicted twice—once performing ritual offerings before the god Amun, and again leading an army into battle. Both figures bore the same cartouche—the younger Menkheperre—yet the accompanying text referred repeatedly to the soul of his father, the great Thutmose III, residing within him, guiding his actions, empowering his rule.

"It's a remarkable theological claim," Maddison murmured, adjusting his glasses. "Not mere inheritance or divine approval, but actual spiritual inhabitation. The ancient Egyptians believed in various forms of the soul—the ka, the ba, the akh—but this suggests something more concrete, more literal. The son claiming not just his father's throne, but his very essence."

For hours that seemed to pass like minutes, Maddison examined the walls, occasionally breaking the silence with exclamations of discovery or disbelief. Farouk watched in quiet satisfaction, seeing the renowned Egyptologist surrendering completely to the ancient mystery before him.

The air in the chamber grew close and heavy with their breathing, the centuries of perfect preservation disturbed by these modern intruders. Yet there was a sense that the place welcomed them—that these walls had been waiting for eyes that could understand their significance, minds that could interpret their message across the gulf of time.

In one corner, a small stone altar stood, carved with offering scenes. Before it, shallow depressions in the stone floor suggested that liquid offerings—perhaps water, wine, or milk—had once been poured in ritual observance. Maddison knelt to examine these, his mind reconstructing the ceremonies that might have taken place here thousands of years ago—priests moving in solemn procession, the flicker of torchlight on painted walls, the murmur of prayers to gods long forgotten by the world above.

"Farouk," Maddison finally said, turning to his companion with eyes burning with the fever of discovery, "do you comprehend the magnitude of what you've uncovered? This chamber could completely rewrite our understanding of succession politics in the 18th Dynasty. The younger Menkheperre appears to have been positioning himself not merely as his father's heir—he's claiming to be his spiritual continuation, his immortal essence returned in a new form."

Maddison's normally composed demeanor had given way to the excitement of pure intellectual discovery. His hands gestured emphatically as he spoke, his voice resonating in the ancient space where once priests had chanted hymns to forgotten gods.

"So it holds significance?" Farouk asked, though the answer was written across the professor's transformed face.

"Significance?" Maddison laughed, the sound echoing strangely in the ancient chamber. "My dear friend, 'significant' is grotesquely inadequate. This is the archaeological discovery of the decade, potentially of the century." He placed a reverent palm against the cool stone. "And I suspect we've only begun to unravel its mysteries."

His mind was already racing ahead—peer-reviewed papers, conference presentations, perhaps a book contract. Oxford University Press would certainly be interested. His colleagues at Cambridge would be green with envy. And the British Museum might even provide funding for a proper excavation. After decades of meticulous work in the field, Arthur Maddison had stumbled upon the discovery that would cement his legacy.

Three days later, Professor Maddison's eyes were bloodshot from lack of sleep, his normally immaculate appearance disheveled after countless hours of translation and documentation. Having cancelled his flights from Luxor to Cairo and then to London, he had turned the small monastery room into a makeshift research station—but not the one he had originally envisioned.

With his laptop stolen, only pencil sketches of hieroglyphs covered the walls where digital photographs should have been. His camera, with its severely limited memory, had captured only a fraction of what he needed to document. Pages of translation notes lay scattered across the bed and floor, covered in Maddison's spidery handwriting—rough sketches hastily drawn in the natural light streaming through the monastery's ancient windows.

Each morning found him descending into the underground chamber to study the hieroglyphs by torchlight, only to emerge hours later to recreate what he had seen in pencil drawings made under the room's inadequate illumination. The professor had worked with the manic energy of a man possessed, his research hampered by the theft but driven forward by sheer determination, stopping only when physical exhaustion forced brief periods of restless sleep.

The hot Luxor sun streamed through the small window, creating a pool of golden light on the worn carpet. Outside, monastery life continued at its unhurried pace—monks chanting morning prayers, pilgrims seeking blessings, gardeners tending the date palms that provided shade in the courtyard. But within the confines of this simple room, time had ceased to matter as ancient Egypt yielded its secrets word by painstaking word.

Farouk entered carrying a tray of strong coffee and bread, pausing at the threshold as he observed the Englishman's obsessive work. His concern was evident as he took in the professor's haggard appearance— the rumpled clothes, the two-day stubble on his normally clean-shaven cheeks, the feverish gleam in his tired eyes. Maddison had the look of a man consumed by something larger than himself, driven by forces he could neither control nor resist.

"You must rest, Professor," he said gently.

The smell of fresh coffee—dark, strong, and sweetened with cane sugar in the Egyptian manner—filled the small room. Outside, the call to prayer from a nearby mosque floated across the monastery walls, a reminder that time continued to flow in the world above while they remained immersed in ancient mysteries below.

Maddison looked up, his eyes feverish with the particular madness that grips men who have touched history's hidden face. "Rest?" he asked, as though the word were foreign to him. "How can I rest when these walls speak of events that reshape our entire understanding of the 18th Dynasty?"

He gestured for Farouk to join him at the cluttered table, sweeping aside papers to make room for the humble meal.

"It's extraordinary," Maddison continued, tapping a particular photograph with a finger stained with ink and dust. "The narrative begins with the death of Pharaoh Seqenenre Tao II—the catalyst that ignited the war of liberation against the Hyksos. But the perspective..." He shook his head in wonder. "It's unlike anything in the established record."

Farouk poured coffee into two small cups, the rich aroma momentarily overpowering the smell of dust and old books that permeated the room. The simple act of hospitality seemed to ground them both, creating a brief respite from the weight of history that had settled upon their shoulders.

Farouk leaned forward, intrigued despite his concerns for the professor's health. "How so?"

"According to these inscriptions, it all began with a captured runner—a seemingly minor event that the younger Menkheperre claims altered the course of Egyptian history." Maddison's voice took on the rhythmic cadence of a storyteller as he prepared to recount the ancient tale. "The son of the great Thutmose III tells us that everything started with the death of Tao II and a runner being captured by Prince Kamose's soldiers. But his version of events..."

Maddison paused, his scholarly excitement tempered by the weight of what he was about to reveal. "His version suggests that destiny itself was steering these events, that the gods were orchestrating the rise of his dynasty through what others might see as mere chance."

Maddison leaned back in his chair, the coffee growing cold in his hands as his eyes took on the distant look of a man seeing across the centuries. When he spoke again, his voice had changed—no longer the excited tone of a discoverer, but the measured cadence of a storyteller about to unveil an ancient truth.

"Let me tell you what these walls reveal," he said quietly, his gaze fixed on a point beyond the monastery room, beyond the present moment. "Let me tell you the story as the younger Menkheperre recorded it, as he claimed it was whispered to him by the spirit of his father..."

The room fell silent except for the distant sounds of monastery life. Farouk set down his cup, sensing that what was about to unfold was more than mere translation—it was the resurrection of a tale that had lain buried for millennia, waiting for the right moment to emerge into the light.

Maddison's voice grew softer, more reverent, as if he were channeling the very words carved into those ancient walls. "It begins with Egypt divided, the Hyksos controlling the north from their capital at Avaris, while the native pharaohs ruled from Thebes in the south. For over a century, this uneasy balance held. But then came the moment that would change everything—a single messenger carrying a message that would ignite the fires of liberation..."

Chapter 4 - The Council of Hesitation

1542 BC Trade route Thebes, Ancient Egypt

The western trade route of Thebes lay silent beneath the pale morning sky, the wind dragging its fingers across the dunes, reshaping them as it had for millennia. The path, worn smooth by the passage of merchants, envoys, and armies, stretched toward the horizon. A lone runner, his body lean and hard from years of training, moved across the shifting sands, his pace unwavering.

The dawn painted the desert in shades of rose and gold, the first rays of Ra's journey across the sky. In the distance, the limestone cliffs of the western mountains gleamed like polished ivory, guardian sentinels watching over the sacred valleys where generations of nobles rested in their eternal homes. The great royal necropolis that would one day house the mightiest pharaohs remained a dream yet unrealized, waiting for future dynasties to carve their legacy into the living rock.

The runner's feet struck the packed sand with metronomic precision, each stride covering ground with economical grace. His training had begun in childhood, when he had been selected for his natural speed and endurance. Years of running messages between Egyptian outposts had hardened his muscles and expanded his lungs until he could maintain this pace from sunrise to sunset without rest.

Sweat glistened on his bronzed skin, tracing rivulets down his torso. A linen wrap clung to his waist, and in his hand, he carried a reed tube, its seal unbroken—a message bound for the south, to the Nubian strongholds beyond the cataracts. His eyes remained fixed ahead, his breath steady. There was no room for hesitation.

The message he carried was urgent—he had been told that much. The scribe who had pressed the sealed tube into his hand had whispered of its importance, of how its contents might change the balance of power along the Nile. But the runner asked no questions. His was not to know or understand, but simply to deliver.

Too late, he saw the soldiers.

They emerged from behind a cluster of boulders, a half-dozen men clad in leather kilts and armed with bronze-tipped spears. Their shields bore the mark of Kamose, Pharaoh of Upper Egypt. The runner slid to a halt, sand rising around him in a fine mist. His free hand dropped to the dagger at his hip, but they were already closing in.

The soldiers moved with the disciplined precision of men who had trained together for years. Their leather armor bore the scars of previous conflicts, and their eyes held the calculating assessment of experienced warriors. They formed a loose semicircle around the runner, cutting off any hope of escape.

"The letter," the captain said, stepping forward, his voice calm but edged with authority. "Give it to us, and you may yet see another sunrise."

The captain stood half a head taller than his men, his shoulders broader, his arms bearing the elaborate ritual scarification that marked him as a member of the elite corps. A golden armband—reward for valor in some forgotten skirmish—gleamed in the morning light. His eyes, dark and assessing, never left the runner's face.

The runner's eyes flicked from one man to another. Six against one. His duty was clear: deliver the message or die trying. But dying would ensure the scroll never reached its intended hands. Jaw tightening, he unclasped the reed case and thrust it forward.

The reed case passed between them—a simple object containing words that might reshape the destiny of nations. The captain's callused fingers closed around it, claiming it as soldiers had claimed plunder since the beginning of warfare.

The captain took it, snapped the seal with his thumb, and withdrew the papyrus. He studied the foreign script for a moment, then rolled it carefully and secured it within his leather pouch.

"Bind him," he ordered. "Pharaoh Kamose will want to see this... and the man who carried it."

Rough hands seized the runner, stripping away his dagger, binding his wrists with coarse rope that bit into his skin. As they dragged him eastward, toward the distant city of Thebes, he cast one final glance southward—toward the destination he would never reach, toward the Nubian prince who would now wait in vain for a message that would never arrive.

Festive Hall, Thebes

The sands of time had barely settled over the tomb of Pharaoh Tao II. Seventy days had passed since his broken body had been sealed within the necropolis, yet the scent of embalming oils still lingered in the halls of the palace.

The seventy days of mummification had been seventy days of vulnerability for Thebes. Tradition demanded mourning, demanded focus on preparing the dead pharaoh for his journey to the afterlife. But enemies rarely respected periods of grief. While priests had chanted and applied precious resins to Tao's corpse, foreign powers had watched and waited, sensing opportunity in Egypt's moment of transition.

Kamose, his son and heir, stood before the assembled council, his fingers gripping the crook and flail with visible tension. The symbols of kingship sat heavy in his grasp. He had lost more than a father—he had inherited a kingdom teetering on the edge of ruin.

The council chamber was a spacious hall deep within the palace, its walls painted with scenes of pharaohs receiving tribute from foreign lands, of successful hunts in the marshes, of offerings made to the gods. Columns carved to resemble bundled papyrus stalks supported the ceiling, their capitals spreading like the delta itself. Light filtered through narrow clerestory windows, creating bars of brilliance that illuminated floating dust motes.

Around a table of polished acacia wood sat the men who would help determine Egypt's future—commanders who had served Tao II in his campaigns against the Hyksos, priests whose temples controlled vast agricultural estates, nobles whose lineages stretched back to the Old Kingdom. Their faces were solemn, aware of the weight of the moment.

"For too long," Kamose began, his voice ringing across the hall, "Egypt has been divided. While I hold Thebes, an Asiatic usurper squats in Avaris, and the Nubian prince sharpens his knives in Kush. Tell me, my lords, do you find this acceptable?"

His youth was evident in the smooth planes of his face, the lack of lines around his eyes, the fullness of his cheeks not yet whittled away by age and responsibility. But there was nothing youthful in his bearing or in the intensity of his gaze as it swept across the assembled counselors.

The council murmured among themselves. Many had served Pharaoh Tao, had fought beside him, had bled for his cause. But battle scars made men wary, and war was a beast that devoured recklessly.

The flickering oil lamps cast dancing shadows across their faces—men of experience, men of power, men with much to lose should Kamose's ambitions prove ruinous. They had seen war before, had calculated its costs in blood and treasure. Some bore the physical marks of conflict—a missing eye here, a twisted limb there—while others carried invisible scars of decisions that had sent men to their deaths.

Teti-an, an elder statesman with lines of wisdom carved deep into his face, leaned forward. His voice, though calm, carried the weight of caution.

His beard, meticulously braided and oiled in the manner of the court, contrasted with the stern practicality of his words. He had served three pharaohs in his lifetime and had developed the cautious pragmatism that comes from seeing the rise and fall of royal ambitions.

"Great Pharaoh," he said, "the lands remain fruitful. We trade with the Asiatics, our cattle graze unmolested. Though Avaris holds the north, we remain strong in Thebes. Why risk all on war when peace fills our granaries?"

The doors to the chamber burst open before Kamose could respond. A squad of soldiers marched in, dragging a dust-covered prisoner between them. The captain knelt and held out a papyrus scroll.

The interruption violated every protocol of royal council—a transgression that spoke to the urgency of the matter. The soldiers' armor bore the dust of the desert, their faces the grim satisfaction of men who had intercepted something of great importance.

"Forgive the intrusion, Divine One," he said. "We intercepted this man carrying a message from Apophis to the Nubian prince. Our scribe has translated its contents."

A hush fell over the hall. Behind the captain stood a young priest-scribe, his head freshly shaved in the manner of his order, ink stains marking his fingers. He carried a wooden tablet bearing the translation written in clear hieratic script.

Kamose gestured for the scribe to approach. The young man's voice trembled slightly as he read aloud the damning words that would reshape the political landscape of the Two Lands. The formal cadence of his training barely concealed his nervousness at being thrust into such a momentous council session.

"Divine Pharaoh, the message reads thus: 'Apophis writes to the Nubian ruler: Seize the south, and I shall share Egypt with you. Kamose is trapped between us. He will fall as his father before him.'"

The words fell into the silence like stones dropped into a still pond, sending ripples of shock through the assembled council. Conspiracy between Egypt's enemies was the nightmare scenario they had feared but refused to voice—the pincer movement that could crush Thebes between two hostile forces.

The council erupted in whispers. The runner knelt nearby, his head bowed, waiting for judgment.

Some councilors rose to their feet in agitation, while others leaned together in hurried, urgent conversation. The more martial among them placed hands instinctively on sword hilts, as if the enemies might materialize within the chamber itself. The priests murmured prayers, perhaps seeking divine guidance in this moment of crisis.

Kamose's voice was thick with fury. "Can you still counsel patience? This is war. The Hyksos conspire with the Nubians to carve Egypt between them like a butcher's blade through meat!"

His youth seemed to fall away in that moment, replaced by the grim determination of a pharaoh forced to confront existential threats to his nation. The mantle of kingship settled more firmly on his shoulders as he brandished the translated message before the council.

A younger noble, his robes embroidered with the wealth of a hundred harvests, hesitated before speaking. "Perhaps, Pharaoh, we should wait. Act only if Apophis strikes first."

The noble's jeweled fingers betrayed his nervousness, twisting the gold signet ring that marked his authority. His family's estates lay in the borderlands—the first territories that would burn should war erupt. Self-interest mingled with genuine concern for Egypt's welfare in his cautious counsel.

Kamose let out a bitter laugh. "Is this not an act of war? You would wait until his chariots burn Thebes before lifting a blade?"

The young pharaoh stood straighter now, the initial shock of the revelation hardening into resolve. The scroll had confirmed what his father had long suspected—that Apophis was not content to rule the north, that the division of Egypt was merely a temporary condition in the Hyksos king's strategic vision.

Ebana, a warrior with scars older than some of the councilors, stepped forward. His voice was iron, forged in years of battle.

Unlike the nobles in their fine linen and jewels, Ebana wore the simple kilt of a soldier, though the gold collar around his neck spoke of royal favor earned through loyalty and courage. One ear was partially missing—a permanent reminder of a Hyksos blade that had come too close during a border skirmish years earlier.

"We have seen disunity before, but never like this," he said. "The Hyksos wear our garb, but they are not Egyptians. They bow to foreign gods, spit upon our shrines. If we do nothing, we are no better than traitors."

Kamose raised a hand for silence. His eyes swept the room, his mind calculating. He needed the council's support. But he also needed to act.

The weight of the decision pressed down upon him like the massive stone blocks of a temple. For all his royal blood and divine authority, he was one man facing choices that would determine the future of a civilization that had endured for thousands of years before his birth. In such moments, even pharaohs might wish for the clarity of direct communication with the gods.

Nefer-Pehu, the high priest of Amun, stepped from the shadows where he had been observing. His face was an impassive mask beneath his ceremonial leopard skin, but his voice carried the authority of the gods themselves.

The leopard skin draped across his shoulders marked him as Amun's earthly representative—the conduit between the divine realm and the world of men. His head was shaved clean, emphasizing the austere angles of his face and the penetrating quality of his dark eyes. Gold armbands inscribed with sacred texts caught the light as he moved.

"My lords," he said, "the omens are... divided. The stars speak of great upheaval, but whether it comes from action or inaction, even the diviners cannot say." He turned to Kamose. "What we know is this: your father did not die by accident. The wounds on his skull tell a different tale—one of Hyksos assassins in the night."

A collective intake of breath swept through the chamber. Many had whispered of such things, but to hear it spoken aloud by the high priest himself carried a finality that silenced debate.

The official declaration of Tao II's death had mentioned only that the pharaoh had joined the gods—the customary phrasing that revealed nothing of the circumstances. But rumors had circulated among the palace staff, whispers of strange wounds, of blood-soaked royal bedchambers, of guards found with their throats cut.

Kamose's eyes blazed. "Then there is no question. I will march north and avenge my father."

The young king's voice rang with the righteous anger of a son who has discovered his father's murderers—a personal grief transformed into political imperative. His hand closed around the hilt of the ceremonial dagger at his belt, as if he might personally cut the heart from Apophis's chest.

"Vengeance is warranted," Nefer-Pehu conceded, raising a hand to silence the eruption of voices. "But a full-scale war? The treasury is not prepared. The army needs time."

The high priest's pragmatism tempered his spiritual authority—a characteristic that had made him valuable to rulers who needed both divine sanction and practical advice. His gaze moved deliberately around the chamber, assessing the reactions of the council members to his words.

"How much time before the Nubians descend from the south?" Kamose demanded. "This letter proves they plot against us even now!"

The council chamber descended into chaos as voices overlapped, some calling for immediate war, others pleading for caution. Teti-an banged his staff against the floor, restoring a fragile order.

The rhythmic thud of wood against stone cut through the cacophony of competing voices, a primitive sound that nonetheless commanded instant attention. In the sudden silence that followed, the elder statesman's calm voice carried to every corner of the chamber.

"We must vote," he announced. "The divine Pharaoh seeks our counsel, though the final decision rests with him alone."

One by one, the councilors cast their lots. When the tally was complete, Teti-An's shoulders slumped slightly.

Small clay tokens—white for peace, red for war—accumulated in two ceremonial bowls before the pharaoh's throne. As the last councilor returned to his seat, all eyes fixed upon the visible manifestation of Egypt's divided opinion. The white tokens outnumbered the red, but not by a comfortable margin.

Nefer-Pehu stepped forward once more. "Pharaoh, the council has decided. You may go after the killers of Tao II, but no further. A limited campaign—not full war."

The compromise satisfied no one completely—a characteristic of effective political solutions since the dawn of governance. It gave Kamose authorization to act without granting him the unlimited mandate he desired. It acknowledged the threat without committing Egypt to an all-consuming conflict.

Kamose clenched his jaw. It was not what he wanted. But it was a start.

"I accept," he said. "For now."

The qualification hung in the air, noticed by all but acknowledged by none. It was the prerogative of pharaoh to interpret council decisions according to his divine wisdom—a flexibility that had allowed many rulers to gradually expand the scope of initially limited campaigns.

As the council members filed out, Ebana remained. He studied his king, saw the fire in his eyes.

The chamber emptied slowly, councilors departing in small groups, their hushed conversations creating a susurrus of sound that faded as they moved deeper into the palace. Guards took positions at the doorways, their eyes forward, faces impassive, trained to hear nothing and remember less.

"They fear war," he murmured, "because they have grown comfortable with division. But you are of Tetisheri's blood. You have her fire."

The mention of Kamose's grandmother—a woman of common birth who had risen to become the matriarch of a royal dynasty through sheer force of will—was calculated to remind the young pharaoh of his heritage. Tetisheri had kept the flame of Egyptian resistance alive during the darkest days, had nurtured the ambition that now burned in her grandson's veins.

Kamose turned to the kneeling prisoner. "What shall we do with him?"

The runner remained motionless, his forehead pressed to the cool stone floor. He had heard everything—the revelation of the conspiracy, the debate over war and peace, the decision that would set nations on a collision course. He knew too much to be released but had committed no crime worthy of execution.

"He has seen too much," Ebana said. "And he served an enemy's cause. He cannot be allowed to return."

Kamose nodded. "The priests will find a use for him."

The runner's fate was sealed with those words—not death, but service in the temple complexes, where he would be watched for the remainder of his days. His speed and endurance would serve Egypt now, carrying messages between Thebes and the outlying temples, his loyalty ensured by knowing the alternatives to faithful service.

He turned back to Ebana, his voice low. "I need more than fire. I need swift runners, loyal warriors, and a plan."

The young pharaoh's mind was already moving beyond the council's limitations, envisioning not just a punitive expedition to avenge his father but a campaign to reunify Egypt under Theban rule. The scrolls in the palace library told of a time when one pharaoh had ruled from the Delta to the cataracts—a golden age of unity and power that Kamose yearned to restore.

Ebana's lips curled in a grim smile. "The runners are ready. Even now, they prepare to carry your words across Upper Egypt. As for warriors... there are many who remember your father and see in you, his spirit."

That night, under a crescent moon, Kamose summoned his most trusted scribe.

The royal apartments were lit by oil lamps that cast flickering shadows across walls decorated with hunting scenes and religious imagery. The scribe knelt on a reed mat, reed pen poised above a fresh sheet of papyrus, inkwell at his side. His fingers were stained with the black and red inks of his profession—permanent marks of a lifetime dedicated to recording the words of gods and kings.

"Write," he ordered. "To Elephantine, to Abydos, to the nomarchs still loyal to Thebes. Tell them Pharaoh Kamose seeks justice for his father's death. And that justice may require more than the council envisions."

The scribe's pen scratched across the papyrus, the hieratic script flowing from his practiced hand in elegant columns. As he wrote, Kamose dictated the carefully coded language that would alert his allies to prepare for war while maintaining the fiction of a limited campaign. The young pharaoh had learned the art of statecraft at his father's knee—including the vital skill of appearing to follow counsel while pursuing his own vision.

The next day, as the sun rose over the Nile, a dozen runners departed Thebes, their scrolls hidden in hollow reeds. They moved swiftly, cutting across the desert, following the river, carrying words that would change the fate of Egypt.

In Avaris, Apophis sat secure in his stolen throne. In Kush, the prince sharpened his ambitions alongside his blades. And in Thebes, Kamose prepared for a war that would either restore Egypt—or destroy it.

The Two Lands would not remain divided for long.

Chapter 5 - Kamose's Last Battle

1539 BC, The Nile at Avaris

The Egyptian sun blazed overhead as Kamose's single war barge cut through the Nile's muddy waters. Three years of relentless raids had transformed the prince into a hardened rebel, his bronze skin marked by countless skirmishes. Around him, seventy warriors—all that remained of his once-proud army—watched the shoreline with the wary eyes of hunted men.

Three years since he'd knelt before his father's mutilated corpse. Three years since his terrible oath of vengeance. Yet the truth still gnawed at him like a festering wound. Apophis? Aata? Teti-An? Which of them had ordered Seqenenre Tao's murder? Every raid, every battle, and still no answers.

Kamose gripped the barge's rail until his knuckles went white. To the Hyksos, he was nothing more than a desert bandit now—a minor irritation scratching at the edges of their empire. To his own people in Thebes, he'd become an embarrassment, a hot-headed prince whose failed rebellion had only made their subjugation worse.

"My prince," Ahmose-Onkh said quietly, moving beside him. The commander's scarred face bore the weight of three years' defeats. "Perhaps it's time to return to Thebes. Your mother—"

"My mother thinks I'm a fool," Kamose cut him off. "And perhaps she's right." He turned to face his men—seventy souls who'd followed him into this wilderness of failure. "But I'll not return empty-handed. Not again."

Behind them, the great bend in the river opened toward the north. Ahead lay the Delta, the Hyksos heartland, and somewhere in that maze of waterways, the truth about his father's death.

"Seventy men against an empire," Ahmose-Onkh murmured. "The bards will sing of our madness."

Kamose allowed himself a bitter smile. "Let them. At least they'll remember we tried."

The Raid on Avaris

By full darkness, they'd penetrated deeper into Hyksos territory than any Egyptian force in decades. The single barge ghosted through narrow canals toward their target—Avaris itself, the seat of Hyksos power. Intelligence from sympathetic locals had revealed Khamudi was away in Bubastis on administrative business. The capital's defenses would be lighter without the king present.

The night air carried the scent of marsh water and blooming lotus as they approached the great city that had once been Egyptian Hutwaret. Avaris rose before them—the fortress-capital of the Hyksos, its walls pale in starlight, its temples and palaces a testament to foreign occupation of sacred Egyptian soil.

"Now we strike at the serpent's very heart," Kamose whispered, his heart hammering with the audacity of it.

Seventy throats erupted in a war cry that shattered the night's silence. They fell upon the harbor district like hunting hawks, bronze weapons flashing in the moonlight. Guards stumbled from their posts, half-dressed and confused. Foreign merchants and their families fled screaming through the streets.

"Behold the vengeance of Upper Egypt!" Kamose roared, standing tall on his barge as flames began to lick at Hyksos warehouses. "Tell your absent king that no Egyptian city—not even this one—belongs to foreign usurpers!"

They burned granaries, scattered precious goods into the harbor, set fire to a temple erected to foreign gods on what had once been Egyptian sacred ground. For one glorious hour, the very heart of Hyksos power echoed with Egyptian war cries.

But this was theater, not conquest. Seventy men couldn't take and hold the Hyksos capital—only humiliate its rulers and send a message that nowhere, not even their greatest stronghold, was truly safe from Egyptian vengeance.

As they withdrew into the darkness, leaving flames and chaos behind them, Kamose felt fierce satisfaction. This blow would echo throughout the Delta—Egyptians striking at the very heart of Hyksos power.

"He'll come for us now," Ahmose-Onkh said quietly. "Personally."

Kamose nodded. "Good. Let's finish this like warriors, not like bandits skulking in the reeds."

The Ambush

The trap struck the next morning as they approached Bubastis. A fast messenger boat had outrun them in the darkness, carrying news of the raid to Khamudi in the ancient temple city. The Hyksos king had acted with the speed of a striking cobra, positioning his war fleet in the reed beds that lined the river approach.

As Kamose's barge rounded the final bend before Bubastis, Hyksos war boats surged from their concealment, their hulls painted black as night. At their head sailed the royal vessel, its prow carved with the image of Seth—Khamudi's patron god—and its deck crowded with the king's personal guard.

"The messenger had reached him," Kamose said grimly, already drawing his sword. In truth, he'd expected this. The raid had been too bold, too personal. Khamudi could not let such an insult pass.

"Battle positions!" he bellowed. "Form square!"

But there was no time for formations. The enemy vessels crashed into them from three sides; their decks crowded with professional soldiers whose bronze-scaled armor marked them as Khamudi's elite guard.

Khamudi himself stood tall on his flagship, resplendent in gilded armor, his oiled beard curled in foreign fashion. When he spoke, his voice carried easily across the water—a king's voice, accustomed to being obeyed.

"Kamose of Thebes!" he called, his words heavy with cold fury. "You dare defile my own residence? Burn my private temple? Three years I've tolerated your pathetic raids, but this—this demands blood!"

The battle was swift and brutal. Kamose's men fought with the desperation of cornered lions, but they were outnumbered five to one. Bronze clashed against bronze, screams echoed across the water, and the sacred Nile ran red with Egyptian blood.

Kamose fought like a man possessed, cutting his way toward Khamudi's vessel. If he could reach the king, if he could end this with one blade stroke, perhaps his death would have meaning.

An arrow grazed his shoulder. A spear thrust opened his thigh. Still, he pressed forward, his bronze blade weaving patterns of death among the enemy ranks.

"To me!" he called to Ahmose-Onkh, but his faithful commander was already down, pierced through the throat by a Hyksos spear.

When Khamudi's own blade found the gap beneath Kamose's armor, driving deep into his chest, the rebel prince looked up at his killer with something almost like gratitude. At least he would die facing a king, not butchered by common soldiers.

"You fought well, Egyptian," Khamudi said, not without respect. "But you fought for a dream that died with your grandfather."

Kamose's vision darkened as he sank to his knees on the blood-slick deck. Around him, his men fell one by one—all seventy of them, dead or dying in the muddy waters of a river that had once known only Egyptian names.

Forgive me, he thought as darkness claimed him. I was not strong enough. But perhaps... perhaps Ahmose will be.

The Return of the Fallen Kamose

The delegation arrived at Thebes as the sun began its descent toward the western horizon. A single Hyksos vessel flying the banner of truce, its deck crowded with foreign soldiers standing at rigid attention.

In the center of the boat lay a plain wooden coffin—rough-hewn, unadorned, unworthy of royal blood. No gold, no protective spells, no offerings for the afterlife. Just raw planks nailed together like a carpenter's box.

Word had spread through the city. By the time the boat docked, a crowd had gathered at the royal quay—priests, nobles, commoners, all drawn by the terrible certainty that their prince had finally met his end.

Usermaatra, the high priest of Amun, stepped forward as the Hyksos commander disembarked. The priest's face showed no emotion, though his hands trembled within his robes.

"We bring you the last of your rebels," the officer said without ceremony. He was young for such rank, his armor bearing fresh scratches from recent battle. "King Khamudi grows weary of these... disruptions. Let this end them."

Four soldiers carried the coffin down the gangplank and set it before the Egyptian delegation with casual indifference. Another officer presented Usermaatra with a sealed scroll.

"From King Khamudi," he said. "Read it and understand your position."

The Hyksos departed without another word, leaving the body of their prince in the hands of his people. As the coffin was lifted with proper reverence, Usermaatra broke the seal and read Khamudi's message:

To the rulers of Thebes: Your prince dared to raid Avaris itself while I was away—an unforgivable violation of the seat of royal power. His rebellion dies with him. Tribute will be doubled for five years to compensate for damages and disrespect. A permanent garrison will be established at Cusae to prevent future foolishness. Let this be the end of Egyptian delusions. —Khamudi, King of Upper and Lower Egypt

Usermaatra closed his eyes briefly, then turned to address the crowd. There would be time for rage later. For now, they must honor their fallen prince and protect the child who would bear Egypt's hopes.

The Funeral

Seventy days of mourning had passed. The embalmers had worked their sacred art, restoring dignity to a body that had been denied it in death. Now, as the funeral procession wound through Thebes' narrow streets, the entire city turned out to bid farewell to their fallen prince.

Professional mourners led the way, their wailing cries echoing off mud-brick walls. Behind them came priests bearing sacred images, then nobles with offerings for the afterlife. The sarcophagus—now properly adorned with gold leaf and protective hieroglyphs—rode on an ox-drawn sledge.

Walking beside it was the royal family. Ahhotep, queen mother, stood tall despite her grief. At forty, she remained beautiful, but fine lines around her eyes spoke of years of worry. Beside her, young Ahmose gripped his mother's hand, the ten-year-old's face solemn beyond his years.

At the tomb carved into the western cliffs, final rituals were performed. Spells from the Book of the Dead were recited, protective amulets placed among the wrappings, provisions set out for the journey ahead. When the heavy stone doors sealed the burial chamber, Ahhotep stepped forward to address the assembled crowd.

"We've buried a son of Egypt today," she said, her voice carrying clearly through the hushed assembly. "A prince who died fighting for our freedom. I know many of you think his rebellion was folly—that he brought only suffering upon our people."

Her eyes flashed with sudden fire. "Perhaps you're right. Perhaps Kamose was a fool to think seventy men could challenge an empire. But he was our fool, and he died believing in something greater than survival."

She placed a protective hand on Ahmose's shoulder, drawing the boy forward.

"My son stands before you now—a child bearing a crown too heavy for his young head. We've accepted Khamudi's terms because we must. We'll pay the tribute, endure the garrison, bow our heads and wait."

Her voice grew stronger. "But we'll also remember. We'll teach our children who they are, where they came from, what was taken from us. And perhaps—perhaps when the gods will it—Egypt will rise again."

A murmur ran through the crowd—not of rebellion, but of something more dangerous: hope preserved in darkness.

The Vision

That night, as the royal household settled into uneasy sleep, old Tetesheri sat alone in her chambers, staring into the flame of a single oil lamp. At seventy-three, she'd lived through the reigns of three pharaohs, watching Egypt's glory fade with each passing year.

The flame flickered, and for a moment seemed to dance with unusual brightness. In its heart, she glimpsed something that made her gasp—a vision of armies marching beneath Egyptian banners, of foreign walls crumbling, of her grandson grown tall and strong, wearing the double crown of the two lands.

When Ahhotep found her there an hour later, Tetesheri was sitting straight-backed, a strange light in her ancient eyes.

"I've seen it," the old woman said before Ahhotep could speak.

"Seen what, grandmother?"

"The future." Tetesheri's trembling hand reached toward the flame. "Ahmose won't be like his brother—charging headlong at walls too strong to break. He'll be patient. Careful. He'll wait until the time is right."

She grasped Ahhotep's hand with surprising strength.

"Kamose failed because he fought like a rebel. But Ahmose... Ahmose will remember he's a king. And when he comes of age, he'll unite the two lands as they were meant to be."

Ahhotep felt a chill at the certainty in the old woman's voice. "How can you know this?"

Tetesheri smiled, years seeming to fall away from her face. "Because some defeats are just the darkness before dawn. Kamose lit a flame that can't be extinguished—not by tribute, not by garrisons, not by all of Khamudi's armies."

She looked toward the sealed window, as if seeing beyond Thebes itself. "Our boy will finish what his brother began. It's written in the stars."

As she spoke, the lamp flame burned steadier and brighter, casting their shadows tall against the painted walls—walls decorated with images of pharaohs triumphant, of Egypt united and strong.

"Then we'll make sure he lives to see it," Ahhotep whispered, her resolve hardening like bronze in the forge. "Whatever the cost."

Chapter 6 - The Shepherd Spy

1530 BC, Pelusiac Branch of the Nile

By midday, they had reached the grazing grounds where their herdsmen tended the royal cattle. From a distance, the scene appeared peaceful—dozens of long-horned oxen dotting the lush Delta pastures, their hides gleaming copper and black in the sunlight. The beasts moved with languid grace, tearing at the sweet grass with powerful jaws, their tails swishing lazily at flies. This was Egypt's bounty, the wealth of the most fertile land in the known world—and yet a fifth of every herd went to feed foreign invaders.

The chief herdsman, Nakht, a burly man with a face like tanned leather and a chest as broad as a bull's, approached as they disembarked. He squinted at the group of apparent cattle drivers, showing no sign of recognition. His hand moved casually to rest on the dagger at his hip, the gesture of a man who lived on the frontier of two hostile kingdoms.

"What business brings you downriver?" he called, his voice carrying the harsh accent of the Delta, distinct from the more refined tones of Thebes.

Ebana stepped forward, subtly placing himself between the stranger and his king. "We come from Thebes, on the king's business," he replied, using the coded phrase they had arranged months before.

Nakht's eyes widened slightly, then narrowed as he scrutinized the disguised men more closely. His gaze lingered on Ahmose, searching for some familiar feature beneath the grime and deception. The herdsman's nostrils flared like a bull testing the wind for the scent of a predator.

"The king sends such common men on his errands these days?" he asked, voice lowered to prevent the nearby herdsmen from overhearing.

Ahmose stepped forward, and only then, as he moved with the unmistakable grace that years of royal training had instilled, did recognition flash in Nakht's eyes. It was in the way Ahmose carried himself—the subtle lift of the chin, the squared shoulders, the direct gaze that expected obedience. Even covered in filth, a king could not wholly disguise the authority bred into his bones.

"My l—" he began, dropping to one knee, his weathered face suddenly pale beneath its tan.

"Quiet," Ahmose commanded softly, the single word carrying the weight of absolute authority. "Here, I am Senbi, a cattle driver, nothing more."

Nakht recovered quickly, rising and gesturing toward his humble reed hut. "Come, then. You must be hungry after your journey."

The hut stood on a small rise above the floodplain, offering a view across the herds and, in the far distance, the hazy outline of Avaris. It was a simple structure, its walls made of bundled reeds plastered with mud, its roof thatched with palm fronds. Still, it offered blessed shade from the punishing sun.

Inside the hut, safe from prying eyes, Nakht's demeanor changed completely. He fell to his knees, pressing his forehead to the packed-earth floor.

"Forgive me, my king. I did not expect... this." He gestured at Ahmose's disguise, awe and confusion warring in his expression.

"Good," Ahmose replied, allowing himself a small smile that transformed his face. "Neither will the Hyksos."

The interior of the hut was cool and dim, the only light filtering through small gaps in the reed walls. The scent of dried herbs hung in the air, mingling with the earthier smells of cattle and men who lived close to their animals. It was a far cry from the cedar-scented, lotus-adorned chambers of the palace in Thebes, but Ahmose found himself appreciating its honest simplicity.

Over a simple meal of bread, dried fish, and beer, Ahmose explained their mission. The bread was coarse but fresh, still warm from baking in clay ovens. The fish had been dried in the sun until it was leathery and intensely flavored, preserved with salt from the nearby marshes. The beer was cloudy and thick, served in rough clay bowls rather than the gold cups Ahmose was accustomed to. To a man who had spent days on the river, it tasted better than the finest royal vintage.

They needed to select forty of the finest cattle—strong enough to justify their presence near Avaris but not so exceptional as to draw undue attention. Each beast would be chosen not just for its appearance but for its stamina and temperament. The animals would need to travel far and fast when the time came.

"And trustworthy men," Ahmose added, tearing a piece of bread with strong fingers. "Men who can keep secrets even under threat of death."

Nakht nodded, his expression grave. "I have such men. They hate the Hyksos as much as any true Egyptian."

The herdsman's eyes darkened as he spoke, and Ahmose sensed a story behind the simple statement. "Your family has suffered at their hands?"

Nakht's weathered face hardened into a mask of controlled fury. "My eldest daughter was taken ten years ago to serve in their households. We hear she lives still, but as a concubine to one of their captains." He spat on the floor. "They take our cattle, our grain, our women. They desecrate our temples with their foreign gods."

Ahmose reached across the space between them, gripping the herdsman's wrist with surprising strength. "When we march on Avaris, your daughter will be among the first we free. This I swear by Ma'at and all the gods."

Nakht's eyes glistened with unshed tears. "For that promise alone, my king, I would die a thousand deaths."

By sunset, they had selected their beasts—powerful oxen with impressive horns and sturdy legs, but deliberately mixed with a few less impressive specimens to avoid arousing suspicion. The sunset painted the Delta landscape in hues of gold and crimson, casting long shadows across the grazing lands. In the distance, thin columns of smoke rose from cooking fires in the Hyksos settlements, a reminder of how close they were to enemy territory. Jackals began their mournful howling as darkness descended, their cries echoing across the flatlands like the voices of restless spirits.

That night, while the others slept on reed mats in Nakht's hut, their bodies exhausted from the day's labors, Ahmose summoned Ebana to his side. The warrior moved silently, his massive frame somehow avoiding every creaking reed.

"We sail tonight," he whispered, his breath warm against Ebana's ear.

Under the cover of darkness, their small boat slipped silently into the network of canals that fed into the main branch of the Nile. With only the stars to guide them, Ahmose and Ebana navigated the treacherous waterways that led toward Avaris, the heart of Hyksos power. The moon was a slender crescent, offering just enough light to navigate by while keeping them concealed from watchful eyes.

The marshy Delta spread before them like a labyrinth, its channels shifting with the seasons. Papyrus reeds rose high on either side, forming natural walls that both concealed their passage and limited their visibility. Occasionally, the eyes of crocodiles gleamed in the darkness, watching their progress with primeval hunger.

This was dangerous territory—not just because of the Hyksos patrols that occasionally swept the region, but because the waterways themselves could trap and strand unwary travelers. One wrong turn could lead them into a dead-end pool where they might be discovered at dawn, or into quicksand-like shallows that could swallow a man whole.

Ahmose, however, had studied these passages for years through reports from merchants and spies. Now, he needed to see them with his own eyes. He needed to feel the currents, to measure the depths with his pole, to judge whether these waterways could support the fleet of war boats he planned to lead north when the time came.

"There," he whispered, pointing to a narrow canal that branched eastward. The waterway was barely visible, a slightly darker line against the night-black landscape. "That waterway bypasses the main approach to Pi-Ramesses. The Hyksos rarely patrol it because it seems to lead nowhere of value."

Ebana nodded, making careful marks on a scrap of papyrus by the dim light of a covered lamp. The flame was shielded on three sides by curved pottery, allowing just enough light to see their immediate surroundings without betraying their position. "And it connects here?" he asked, indicating another channel.

"Yes. That route would allow us to move supplies and men within striking distance of Tjaru without alerting the main garrison." Ahmose's finger traced the path on the crude map, leaving a faint smudge of river mud.

The night air was cool against their skin, a blessed relief after the day's heat. Insects hummed and chirped all around them, providing a natural cover for the soft sounds of their passage. From somewhere in the darkness came the deep, guttural roar of a hippopotamus—a reminder that human enemies were not the only danger they faced.

For three nights they continued this dangerous survey, mapping tributaries and marking the positions of Hyksos watchtowers. They observed the foreign soldiers' patterns—when guards changed, which posts were undermanned, where the defensive walls were most vulnerable. They noted the locations of granaries and arsenals, counting the number of chariots visible in the moonlight, estimating the strength of the forces that would oppose them.

Each observation was meticulously recorded, each detail memorized. Ahmose knew that a single missed detail could mean the difference between victory and annihilation when the time came for war.

Most crucially, they confirmed what their spies had long suspected: the Hyksos had grown complacent in their dominance. Their patrols were predictable, their vigilance diminished by years of unchallenged rule. Guards dozed at their posts or gathered to gamble with knucklebones, leaving sections of wall unwatched for hours at a time. Officers drank themselves into stupors in taverns near the barracks, their weapons left carelessly aside.

"They believe we are broken," Ahmose remarked on their final night of reconnaissance, as they observed a Hyksos guard post from the concealment of reeds. The guard tower rose like a dark finger against the star-strewn sky, its platform occupied by a single sentry who paced with lazy indifference. "They think we accept their yoke."

Ebana's eyes gleamed in the darkness, reflecting the distant torchlight from the Hyksos fortress. "They will learn otherwise, my king."

Ahmose nodded, his face set like flint. "Yes. But first, we must play our parts one last time."

Payment of Tribute

On the final leg of their journey, Ahmose led his cattle south, moving toward Memphis, where Thebes was required to pay its tribute to the Hyksos tax collectors. The procession moved slowly along the dusty riverbank, forty beasts lowing under the midday sun. The air shimmered with heat, the horizon wavering like a mirage, promising water that wasn't there.

Ahmose walked at their head, staff in hand, every inch the experienced herdsman. The wooden rod was smooth from years of use, inherited from the real herdsman whose identity he had borrowed. His skin was now truly weathered; his hands genuinely calloused from days of handling the powerful beasts. The disguise had become, in some ways, a second skin.

But when they arrived at the collection point, Ahmose's blood ran cold.

He found Khamudi waiting.

The Hyksos king stood tall in his foreign robes of imported Canaanite fabric, patterned with geometric designs in vibrant hues of purple and crimson. His chariot gleamed in the sun like a blade of bronze, its sides inlaid with electrum and ivory, its framework crafted by the finest Egyptian artisans working under Hyksos whips. The horses that drew it were magnificent Arabian stock, their coats gleaming like burnished copper, their manes plaited with gold thread. Gold glinted from Khamudi's wrists and throat—Egyptian gold, plundered from the land he now ruled. A pectoral of carnelian and turquoise lay against his chest, depicting Sutekh, the storm god the Hyksos had adopted as their patron deity. His beard was oiled and curled in the Asiatic style; his eyes lined with kohl in a poor imitation of Egyptian nobility.

His soldiers—some of them Egyptian defectors—stood at his side, watching the Theban herdsmen with predatory attention. Their spears caught the sunlight, the metal tips promising swift death to any who showed disrespect to their foreign master.

Ahmose had not anticipated this. The Hyksos king rarely attended such mundane matters as tax collection. Something had drawn him here—perhaps suspicion, perhaps mere chance. Either way, danger hung in the air like the scent before a storm.

With practiced humility, Ahmose directed his men to separate eight of the finest cattle from the herd—the required tribute. He kept his face turned down, hoping the king's interest would pass quickly. Sweat trickled down his spine, not just from the heat but from the tension that coiled within him like a desert cobra preparing to strike.

But fate was not so kind.

Khamudi's sharp eyes swept over the gathering, then landed on Ahmose like a hawk spotting prey. The foreign king stepped forward, his jeweled sandals raising small puffs of dust with each deliberate step.

"You," he said, stepping forward. His Egyptian was fluent but carried the harsh accent of his homeland, each word precise but lacking the musicality of a native speaker. "You look familiar."

The world seemed to slow. Ahmose could feel Ebana tensing nearby, hand drifting toward his concealed dagger. With the slightest shake of his head, Ahmose warned him to stand down. Violence here would mean death for them all—and more importantly, would alert the Hyksos to their plans before they were ready to strike.

He bowed his head, keeping his voice steady and rough, as befitted his disguise. "My lord, I am but a herdsman, come to deliver what is owed."

Khamudi studied him for a long moment. The king's eyes were the pale blue of distant mountains, cold and calculating, set in a face weathered by desert winds and hardened by years of brutal rule. Then he smirked, the expression like oil spreading across water.

"A herdsman, you say? Then tell me... why do your hands bear the marks of a warrior?"

For a moment, silence hung in the air like a suspended blade. Even the cattle seemed to sense the tension, growing still and watchful. Ahmose knew he had only seconds to act before Khamudi's suspicion hardened into certainty.

He laughed—a coarse, genuine sound that surprised even himself—and held up his hands. The calluses were real enough, though earned from sword practice rather than a herdsman's staff. Years of weapons training had hardened his palms in distinctive patterns that a keen observer might recognize.

"Hard work, my lord! The cattle in Thebes are not gentle. A man must be part warrior to manage them."

He gestured toward one of the larger bulls, which snorted and pawed at the ground as if on cue, its massive horns gleaming wickedly in the sunlight. A magnificent beast with a temper to match its size. "That one there gored my brother last season. Nearly sent him to meet Osiris, it did."

Khamudi's gaze lingered, probing for the lie beneath the truth. His eyes narrowed as he studied Ahmose's face, searching for some hint of nobility that might have survived the disguise. The moment stretched until Ahmose could hear his own heartbeat thundering in his ears like distant war drums.

For a terrible moment, Ahmose thought he saw recognition dawn in the Hyksos king's eyes. A flicker of suspicion, sharp as a dagger's point. But then Khamudi waved a dismissive hand, already bored with the exchange, his arrogance overriding his intuition.

"Take your beasts and go," he sneered.

As the scribe noted the transaction on a sheet of papyrus, his reed pen scratching softly across the surface, Khamudi's attention returned briefly to Ahmose. There was something in his gaze now—a lingering doubt, perhaps, or simply the casual cruelty of a man who enjoyed exercising power over others.

Ahmose bowed low, hatred burning in his chest like a coal. Every fiber of his being wanted to seize his hidden knife and plunge it into the foreigner's heart—but that would be the act of a boy, not a king. True vengeance required patience.

"As my lord commands."

He gathered his remaining cattle, careful not to move too quickly, not to show relief or fear. They departed without looking back, though Ahmose could feel Khamudi's eyes boring into his back until they were beyond the settlement's edge. Only when they had travelled a league downriver did he allow his shoulders to relax slightly.

When they were safely away, Ebana moved closer to his king.

"That was too close," he murmured, his voice barely audible above the lowing of the cattle and the soft thuds of their hooves on the packed earth of the riverbank path.

Ahmose nodded, his jaw tight. "But revealing as well. Did you see how he surrounded himself? Four guards, no more. And only two chariots in his retinue. He travels with less protection than a minor noble."

"Arrogance," Ebana agreed, spitting into the dust.

"Arrogance that will be his undoing."

That night, as Ahmose and Ebana rode south toward Thebes, the weight of their gathered intelligence more precious than gold, the king's mind was already racing with plans. The terrain they had mapped, the weaknesses they had discovered, the complacency they had witnessed— all would factor into the campaign to come.

They made camp in a grove of sycamore trees, the sacred trees of Hathor, whose fruit had fed generations of Egyptians. As they sat around a small fire, eating a simple meal of bread and dried meat, Ahmose looked at the face of his companion. Ebana was more than a warrior—he was the brother fate had given him to replace the one the Hyksos had taken. Their bond had been forged in the furnace of shared purpose, tempered by years of patient planning.

The night was alive with sounds—the grunting of hippos from the nearby river, the occasional roar of a lion prowling the distant hills, the constant chorus of frogs and insects. Above them, the stars of Nut's body arched across the heavens, the same stars that had watched over Egypt since the beginning of time.

The Hyksos had let their guard down. They did not see the war coming. They could not imagine that the subjugated people of Upper Egypt would dare to challenge their rule after so many years of submission.

And soon, they would pay for their arrogance with blood and fire.

Ahmose looked to the stars, thinking of his brother's unmarked grave, of the years of humiliation, of the tribute cattle that should have fed Egyptian children. Of his mother Ahhotep, who had guided him from boyhood to manhood with unwavering strength. Of his grandmother Tetesheri, whose prophecy had named him Egypt's liberator. Of the people who looked to him for salvation from the foreign yoke.

"Soon," he promised the night, the word a sacred vow to gods and ancestors alike. "Soon."

The stars glittered in silent witness to his oath—an oath that would change the course of Egypt's destiny, an oath that would be written in Hyksos blood and commemorated in stone for all eternity.

Chapter 7 - The Liberation Begins

1529 BC Palace of Ahmose, Thebes

The night air hung heavy over Thebes, thick with lotus blossoms and sacred oils. The cloying sweetness mingled with earthier aromas drifting up from the Nile. Tetisheri, grandmother of princes and matriarch of a dynasty not yet born, tossed upon her sleeping couch. The fine linen sheets tangled around her frail frame like burial wrappings. Her once regal and commanding body had withered with the passage of years, but her mind remained as sharp as a hunter's spear, and tonight it pierced the veil between worlds with uncanny precision.

In her dream, she stood upon the sacred waters of the Nile, her feet dry as though the river itself acknowledged her divine right. Her toes felt the coolness beneath them without the wetness that should accompany it—a miracle that even in dreams left her breathless with wonder. Before her stretched the Two Lands, fractured and bleeding under foreign occupation. The rich black soil of the valley had turned gray and barren in patches where Hyksos boots had trampled the earth for too long. The Asiatic invaders who had seized Lower Egypt and ruled from Avaris had held their boot upon Egypt's throat for generations, squeezing the life from a once-proud civilization.

"No more," she whispered, and in her dream, the words carried on the wind across the entirety of the land, from the delta marshes to the cataracts of the south. "No more shall the sons of Set rule where Horus should reign."

She turned northward, toward the delta where the Hyksos had built their stronghold at Avaris. Through the veil of dream-sight, she could see it burning already, not with the destructive flames of chaos but with the purifying fire of Ma'at—divine order returning at last. The flames were golden rather than red, like the sun itself had descended to cleanse the land of foreign taint.

When she awoke, her handmaiden Meryt was already at her side, concern etched into her young face, her eyes wide with the fear of one who has witnessed the divine touching the mortal.

"My lady, you called out in your sleep," Meryt said, pouring fresh water into a silver cup. Her hands trembled slightly. "The guards heard you from the corridor."

Tetisheri accepted the drink, her hand steady despite her years. The cool liquid soothed her throat, parched from speaking prophecies to the empty night. She studied the handmaiden's face, noting the shadows beneath her eyes—the girl had likely been watching over her for hours.

"Summon my daughter Ahhotep," she commanded, her voice carrying the weight of royal authority despite her informal position. "And my grandson, Prince Ahmose. A vision and a dream, confirmation. The time of waiting is over."

Meryt bowed low, her forehead nearly touching the polished limestone floor. "At once, my lady. They await your call in the antechamber already. The prince returned from the temple of Amun only moments ago."

So the gods have orchestrated this meeting, Tetisheri thought. Amun himself has prepared my grandson's heart to receive my vision.

The Great Royal Wife Ahhotep entered her mother's chambers with the quiet dignity that had sustained Egypt through its darkest hours. The golden uraeus serpent gleamed upon her brow, symbol of a sovereignty that foreign invaders had tried and failed to extinguish. After the brutal murder of her husband, Pharaoh Tao II, she had shouldered the burden of keeping Thebes—the last Egyptian stronghold—from falling to the Hyksos. The weight of that responsibility had etched fine lines around her eyes and mouth, but had only strengthened the steel in her spine.

At her side walked her son Ahmose, a young man of twenty, his muscular frame testament to years of military training. His eyes held the same determination that had marked his father and his slain brother Kamose, yet something deeper lurked there too—a calculating patience, a willingness to sacrifice today for tomorrow's victory. Unlike his impetuous brother, Ahmose had learned the value of timing.

"You summoned us, Mother?" Ahhotep asked, bowing her head slightly in respect, the golden beads in her elaborate wig catching the lamplight.

Tetisheri gestured for them to sit upon the carved cedar chairs that flanked her couch. "I have seen Egypt whole again," she said without preamble, her voice dropping to ensure only they could hear her words. "Not as a wish or a prayer, but as a truth that waits for us to claim it."

Prince Ahmose's jaw tightened, the muscles bunching beneath his smooth-shaven skin. Since his father's violent death—skull crushed by a Hyksos war axe—and his brother's mysterious demise, the responsibility of vengeance and restoration had fallen to him. He was no longer the second son, the spare prince. He was Egypt's last hope, and the knowledge of it had aged him beyond his years.

"Grandmother," he said, his voice carrying the hardened edge of a warrior who had already seen too much bloodshed, "I have been training the army. We are stronger than when Kamose launched his attack, but is it enough to take Avaris? The Hyksos walls are high, their chariots swift, their archers skilled."

"Not Avaris first," Tetisheri replied, surprising them both. She leaned forward, her weathered fingers tracing an invisible map upon the linen sheet. "The vision showed me the path. The Hyksos draw their strength from Memphis and their supply routes to the east. Cut these, and Avaris becomes vulnerable, like a lotus severed from its roots."

Ahhotep nodded slowly, understanding dawning in her eyes. She had been a military commander's wife long enough to grasp strategy. "A siege, then. Starve them out rather than a direct assault. Kamose tried to take Avaris with brute force and failed."

"The lioness understands the hunt," Tetisheri smiled at her daughter, pride warming her ancient voice. "When the prey is strong, one does not attack its horns but waits for hunger to weaken it."

"Ahmose, you have a commander, the son of Ebana? The naval officer?" Tetisheri continued, recalling tales of an innovative young captain who had risen through the ranks not by birth but by brilliant tactical thinking.

"Yes," Ahmose confirmed, leaning forward, his interest piqued. "A brilliant tactician. He believes our strength lies in combining land forces with river attacks. The Hyksos may have superior chariots, but they have never mastered the Nile as we have. Their ships are clumsy, designed for the open seas of their homeland, not our sacred river."

"Then it is as I saw it," Tetisheri said, sitting straighter, her spine uncurling like a cobra preparing to strike. "Ahmose, grandson of my heart, hear me well. You will not merely drive the Hyksos back to their lands. You will become the first king of a new Egypt, a unified Egypt. The founder of a new dynasty."

The prince did not smile at this prophecy. Instead, he knelt before his grandmother, taking her aged hands in his calloused ones. His palms bore the hardened calluses of daily weapons training; his knuckles scarred from countless practice bouts.

"By my father's blood and my brother's spirit, I swear it," he vowed, his voice dropping to a whisper that nevertheless carried the force of thunder. "The Hyksos king Khamudi will kneel before Egyptian power, or he will not live to see the next flood season."

Ahhotep placed her hand upon her son's shoulder, completing the circle of three generations. "Then let it begin," she said. "While the Hyksos believe us to be wounded after Kamose's defeat, we will prepare as never before."

Tetisheri nodded, feeling the presence of the gods in the room, invisible witnesses to this moment of destiny. "Go now," she told her grandson. "When next we speak, may it be as prince to a conquering commander."

As Ahmose rose and bowed, Tetisheri caught a glimpse of the future king in his bearing—the pharaoh who would reunite the Two Lands after a century of division. The gods had chosen well.

June 1529 BC Thebes

The shipyards of Thebes buzzed with activity as dawn broke over the eastern horizon, painting the limestone cliffs with streaks of gold and crimson. Sawdust filled the air, mingling with the smells of pitch and cedar oil. Ahmose, son of Ebana, directed the final preparations of the naval fleet that would sail north alongside Prince Ahmose's ground forces. Though both men were named Ahmose, the naval commander had risen from common origins through merit and cunning rather than birth—a fact that had initially caused grumbling among the nobility until his tactical brilliance silenced all critics.

"The last of the provisions are being loaded, my prince," he reported as the royal heir inspected the ships. He wiped sweat from his brow, leaving a streak of dirt across his copper-colored skin. "Hardtack enough for three months, dried fish and beer for two. We can sail with the midday tide when the wind shifts in our favor."

Prince Ahmose nodded, watching as soldiers filed aboard the cedar vessels, their bronze-tipped spears catching the morning light like a forest of metallic reeds. Each man was armed with weapons freshly forged in the temple workshops, their shields of stretched hide painted with symbols of divine protection.

The river would carry them swiftly toward their destiny, its current an ally as faithful as any soldier. Ahmose offered a silent prayer to Hapi, god of the inundation, asking for his blessing upon their journey.

"How many ships?" the prince asked, calculating in his mind the logistical needs of the campaign ahead.

"Forty combat vessels and twenty supply barges," the commander replied, pride evident in his voice. "The largest fleet assembled since the Old Kingdom, enough to control the river from Thebes to Memphis."

"And the land forces?"

"Five thousand men, as you ordered. The chariots will follow the east bank, where the ground is firmer. The infantry takes the western route, with scouts ranging ahead to warn of ambush." The commander's face hardened. "We've trained them as you commanded, my prince—not as individuals but as units. They fight as one, shields locked, spears advancing in waves."

Prince Ahmose turned to see his mother approaching, flanked by her personal guard. These men, handpicked veterans who had survived the battle that claimed her husband's life, would die to the last man before allowing harm to come to her. Ahhotep had forgone her royal finery for a simple linen dress, belted with gold that glinted in the morning sun. Around her neck hung the Golden Flies of Valor—awards for bravery usually reserved for warriors. She had earned them during the defense of Thebes after her husband's murder, rallying the citizens when all seemed lost.

"The men should see you before you depart," she told her son, her voice carrying easily over the din of preparation. "They need to know what they fight for—not just a prince, but the future of Egypt itself."

The prince understood. With a nod to the commander, he followed his mother to a raised platform where he could address the assembled army. Five thousand men stood in formation—spearmen with their bronze-tipped weapons held vertically like a forest of reeds, archers with quivers full of arrows fletched with hawk feathers, charioteers standing beside their vehicles of war. Their faces were turned upward, waiting, hope and fear mingling in equal measure.

Ahhotep spoke first, her voice strong and clear, trained by years of command to carry across crowds without shrieking like a market woman.

"Sons of Egypt! For a hundred years, our land has suffered under the Hyksos heel. They have claimed the title of pharaoh, though their blood is not of the Black Land." She paused, letting her words sink in. "They have worshipped strange gods and made us bow to foreign ways. They have taken our grain and our gold, leaving us to starve while they feast in our palaces."

A murmur of anger rippled through the troops, like wind through papyrus reeds. She raised her hand for silence, the golden bracelets on her wrist catching the sunlight.

"But they made one mistake," she continued, her voice dropping so the men would strain to hear, drawing them into her words like conspirators. "They left us Thebes. They left us our pride." Her voice rose again. "They left us the memory of what Egypt once was—and what it will be again. And they left us my son, Prince Ahmose, blood of Tao, brother of Kamose, who will reclaim what is ours!"

The prince stepped forward as cheers erupted, the sound reverberating off the temple walls behind them. He waited until they subsided before speaking, conscious that many of these men had heard similar speeches before Kamose's failed campaign.

"I do not promise you an easy victory," he began, his voice less practiced than his mother's but no less commanding. The men fell silent, straining to catch every word. "The Hyksos have horses and chariots. They have walled cities and foreign alliances. They are fierce and cunning, and they will not yield Egypt without blood."

He paused, letting the stark reality of his words sink in. These were not mercenaries to be swayed by promises of gold and women. They were Egyptians fighting for their homeland.

"But we have the blessing of Amun-Ra," he continued, gesturing toward the great temple behind them where prayers and sacrifices had been offered since dawn. "We have right on our side. We have the wisdom of our ancestors guiding our plans." His voice rose with passion. "And we have a hundred years of rage in our hearts!"

The roar from the troops shook the very ground, dust rising from thousands of stamping feet. Spears hammered against shields in rhythmic approval, the sound like thunder across the valley.

"Today we sail north," Ahmose continued, his voice rising with the fervor of the moment. "Not as raiders or scouts, but as liberators. We do not fight just for ourselves, but for our children and their children after them. By the next full moon, Memphis will be Egyptian again. By the next flood, all of Egypt will be united under one crown—our crown!"

The celebration that followed was deafening. Ahmose caught his commander's eye and nodded slightly. It was time. The words had been spoken; now action must follow, or they would become as empty as the promises of defeated kings before him.

As the sun reached its zenith, the first ships pushed away from the docks, their sails of tightly woven linen catching the northerly wind. The sacred bark of Amun-Ra led the procession, bearing priests who would offer continuous prayers throughout the journey. Behind it came the royal vessel, its prow carved in the likeness of a falcon—Horus, divine protector of the kingship.

On the banks, the infantry began their march, standards held high. Each company carried totems of their patron deities—Montu the war god, Sekhmet the lioness, Nekhbet the vulture goddess. They would march through territories long abandoned to Hyksos rule, through villages where Egyptian customs had begun to fade under foreign influence.

Prince Ahmose stood at the prow of the lead military vessel; his gaze fixed on the horizon where destiny awaited. The weight of Tetisheri's prophecy pressed upon his shoulders, neither crushing him nor bowing his back, but strengthening his resolve like the counterweight of a balance scale.

Behind him, standing on the palace balcony, Tetisheri watched her vision begin to unfold. Her lined face broke into a smile of grim satisfaction. Soon, very soon, Egypt would be whole again. She could almost see the threads of fate weaving themselves into the pattern she had glimpsed in her dream—a tapestry of blood and glory, defeat and triumph, death and rebirth.

"May Amun guide you," she whispered as the last sail disappeared around the river bend. "May Sekhmet lend strength to your arm. May Thoth grant you wisdom in your strategies."

And as an afterthought, spoken so softly that even Meryt standing beside her could not hear: "And may you return to us alive, grandson of my heart."

Over the following weeks, Prince Ahmose's forces moved methodically northward, reclaiming Egyptian territory with surgical precision. Unlike his brother Kamose's headlong charges, Ahmose employed patient strategy—isolating Hyksos garrisons, cutting supply lines, and securing the loyalty of liberated towns before advancing. Each victory strengthened his army and weakened enemy morale. By midsummer, the time had come for the boldest gambit yet.

July 1529 BC - Memphis and Heliopolis

The heat rose in shimmering waves from the desert floor as Prince Ahmose's army approached the approaches to Memphis, Egypt's ancient capital. Not the gentle warmth of southern Thebes, but the fierce, punishing heat of the northern desert, where even scorpions sought shelter during midday. For nearly a month, they had been systematically reclaiming Upper Egypt, consolidating their gains, ensuring loyalty from liberated territories before pressing northward. Each town, each temple complex, each strategic crossroads had been taken with minimal Egyptian casualties—not through overwhelming force but through carefully orchestrated movements that isolated Hyksos garrisons and cut their supply lines.

Now, the real prize lay before them—Memphis, Egypt's traditional capital, the jewel that had fallen to foreign hands generations ago. Beyond Memphis, to the northeast, lay Heliopolis, the sacred city of Ra. And beyond both, the ultimate target: Avaris itself, the Hyksos stronghold in the Delta.

"The scouts report Hyksos forces are concentrated at Memphis," said Ahmose, son of Ebana, pointing to a crude map drawn in the sand of the command tent. Sweat trickled down his temples despite the shade, and flies buzzed incessantly around the lamp oil used to mark enemy positions. "They've reinforced the garrison there with troops from outlying areas. They expect us to strike there first."

Prince Ahmose studied the map, his face betraying nothing of his thoughts. A month of warfare had hardened him further, adding new scars to his bronzed skin and a calculating patience to his military mind. Where once he might have lunged for the obvious target, now he sought the vulnerable underbelly, the undefended flank.

"And that is precisely what we shall not do," he replied at last, his voice low so that only his inner circle of commanders could hear. "How quickly can we bypass Memphis and take Heliopolis instead?"

The naval commander raised his eyebrows in surprise, the scar tissue around his left eye puckering. "Bypass Memphis? It's risky, my prince. We would leave a significant enemy force at our backs. If they sortie while we're engaged elsewhere..."

"Not if we position troops here and here," Ahmose indicated positions on both sides of the Nile, his finger tracing lines in the sand with the precision of a scribe. "Look at the geography. Heliopolis controls the approaches from the northeast—the supply routes between Memphis and Avaris. We don't need to take Memphis yet—only isolate it. Cut it off from Avaris and from any reinforcements moving south."

Understanding dawned in the commander's eyes. "A chokehold rather than a dagger thrust."

"Precisely," the prince nodded, a grim smile briefly crossing his features. "The Hyksos have ruled through fear and superior weaponry, not superior numbers. Their chariots are fearsome in open battle, but useless in siege warfare. If we separate their forces, they cannot bring their full might against us at any one point."

The other officers leaned closer, the strategy capturing their imagination. This was not the headlong charge that had doomed Kamose; this was the patient stalking of a leopard, choosing the moment to strike with lethal precision.

"We will need to move quickly," said an older commander, his beard gray with years but his eyes sharp as a hawk's. "Before they realize our intent and reinforce Heliopolis."

"Tonight," Ahmose decided. "We move tonight."

As darkness fell, the Egyptian camp appeared to settle in for the night, cook fires burning low, sentries pacing in plain sight of any watching Hyksos scouts. But beneath this façade of routine, preparations were already underway. Weapons were checked and rechecked, sandals wrapped with cloth to muffle footsteps, orders passed in whispers from officer to soldier.

Under cover of darkness, the Egyptian army split into three divisions. The smallest remained to establish a blockade of Memphis from a safe distance, their orders to create the illusion of a larger force through multiple campfires and constant movement. The second, led by the naval commander, secured the river routes, positioning ships at strategic points to intercept any Hyksos vessels attempting to bring reinforcements or supplies.

The largest force, under Prince Ahmose himself, made a forced march through the night, circumventing known Hyksos patrol routes. The men moved in silence, each step bringing them closer to their objective. By the time false dawn painted the eastern sky with the first hint of gray, they stood poised outside the walls of Heliopolis, hidden among date palms and irrigation ditches.

The city of Ra, center of solar worship since time immemorial, slumbered unaware of the liberation—or doom—that awaited it with the rising sun.

Ahmose surveyed the walls through the pre-dawn gloom, noting with satisfaction that they appeared lightly manned. The Hyksos had grown complacent here, so close to their strongholds, so far from the traditional fronts of battle. The guards paced with the bored shuffle of men who expected no danger, their spears carried casually rather than at the ready.

"Have the men in position," he whispered to his sub-commanders. "When the sun touches the temple rooftops, we move."

The priests of Ra were the first to surrender, opening the eastern gate before a single arrow flew. Whether through Egyptian patriotism or simple self-preservation, they recognized the tide of history when it appeared before their walls. By midday, the city's Hyksos garrison found themselves surrounded, cut off from reinforcement, their commander trapped in his own headquarters.

"They are offering terms, my prince," reported a scout, kneeling before Ahmose's makeshift throne in what had once been the governor's palace. Blood stained the man's linen kilt, though whether his own or an enemy's was impossible to tell.

"Their terms are irrelevant," Ahmose replied coldly, fingering the hilt of his khopesh. The curved blade had tasted Hyksos blood many times in the past month, and he had no intention of denying it another feast. "They will surrender unconditionally, or they will die to the last man."

The scout hesitated, then added, "Their commander asks to speak with you directly, my prince. He claims to have information regarding Memphis' defenses."

That gave Ahmose pause. Information was as valuable as bronze in warfare, often more so. "Bring him, then. But strip him of weapons first, and have archers ready should he try anything foolish."

By sunset, the Hyksos commander knelt before the Egyptian prince, his foreign armor stripped away, his neck bare to the blade. He was older than Ahmose had expected, his beard streaked with gray, his skin weathered by decades of Egyptian sun despite his northern blood.

"You fight without honor," the defeated man spat, his Egyptian heavily accented but understandable. "Sneaking around like desert jackals rather than meeting us in open battle where your chariots could test themselves against ours."

Ahmose leaned forward, his eyes hard as obsidian. The braziers in the chamber cast his shadow large upon the wall behind him, creating the illusion of a giant looming over the kneeling prisoner.

"You speak of honor?" he asked quietly, the softness of his voice more terrifying than any shout. "Your king's assassins crushed my father's skull while he slept. Your people have occupied our land for a century. You have desecrated our temples, stolen our wealth, enslaved our people. There is no honor between us—only survival."

He stood, circling the kneeling man like a jackal around wounded prey. "Now, I'm told you have information about Memphis. Speak it plainly, and you may yet live to see another sunrise."

The Hyksos commander stared up at him, hatred burning in his pale eyes. "Kill me if you wish, Egyptian. I will not betray my king."

Ahmose smiled, a cold expression devoid of mirth. "Your king? Khamudi sits in Avaris feasting while you kneel here awaiting death. Do you think he would hesitate to sacrifice you if your positions were reversed?"

A flicker of uncertainty crossed the commander's face—brief, but not brief enough to escape Ahmose's notice. The prince pressed his advantage.

"Your garrison at Memphis is already cut off. No reinforcements will reach them. Your king has abandoned them, just as he has abandoned you. How long before they realize this and surrender as well?"

"Memphis will never fall," the man insisted, but his voice lacked conviction.

"Memphis has fallen before," Ahmose countered. "It fell to your people a century ago. Now it will return to its rightful rulers. The only question is how many must die before that happens."

With a gesture, he had the man dragged away to join the other prisoners. The Hyksos soldiers would be useful as laborers; their commanders would make valuable hostages. Later, perhaps, some might be ransomed back to their families in Canaan or Syria, but for now, they would help rebuild what their occupation had destroyed.

Three days later, word reached them of another victory. The Egyptian forces had successfully isolated Memphis, cutting off all supply routes from the north and south. The Hyksos fortress at Cusae had been abandoned without a fight, its garrison retreating northward to reinforce Avaris.

Ahmose received this news in the temple of Ra, where priests who had spent their entire lives under Hyksos rule now offered prayers of thanksgiving for their liberation. The golden rays of the setting sun streamed through the hypostyle hall, bathing the scene in an ethereal light that seemed to sanctify the moment.

Standing atop the temple pylon afterward, Prince Ahmose gazed northward toward the horizon where Avaris, the Hyksos capital, lay waiting. The victory at Heliopolis had come more easily than expected, but he harbored no illusions about the challenges ahead. Avaris was no mere garrison town; it was a fortress city built to withstand anything Egypt could throw against it.

His heart beat with the same rhythm as the war drums that had not ceased their pounding since they left Thebes. Each beat brought him closer to fulfilling his grandmother's prophecy, closer to avenging his father and brother, closer to reuniting the Two Lands under native rule.

"We march for Avaris," he announced to his commanders gathered behind him. The setting sun cast long shadows across the temple complex, turning men into giants upon the ancient stones. "And we will not stop until the Hyksos king Khamudi is on his knees before me."

One of the older commanders cleared his throat hesitantly. "My prince, our supply lines are stretched thin. Perhaps we should consolidate our gains before—"

"No," Ahmose cut him off, turning to face the assembled officers. "We have momentum now. The Hyksos are reeling, confused by our strategy. They expected a frontal assault on Memphis and instead find themselves outflanked. We must press our advantage before they recover."

He pointed north, toward invisible Avaris. "Every day we delay gives Khamudi time to summon allies from Canaan. Every day strengthens their walls and weakens our resolve. We have waited a century for this moment—I will not wait a day longer than necessary."

The commanders exchanged glances, then nodded as one. Who were they to argue with a prince whose strategies had already confounded the enemy?

That night, messengers were dispatched to Thebes, carrying news of their victories and requests for additional supplies to be sent downriver. Ahmose penned a personal message to his mother and grandmother, the papyrus roll sealed with dark amber resin, the precious substance hardened against the desert heat to protect the sacred writings within.

To the Great Royal Wife Ahhotep and the Royal Mother Tetisheri, greetings from your son and grandson Ahmose, by the grace of Amun-Ra. Heliopolis is ours. Memphis is isolated. We march for Avaris within the week. The vision unfolds as grandmother foresaw. May the gods continue to favor our cause.

He allowed himself a moment of reflection. A month ago, he had been a prince with an army of questionable readiness and a dream that seemed impossible. Now he commanded veterans of multiple victories, men who believed not just in Egypt's cause but in his leadership.

Tetisheri's prophecy was coming true, step by inexorable step. Soon, very soon, Egypt would be whole again.

Chapter 8 - City under Siege

August 1529 BC - Avaris

The stench of Avaris reached them long before its walls came into view—a miasma of too many people crowded into too small a space, of slaughterhouses and tanneries, of canals used as sewers. Built upon the ruins of an older Egyptian settlement, the Hyksos capital sprawled across the eastern delta, its northern district—Pi-Ramses—fortified with walls unlike anything seen in Egypt before. Foreign architecture jutted against the sky, an offense to Egyptian eyes accustomed to the elegant symmetry of their own monuments.

Prince Ahmose surveyed the city from a ridge overlooking the marshy approaches. The summer sun beat down mercilessly, turning armor into ovens and causing mirages to shimmer across the distant landscape. Behind him stretched his army, now swelled with liberated Egyptians eager to throw off the last vestiges of Hyksos rule. Men who had been slaves or servants months ago now stood as soldiers, their bodies leaner, their eyes harder, their spirits forged in the crucible of war.

The sight before him represented more than just another siege. Within those alien walls cowered the last stronghold of a century-long occupation, the final cancer that had to be cut from Egypt's body. Every stone of those foreign fortifications mocked the memory of his murdered father and brother, every banner that flew above them a reminder of Egyptian humiliation.

"Their walls are formidable," observed his chief architect, a young man named Ineni who had been brought along specifically to advise on siege tactics. Sweat beaded on the architect's shaven head as he studied the distant fortifications with the calculating eye of one who built such structures. "But not impregnable. They built for defense against Asiatic raiders, not an Egyptian army."

Ahmose nodded, appreciating the man's professional assessment. Ineni had proven himself invaluable during the campaign, his understanding of construction allowing him to identify weak points that others might miss. The prince had learned to value such expertise—the difference between a good commander and a great one often lay in knowing which advisors to trust.

"How long to breach them?" Ahmose asked, passing a waterskin to the older man. Water was precious here, with the Nile's branches controlled by the enemy, but he needed the architect's mind sharp.

Ineni drank sparingly before answering. "With rams and scaling ladders? Perhaps a month, and at terrible cost in lives. With a proper siege?" He squinted at the distant walls, measuring angles with his eye as though already planning the assault. "Longer, but with fewer casualties among our men."

The prince considered this, weighing options against time. A direct assault would cost many lives, but a prolonged siege would give the Hyksos time to summon allies from Canaan and beyond. Reports from scouts indicated that messengers had already slipped through their lines, racing eastward to beg assistance from Khamudi's allies. What troubled him more were the whispers of movement elsewhere—scattered reports of armies gathering in the south, of old enemies stirring while his forces were committed here.

He pushed these concerns aside for now. The siege of Avaris was the keystone of Egypt's liberation. Without removing this final Hyksos stronghold, all their previous victories would be meaningless. Khamudi and his foreign lords would simply wait, rebuild their strength, and strike back when the moment was right.

"We begin with encirclement," he decided, the military pragmatism of his father asserting itself. "Cut off all access to the river. Poison their wells if possible. Prepare for both options—assault and siege."

As his orders were carried out, runners established the first perimeter around the city, marking positions for the various divisions. Camp followers set up field kitchens and makeshift infirmaries, preparing for the wounded that would inevitably come. The sight of so many Egyptian banners surrounding the Hyksos capital filled every man with pride—for the first time in living memory, it was Egyptian forces doing the besieging rather than cowering behind their own walls.

Another messenger arrived from the east, dust-covered and exhausted. "My prince," the man gasped, falling to his knees. His lips were cracked from dehydration, his skin burned dark by days under the relentless sun. "News from Commander Pennekh's division at Tjaru!"

Tjaru—the easternmost fortress of Egypt, guarding the Way of Horus that led to Canaan and serving as the Hyksos' supply line to their homeland. Ahmose had dispatched a force there weeks ago, considering it essential to isolate Avaris completely. The capture of that fortress would cut Khamudi off from any hope of reinforcement from his Asiatic allies.

"Speak," Ahmose commanded, motioning for a servant to bring the messenger water.

The man drank gratefully before continuing, his voice steadier. "Tjaru has fallen, my prince! The garrison surrendered after only three days of siege. Some of the Hyksos soldiers escaped towards Sharuhen in Canaan, but our forces have secured the fortress itself. The road east is now under Egyptian control."

A cheer went up from the officers gathered around their prince. Ahmose allowed himself a small smile—the first in many months. The noose was tightening around Khamudi's neck, one strand at a time. With Tjaru secured, the Hyksos king would find no succor from his traditional allies in Canaan. The foreign rulers who had once seemed so powerful were discovering that their Egyptian subjects had not forgotten how to fight.

"Send word to Commander Pennekh. He is to secure the fortress and make sure that no supplies reach Avaris from Canaan. Any messengers attempting to leave Egypt are to be intercepted. I want Khamudi blind to events beyond his walls."

Yet even as he gave these orders, a nagging concern gnawed at the back of his mind. The timing of recent intelligence reports troubled him—whispers of movement in the south, of old enemies who had remained quiet suddenly showing signs of activity. It could be coincidence, but Ahmose had learned not to trust coincidence in warfare.

The greatest danger often came not from the enemy you were fighting, but from the one you weren't watching.

As night fell, Prince Ahmose climbed alone to the highest point of their encampment, dismissing even his personal guard. Below him, thousands of campfires dotted the landscape, surrounding Avaris like a net of stars drawn tight around prey. Within those walls cowered Khamudi, the Hyksos king who had orchestrated the murder of Ahmose's father and brother.

The sight filled him with grim satisfaction, but also with an awareness of how much depended on this siege. His entire army was committed here; every division focused on this single objective. If enemies struck elsewhere while his forces were tied down at Avaris, he would face the same impossible choice that had plagued Egyptian commanders for generations—abandon what they had fought to achieve, or watch the rest of Egypt burn.

"I am coming for you," Ahmose whispered into the darkness, his hand resting on the hilt of his father's khopesh. "All of Egypt is coming for you."

The night air carried the sounds of a city under siege—the distant calls of sentries, the hammering of carpenters working by torchlight to complete siege towers, the low murmur of men around campfires sharing stories of home and hopes for victory. These were the sounds of Egypt awakening from a century-long nightmare.

From within the walls of Avaris, watchfires burned like fallen stars, each one representing Hyksos soldiers who would soon face Egyptian justice. Ahmose wondered if Khamudi stood similarly on his own walls, looking out at the encircling Egyptian forces and contemplating his rapidly diminishing options. More troubling still, he wondered what other plans the Hyksos king might have set in motion—what final desperate gambit he might attempt when the walls finally began to crumble.

The end was approaching for one of them. After a century of occupation, destiny hung balanced on the edge of a blade—specifically, the blade that now rested at Prince Ahmose's side, hungering for the blood of his father's murderers.

February 1526 BC - The Siege Continues

Two and a half years had passed since Prince Ahmose began the siege of Pi-Ramses, the northern stronghold of Avaris. The war of attrition had become a familiar rhythm—Egyptian forces slowly tightening their grip while the Hyksos behind their walls grew weaker with each passing season. Victory seemed inevitable, a matter of time rather than uncertainty.

The Nile's annual flood had come and gone twice, marking the seasons with ancient reliability even as men waged their temporary wars upon its banks. Egyptian soldiers had settled into the dull routine of siege life—training, patrols, and the endless waiting that tested courage more thoroughly than any battlefield charge. Yet beneath the routine, tension simmered like water in a covered pot. Reports from scouts and merchants spoke of stirrings throughout Egypt, of old enemies growing bold while the prince's forces remained committed to the siege.

Prince Ahmose stood on the observation platform his engineers had constructed, studying the walls of Avaris through the morning haze. The city showed clear signs of privation now—fewer cooking fires, garbage piling up in areas where the inhabitants had given up on disposal, the occasional desperate sortie as defenders tried to break through to the river for water. His strategy was working, but slowly, and time was becoming his enemy rather than his ally.

"My prince," called his aide-de-camp, approaching with the diffidence of one bearing unwelcome news. "Urgent message from the south."

The afternoon sun blazed mercilessly over the Delta when a lone runner appeared on the southern horizon, his legs pumping with desperate urgency despite obvious exhaustion. Even at this distance, the urgency in his movement spoke of dire news—the kind of report that could shatter carefully laid plans and force impossible decisions.

This messenger was different from the usual dispatches. Where others had carried routine intelligence or requests for supplies, this man moved with the desperate haste of one carrying news that could not wait.

Ahmose felt his stomach tighten with foreboding even before the man reached their lines.

"Captain!" the messenger gasped as he staggered into camp. Dust and grime caked his face, and his voice cracked from thirst. "Prince Ahmose! Memphis is under attack! Lord Teti-Ann has emerged from hiding with a vast army—they struck at dawn!"

Ahmose felt ice form in his veins despite the desert heat. Memphis, the ancient capital, the key to all Egypt's northern defenses. If it fell, the entire strategic situation would collapse. Every mile his army had advanced, every victory they had won, would become meaningless if Teti-Ann could establish himself in the heartland while the Egyptian forces were tied down besieging Avaris.

The prince's mind raced through implications and possibilities. This was no coincidence—the timing was too perfect, the coordination too precise. While he had focused all his attention on Khamudi and the Hyksos, other enemies had been moving in the shadows, waiting for the moment when he would be most vulnerable.

"How many men does the traitor command?" Ahmose demanded, helping the exhausted runner to steady himself.

"Over a thousand, my lord. Chariots, infantry, siege engines—this is no raiding party. The garrison commander at Memphis sent word that they cannot hold beyond two days, perhaps three if the gods favor them."

A thousand men with siege equipment. Teti-Ann had been preparing for this moment, gathering forces and materiel while pretending to remain in exile. The prince realized with growing horror that he had been outmaneuvered—his enemies had let him commit his entire army to the siege of Avaris, then struck at the undefended heartland behind him.

"Double the guard on all approaches," he ordered his officers, his mind already calculating distances and marching times. "Send scouts south and west—I want to know if this is part of a larger coordinated attack. And bring me our best map of the region between here and Memphis."

As his officers hurried to comply, Ahmose stared south toward the smoke that was beginning to rise on the horizon. The dilemma he had always feared was upon him: abandon the siege that represented years of sacrifice and progress, or watch the rest of Egypt burn while he pursued his vendetta against Khamudi.

The choice tore at him. Every day spent at Avaris had cost lives, treasure, and the patience of his allies. To abandon it now would mean all those sacrifices had been in vain. Yet to remain while Memphis fell would be to hand his enemies the very prize he had fought so hard to protect.

The Race to Save Egypt

The decision, when it came, was as inevitable as the Nile's flood. Egypt came before vengeance, the living before the dead. With a heavy heart, Ahmose gave the orders that would transform his carefully constructed siege into a forced march.

"We break camp within the hour," he announced to his assembled commanders. "Leave sufficient force to maintain a screen around Avaris—I want Khamudi to think we're still here in strength. The rest of the army marches south immediately."

The logistics of moving an army were staggering under the best circumstances, but to do so with such haste invited disaster. Supply trains had to be reorganized, siege equipment abandoned or hastily loaded onto carts, the wounded either left behind with the screening force or loaded onto stretchers that would slow the march. Every minute spent in preparation was another minute that Memphis might be falling, another chance for Teti-Ann to consolidate his position.

As the army formed up for the march, word came from scouts that Heliopolis was also under attack. The pattern was becoming clear now—this was indeed a coordinated assault, timed to perfection. While Ahmose had focused on the obvious threat at Avaris, his enemies had struck at the foundations of Egyptian power itself.

The march south became a race against time and disaster. Under the merciless sun, Egyptian soldiers covered ground at a pace that left weaker men collapsing by the wayside. The prince himself set the example, marching on foot with his men rather than riding in comfort, sharing their hardships and their determination to reach Memphis before it was too late.

As they crested a rise overlooking the approaches to Heliopolis, the first sounds of battle reached them—the clash of bronze on bronze, the screams of wounded men, the thunder of collapsing masonry. Smoke rose from multiple points within the city, telling a story of fierce street-fighting and buildings set ablaze.

"The garrison still holds," observed General Kheti, studying the patterns of smoke and the positions of various banners visible on the walls. "But barely. They've been pushed back to the temple complex."

Ahmose nodded grimly. Captain Nehesi and his men had bought them precious time with their blood, holding out far longer than anyone had a right to expect. Now it was time to repay that sacrifice with interest.

The attack came without warning or formal challenge. Ahmose had learned that in warfare, surprise was worth more than honor, speed more valuable than ceremony. His chariots struck Teti-Ann's rear guard while they were still focused on reducing the temple complex, turning an assault into a rout within minutes.

Now he drove his chariot straight into the heart of Teti-Ann's forces, his bronze-tipped spear claiming lives with each thrust. His charioteer, a Nubian named Intef who had served him since boyhood, guided the horses with practiced skill through the chaos of battle, anticipating the prince's needs without requiring orders.

Behind Ahmose came his guard, and behind them the infantry, their battle cries reaching even the beleaguered defenders inside the temple: "Amun! Thebes! Ahmose!" The sound washed over the battlefield like the annual flood, bringing life and hope where there had been only dust and despair.

Teti-Ann's men, caught between the newcomers and the desperate sortie led by Nehesi's survivors, began to waver. Their advantage of numbers meant little now that they were the ones surrounded. Panic spread through their ranks, the contagion of fear turning an organized army into a disintegrating mass as men began to think of survival rather than victory.

Prince Ahmose fought with cold precision, his every movement economical and deadly. This was not the raw youth who had left Thebes years earlier but a seasoned commander who had learned the brutal arithmetic of warfare—how many lives must be spent to purchase victory, which losses were acceptable and which catastrophic. His face, once boyishly handsome, had been hardened by the sun and wind of countless campaigns. A scar ran from temple to jaw on the left side, the legacy of a Hyksos axe that had nearly ended his story before it properly began.

Through the chaos of battle, he caught sight of an ornate chariot breaking away from the main force, heading southwest toward Memphis. Even at a distance, he recognized the distinctive armor of Lord Teti-Ann—the traitor was fleeing, abandoning his men to save his own skin while they died fighting his battle.

"With me!" Ahmose shouted to his guard, wheeling his chariot in pursuit, the horses responding instantly to Intef's expert guidance. "The snake tries to escape!"

Teti-Ann had a good lead, but his chariot was heavier, designed more for ceremony than speed. Its golden fittings and elaborate decorations, symbols of his status gained through betrayal, now served only to slow his flight. The gap closed steadily as they raced across the flat plain between Heliopolis and Memphis, dust billowing behind them like the wake of ships upon the Nile.

The pursuit ended abruptly when Teti-Ann's chariot struck a hidden irrigation ditch, the impact throwing the vehicle forward with such force that one of its wheels shattered, sending wooden fragments spinning through the air. The horses screamed in panic, one falling with a broken leg while the other thrashed in its harness. The traitor lord was thrown clear, tumbling across the hard-packed earth before regaining his feet, dust and blood marking his once-fine garments.

By the time he regained his feet, Prince Ahmose was upon him, leaping from his own vehicle with spear levelled. The prince's guard formed a circle around the two men, ensuring there would be no interference in what was about to become a matter of personal honor rather than warfare.

"So," Teti-Ann sneered, drawing his khopesh—the curved sword favored by Egyptian nobility. The blade gleamed in the sunlight, well-maintained despite the chaos of battle. "The son comes to avenge the father. How poetic."

Up close, Ahmose could see that the years had not been kind to Teti-Ann. Though still powerful, his once-handsome face had grown bloated, his eyes yellowed and rheumy. The wealth and status gained through betrayal had exacted their own price on his body, if not his conscience. This was the man who had voted against Kamose in council, who had chosen foreign masters over Egyptian honor, who had opened the gates to assassins in the night.

"You betrayed Egypt," Ahmose replied, circling warily, his spear held at the perfect angle to strike or defend. "You chose foreign masters over your own people. You opened the gates to murderers who came in darkness."

Teti-Ann's laugh was bitter as aloes, a sound devoid of any true humor. "I chose the winning side, boy. The Hyksos have ruled here for a hundred years. What makes you think you can change that? Your father thought as you do, and look where it brought him—to a tomb before his time, his skull crushed by superior strength."

The taunt struck deep, but Ahmose's expression remained impassive. He had learned to master his emotions, to channel rage into precision rather than blind fury. His eyes never left Teti-Ann's, watching for the telltale shift that would presage an attack.

"This," said Ahmose, and attacked.

What followed was not the ceremonial combat of ritual duels but the savage exchange of men intent on killing. Teti-Ann, despite his years and debauchery, moved with the fluid grace of an experienced fighter. His khopesh whistled through the air, seeking Ahmose's throat, the curved blade designed to slip past defenses and hook flesh with its inner edge.

The prince parried with his spear shaft, the bronze head scoring a line across Teti-Ann's breastplate. Metal screeched against metal, sparks flying from the contact. They separated, circling again, each measuring the other with new respect. This would not be the easy victory either man had hoped for.

"You fight well," Teti-Ann acknowledged, breathing heavily, sweat running in rivulets down his dust-streaked face. "Better than your father. But not well enough."

With a sudden feint, he slipped past Ahmose's guard and slashed at the prince's leg. The blade bit deep, drawing blood that darkened the sand beneath their feet. Pain flared, hot and immediate, but Ahmose had known worse. He turned the wounded leg away, adjusting his stance to compensate without betraying weakness.

"First blood to you," Ahmose conceded, his voice controlled despite the pain. "But battles are not won by first blood alone."

They clashed again, weapons meeting with enough force to send sparks flying from the metal. Ahmose's spear darted forward, seeking vulnerable points—throat, armpit, groin—while Teti-Ann's khopesh swept in deadly arcs, forcing the prince to give ground or risk dismemberment. The duel became a dance of death, each man pushing the other to the limits of skill and endurance.

Time seemed suspended as the two men fought, their personal combat a microcosm of Egypt's larger struggle. Around them, the prince's guard stood silent, witnesses to a confrontation that would determine not just the fate of these two men, but the direction of Egypt's future.

Ahmose staggered but did not fall when the blade caught him a second time. His counterthrust caught Teti-Ann in the shoulder, penetrating the joint of his armor with a wet sound of tearing flesh. The traitor dropped his sword, cursing as his arm went suddenly limp, rendered useless by severed tendons.

"It seems your gods have abandoned you," Ahmose said coldly, levelling his spear at Teti-Ann's throat, close enough that the traitor could feel the cold bronze against his skin, could see his own reflection distorted in its polished surface.

The fallen noble glared up with undisguised hatred, defiance still burning in eyes now clouded with pain and the approaching shadow of death. Blood soaked the front of his once-fine tunic, spreading in a dark stain that told of mortal damage within.

"Kill me then, princeling," he spat, blood flecking his lips. "It changes nothing. The Hyksos are too strong. They crushed your father. They killed your brother. They will destroy you just as thoroughly."

Ahmose pressed the spear tip against Teti-Ann's skin, drawing a bead of blood but not yet delivering the fatal thrust. There was something he needed to know first, a question that had haunted him since the night messengers had arrived in Thebes bearing news of his father's murder.

"Before you die," Ahmose said, his voice dropping to ensure this exchange remained between them alone, "tell me this: Were you there when my father was murdered? Did you help the assassins enter his chambers?"

Something shifted in Teti-Ann's eyes—a flash of pride stronger than his fear of death, a need to claim his greatest accomplishment before the darkness took him. His lips curled in a bloody smile, revealing teeth-stained crimson.

"I didn't merely help them, boy," he rasped, each word clearly causing him pain yet delivered with savage satisfaction. "I led them. It was my khopesh that crushed Tao's skull as he slept. He never even woke to see who sent him to the afterlife."

Rage, cold and clarifying, swept through Ahmose. With deliberate slowness, he lowered his spear and instead drew his own dagger—a blade of black flint traded from distant lands, sharper than any bronze and reserved for ritual significance rather than common combat.

"Then by my father's name," he said with terrible quietness, "your death will not be quick. When you enter the Hall of Two Truths, you will do so in pieces, your body too damaged to serve you in the afterlife."

The gathering of Ahmose's guard turned their faces away, knowing what would follow and having no wish to witness it. Even in war, there were things better left unobserved by those who would need to sleep peacefully in days to come.

The Bitter Victory

When it was finished, Prince Ahmose stood over the remains of his father's murderer, feeling not triumph but a strange emptiness. Justice had been served, but the cost seemed higher than the satisfaction gained. Teti-Ann was dead, but Khamudi still lived behind the walls of Avaris, and now new threats were emerging from shadows he hadn't even known existed.

As his men prepared to resume the march toward Memphis, another messenger arrived—this one from the deep south, bearing news that made Ahmose's blood run cold. The message was brief, written in his mother's own hand, but its implications were staggering:

"My son—Thebes is under attack. The Nubian Aata has come with a great army. The city holds, but barely. Come quickly if you can. If you cannot, know that Egypt remembers its sons with pride. Your mother, Ahhotep."

Ahmose stared at the papyrus until the hieroglyphs blurred before his eyes. Three coordinated attacks—Avaris holding him in place while Teti-Ann struck from the south and Aata from the deep south. The strategic brilliance of it was undeniable, even as it filled him with dread. His enemies had outthought him completely, using his own greatest strength—his determination to finish what his father started—against him.

Seven hundred kilometers. Seven hundred kilometers of desert and river between his army and Thebes, where his mother and the remnants of the royal court faced a Nubian army alone. Even if he marched immediately, abandoning Memphis to its fate, he could not reach Thebes in time to affect the outcome.

The prince looked around at his assembled officers, seeing his own anguish reflected in their faces. They understood as well as he did what this meant—the royal family, the ancient capital, everything they had fought to preserve, hanging by the thinnest of threads while they stood powerless to intervene.

"We march for Thebes," Ahmose announced, his voice carrying across the assembled ranks. "Maximum speed. Leave the wounded at Memphis, abandon all non-essential equipment. If any man cannot keep the pace, he stays behind."

As his army prepared for the longest, most desperate march of the war, Prince Ahmose gazed south toward home. Somewhere beyond the horizon, his mother faced the test of her life, defending not just a city but the future of Egypt itself. All he could do was march, and pray to all the gods that she would prove as formidable as the enemies who thought to crush her while her son was far away.

The race to save Egypt had begun, and its outcome would determine whether the royal line of Thebes would survive to see another dawn.

Chapter 9 - Ahhotep the Brave

February 1526 BC - Elephantine

Seven hundred miles to the south, while Prince Ahmose pressed his siege against the walls of Avaris, a different yet equally dangerous threat emerged from the shadows of the Nubian frontier. The coordination was no coincidence—though neither Egyptian ruler yet understood the web of conspiracy that had been spun around them.

Aata, a chieftain who had long harbored ambitions of carving out his own kingdom from Egypt's southernmost territories, had received his instructions through channels that wound back to the besieged city of Avaris itself. Khamudi's reach extended far beyond his fortress walls, his network of spies and allies still functioning despite the Egyptian stranglehold on his capital.

The Nubian chieftain's skin gleamed like polished ebony in the harsh desert sun as he surveyed his assembled warriors—fierce men adorned with ostrich feathers and leopard skins, their eyes eager for combat and plunder. For months, his scouts had watched the Egyptian garrisons along the First Cataract, near Elephantine, noting the reduced numbers and lax vigilance that came with prolonged peace. Every able-bodied soldier had been drawn north to feed Ahmose's endless appetite for troops at Avaris.

"The jackal strikes when the lion hunts elsewhere," Aata told his sub-chiefs, his white teeth flashing in a predatory smile beneath his neatly trimmed beard. "While the Egyptians look north, we shall strike from the south. Their prince thinks he has only one enemy to face."

His war council gathered around him in the pre-dawn darkness, their weapons gleaming dully in the light of dying coals. These were not mere raiders but seasoned warriors who had fought the Egyptians before, men who understood that opportunity such as this came perhaps once in a generation. With Egypt's strength concentrated at one point, the rest of the kingdom lay exposed like a gazelle separated from the herd.

"What of reinforcements?" asked one sub-chief, a scarred veteran whose left eye had been taken by an Egyptian spear years before. "If they break off from their siege..."

"They will not," Aata replied with confidence born of secret knowledge. "Trust me in this—Ahmose faces more than just our spears. He cannot be everywhere at once, and soon he will learn the price of overreaching his grasp."

With the bulk of Egypt's forces committed to the north, the cities along the First Cataract lay vulnerable as sleeping children. Elephantine, gateway to Nubia and keeper of the southern border, had only a token garrison supplemented by local militia—merchants and farmers who practiced with weapons once a month and prayed they would never need to use them in earnest.

The night air carried the scent of doom across the water as Aata's warriors prepared their boats. Each man checked his weapons in silence, the ritual movements of soldiers who had done this dance of death many times before. Spears were tested for straightness, bowstrings examined for fraying, shield straps adjusted for comfort. Death was a familiar companion to these men, and they prepared to greet him as an old friend.

Aata struck at dawn, his warriors crossing the Nile in dozens of small boats, their paddles barely disturbing the water's surface in the gray pre-dawn light. The mist rising from the river's surface provided additional concealment, wrapping the raiders in ghostly tendrils that made them seem like spirits emerging from the underworld itself.

Unlike Teti-Ann's disciplined assault on Heliopolis far to the north, this was a raid of swift brutality—burning, looting, killing anyone who resisted. The air filled with the screams of victims and the roar of flames devouring reed-thatched roofs. Children scattered like frightened birds before the Nubian advance, their cries adding to the symphony of terror that announced Aata's arrival.

The garrison commander, a grizzled veteran named Khaemwaset who had served under three pharaohs, died with his sword in his hand at the gates of his own fortress. Around him fell his men, overwhelmed by numbers and the savagery of warriors who fought without the restraints of civilized warfare. Their bronze weapons, superior in quality to Nubian stone and copper, could not compensate for being outnumbered three to one.

By noon, Elephantine was a smoking ruin. The ancient granite quarries that had built the pyramids now echoed with the triumphant war cries of Nubian raiders. The sacred isle of Khnum, protector of the Nile's source, bore witness to devastation that would have made the ram-headed god weep tears of blood.

But Aata's appetite was not yet satisfied. Abu fell next, then Syene, each town offering less resistance than the last as word of the raiders' approach sent defenders fleeing northward like leaves before a storm. The local militia, faced with professional warriors, melted away like morning mist. Only the gods knew how far north these jackals might push before meeting organized resistance.

March 1526 BC - Thebes

The news reached Thebes eight days later, carried by a blood-spattered messenger who collapsed at the palace gates like a dying bird. Guards rushed to help the man—a young lieutenant whose left arm hung useless at his side, a Nubian spear having pierced it cleanly through. His horse, a magnificent stallion that had once been the pride of the royal stables, stood with foam-flecked flanks and eyes wild with exhaustion.

"Nubians," he gasped as they carried him into the palace, his voice hoarse from dust and desperate travel. "Aata has crossed the border with hundreds of warriors. Elephantine burns. Abu has fallen. They move north unchecked, slaughtering all who stand before them."

The messenger's words rang through the palace corridors like the tolling of funeral bells. Servants stopped their work to cross themselves and whisper prayers to household gods. Even the sacred cats that roamed the palace seemed to sense the doom that stalked Egypt's borders, their usual languid grace replaced by nervous alertness.

Ahhotep, mother of Prince Ahmose and regent in his absence, listened to the report with a face carved from stone. The years had lined her features but not weakened her spirit—if anything, the trials of recent decades had forged her into something harder than bronze, more enduring than granite. Around her gathered the remaining members of the royal council, old men mostly, whose courage resided more in their tongues than their sword arms. She could sense their fear, smell it like a predator scents weakness in the herd.

The council chamber felt smaller with each word the messenger spoke, the walls seeming to press inward as if the very stones reflected the crushing weight of crisis. Painted reliefs of victorious pharaohs looked down from the walls—Mentuhotep, Sesostris, mighty kings who had extended Egypt's borders and cowed her enemies. Their stone eyes seemed to judge the current generation and find it wanting.

"It seems," observed the High Priest of Amun with undisguised anxiety, his plump fingers nervously adjusting the folds of his pleated robe, "that our enemies have coordinated their attacks. North and south simultaneously—this cannot be coincidence."

The priest's words confirmed what Ahhotep had already suspected. Three major attacks, all timed for when Ahmose was committed to his siege—this bores the stamp of Khamudi's cunning mind. Even trapped in Avaris, the Hyksos king was still weaving his web of destruction.

"Of course it is not," Ahhotep agreed, her voice steady despite the fear clutching at her heart like cold fingers. She stood straighter, refusing to let her posture betray the turmoil of her thoughts. "Teti-Ann has always been cunning, but this... this speaks of coordination from Avaris itself. Khamudi plays his final gambit."

Sunlight streamed through the high clerestory windows, illuminating motes of dust that danced like spirits above the worried councilors. The cool of the stone floor beneath her sandaled feet anchored Ahhotep as her mind raced through possibilities, each more desperate than the last. Her son faced the greatest siege in Egyptian history, unaware that his kingdom was being devoured from behind.

The irony was bitter as wormwood on her tongue. For two years, every resource had been poured into the siege of Avaris, every available man marched north to break the Hyksos stranglehold. Now, with victory perhaps within Ahmose's grasp, Egypt's enemies struck at her exposed flanks like hunters converging on wounded prey.

"What do we do?" asked the treasurer, his hands fidgeting with the gold rings that adorned his plump fingers—symbols of wealth and position that suddenly seemed meaningless in the face of invasion. "Our army is committed to Avaris. We have only the palace guard and what remains of the temple militias."

The question hung in the air like incense smoke, heavy with implications. Send word to Ahmose, and he might abandon his siege—years of sacrifice and thousands of lives lost for nothing. Remain silent, and watch Egypt's heartland fall to barbarian raiders while her prince hammered uselessly against Khamudi's walls.

Ahhotep rose from her chair, and though she was a woman well into her fifth decade, her bearing was that of a queen born to command. Years of hardship had etched lines into her once-smooth face, but they were the marks of character rather than defeat. Her eyes—dark and penetrating as a falcon's—swept over the assembled councilors, measuring each man and finding most wanting.

"We send no word to my son," she declared, her voice cutting through their murmurs like a bronze blade through papyrus. "He fights the greatest battle of our age. I will not weaken his resolve with problems he cannot solve from seven hundred miles away."

The councilors shifted uncomfortably, some nodding agreement while others looked as if they had swallowed bitter medicine. The logic was sound but the risk enormous—if they failed here, Ahmose might return victorious from Avaris only to find his kingdom in ashes.

"Summon the veterans," she ordered, her voice gaining strength with each word. "Every man who has ever carried a spear for Egypt. Arm the temple guards and the palace servants. Raid the tomb guards from the Valley of Kings if necessary. I will not lose the south while my son reclaims the north."

Her words hung in the air, bold and defiant as a war cry echoing across a battlefield. The councilors exchanged glances, some doubtful, others calculating what advantages or disasters this decision might bring to their own positions. In their faces, she read the eternal story of courtiers faced with crisis—some would rise to the occasion while others would seek to protect only themselves.

"But, Your Highness," protested the treasurer, sweat beading on his forehead despite the chamber's coolness, "who will lead them? We have no commanders remaining in Thebes. Every general, every captain has gone north with Prince Ahmose."

The objection was valid—Egypt's military leadership had been drawn to Avaris like iron to a lodestone. Those who remained were either too old, too young, or too inexperienced to face a warrior like Aata. The local militia commanders were farmers and merchants playing at soldier, not men who could stand against seasoned Nubian raiders.

Ahhotep's eyes flashed with a fire that silenced the council chamber. The golden beads in her elaborate wig caught the sunlight as she turned to face the treasurer directly, her shadow falling across him like a physical manifestation of her authority. In that moment, she looked less like a woman and more like a lioness preparing to defend her cubs.

"I will lead them," she declared, each word striking like a hammer on bronze. "I am the daughter of Tao I, wife of Tao II, mother of Kamose and Ahmose. The blood of warriors flows in my veins no less than in my son's. While he fights for Egypt in the north, I shall defend her in the south."

The silence that followed was profound, broken only by the distant sound of temple bells marking the passage of time. Several councilors opened their mouths to protest, then thought better of it as they met her gaze. This was not a woman asking for permission—this was a queen announcing her decision.

"Unless," she added with a dangerous softness that made more than one councilor step backward, "you wish to volunteer for the task yourself?"

The treasurer blanched, his protests dying in his throat like flowers touched by frost. No one dared argue further with the queen mother, whose reputation for both wisdom and fierce determination was known throughout the kingdom. She had earned her gold flies through blood and courage, not through birth or marriage alliances.

By nightfall, a motley army had assembled in the courtyard of the great temple of Amun—old soldiers with graying beards standing alongside boys barely old enough to lift a shield, priests and scribes now awkwardly holding weapons instead of scrolls and papyri. The scene would have been comical if not for the desperate seriousness of their situation.

Torches illuminated the gathering, casting long shadows and gleaming off hastily distributed weapons—some from the royal armory, others family heirlooms brought out of retirement for one last campaign. The air hummed with tension and whispered prayers to various deities, each man seeking protection from his preferred god. Veterans checked the grip of unfamiliar spears while young scribes tried to remember which end of a sword was meant for holding.

Ahhotep appeared before them dressed not in the finery of a royal woman but in the simple linen kilt and leather breastplate of an Egyptian commander. The transformation was remarkable—gone was the elegant queen mother, replaced by something far more dangerous. Around her neck gleamed the Gold of Valor—the fly-shaped medals awarded for exceptional bravery in battle, each one earned through blood and courage rather than birth.

Her hair was bound tightly beneath a simple cloth headpiece, practical for the combat to come. In her hands, she carried the khopesh sword that had belonged to her husband Tao II, its bronze blade bearing the nicks and scars of real warfare. The weapon seemed to sing in her grasp, eager for one more taste of battle.

"Men of Thebes," she addressed them, her voice carrying clearly in the evening stillness, resonating off the massive stone columns that surrounded the courtyard. "Today we fight not for conquest or glory, but for survival. While my son Prince Ahmose battles the Hyksos in the north, another enemy threatens our homes from the south."

The assembled faces turned toward her—uncertain, afraid, but resolute. These were not professional soldiers but citizens transformed by necessity into warriors. Shopkeepers stood beside scribes, farmers next to priests, all united by the common thread of desperation and the fierce love of homeland that burned in every Egyptian heart.

"Aata of Nubia believes we are weak," she continued, her voice growing stronger with conviction, filling the courtyard like a battle hymn. "He thinks our cities lie undefended, our people helpless. He has counted our armies at Avaris and believes the rest of Egypt lies naked before his spears."

She paused, her gaze sweeping across the assembled faces, seeing in their eyes not just fear but determination—the stubborn pride of a people who had endured foreign domination for a century and were now fighting to reclaim their destiny. In the flickering torchlight, they looked less like an improvised militia and more like the inheritors of a warrior tradition stretching back to the pyramid builders.

"He is mistaken," she declared, her voice rising to carry to the farthest corners of the courtyard. "For as long as one Egyptian draws breath, our land is never undefended. Tomorrow, we march south to meet Aata's raiders. We will drive them back across the cataracts and teach them the price of violating Egypt's sacred soil!"

A ragged cheer went up—not the confident roar of professional soldiers but the determined cry of citizens protecting their families, their homes, their very way of life. The sound echoed between the temple walls, startling a flock of ibises roosting atop the pylons. It would have to be enough. It was all they had.

As the strange army prepared for departure, checking weapons and gathering supplies with varying degrees of competence, Ahhotep retreated to the inner sanctuary of the temple where her mother-in-law Tetisheri waited in silent prayer. The old woman had been the steel in the royal family's spine through the darkest years, and Ahhotep needed that strength now more than ever.

The sanctuary was dimly lit by oil lamps, their flickering light casting dancing shadows across the painted reliefs of gods and goddesses that adorned the walls. The scent of incense hung heavy in the air—kyphi mixed with myrrh, sacred scents believed to please the divinities and carry prayers heavenward on their fragrant smoke.

"Do you think we can succeed?" Ahhotep asked softly, suddenly feeling the weight of her years and responsibilities. In this sacred space, away from the eyes of those she must lead, she could allow herself a moment of vulnerability. The goddess Mut gazed down from the painted walls, her protective wings spread wide in eternal guardianship.

The old woman, now bent with age but still fierce of spirit, her once-ebony hair now white as river foam, nodded slowly. The gold and carnelian beads in her elaborate wig clicked softly with the movement, a sound like distant sistrum rattles. Her eyes, though clouded with age, still held the fire that had sustained the royal family through decades of struggle.

"Aata expects to find weakness," Tetisheri replied, her voice thin but unwavering as the flame of a temple lamp. "Show him instead the lioness defending her cubs, and he will flee. Remember what you told Kamose before his first campaign—it is not the size of the force but the strength of its heart that determines victory."

The mention of her fallen son sent a sharp pang through Ahhotep's chest, but she mastered it quickly. This was no time for grief. Tetisheri was right—she must embody the protective fury of Sekhmet, the lioness goddess who defended Ra against his enemies. The temple walls seemed to pulse with divine presence, as if the gods themselves were preparing for the coming battle.

Ahhotep touched the gold flies at her throat—awards she had earned not through birth but through blood, defending Thebes after her husband's murder. The cool metal against her skin reminded her of her own strength, tested and proven in crucibles of fire and loss. Each fly represented a moment when she had chosen courage over safety, duty over comfort.

"May Sekhmet guide my hand," she whispered, the prayer rising with the incense smoke toward the painted ceiling where the sky goddess Nut stretched her star-spangled body across the heavens. "And may the strength of my ancestors flow through my sword arm."

Tetisheri reached out with gnarled fingers, gripping Ahhotep's forearm with surprising strength. Her touch conveyed more than words—the accumulated wisdom of a lifetime spent navigating the treacherous currents of palace politics and royal duty. "And may Neith sharpen your wisdom alongside your spear. Remember, you fight not just for today but for Egypt's tomorrow."

The weight of that responsibility settled on Ahhotep's shoulders like a pharaoh's crown. She was not merely defending territory but preserving the possibility of her son's ultimate triumph. If she failed here, Ahmose might win at Avaris only to find his kingdom carved up by ambitious neighbors.

With these words of blessing fortifying her spirit, Ahhotep returned to the courtyard where her improbable army awaited. As the eastern sky began to lighten with promise of another dawn, they marched south toward uncertainty, danger, and the hope of salvation.

The Battle at the First Cataract

Four days of hard marching brought them to the sound of battle— the clash of weapons and the cries of dying men carried on the desert wind like an evil omen. Ahhotep's makeshift army had intercepted Aata's raiders near the First Cataract, where the Nile's waters churned white over hidden rocks, the roar of the river providing a constant backdrop to the preparations for combat.

The terrain here favored defense—rocky outcroppings and narrow approaches between river and cliff that would neutralize the Nubians' advantage in numbers and ferocity. Ahhotep had chosen the battlefield carefully, consulting with her veteran officers while studying the land herself, walking the ground until she understood every contour that might determine life or death in the coming clash.

Her opponents were already visible across the killing ground— Nubian warriors in their leopard skins and ostrich plumes, their dark skin gleaming with oils and ritual scarifications. They moved with the fluid grace of predators, supremely confident in their superiority over what they perceived as a desperate collection of farmers and shopkeepers.

The Nubian chieftain had not expected organized resistance, much less an army led by Ahhotep herself. When his scouts brought word that the Queen Mother personally commanded the Egyptian force, Aata had laughed—surely this was some desperate deception, a false standard meant to inspire hopeless militiamen.

His advantage lay in his warriors' ferocity and experience; hers in superior Egyptian weaponry and the desperate courage of people defending their homeland. Bronze-tipped spears gleamed in Egyptian hands while the enemy bore weapons of stone and copper. The technological gap was not vast, but in battle, even small advantages could mean the difference between victory and annihilation.

The sun blazed overhead, its heat shimmering off the rocks and sand, turning the battlefield into an oven that tested endurance before combat even began. Nubians and Egyptians alike sought what shade they could find as they prepared for battle, checking weapons and offering prayers to their respective gods. Vultures circled high above, drawn by some instinct that told them death would feast well here today.

Ahhotep commanded from a war chariot positioned on a small rise that offered a view of the entire field—not fighting directly but directing her forces with the tactical acumen she had absorbed from a lifetime among military men. Her charioteer, an old palace guard who had once served her husband, kept the horses steady despite their nervous shifting in the presence of so many armed men.

The beasts could smell the fear-sweat and weapons oil, their nostrils flaring as they tossed their heads and pawed the rocky ground. Their bronze-sheathed hooves struck sparks from the stone, as if the very earth was eager for the blood that would soon water it.

The veterans who formed her officer corps executed her orders without question, positioning archers on the high ground and infantry in tight formations along the riverbank. They had looked dubious when she first appeared to lead them, but those doubts had faded during the march south, as her knowledge of military matters and natural authority became apparent.

"Archers to the ridgeline," she commanded, her voice carrying over the pre-battle tension. "Infantry in phalanx formation, shields overlapped. When they charge, let them break themselves against our bronze like waves against a seawall."

The deployment was textbook Egyptian tactics, learned from campaigns stretching back generations. Her husband had taught her to read terrain, her sons had shown her the art of command, and bitter experience had honed her understanding of what men would do when death stalked the battlefield.

When Aata realized he faced not a disorganized militia but a structured Egyptian force, he attempted to withdraw his raiders back across the river. The surprise on his face was visible even at a distance when he recognized Ahhotep's royal standards—the realization that he faced not just any Egyptian commander but the Queen Mother herself seemed to give him pause.

But the Nubian chieftain had not survived twenty years of raiding by being indecisive. If he could not retreat unseen, he would attack with overwhelming force and scatter these Egyptians like chaff before the wind. His war cry rose above the cataract's roar, a sound like a hunting lion's roar that sent ice through Egyptian veins.

Ahhotep would not allow his moment of hesitation to become an opportunity for escape. She had not marched her people this far to watch the enemy withdraw intact, only to return when Egypt's defenses were even weaker.

"Press them!" she commanded, her voice carrying over the din of preliminary skirmishing. "Drive them against the water's edge! Let them choose between our spears and the crocodiles!"

The Egyptians surged forward, their shields forming a wall of protection against Nubian javelins. The clash of weapons rose above the river's constant roar—bronze against stone, wood against flesh, the universal language of combat that needed no translation between cultures.

What followed was not the clean, heroic battle of royal inscriptions but the brutal reality of men killing men with sharp metal. Spears thrust through bodies, swords opened arteries, and the sand grew dark with blood that would feed the desert for months to come. The stench of voided bowels and spilled blood filled the air, mixing with the acrid smoke of disturbed dust.

Step by step, the Egyptians pushed the raiders back until they stood with the cataract at their backs, trapped between bronze spearpoints and raging waters. The smell of blood and fear hung heavy in the air, mingling with dust kicked up by hundreds of sandaled feet. Men screamed prayers in a dozen dialects as they died, calling out to gods who seemed deaf to their pleas.

Aata himself fought like a cornered lion, his massive frame towering over most of his opponents. With each swing of his great axe, an Egyptian fell. The weapon's stone head, shaped from diorite harder than any metal, shattered shields and crushed bones with equal ease. It seemed he might yet cut an escape path through their ranks, his warriors rallying around his imposing figure like iron filings drawn to a lodestone.

The Nubian chieftain's axe work was poetry written in blood and broken bone. He moved with the fluid grace of a dancer, each strike flowing into the next in a rhythm that hypnotized his opponents even as it killed them. Around him, Egyptian militiamen fell like grain before the scythe, their untrained movements no match for a lifetime of warfare.

Then Ahhotep's chariot drove directly toward him, her driver navigating the rocky terrain with practiced skill born of decades in royal service. The horses' eyes rolled white with terror as they thundered through the battlefield, their bronze-shod hooves striking sparks from stone and crushing fallen weapons beneath their weight.

The queen mother herself stood tall, a ceremonial bow in her hands—not a weapon of war but a symbol of royal authority. Her face was set in lines of determination, showing neither fear nor uncertainty despite the chaos of battle surrounding her. In the afternoon sun, she looked like a goddess of war descended to earth.

"Aata of Kush!" she called out, her voice somehow carrying over the noise of combat and flowing water. "Look upon the face of your defeat!"

The Nubian chieftain turned, surprise registering in his eyes at the sight of a royal woman on the battlefield. That moment of distraction was all her guardsmen needed. They closed in from both sides, their spears finding gaps in his leather armor. Bronze points, honed to razor sharpness, slid between ribs and found the soft places where life could be ended with a single thrust.

Aata fell to his knees, blood darkening the sand beneath him to a rich crimson pool that spread outward like the Nile's annual flood. His massive frame, which had moments before towered above the Egyptian spearmen like a granite colossus, now sagged as strength fled his limbs. The great diorite axe slipped from nerveless fingers, its weight too much for arms that had once wielded it like a reed.

Around him, his warriors began throwing down their weapons, the clatter of discarded bronze a surrendering chorus that swept through their ranks like wildfire. They stood frozen with indecision, their dark eyes shifting between their fallen leader and the approaching Egyptian queen. The sight of their mighty chieftain brought low broke their spirit more surely than any Egyptian spear.

The battle was over, decided not by numbers or superior weapons but by the simple mathematics of morale. With their leader down, the Nubian raiders lost the fierce unity that had made them dangerous. They were once again merely individual warriors far from home, facing an enemy that had proven stronger than expected.

Ahhotep approached on foot now, her guardsmen forming a protective circle around her, their shields creating a moving fortress of painted cedar and bronze. Sweat ran freely down their muscled bodies, mingling with blood both their own and their enemies'. The queen walked with the measured step of royalty; her chin lifted in the same proud angle that graced temple reliefs of her ancestors.

Despite the dust of battle that clung to her simple linen kilt and leather breastplate, she carried herself with an innate dignity that no crown could have enhanced. This was leadership in its purest form—not the ceremonial authority of the throne room but the earned respect of those who had followed her into deadly peril.

She stood before the wounded chieftain, studying him with the calculating gaze of a ruler rather than the hatred of an enemy. Up close, she could see that despite his fearsome reputation, Aata was hardly more than forty summers—a man grown powerful through ferocity and cunning rather than age and wisdom. His obsidian eyes glared up at her from beneath a furrowed brow ridged with ritual scars.

Blood frothed at the corners of his mouth, pink bubbles that spoke of internal wounds that would not heal. Yet his gaze remained defiant, unbroken even in defeat. Here was a warrior who would die before he begged, a quality that Ahhotep could respect even in an enemy.

"You have courage," she acknowledged, her voice carrying the smooth authority of one born to command. "But you chose the wrong time and the wrong enemy."

Aata spat blood onto the ground, the crimson spittle landing near her feet in a final act of defiance. His voice, when he spoke, was thick with blood and the growing weakness of approaching death. "Kill me then, Egyptian woman. My sons will avenge me. They will sweep down from the hills like jackals and feast on your lands."

"No," Ahhotep replied calmly, her weathered face revealing nothing of her inner thoughts. The Gold of Valor flies around her neck caught the merciless desert sun, reminding all present that this was no ordinary woman, but one who had earned the right to stand among warriors. "Your sons will serve Egypt, as will you. Your life in exchange for peace along our southern border."

She stepped closer, her shadow falling across his kneeling form, her voice dropping so only he could hear. The scent of battle clung to them both—sweat, blood, and the peculiar coppery tang of fear. Around them, the surviving warriors of both sides watched this moment of decision that would determine the fate of the southern frontier.

"Your warriors will return to their homes, and you will ensure no Nubian raids cross into Egypt for as long as you draw breath. Refuse, and we will not stop at driving you back. We will pursue your people beyond the Fourth Cataract, burning every village in our path."

Her words carried the weight of absolute conviction. This was not the empty threat of a desperate commander but the cold promise of a queen who had the will and means to carry out exactly what she promised. The vultures circling overhead seemed to sense the moment's gravity, their harsh cries echoing off the canyon walls.

"The vultures will grow fat on Nubian flesh," she continued, her voice never rising above a conversational tone, "and your family name will be erased from memory. Even your gods will forget you ever existed."

Aata's eyes widened slightly, the whites showing around the dark irises as he recognized the steel behind her words. This was no idle threat from a woman playing at war—this was the cold promise of a queen who had already survived assassination attempts, palace intrigues, and battles that would have broken lesser souls. She would do exactly as she promised, with the same methodical determination that had kept her son's claim to the throne alive through years of Hyksos oppression.

The silence stretched between them, broken only by the eternal roar of the cataract and the groans of wounded men. In that moment, the fate of Egypt's southern border hung in the balance, decided not by armies or treaties but by the will of two strong individuals locked in a contest of determination.

"I accept your terms," he growled finally, his massive hands clenching into fists that sank into the blood-soaked sand. Pain and defeat warred in his expression, but beneath both lay a grudging respect for the enemy who had outmaneuvered him. "But know this: one day Egypt will grow weak again, and we will be waiting. The desert remembers, Egyptian. The stones remember."

Ahhotep merely smiled, a cold expression devoid of warmth that didn't reach her eyes. Like a cobra regarding its prey, she measured him with her gaze, seeing not just the man before her but the generations of potential enemies he represented. "Then pray to your gods that day does not come during your lifetime, Aata of Kush. For I do not grant second chances."

She turned away, the matter settled in her mind, and gestured to her officers. "Bind his wounds. He returns to Kush alive—but first, he will witness the strength of Egypt that his people have challenged."

The Aftermath

By nightfall, the surviving Nubian raiders had been disarmed and escorted back across the river. They moved like a dark shadow across the landscape, their defeated slump a stark contrast to the proud warriors who had come boasting of conquest mere days before. The setting sun painted the Nile blood-red, as if the great river itself acknowledged the day's sacrifice.

The crossing was a funeral procession in reverse—instead of the dead being carried to their rest, the living were being returned to contemplate their mortality. Egyptian guards watched from the banks as the boats disappeared into the gathering dusk, their occupants bearing word of a queen who fought like a goddess and showed mercy like a pharaoh.

Under the light of camp fires that dotted the battlefield like fallen stars, Ahhotep dictated a message to be sent north by the fastest courier—a wiry Medjay runner who could cover distances that would exhaust ordinary men. Her voice was steady despite the exhaustion that made her bones feel like water.

"To Prince Ahmose, Son of Ra, Beloved of Amun," she began, the formal titles rolling off her tongue with practiced ease. "The southern threat is eliminated. Egypt's border stands secure. The Nubian chieftain Aata has submitted and pledged peace. Glory to Prince Ahmose in his great endeavor."

The words were simple, diplomatic in their phrasing, but behind them lay the weightier message that only her son would fully comprehend: I have kept my promise. I have held the south while you reclaim the north. The dream of reunification lives, and you need not divide your attention between multiple enemies.

She sealed the papyrus with her personal seal—the image of a lioness rampant, jaws open in eternal defiance. The wax pressed clean and sharp, bearing the mark of royal authority that would ensure the message's swift delivery to wherever her son might be found.

As the messenger departed, disappearing into the darkness with the speed of a hunting falcon, Ahhotep finally allowed herself a moment of private weakness. She sagged against her chariot with the bone-deep weariness of command, her body protesting the day's exertions with aches that radiated through muscle and bone.

Her hands, steady throughout the battle, now trembled slightly as the aftermath of crisis settled upon her like a heavy cloak. The responsibility she had carried—not just for the battle but for Egypt's southern frontier—had weighed more heavily than bronze armor. Now, with victory secured, she could feel every one of her years.

"Water for the queen," ordered Meryt, her personal handmaiden who had refused to remain behind in Thebes. The girl approached with a fresh cup and a damp cloth to wipe the dust from her mistress's face. Even in the midst of military encampment, she maintained the protocols of royal service.

"Thank you, child," Ahhotep murmured, accepting both with gratitude that she would show to few others. The water was warm and tasted of leather from the water skins, but it was the sweetest drink she had ever tasted. Victory had its own flavor, bitter and satisfying in equal measure.

Around them, the camp settled into the routines of aftermath— tending wounded, collecting weapons, and preparing the dead for their journey to the afterlife. Egyptian and Nubian bodies alike would receive proper burial rites, for even enemies deserved respect in death. The priests accompanying the army moved among the fallen, performing the necessary ceremonies that would ease their passage to the realm of Osiris.

She had preserved the south for her son, maintained the ancient borders that had defined Egypt since the time of the pyramid builders. The victory here would free Ahmose to concentrate his full attention on Avaris, knowing that his rear was secure from ambitious neighbors. No longer would he need to divide his forces or worry about coordinated attacks on multiple fronts.

"My lady," ventured one of her veteran officers, approaching with the respectful caution due to royalty, "what are your orders for the return to Thebes?"

The question brought her back to immediate concerns. They had won the battle, but wars were won through the accumulation of such victories, each one building upon the last. This triumph needed to be consolidated, its lessons absorbed, its benefits maximized.

"We return by stages," she decided, her mind already moving beyond the battlefield to the wider implications of their success. "Leave strong garrisons at key points along our route. The Nubians must see that Egypt's strength extends beyond this single victory."

The officer nodded, understanding the wisdom of the command. A visible Egyptian presence would reinforce the psychological impact of Aata's defeat, reminding potential raiders that the southern border was no longer undefended. Fear, properly applied, was often more effective than walls or armies.

As darkness claimed the land and the stars emerged like scattered gems across the indigo vault of heaven, Ahhotep allowed herself to envision a greater victory—not just here in the southern reaches, but across all Egypt. She imagined the Hyksos driven back to their distant homelands, the Two Lands united once more under native rule, and her son seated upon the throne of his forefathers.

The camp fires cast dancing shadows across her face as she gazed northward, toward where her son fought his own desperate battle. The smoke rose straight up in the still air, carrying prayers and hopes toward the star-filled sky. Somewhere beyond the curve of the earth, Ahmose was perhaps looking at these same stars, wondering about the fate of his kingdom's southern border.

"Send another message," she commanded suddenly, the thought crystallizing as she watched the smoke rise. "To the governors of all southern nomes. Tell them that the Queen Mother has secured the frontier. Tell them that Egypt's enemies have learned the price of aggression."

The message would spread faster than any courier could travel, passed from village to village by traders and travelers until all of southern Egypt knew of their victory. Morale was as important as military success—a people who believed in their strength would fight harder to preserve it.

Her thoughts turned to the broader conflict that had shaped their world for over a century. The Hyksos had ruled northern Egypt through superior weapons and tactical innovation, but they had always been foreigners, ruling through force rather than the divine mandate that legitimized native pharaohs. Now, for the first time in generations, that foreign domination was being challenged successfully.

The coordination of today's attacks—Teti-Ann in the north, Aata in the south, timed to coincide with Ahmose's greatest effort at Avaris— spoke of sophisticated planning. Even besieged, Khamudi had shown he could still orchestrate complex strategies across vast distances. It was the mark of a formidable enemy, one who understood that warfare extended far beyond the clash of armies.

But understanding an enemy's strength was the first step toward defeating it. Khamudi's network of allies and agents was also his weakness—the more complex his plans became; the more opportunities existed for disruption. Today's victory was proof that even the best-laid schemes could be undone by determined resistance at the crucial moment.

"Soon," she whispered to the night sky, where the goddess Nut spread her star-spangled body across the heavens. "Soon Egypt will be whole again."

The words carried on the desert wind, mixing with the smoke of their fires and the eternal sound of the cataract. Somewhere in that vast darkness, her message was already racing toward her son, carrying news that would lift the burden of worry from his shoulders and allow him to focus entirely on the siege that would determine Egypt's future.

She had done her part, held her section of the line against overwhelming odds. Now it remained for Ahmose to complete the great work they had all sacrificed so much to achieve. The reunification of Egypt, the restoration of native rule, the end of foreign domination—all these dreams hung in the balance at the walls of Avaris.

But tonight, at least, the south was secure. The ancient border held firm, defended not by professional armies but by the fierce determination of a mother protecting her son's inheritance. It would be enough. It had to be enough.

As she finally retired to her tent, Ahhotep carried with her the satisfaction of duty fulfilled and the hope of greater victories to come. Behind her, the camp settled into the quiet vigilance of soldiers who had earned their rest through blood and courage. Tomorrow would bring new challenges, but tonight belonged to Egypt and her defenders.

The message to Ahmose, sealed with the lioness of her personal seal, traveled north through the darkness, carrying more than mere words. It carried the promise that Egypt's enemies would never again catch her divided and vulnerable. The coordination that had seemed so clever in the planning had become the very instrument of its own defeat.

Three enemies had struck simultaneously, believing they faced a kingdom weakened by the concentration of its forces at a single point. Instead, they had discovered that Egypt's strength lay not just in her armies but in the indomitable will of her people. One by one, they would learn the price of underestimating the land of the pharaohs.

The south was secure. The message was sent. Now all that remained was to await word from the north, where the greatest battle of their age continued to unfold at the walls of Avaris.

Chapter 10 - Glory before the Siege

April 1526 BC - Thebes

The royal procession wound its way through the streets of Thebes, sunlight glinting off polished bronze spearheads and golden chariots. The avenue of sphinxes leading to the great temple of Amun-Ra had been strewn with fresh rushes and lotus blossoms, their sweet scent temporarily overpowering the usual aromas of the city—bread baking, incense burning, and the earthy smell of the river that gave Egypt life.

At the procession's center rode Prince Ahmose, victorious from his campaign against Teti-Ann, his wounds from the battle still visible though healing well. His skin, darkened by months under the northern sun, contrasted with the pristine white of his kilt and the gleaming gold of his ceremonial collar. Despite his youth, there was nothing boyish about him now—his eyes held the steady gaze of a man who had looked upon death and dealt it with his own hands.

Citizens lined the route, women ululating in the traditional cry of celebration, men raising their arms in salute, children darting forward to touch the wheels of the prince's chariot for luck. They tossed lotus blossoms before the horses' hooves and chanted praise to Amun for delivering their prince safely home. Beautiful young women leaned from upper windows, deliberately catching his eye before dropping flowers or small tokens of admiration.

"The Son of Ra returns!" "Blessed be the arm of Ahmose!" "Death to the Hyksos oppressors!"

The cries rose from the crowd like birds taking flight, but beneath the celebration ran an undercurrent of tension that the perceptive prince did not miss. This was only a brief respite in the larger campaign—a moment to honor a victory against a traitor while the main battle against the foreign occupiers continued in the north under the command of Ahmose's namesake, the son of Ebana.

The procession reached the temple, where priests in leopard skins and white linen awaited with smoking censers that released clouds of kyphi—the sacred temple incense whose recipe was known only to the highest-ranking clergy. The High Priest of Amun, Thuty, stood at the forefront, his shaved head gleaming with sacred oils, his eyes lined with kohl that extended in the style favored by those who served the divine.

"Welcome home, Great One," the priest intoned, bowing deeply. "Amun-Ra has heard our prayers and guided your spear against the traitor. May He continue to grant you victory until all of Egypt lies once more under rightful rule."

Prince Ahmose dismounted from his chariot with fluid grace that belied his recent wound. He acknowledged the priest's greeting with the measured dignity expected of a future pharaoh—neither overly familiar nor coldly distant. "The victory belongs to Egypt and her gods," he replied, his voice carrying to the assembled nobles and priests. "I am merely their instrument."

It was the expected answer, humble yet authoritative, and it drew approving nods from the elders who had known him since childhood. This was no longer the impetuous youth who had departed Thebes two years earlier but a commander tempered by battle and responsibility.

The formal ceremonies lasted until midday—offerings to the gods, purification rituals, the official recounting of the campaign against Teti-Ann for the temple records. Through it all, Ahmose maintained the proper expression of grave attention, though his mind often strayed northward to the continuing siege of Avaris. He had left his best commanders there, men he trusted with his life, but the burden of ultimate responsibility still weighed upon him like the desert sun.

In the great hall of the palace, Ahmose finally embraced his mother Ahhotep, their public reserve giving way to genuine emotion now that they stood away from official eyes. He marveled at the core of steel that lay beneath her graceful exterior. Though approaching her fifth decade, she stood straight-backed and clear-eyed, her arms still strong enough to wield a bow or command an army.

"It seems I am not the only warrior in our family," he said with genuine admiration, noting the fresh scar that marked her forearm—a token from the southern campaign that she had not mentioned in her messages.

Ahhotep merely smiled, the expression softening the stern lines that responsibility had carved into her once-beautiful face. "I did what was necessary, as did you." Her hand reached up to touch his cheek in a rare gesture of maternal affection. "The blood of Tao runs strong in both of us."

Her expression grew more serious, her voice dropping so that even the nearest attendants could not overhear. "And Teti-Ann?"

A shadow crossed the prince's face, darkening his eyes to obsidian. The memory of that final confrontation rose unbidden—the traitor lord kneeling in the sand, blood pooling beneath him, his last words a mixture of defiance and perverse pride.

"He is dead. By my hand," Ahmose replied simply, though the full truth was far more complex and brutal than those four words conveyed.

"Good," she said simply, her tone suggesting that had Teti-Ann somehow survived to be brought back as a prisoner, his fate would have been far worse. There was no need to ask if he had suffered—she knew her son too well to doubt it. The betrayal of Egypt was bad enough; the murder of her husband demanded a reckoning written in pain.

Tetisheri joined them, moving slowly now with the aid of a cedar staff inlaid with ivory and gold. Age had bent her frame but not her spirit nor the piercing clarity of her dark eyes, which still missed nothing. Her once-black hair had turned completely white, giving her the appearance of one already half-transformed into a venerable ancestor spirit.

"So the traitor has paid his debt," she observed, her voice thin but unwavering. She settled onto a chair cushioned with leopard skin, appropriate to her status as the matriarch of the royal line. "Did he speak of your father before the end?"

Ahmose's jaw tightened visibly, the muscles working beneath his smooth-shaven skin. He had not intended to share this with his mother and grandmother, wishing to spare them the pain that had lanced through him at Teti-Ann's confession. But they deserved the truth, bitter though it might be.

"He boasted of it," the prince said quietly, the controlled rage in his voice more frightening than any shout could have been. "It was his khopesh that killed father. Not merely on his orders, but by his own hand."

Ahhotep closed her eyes briefly, absorbing this confirmation of what she had long suspected. Her fingers sought the amulet she wore beneath her robes—a small carving of Osiris, judge of the dead, to whom her murdered husband had gone.

Tetisheri merely nodded, as if a piece of a puzzle had finally fallen into place. The old woman's face remained composed, but those who knew her well could see the brief flicker of vindication in her eyes. "What did you do with the weapon?" she asked, ever practical even in matters of vengeance.

Ahmose reached to his belt and withdrew an ornate khopesh, its curved blade cleaned of blood but still bearing the distinctive shape of a weapon designed to crush as well as cut. The bronze gleamed dully in the filtered light of the chamber, and elaborate hieroglyphs ran along its length—boastful inscriptions of victories that now meant nothing.

"I took it from him," he said, his voice low with controlled emotion. "The blade that killed my father will now help me avenge him completely. When I face Khamudi, it will be with this sword in my hand."

Tetisheri reached out, her fingers—once nimble and strong, now gnarled with age but still adorned with the rings of her rank—tracing the hieroglyphs engraved on the bronze. Her lips moved slightly as she read the boastful inscriptions: claims of enemies defeated, territories conquered, wealth acquired.

"Yes," she murmured, satisfaction coloring her thin voice. "There is symmetry in this. The wheel turns, justice follows." Her eyes, still sharp despite her years, fixed on her grandson's face. "You will complete what your father and brother began. The circle must be closed."

Their reunion was interrupted by the arrival of a messenger, dust-covered and clearly exhausted from hard riding. The young man's face was burned dark by the sun, and his feet were wrapped in blood-stained bandages—evidence of his determination to deliver his news without delay.

"My prince," the man gasped, dropping to one knee. His chest heaved with exertion, and servants rushed forward with water, which he gulped gratefully before continuing. "News from Avaris!"

Ahmose tensed, his hand unconsciously moving to the hilt of his sword. Two years of warfare had conditioned him to expect the worst. "Speak. Has the siege been broken?"

"No, my lord. But Commander Ahmose son of Ebana sends word that the Hyksos position grows desperate." The messenger's eyes gleamed with suppressed excitement. "Their last supply route through the marshes has been discovered and cut off. The enemy burns their dead by night, and disease spreads within their walls. He believes they cannot hold out much longer."

A ripple of excitement passed through the assembled court officials who had edged closer to hear the news. After more than two years of warfare, could victory finally be within reach? Whispers spread like wind through reeds: "The end approaches." "Egypt will be whole again." "The prophecy is fulfilled."

Prince Ahmose's expression remained carefully neutral—the face of command that his men had come to know well. Celebration before victory was secured invited the displeasure of the gods. "Rest tonight," he told the messenger, his tone making it clear that the audience was concluded. "Tomorrow you will return to Avaris with my reply."

The court dispersed slowly, officials and nobles breaking into small groups to discuss the news. Only when the last of them had departed did Ahmose allow his guard to drop, if only slightly.

Later, alone with his mother and grandmother in the private royal apartments where even servants were excluded, he allowed his true thoughts to emerge. Oil lamps cast flickering shadows across walls painted with scenes of royal dignity and divine favor—reminders of the legacy he had been born to uphold.

"I leave for Avaris at dawn," he announced without preamble. There was no need for explanation or justification; they had known from the moment the messenger arrived that he would go. The prince poured wine with his own hand, a rare breach of protocol that emphasized the private nature of their council.

"I will not entrust the final victory to anyone else, no matter how loyal or capable. The task begun by my father and continued by my brother will be completed by me—or it will not be completed at all."

Neither woman attempted to dissuade him. They understood too well the weight of destiny that had settled upon his shoulders from the moment of his birth—a burden made heavier by the deaths of those who should have carried it before him.

"Take the khopesh," Tetisheri said, pointing to Teti-Ann's weapon which now lay on a table of imported cedar. "Complete the circle of vengeance. Let your father's murderer provide the means of his final justice."

Ahhotep touched her son's arm, her callused fingers a reminder that she too had wielded weapons when necessity demanded. The gold flies of valor around her neck caught the lamplight, symbolic of courage beyond what most men would ever know, much less a woman of royal birth.

"When you face Khamudi, remember that he is more than just a Hyksos king," she said, her voice taking on the cadence of formal instruction. "He is the embodiment of all they have done to Egypt—the murders, the desecration of our temples, the humiliation of our people. Show him no mercy, for he would show none to you."

Her eyes, so like her sons in their unwavering intensity, held his gaze. "Make him understand before the end that the Egypt he sought to crush has risen again, stronger for the trial. Let that knowledge be the last thing he carries into the darkness."

Ahmose clasped his mother's hand, feeling the strength that still resided in her grip despite her years. "When next we meet, it will be in a unified Egypt. I swear it by father's spirit and brother's memory."

Thebes to Avaris

Before first light the next morning, he departed Thebes with his personal guard—two hundred men who had proven their loyalty from the first battles along the Nile to the recent victory at Heliopolis. The city still slept as they rode out, only temple priests and early market vendors witnessing their departure.

As they passed through the massive pylon gates that marked the city's boundary, the morning star—Sirius, beloved of Isis—gleamed bright on the eastern horizon like a divine blessing or a distant watchfire guiding their way. Ahmose noted it with satisfaction; the gods had sent a favorable sign.

They left behind the celebrations and comfort of home for the grim reality of the siege lines at Avaris. The Hyksos had occupied Egypt for a century. A few more weeks of discomfort seemed a small price to pay for their final expulsion.

As he rode, Teti-Ann's khopesh hung at his side, its weight a constant reminder of both loss and purpose. The bronze had been purified in temple fires and blessed by the priests of Amun, transforming it from an instrument of treachery to a tool of divine justice. The blade that had brought death to his father would soon bring liberation to his country.

Behind him, the soldiers who had fought at Heliopolis and survived Teti-Ann's treachery marched with renewed determination. These were no longer ordinary men but living extensions of their prince's will—selected warriors who had proven themselves in the crucible of combat. They moved with the disciplined rhythm of veterans, their shields and spears creating a moving forest of bronze that caught the morning light.

The journey north took them through lands bearing the scars of years of conflict. Fields that should have been green with crops lay fallow or burned. Villages stood empty, their inhabitants fled to the safety of walled cities or hiding in the marshes until the war's conclusion. Here and there, the bloated corpses of the unburied dead—victims of raids or disease—drew circles of gorging vultures.

Near the ruins of Teti-Ann's stronghold south of Memphis, they passed a gruesome reminder of the price of treachery. The bodies of captured collaborators hung from makeshift gallows, their flesh blackened by the sun and picked clean by birds, left as a warning to any who might consider aiding the Hyksos cause.

Ahmose did not order them cut down. In war, mercy had its place, but not for those who betrayed their own people. The time for reconciliation would come after victory was secured, not before.

As they continued northward, the prince's thoughts turned to the final confrontation that awaited him. Khamudi, the Hyksos king, was no fool. Cornered and desperate, he would be at his most dangerous—like a wounded crocodile that fights with greater ferocity as its strength ebbs.

But so too was Ahmose. With Teti-Ann's confession still burning in his ears and his father's murderer's weapon at his side, he rode toward Avaris not merely as a commander seeking military victory but as the instrument of Egypt's long-delayed vengeance. The blood of three generations of Theban royalty—his grandfather, his father, his brother—cried out for justice. He would not fail them.

When he reached the siege lines twenty days later, the first thing that struck him was the smell—the unmistakable stench of a city under prolonged siege. Disease, rotting food, too many bodies confined in too small a space with inadequate sanitation. It hung like a miasma over the battlefield, a silent ally to the besiegers more effective than any weapon.

His commander, Ahmose, son of Ebana, greeted him with the formal salute due his rank but also the embrace of a brother-in-arms. The naval commander's face was leaner than when the prince had left him in charge of maintaining the siege, his eyes sunken from months of vigilance and hard decisions.

"Welcome back, my prince," he said, his voice rough from shouting commands across battle lines. "Your return brings new heart to the men."

"And what news do you bring me?" Ahmose asked, dismounting and handing his reins to a waiting attendant. "Does your message speak true? Is the enemy truly at breaking point?"

"The commander nodded, satisfaction evident in his weather-beaten features. "The Hyksos grow more desperate with each passing day, their strength sapped by the close confines of their crowded walls. Their once-proud warriors now fight with diminished vigour, weakened by dwindling supplies and broken morale. We've intercepted deserters trying to slip away by night. They speak of quarrels between Khamudi and his commanders, disagreements over whether to seek terms or fight to the end. "He gestured toward the distant walls of Pi-Ramses where Hyksos banners still flew in defiance, though notably fewer than when the siege began. "They cannot last another month. Perhaps not even another week."

Prince Ahmose nodded, gazing at the city that had defied him for so long. Soon it would fall, and with it, the last vestige of Hyksos rule in Egypt. "Then we will give them one last chance to surrender. After that, we storm the city and put every Hyksos warrior to the sword."

The siege had entered its final phase. Soon, the lands of Egypt would be unified once more under native rule, just as Tetisheri had prophesied in her dream three years before. The wheel of fate had turned full circle, bringing the moment of redemption within reach at last.

As night fell over the encampment, Ahmose stood alone on a small rise overlooking the besieged city. Around him, campfires dotted the darkness like earthbound stars, each one representing Egyptian soldiers who had given years of their lives to this campaign. Some would not live to see its conclusion; others would return home bearing scars both visible and hidden. All had earned their place in the songs that would commemorate this struggle for generations to come.

In his hand he held Teti-Ann's khopesh, the moonlight catching its curved edge and transforming the bronze to silver. The weapon seemed to pulse with its own energy, as if the metal itself recognized the approaching moment of reckoning.

"Soon," he promised the spirits of his father and brother that he felt sure were watching from the Field of Reeds. "Soon you will rest easy in the afterlife, knowing your deaths have been avenged. The scepter stolen by the Hyksos will return to Egyptian hands, and the Two Lands will be one again under the rule of the house of Tao."

The end was approaching for one of them. After a century of occupation and three years of war, destiny hung balanced on the edge of a blade—specifically, the blade that now rested in Prince Ahmose's hand.

Chapter 11 - The Siege of Avaris

June 1526 BC - Avaris

The morning sun blazed across the eastern horizon like molten gold poured from Ra's celestial crucible, casting long purple shadows over the siege lines surrounding Avaris. Prince Ahmose stood atop a makeshift observation platform of sun-bleached acacia wood, his muscled frame silhouetted against the dawn sky. Desert winds tugged at his royal kilt and the leopard skin draped across one shoulder, symbols of his royal blood that meant nothing without victory. The khopesh of Teti-Ann hung heavy at his side, its curved blade promising justice long delayed.

From this vantage point, he surveyed the vast Egyptian camp that stretched like a living creature around the besieged city. Thousands of battle-hardened warriors moved with purpose through a labyrinth of tents and cooking fires, preparing for what might be the final assault on the Hyksos stronghold. The air thrummed with anticipation, with destiny. Ahmose could taste it—metallic like blood, sweet like vindication.

The prince's dark eyes narrowed as he studied the enemy fortifications. Avaris had withstood his army for nearly three years now, its adobe walls still standing. Inside those walls cowered Khamudi, the Hyksos usurper who had stolen his father's life and his brother's future. The thought made Ahmose's jaw tighten until his teeth ached.

A thunderous cheer erupted from the northern approach, rolling across the camp like desert thunder. Ahmose turned sharply, hand instinctively finding the hilt of his weapon, the weapon that had taken his father's life. The sound swelled, drawing closer, sweeping through the camp like a flood along the Nile's fertile banks.

"What is it?" he demanded of the officer beside him, a grizzled veteran whose face bore the scars of a dozen campaigns.

"Reinforcements, my prince," the man replied, eyes wide with excitement, a rare smile breaking through his battle-weathered features. "They march under your banners."

Ahmose descended rapidly from the platform, striding through throngs of soldiers who parted before him like reed grass before the desert wind. Men touched their foreheads in respect as he passed, some reaching out to brush his garments for luck. Their eyes gleamed with a fervor that went beyond military discipline—these men followed him not just as a commander but as living embodiment of Egypt's hope, its rightful future.

As he approached the northern edge of the encampment, the cheering grew deafening, a wall of sound that seemed to physically push against his chest. Through the heat haze of the Delta morning, a column of men materialized like spirits from the afterlife.

There they came—the vanguard he had dispatched to secure the routes from Canaan, now returning triumphant. At their head rode Commander Pennekh, his bronze armor glinting in the morning light, his face weathered by weeks of hard campaigning. Blood-stained bandages wrapped his left forearm, testament to battles fought and won in the prince's name.

The soldiers surrounding the prince took up the chant: "Ahmose! Ahmose! Avenger of Egypt!"

Each repetition of his name struck the prince like a physical blow. Not mere adulation but affirmation of his sacred purpose, the destiny that had been thrust upon him with his father's murder and brother's assassination.

The prince stood immobile as Commander Pennekh dismounted and approached, dropping to one knee before him, head bowed in deference that carried the weight of absolute loyalty.

"Rise, loyal friend," Ahmose commanded, voice cutting through the continuing cheers. "What news do you bring?"

Commander Pennekh rose, revealing a face transformed by weeks of warfare, leaner and harder yet alight with triumph. A fresh scar traced a jagged path from his left ear to his chin, still pink and angry against his sun-darkened skin.

"Victory, my prince," the commander replied, his voice carrying to the men gathered around them. "The last Hyksos outposts between here and Canaan have fallen. Their reinforcements are scattered or dead. We caught their supply caravan three days' march east—fifty chariots laden with grain and weapons." His eyes gleamed with savage satisfaction. "Their bodies now feed the jackals, and their supplies feed our men."

He paused, savoring the moment before delivering the coup de grace: "Avaris stands alone."

Another cheer erupted, so powerful it seemed the very walls of the besieged city must tremble at the sound. Men beat their spears against their shields, creating a cacophony of bronze and leather that echoed across the plain.

Ahmose clasped his commander's forearm, feeling the corded muscle beneath the skin, the strength of a man who had risen from common birth to become one of Egypt's greatest warriors.

"You have done well," he said, his voice pitched for his commander's ears alone. "The gods of our ancestors smile upon your deeds."

Then, louder for all to hear: "Now join me, for we have a king to dethrone."

Khamudi's dilemma

Within the adobe walls of Pi-Ramses, north of Avaris, King Khamudi paced the confines of his audience chamber like a caged leopard. His sandaled feet traced and retraced a path worn into the polished limestone floor over weeks of siege. The distant roars from the Egyptian camp penetrated even these thick walls, carrying with them the scent of doom.

Khamudi's once-immaculate royal garments hung loose on his frame, testament to weeks of dwindling supplies and mounting desperation. The gold and lapis lazuli collar around his neck—symbol of his kingship—now seemed to weigh like a millstone, dragging him toward an inevitable fate. His beard, once carefully oiled and braided in the Egyptian fashion he had adopted to legitimize his rule, had grown unkempt, streaked with gray that had not been there when the siege began.

"What is happening out there?" he demanded of his cowering steward, a thin Egyptian who had served the Hyksos court for decades with the fluid loyalty of one who knows where true power resides.

The man trembled visibly, his eyes fixed on the floor tiles. "Another Egyptian force has arrived, Divine One. Their numbers grow while ours..." He trailed off, unwilling to complete the thought.

Khamudi silenced him with a savage gesture. "And Teti-Ann? Any word from our agent in their camp?"

"None, my king," the steward whispered, shrinking further into himself. "We must assume—"

"Assume nothing!" Khamudi snarled, hurling a golden chalice across the room. It clattered against the wall, spilling the last of his precious wine across the painted plaster where hunting scenes depicted a bounty long vanished from the besieged city. "That Egyptian serpent was our last hope."

The wine traced crimson rivulets down the wall, pooling on the floor like blood. Khamudi watched it spread with a detached fascination, seeing in it an omen he dared not interpret.

He stalked to the narrow window that overlooked his beleaguered city. The air that drifted through carried the stench of too many bodies in too small a space—sweat and waste and fear combining into a miasma that even the burning of precious incense could not disguise.

Beyond the palace complex, the streets of Avaris teemed with frightened faces—not just soldiers now, but civilians. Women clutching children to their breasts, their eyes hollow with hunger. Old men leaning on staffs, their life's belongings bundled on their backs. Merchants with whatever valuables they could carry, desperately seeking to trade gold and gems for food that no longer existed.

They had come from every Hyksos settlement across the Delta as the Egyptian tide rose inexorably against them, fleeing before Ahmose's advance like chaff before the wind. Now they huddled within the walls of Pi-Ramesses, their last stronghold, looking to him for salvation. Him—Khamudi, last king of a dynasty that had ruled Egypt for a century, now facing extinction.

Khamudi's fingers tightened on the window ledge until his knuckles showed white beneath his skin. His plan with Teti-Ann had been masterful—divide the Egyptian force, assassinate their prince, shatter their momentum. Yet here he stood, watching it all crumble like a sand castle before the rising flood.

"My king," his commander ventured cautiously, approaching from the shadows of the chamber where he had been silently observing his ruler's agitation. The man was Khamudi's age, born in Egypt to Hyksos parents, straddling two worlds just as his king did. His armor bore dents and scratches from numerous sorties against the besiegers, each one less successful than the last.

"Speak," Khamudi commanded without turning.

"Perhaps we should consider—"

"Consider what?" Khamudi rounded on him, eyes blazing with the desperate fury of a cornered predator. "Surrender? To these barbaric southerners who would feed our children to their crocodile gods? Who would erase a century of Hyksos rule as though we were a stain upon their precious Two Lands?"

The commander met his gaze steadily, one of the few men in the kingdom with the courage to do so. In his eyes, Khamudi saw not the blind loyalty he craved but something worse—pity.

"Consider our people, Divine One," the commander said quietly. "Look below." He gestured toward the window. "This is no longer a siege of soldiers. It is the siege of a nation."

Khamudi turned back to the window, forcing himself to truly see what his pride had been avoiding. The streets had become a vast, impromptu camp of refugees. Tents and makeshift shelters filled every available space, blocking alleys and courtyards. Cooking fires sent thin tendrils of smoke skyward, burning dung and refuse for lack of proper fuel. Children wailed from hunger, their cries a constant backdrop to the city's slow death. This was no longer a military contest but a fight for survival itself—and one they were losing by increments each day.

"How long?" he asked, his voice suddenly weary, stripped of royal pretence.

"The granaries will be empty within twenty days," the commander replied without hesitation. "Less if we continue to feed the civilians at current rations. The wells remain sweet, but without food..."

Khamudi nodded slowly, the implications clear. Starvation before surrender. Death before dishonor. The warrior's way—but could he condemn thousands of his people, including women and children, to such a fate?

"Twenty days," he murmured, trying to convince himself. "Perhaps help will come from our cousins in Canaan by then."

The commander said nothing, but his silence spoke volumes. They both knew the truth—Canaan would not risk Egyptian wrath by sending aid to a doomed king. The vultures were already circling, waiting to pick clean the bones of the Hyksos empire.

As darkness fell, Khamudi climbed to the highest tower of his palace, dismissing his guards with a gesture. He wanted—needed—to be alone with the weight of decision, the burden of a king's final choice.

From here, he could see the Egyptian camp fires stretching in a vast semicircle around his city, countless pinpricks of light in the gathering gloom like fallen stars come to earth. Beyond them, the fertile black land of the Delta stretched away, the land his ancestors had ruled for a century.

A land that might soon reject them entirely.

Khamudi closed his eyes, feeling the cool night breeze against his face, carrying the distant sounds of Egyptian revelry. They were celebrating already, confident in their inevitable victory. And perhaps they were right.

He opened his eyes again, focusing on the brightest light in the Egyptian camp—surely the fire before the prince's tent. Even at this distance, he could imagine Ahmose planning tomorrow's assault, the son of Seqenenre plotting the final vengeance for his father's blood.

"Sleep well, prince of Egypt," Khamudi whispered to the night. "Dawn brings decisions for us both."

July 1526 BC Surrender of the Charioteers

The dawn broke sullen and gray over the siege lines, unusual weather for Egypt. A mist hugged the ground, transforming the landscape into something otherworldly, as though the barrier between this world and the next had grown thin. Prince Ahmose had slept little, troubled by dreams of his father's death and brother's murder—vivid nightmares where their blood-drenched faces accused him of delay, of inadequate vengeance.

Now he stood with his commanders around a table of beaten copper, its surface etched with a map of Avaris. His finger traced the city's outline, lingering on the western wall where deserters had indicated a weakness.

"Here," he said, his voice rasping from lack of sleep. "We concentrate our attacks here while the archers provide covering fire from these positions." He marked the locations with carved stone markers, each placement deliberate, final.

His commanders nodded in agreement, faces solemn in the amber light of oil lamps. These men had followed him from Thebes, through battles and hardships, driven by the same hunger for justice, for restoration of proper order.

"My prince!" A sentry's cry pierced the morning stillness, urgent and alarmed. "Movement at the western gate!"

Ahmose was instantly alert, head snapping up, hand instinctively reaching for his father's khopesh. "Attack formation," he barked.

"No, my prince," the sentry interrupted, an unthinkable breach of protocol that spoke to his agitation. His chest heaved from the exertion of his run, sweat mingling with the morning dew on his brow. "Not an attack. Chariots approach, but slowly. Their weapons are sheathed."

Ahmose narrowed his eyes, exchanging glances with his commanders. In those brief looks passed volumes of suspicion, of hard-earned wariness. The Hyksos were known for their cunning as much as their cruelty.

"Show me," he commanded.

Outside, the morning mist was beginning to burn away under the strengthening sun. Through the haze, he could make out a line of war chariots emerging from Avaris's eastern gate. They moved at a deliberate pace, not the thundering charge of an assault, their distinctive curved sides catching the light.

"A trap?" Ahmose, son of Ebana, muttered at his side. His hand rested on his sword hilt, knuckles white with tension.

"Perhaps," the prince conceded, studying the approaching formation with the experienced eye of a man who had fought the Hyksos for years. "Form the men anyway. If this is some Hyksos trick, let them find us ready."

Orders flew throughout the camp, transforming it from a morning routine into a battle-ready stance within moments. Spearmen formed lines, archers nocked arrows, shield-bearers created walls of protection. The discipline of the Egyptian army—forged through bitter defeats and hard-won victories—displayed itself in the smooth precision of their movements.

But as the chariots drew closer, the mystery deepened. They carried the distinctive markings of Hyksos elite forces—the red and gold paint, the high sides for added protection—yet they made no aggressive moves. When they reached the halfway point between city and camp, they halted in perfect formation.

Then, one by one, the charioteers stepped down from their vehicles. In unison, they placed their weapons upon the ground—curved swords, axes, bows, and quivers. Without their chariots, standing in the open plain, they began walking toward the Egyptian lines.

"What sorcery is this?" breathed an Egyptian officer, his face contorted with confusion.

Ahmose studied the approaching men with narrowed eyes, noting their straight backs, their measured pace. This was no trick but something far more significant.

"Not sorcery," he said softly. "Surrender."

The realization rippled through the watching troops like wind through a wheat field. These were Hyksos charioteers—Egyptian-born men who had served the foreign kings, the most elite of the enemy forces. And they were laying down their arms.

As they approached the Egyptian lines, their leader stepped forward. He crossed the weathered stone bridge spanning the narrow canal between Pi-Ramses and Avaris, his footsteps echoing in the tense silence as he approached the waiting Egyptian prince. Then he prostrated himself before Prince Ahmose. The man was middle-aged, his body bearing the scars of countless battles, his armor of the finest quality despite weeks of siege.

"Great One," he said in perfect, unaccented Egyptian, forehead pressed to the earth in absolute submission, "we come to offer our services to the true lord of the Two Lands."

Ahmose's hand remained on his khopesh, fingers caressing the hilt that had once belonged to his father's killer. "You would betray your king so easily?" His voice carried contempt, but also curiosity.

The charioteer raised his head slightly, revealing eyes that held not shame but conviction. "We are Egyptians first, Great One. Though our fathers served the Hyksos, and we after them, Egypt's blood runs in our veins. We served the Hyksos because we had no choice. Now we choose to serve Egypt's rightful ruler."

"And you expect me to trust you?" Ahmose's voice was cold as a desert night, sharp as obsidian. "The men who have killed my soldiers, who have defended the murderer of my kin?"

"We bring gifts, Great One," the charioteer replied, his gaze unwavering despite the hundred arrow points trained upon him and his men. "Knowledge of Avaris's defenses. The location of their food stores. The weakness in their western wall where the brick was laid poorly during recent repairs." The man's eyes gleamed with a fierce intelligence. "And news that Khamudi's water cisterns run lower than he admits to his own people. The wells grow brackish while he tells them sweet water remains plentiful."

Ahmose exchanged a glance with son of Ebana, whose face showed the calculations running behind his eyes. Such intelligence could shorten the siege by weeks, saving countless Egyptian lives. Yet the risk of treachery remained.

"Take them," he ordered after a moment's consideration, his voice carrying the weight of royal authority across the battlefield. Nearly six hundred charioteers crossed the bridge behind them, already unarmed, each leading their valuable horses by the reins across the weathered stone toward the vast open field to the west of the city. Ahmose's eyes narrowed as he studied the procession, calculating their worth. "Separate them for questioning. If their words prove true, they may yet live to serve Egypt."

As the surrendered charioteers were led away, Ahmose turned back toward Avaris. The mist had cleared entirely now, revealing the city in stark detail—its high walls, its teeming streets visible even at this distance. Something had changed in the balance of this siege. He could feel it in his bones, in the blood that carried the legacy of eighteen kings before him.

Destiny was accelerating, rushing toward a conclusion written in the stars before his birth.

Khamudi's decision

Within the palace of Pi-Ramses, King Khamudi received the news of the charioteers' desertion with eerie calm. He dismissed the trembling messenger with a wave, then sat motionless upon his throne for long minutes, his face a mask of stone. Only the rapid rise and fall of his chest betrayed the storm raging within.

The audience chamber had emptied of all but his most trusted advisors, men who had tied their fates to his and now watched him with poorly concealed fear. The palace felt hollow, echoing with absences. Servants who had disappeared in the night. Guards who had failed to report for duty. The slow bleeding away of loyalty as the inevitability of defeat pressed against the city walls.

When at last Khamudi spoke, his voice was hollow, devoid of the imperious tone that had once made men tremble. "How many remained loyal?"

His commander shifted uncomfortably, the movement causing his armor to creak like an old boat. "Perhaps a thousand foot soldiers and three hundred bowmen, Divine One. Not enough to mount an effective defense of the outer walls."

Khamudi nodded slowly, absorbing this latest blow with the resignation of a man who has been beaten too often to feel the individual blows. "And our people continue to suffer."

"The situation grows dire, my king," the commander admitted, his eyes flickering toward the window where the sounds of the city filtered through—crying children, arguing adults, the background murmur of thousands pressed together in fear. "There was fighting at the granaries this morning. Three dead, a dozen injured. The stores meant to last another ten days will be gone in five at this rate."

The king rose abruptly from his throne—a massive construction of cedar and gold, carved with scenes of Hyksos triumph that now seemed like mockery. He crossed to a cedar chest inlaid with ivory and gold that stood in a shadowed corner of the chamber. From it, he withdrew a clay tablet and a stylus, handling them with unusual care, as though they represented his last connection to dignity.

"What choice remains to us?" he murmured, more to himself than his commander. The weight of accumulated decisions, of a dynasty's fall, bent his shoulders beneath his royal regalia. "We fight and die to the last man, our women and children starving in the streets? Or..."

His hand hovered over the tablet, trembling slightly. Then, with sudden decisiveness, he began to write, the stylus scratching across the clay with furious intensity.

"Summon my scribes," he ordered without looking up. "And prepare my royal seal. There is little time."

The commander bowed and withdrew, relief visible in every line of his body. He had feared being ordered to lead a suicidal final charge, to die pointlessly for a lost cause. Instead, Khamudi had chosen the path of pragmatism, of survival—at least for his people, if not his dynasty.

Alone, Khamudi continued to write, each symbol pressed into the soft clay with deliberate care. When he finished, he sat back, studying what he had written. The words that would end a century of Hyksos rule in Egypt. The admission of defeat that would follow his name through history.

But also, perhaps, the decision that would save thousands of lives.

He pressed his seal into the bottom of the tablet and called for the messenger who would carry it to the Egyptian camp.

Khamudi's withdrawal proposal

The Egyptian camp buzzed with activity as Prince Ahmose received the Hyksos messenger. The man approached under a flag of truce, bearing a sealed clay tablet. His eyes darted nervously from side to side as Egyptian soldiers escorted him through rows of tents and cooking fires, past the trophies of previous victories displayed on poles—Hyksos shields, helmets, weapons.

After careful inspection for hidden weapons or poisons— conducted with methodical thoroughness that left the messenger pale and shaking—he was brought before the prince in the command tent.

Ahmose broke the royal seal and read the message carefully, his expression revealing nothing. The tent was silent save for the distant sounds of the camp and the messenger's labored breathing.

"Your king proposes terms," he said finally, looking up from the tablet. "He offers to abandon Avaris peacefully and withdraw his people to Canaan, in exchange for safe passage."

Ahmose, son of Ebana, scoffed, his scarred face contorting with derision. "After a century of occupation, after the murder of your brother and father, he expects mercy? The jackal demands safe conduct after savaging the flock?"

The prince said nothing, reading the tablet once more. This was unexpected—a complication in what had seemed a straightforward, if bloody, conclusion to his campaign. The Hyksos king was offering to yield the prize without further Egyptian casualties. Yet allowing the enemy to escape intact felt like an incomplete victory, a partial fulfilment of the oath he had sworn over his father's mutilated body.

His fingers traced the carved hieroglyphs of his father's name on the hilt of Teti-Ann's khopesh. What would Seqenenre have done, faced with this choice? What would Kamose have counselled? The dead offered no answers, only the weight of expectation, the demand for vengeance.

"Return to your master," Ahmose told the messenger. "Tell him his proposal is... under consideration. I will send my answer before sunset."

When the messenger had departed, he summoned his war council, the men who had followed him from Thebes to Memphis to this final confrontation. They gathered quickly, faces grimy from weeks of campaign, eyes alert with curiosity about this unexpected development.

"The Hyksos king offers surrender," he announced without preamble, holding up the clay tablet. "He will abandon Avaris and withdraw his people to Canaan if we grant them safe passage."

A murmur ran through the assembled commanders, a mixture of surprise and suspicion.

"It is a trick," one insisted, slamming his fist on the table. "They seek only to escape our justice, to preserve their strength for another day. Once safely in Canaan, what prevents them from rebuilding their army and returning?"

"Perhaps," Ahmose acknowledged, setting the tablet down carefully. "But consider our position. We have them surrounded, their supplies dwindling. Victory is assured—but at what cost in Egyptian lives? And how many months more of siege?" He looked around the circle, meeting each man's eyes. "Every day we remain here is a day our enemies elsewhere might take advantage of our absence."

"The men expect blood," another commander warned, an older man whose campaigns stretched back to Ahmose's grandfather's time. His voice carried the weight of experience. "They have marched far and suffered much. They have seen comrades fall to Hyksos arrows and swords. They will not be satisfied with an enemy that simply walks away."

Ahmose paced the length of the tent, weighing options, calculating costs. The Hyksos had ruled Egypt for a century, had murdered his father and brother. The scales of Ma'at demanded balance, demanded justice.

And yet... the sight of starving children within Avaris's walls, glimpsed during reconnaissance, haunted him. Children bore no responsibility for their parents' crimes. Women had not chosen this war. And even among the men, many had been born to Hyksos service as their fathers before them. Could he condemn them all for the sins of Khamudi and his predecessors?

"I will accept their withdrawal," he announced finally, turning to face his commanders. The decision solidified within him as he spoke, bringing with it not satisfaction but certainty. "But with conditions. Khamudi himself must remain. And they leave their weapons, their treasure. They march into exile with only what they can carry on their backs."

His commanders exchanged glances. It was not the bloodbath many had anticipated, but it was victory nonetheless. Egypt would be whole again, united under native rule for the first time in generations.

"And what of Khamudi?" asked Ahmose, son of Ebana, the question that hung in all their minds.

The prince's hand tightened on his khopesh, feeling the weight of history, of vengeance, of a son's duty to his murdered father. "Justice will be served," he promised, his voice soft but implacable. "Ma'at will be satisfied."

Chapter 12 - The Hyksos Exodus

July 1526 BCE Hyksos leaving Avaris

The merciless Egyptian sun climbed toward its zenith, a molten copper disk suspended in a sky bleached white by heat, pouring its punishing intensity upon the teeming streets of Avaris. The air hung thick with dust and desperation, carrying the mingled odors of sweat, fear, and the cloying sweetness of rotting food abandoned in the markets.

Within the city that had stood proud as the Hyksos capital for a century, chaos now reigned supreme. The wide sandstone avenues and labyrinthine alleyways alike were choked with humanity—men with hollow eyes, women clutching precious heirlooms, and children too stunned by the sudden upheaval to cry.

Nakhthonsu, his once-muscular frame now leaner from months of dwindling provisions, stood amid the wreckage of his former prosperity. The copper amulet of Seth that had never left his neck since boyhood felt unnaturally heavy against his skin. He surveyed the empty timber shelves of his warehouse where exotic spices from distant lands had once been stored in labeled clay jars, where bolts of fine linen and cedar oil from Lebanon had made him wealthy. Now stripped bare, its valuable contents traded weeks ago when the siege had tightened like a serpent's coils around the city's throat. All that remained to show for twenty years of shrewd trading and calculated risks was a single braying donkey, its flanks quivering beneath hastily packed bundles.

"Take only what sustains life," he instructed his wife, Tani, whose once-plump cheeks had hollowed during the siege. She clutched their youngest child to her breast while the older two clung to her indigo-dyed skirts. "The journey to Sharuhen crosses two hundred and fifty kilometers of hostile land, and the Egyptian sun shows no mercy to those who travel slowly."

Tani nodded, her kohl-rimmed eyes red from weeping yet dry now, hollowed by the resignation that had settled upon her like a funeral shroud. The silver anklets that had jingled merrily when she danced during happier times were gone—traded for grain in the second month of the siege. Her fingers, once adorned with carnelian rings, were bare and cracked from washing clothes in increasingly precious water. "What of your father's scrolls?" she asked, her voice catching on the words. "They carry the legacy of your blood. How will our children know their lineage if we abandon the stories?"

She gestured toward the cedar chest inlaid with ivory that contained three generations of merchant records, family histories, and the stories of their people's arrival in Egypt. Her hands trembled as she spoke, revealing the depth of her own attachment to these tangible links to their past.

Nakhthonsu's face darkened, the scar along his jaw—legacy of a merchant dispute in his youth—whitening as he clenched his teeth. He moved to the chest and lifted its lid, his calloused fingers tracing over the neat columns of his father's script. The familiar handwriting brought a flood of memories: his father's voice reciting the oral histories of their Canaanite ancestors, the pride in his eyes when young Nakhthonsu had first helped compose a trade agreement.

"Leave them," he finally commanded, his voice rough as desert stone, though his hand lingered over a particular scroll that bore his grandfather's seal. "Words written on papyrus will not feed our children in the wilderness. The Egyptians can burn them with the rest of our history." The lid closed with a soft thud that seemed to echo in the hollow warehouse.

"But Papa," his eldest son, Khenti, spoke up for the first time that morning, his voice wavering between childhood and the premature adulthood that crisis brings. "What about the story of great-grandfather's journey? You said I would tell it to my sons." The boy's eyes, so like his father's, were wide with the first real understanding of loss.

Nakhthonsu knelt before his son, placing both hands on the boy's thin shoulders. "The stories live here," he said, touching the child's forehead gently. "And here," he added, placing his hand over the boy's heart. "Words on papyrus can be burned, but the tales we carry within us will survive even the desert crossing. You will tell your sons—in Canaan."

Around them, similar scenes of heartbreak played out in every household across the once-great city. Through open doorways, Nakhthonsu glimpsed families arguing over which ancestral treasures to abandon, which to carry into an uncertain future. The wails of women merged with the authoritative shouts of Egyptian officials, creating a cacophony of defeat that echoed off stone walls soon to be reclaimed by the victors.

The Hyksos elite—those who had served in King Khamudi's glittering court and commanded his once-feared chariots—had already departed at dawn, taking the choicest animals and cushioned wagons. Now it was the turn of the merchants, the artisans, the ordinary people who had built lives here over generations, considering themselves Egyptian until Ahmose's armies had reminded them they were forever foreigners.

"By sunset, all must be beyond the eastern marker stones!" an Egyptian officer announced, his voice carrying over the crowd's desperate murmur. He stood atop an overturned Hyksos chariot, its once-proud decoration of gold leaf and electrum now stripped away, leaving only bare wood. "Those who remain will be considered enemies of Pharaoh Ahmose, Beloved of Amun, Lord of the Two Lands, Uniter of Upper and Lower Egypt!"

Each title hammered into Nakhthonsu's heart like a nail into a coffin lid. The final proclamation—Lord of the Two Lands—hung in the air like the death knell of Hyksos dreams. Egypt, divided for a century, was whole again under native leadership. And they, the defeated, were being cast out into the wilderness like chaff before the threshing floor.

Nakhthonsu spat in the dust, the gesture containing all the venom and bitterness of the defeated. "So ends a hundred years of our rule. Not with glorious battle but with begging bowls and bent backs."

An old man nearby—Pashenuro, once a scribe in the king's court whose fingers were permanently stained with ink—leaned heavily on a staff carved from Lebanon cedar. His face was deeply creased with the wisdom and wounds of decades; his eyes clouded with cataracts yet still perceiving truths others missed. "Did you expect differently, merchant?" he asked, his voice thin but carrying the cadence of education. "The gods of this land never truly accepted us. We were always strangers drinking from a borrowed cup. Now the cup's true owner has returned to claim it."

The temple of Seth, where Khamudi had once made offerings for the prosperity of his people, now witnessed the hurried exodus of its priests. In its shadow, shaven-headed figures moved with practiced efficiency, removing sacred objects from the inner sanctuary. Golden vessels, ritual implements, sacred texts—all packed into wooden crates with the reverence due to holy things, yet with the urgency of those who knew Egyptian priests already waited to reconsecrate the space to Amun-Ra.

By midday, when the sun's heat had become a living thing that pressed against flesh like molten bronze, a vast column of humanity stretched from the eastern gate of Avaris across the fertile plain. The procession moved like a great, wounded serpent, raising dust that shrouded the refugees in a golden haze that would have been beautiful were it not born of such misery.

From the highest tower of the palace, Ahmose son of Ebana watched the exodus unfold with the calculating gaze of a veteran commander. The gold collar of valor rested heavy around his neck, reward for being the first to breach the city walls. His face, a tapestry of battle scars earned in thirty years of service, revealed nothing of his thoughts as he observed the consequence of victory.

"How many, Commander?" asked a young lieutenant at his side, his smooth face marking him as untested before this campaign.

"Twenty thousand, perhaps more," replied son of Ebana, his experienced eye calculating distances and provisioning with automatic precision. "Most will not survive the journey to Sharuhen. The desert shows no mercy to the unprepared, and these people have known only the luxury of delta living for generations."

The veteran commander's assessment proved prescient as the column moved eastward. Overloaded wagons began shedding their burdens almost immediately—a carved chair here, a copper mirror there, a child's painted wooden toy abandoned as the brutal reality of the journey's demands became clear with each passing furlong.

Nakhthonsu and his family joined the great river of displaced humanity, their donkey braying in protest at its burden. As they passed through the eastern gate where Hyksos guards had once challenged all visitors, Tani turned for one last look at the city of her birth. Tears coursed down her dust-streaked face, cutting pale channels through the grime as she beheld the Egyptian standards already flying from the walls.

"Do not look back," Nakhthonsu told her, though his own voice cracked with emotion. His hand closed around her upper arm with urgent purpose. "What lies behind us is no longer ours. We must look to Sharuhen, to Canaan beyond. There we will build again, as our grandfathers built here when they first came to this land."

As they crossed the marker stones, an Egyptian guard stepped forward from his post. Unlike his companions, who stared through the refugees as if they were already ghosts, this man's eyes held something akin to pity. A small copper scar on his forearm suggested he had faced Hyksos weapons in battle and lived to tell of it.

"For the children," he said gruffly, extending a water skin still beaded with moisture from the well. He avoided their direct gaze as custom demanded when addressing the defeated, but his voice carried an unexpected gentleness. "I have little ones of my own. The road ahead is harsh."

Nakhthonsu hesitated, pride warring with necessity as he watched his children's parched lips and fevered skin. The sight of their need overrode all else. He accepted the offering with a curt nod, the gesture containing the last remnants of his dignity.

"The smaller wells three leagues east still hold water," the guard added in a low voice, glancing around to ensure his words went unheard by his superiors. "The larger ones have been fouled by those who went before. And..." he paused, seeming to wrestle with himself, "there are caves in the red rocks where the sun cannot reach. Rest there during the heat of day."

Even in defeat, small mercies persisted. Small kindnesses that pierced the armor of hatred Nakhthonsu had begun to build around his heart. He met the soldier's eyes briefly, acknowledging their shared humanity despite the bitter divisions of war and conquest.

The endless column trudged onward into the afternoon heat, leaving behind the fertile black soil of Egypt for the harsh embrace of the eastern desert. The air shimmered above the sand, creating mirages that tantalized with visions of water and shade. The sun beat down upon bent backs, turning exposed skin red and blistered. The wind carried away their lamentations, scattering grief across the dunes like seeds that would find no purchase in the barren soil.

Thus ended a century of Hyksos presence in the land of the Nile—not with the glory songs would commemorate, not with honorable defeat in battle where men could preserve their pride even as they lost their lives, but with the quiet humiliation of expulsion. With children whimpering for water, with women concealing family treasures where searching hands might not find them, with men whose sleepless nights showed in their red-rimmed eyes as they contemplated an uncertain future.

Behind them, in the suddenly diminished city of Avaris, Egyptian soldiers began the methodical process of reclamation. Temples were cleansed, granaries inventoried, palace treasuries sealed for transport to Thebes. The physical traces of Hyksos rule would be erased, stone by stone, inscription by inscription, until only memory remained. And even memory, in time, would be reshaped by the victors' hands.

As night fell across the desert, the first casualties of the exodus were already being buried in shallow graves scratched from unyielding soil. Nakhthonsu counted twelve funeral fires within sight of their meager camp, each marking another soul who would never see the promised safety of Sharuhen. The very old, the very young, those weakened by siege—the desert claimed them with impartial cruelty.

His daughter, Nefret, barely eight summers old, pressed close to his side as they sat around their own small fire. "Will we ever go home, Papa?" she asked, her voice small in the vast darkness.

Nakhthonsu gazed westward, where the lights of Avaris—his home for all his forty-two years—glimmered in the distance like a taunt. Then he turned resolutely eastward, toward the darkness where no lamps beckoned, no familiar landmarks offered comfort. Somewhere beyond that vast emptiness lay Canaan, the land his grandfather had left three generations ago seeking Egyptian wealth.

"We carry our home with us," he said, gathering his daughter closer. "In our blood, in our stories, in the love that binds us together. That cannot be taken by any pharaoh."

Beside him, Tani wrapped their youngest child tighter in a scrap of linen, her eyes fixed on the eastern horizon where their future lay. "Our ancestors survived the journey once," she whispered, finding new strength in her voice. "We carry their blood. We will endure."

Above them, indifferent to human suffering yet somehow eternal in their constancy, the stars emerged one by one. The same stars that had guided their ancestors to Egypt five generations earlier would now lead their exodus home. In their ancient light, the Hyksos began the long journey back to the land of their fathers, carrying with them the weight of a century's dreams and the fragile hope of new beginnings.

Chapter 13 - Assassination of Khamudi

July 1526 BCE, - Avaris

As twilight gathered over the delta, painting the western sky in hues of amber and crimson that bled across the horizon like wounds in the flesh of heaven, a different scene unfolded before the massive cedar gates of Avaris. The heat of the summer day still radiated from the trampled earth, making the air shimmer like water above sunbaked stones. A wooden platform had been hastily constructed from the wreckage of Hyksos war chariots, elevated enough that all could witness what was to come, its rough-hewn planks still smelling of fresh-cut timber and conquest. Hundreds of Hyksos soldiers—those who had surrendered in the final desperate days of the siege—knelt in precise rows before the platform, their wrists raw and bleeding where hemp ropes bit into flesh, their once-proud faces now hollow with the knowledge of defeat. Egyptian guards stood vigilant behind them, spear butts planted firmly in the trampled earth, eyes watchful as desert hawks.

These men, with their foreign features and bowed postures, represented the last remnants of Khamudi's once-mighty army that had held the rich delta lands for generations. Most would be offered the same choice as their civilian counterparts—exile eastward to the harsh lands of Canaan or service in Egypt's own forces under close supervision, their loyalty tested daily under the merciless Egyptian sun. But first, they would witness the consequence of their king's defiance, a lesson written in blood that would echo through time.

Torches blazed around the platform, their flames dancing wildly in the gathering darkness, casting long, distorted shadows across the assembled crowd that seemed to writhe like demons from the underworld. The heat from the pitch-soaked brands pressed against exposed skin like invisible hands. The air hung heavy with tension, with anticipation, with the metallic scent of fear that rose from the kneeling men like steam from the Nile marshes. The smell of sweat and despair mingled with the acrid smoke of the torches, creating a pungent fog that clung to every breath and coated the back of the throat.

A drum began to beat, slow and sonorous like the heartbeat of some great beast awaiting sacrifice. The sound seemed to come from the earth itself, reverberating through the bones of all who heard it. From within the conquered city emerged a procession led by Prince Ahmose himself, his lean body silhouetted against the torchlight within the gate. He walked with the steady, inexorable purpose of a man fulfilling a destiny written in the stars long before his birth, each step measured and deliberate, marking the transition from warrior prince to pharaoh-in-waiting. His royal kilt of finest pleated linen gleamed white in the fading light, and the spotted leopard-skin cloak draped over one muscular shoulder marked him as one of royal blood, its preserved claws clicking softly with each step. The khopesh of Teti-Ann hung at his side, its curved blade—shaped like the jaw of a crocodile—catching the torchlight as he moved, seeming almost to drink in the orange glow with an ancient hunger.

The young prince's face told its own story. Not yet twenty-five years of age, Ahmose had already witnessed more blood and treachery than men three times his age. The death of his father had etched lines around his mouth that spoke of grief hardened into resolve; the murder of his brother had left a coldness in his eyes that no victory feast could warm. Tonight, those eyes reflected only the dancing flames as he approached the platform, his gaze fixed on some point beyond the horizon, perhaps seeing not just this moment but the dynasty he would forge from the ashes of war.

Behind him, dragged between two burly guards whose arms bulged like granite beneath their bronze-scaled armor, came Khamudi. The former king had ruled as prince-regent under Apophis for seven years before ascending to full kingship upon his predecessor's death, making his total dominion over the northern lands span twenty-two years of iron rule. His finery had been stripped away, his jewels and gold armbands distributed among Ahmose's captains, leaving him in a simple linen kilt stained with dust and dried blood that emphasized the stark diminishment of his circumstances. His once-oiled beard was matted with filth, and dried blood crusted at a split in his lower lip. Yet he walked with his head high, his shoulders squared despite the rough hands that propelled him forward, his eyes—dark as obsidian and just as hard—fixed straight ahead, refusing to be broken even in defeat.

Khamudi had been a man of imposing stature in his prime, broad-shouldered and powerful, his voice capable of commanding armies across blood-soaked battlefields. Now, as he staggered forward under the guards' rough handling, that power seemed leached from him, leaving only the hollow shell of authority. Yet something in his bearing, in the set of his jaw and the unbroken pride in his eyes, suggested that even stripped of crown and kingdom, the man remained unconquered in spirit.

A murmur rippled through the kneeling soldiers as they beheld their king—some whispered prayers to foreign gods with strange names, others turned away, unable to bear the sight of majesty so reduced. A few, perhaps those who had served in his personal guard, struggled against their bonds, their faces contorted with helpless rage. One grizzled veteran, his scarred face wet with tears, raised his voice: "Khamudi! We remember the victory at Memphis! We remember—" The Egyptian guards struck those who moved with the butts of their spears, the dull crack of wood against flesh punctuating the evening like the sound of distant thunder, restoring silence.

Prince Ahmose ascended the platform first, his sandaled feet making little sound on the wooden planks. He turned to face the assembled Hyksos soldiers, his young face, illuminated by torchlight, seemed carved from the same red granite used for the statues of his ancestors—implacable, unyielding, a visage of justice long delayed but finally at hand. In that moment, with the light playing across his features, the resemblance to his slain father was so striking that some of the older Egyptian soldiers involuntarily touched their amulets of protection.

"Men of Avaris," he began, his voice carrying across the hushed assembly like the cry of a desert falcon, clear and piercing. "Your king has surrendered. Your women weep. Your children now learn Egyptian prayers. Your people march east to a new homeland by my mercy—a mercy your kind never showed to Egypt during the long years of occupation." He paused, letting the words sink into the gathering darkness, feeling the weight of history settling upon his shoulders like a pharaoh's double crown. "But before you join them on the road to exile, you will witness the price of treachery against the Two Lands."

Khamudi was dragged up the steps to stand beside Ahmose, the guards' fingers digging cruelly into the flesh of his upper arms, leaving white impressions that slowly flushed red. Despite the rough handling, the former king maintained his dignity, straightening as best he could with his bound hands, drawing himself up to his full height so that he stood almost eye to eye with his conqueror. For a moment, the two men studied each other—the young pharaoh-to-be and the fallen sovereign—each recognizing something of himself in the other's unwavering gaze.

"My soldiers," Khamudi said suddenly, his voice carrying the authority of two decades of rule, "you have served with honor. Remember that when you reach the eastern lands. Remember that you fought for something greater than yourselves." His eyes swept over their faces, committing each to memory. "A king's first duty is to his people, even in defeat."

"Tell them," Ahmose commanded, turning to face his captive, his voice dropping to a dangerous whisper that nevertheless carried in the utter silence that had fallen. "Tell your men how my brother died."

For a long moment, Khamudi said nothing, his eyes—still sharp and intelligent despite his fallen state—scanning the faces of his former soldiers as if drawing strength from their presence one final time. When he spoke, his voice was hoarse from thirst but clear as temple bells, the voice of a king even in defeat.

"I organized the death of Prince Kamose," he admitted without flinching, the words falling like stones into a still pond. "I would have killed any person who threatened my kingdom, as any king would." There was no remorse in his tone, only the cold calculation of a ruler who had made the decisions required by his position and would make them again if given the chance. "The strong survive. The weak perish. This is the way of kingdoms."

A collective intake of breath came from the assembled soldiers, the sound like wind through a burial chamber. Most had known or suspected the truth, the whispers of assassination having spread through the ranks during the final days of the siege, but to hear it confirmed from their king's own lips was another matter entirely. Some closed their eyes in shame, others nodded imperceptibly, understanding the harsh logic of power.

Ahmose let the confession hang in the air for a moment before speaking again, his voice now carrying the weight of formal judgment. "For this alone, your life would be forfeit." He turned to address the kneeling soldiers directly. "Your lives are spared. By sunset tomorrow, you will be escorted to join your families on the road to Sharuhen. This is more mercy than your king showed my brother, whose body was returned to us bearing seventeen wounds, any one of which would have been fatal."

The prince's hand trembled slightly at this—the only sign of emotion he had displayed thus far—before he mastered himself once more. The memory of Kamose's broken body, displayed before him as proof of death, flickered behind his eyes like lightning in a summer storm. "Before you stand witness to justice, know this—I hold here the confession of Teti-Ann, the traitor who slew my father with this very blade." He patted the khopesh at his side, the metal making a dull sound against his knuckles. "Before his execution, as the interrogators applied their arts with particular dedication, he revealed how your king ordered not just my brother's death but my father's as well, while serving as prince-regent under Apophis."

The young prince's eyes flashed dangerously as he spoke his father's name, the memory of Seqenenre Tao's shattered skull—displayed to him when he was barely seven—momentarily visible in the tightening of his jaw.

Khamudi's composure finally cracked, the façade of royal dignity shattering like thin ice beneath a warrior's boot. "Lies!" he shouted, spittle flying from his lips as he lunged against his captors' grip. "Your father raised arms against my predecessor! He plotted rebellion from Thebes! Teti-Ann acted on his own initiative—I never gave such an order!" His voice rose to a desperate pitch. "I commanded armies, not assassins!"

"The dying rarely lie," Ahmose replied coldly, unmoved by the outburst. "Especially when truth buys a quicker end to suffering. And Teti-Ann died very slowly indeed." Something in the prince's tone suggested he had witnessed this death personally, had perhaps even guided the interrogator's hand at crucial moments. "He spoke your name with his final breath."

The former Hyksos king seemed to deflate before their eyes, like a sail suddenly robbed of wind, the last vestige of his authority crumbling like a sand sculpture before the rising tide. His shoulders slumped, and for the first time, he looked his age—a man past fifty who had known power all his life only to see it vanish like morning mist. He turned to face his men, perhaps hoping to find some support, some loyalty in their eyes that might sustain him in these final moments. But he found only resignation, acceptance, the severed bond between a failed king and his abandoned soldiers.

Yet in that moment of looking upon his men, something of his old majesty returned. He straightened his spine, lifted his chin, and spoke with the voice that had once commanded from palace balconies: "Remember me not as I am now, but as I was. Remember that we held the delta for a century, that we built cities and commanded trade routes, that we were kings when these Egyptians knelt in the mud of Thebes."

"You were once great rulers of a mighty people," Ahmose acknowledged, his voice almost gentle now, as one might speak to a fallen adversary worthy of respect. "Your ancestors swept across our borders like a desert storm, conquering the Two Lands through strength and cunning when Egypt was weak and divided. But what was taken by force can be reclaimed by force. The wheel of time turns for all men, even kings." He placed a hand on the hilt of his father's khopesh, feeling the worn leather binding beneath his fingers, still warm from the day's heat. "Tonight, the wheel completes its circle."

With a gesture to his guards—a simple downward flick of his wrist that seemed almost casual—Ahmose ordered Khamudi forced to his knees in the center of the platform. The wooden boards creaked beneath the sudden weight, the sound unnaturally loud in the hushed night. The former king did not resist, accepting his position with the fatalism of one who has already seen the end written in the stars and knows the futility of struggling against destiny.

As he knelt, Khamudi closed his eyes briefly and moved his lips in what might have been a prayer to Set, the god of his people, or perhaps merely a final farewell to the life he had known. When he opened them again, they held the calm acceptance of a man who had made peace with his fate.

"Look upon your king one last time," Ahmose commanded the kneeling soldiers. "Remember his face when you reach Sharuhen. Remember what becomes of those who rule Egypt through fear rather than Ma'at."

Khamudi knelt straight-backed on the rough planks, his knees surely pained by the splinters digging into flesh, yet giving no sign of discomfort. Blood from his split lip had dried in a dark rivulet down his chin, giving him a savage appearance at odds with his composed posture. The torchlight played across his weathered features, revealing a face that had known both triumph and defeat, both the heights of power and the depths of humiliation.

"For the murder of my father, Seqenenre Tao, whose skull was split by seven blows while he slept, and my brother, Prince Kamose, rightful heirs to the throne of Egypt, I, Ahmose, son of Seqenenre, pronounce sentence of death." The formal words echoed across the silent assembly with the finality of tomb doors closing. "May the gods judge whether justice is served this night."

The prince unsheathed the khopesh with deliberate slowness, the distinctive scrape of bronze against leather scabbard raising the hair on the necks of all who heard it. This was the same weapon that had taken his father's life, its curved blade—designed to slip between the ribs and find the heart—now held aloft so that all could see it catch the torchlight, seeming to glow with an inner fire of its own. The symbolism was lost on none present—the instrument of death would become the instrument of justice, completing a circle begun years ago in a royal bedchamber in Thebes.

Khamudi raised his head, the cords in his neck standing out like ropes, meeting Ahmose's gaze directly. Their eyes locked, captor and captive, victor and vanquished, the space between them charged with the weight of history being written in this moment. In that silent exchange, each man saw something of himself reflected in the other—the burden of kingship, the weight of difficult choices, the loneliness of command.

"Remember this moment, son of Seqenenre," Khamudi said, his voice steady despite everything, carrying the authority of prophecy. "For one day, you too will kneel before death, and all your victories will mean nothing. The kingdoms of men are but sandcastles before the tide of time."

"Perhaps," Ahmose acknowledged, a flicker of something—respect, perhaps, or recognition of a shared understanding of power's ultimate limitations—passing across his features. "But I will meet my end as a pharaoh of Egypt, not as a foreign usurper stripped of stolen glory. Your name will be chiseled from monuments, your face scratched from reliefs, while mine will endure as long as the stones of Egypt stand against the desert wind."

Khamudi's lips curved in what might have been a smile. "We shall see, young pharaoh. We shall see."

The moment stretched between them, a final acknowledgment of mutual respect between enemies. Then Ahmose raised the blade, its bronze surface catching the last rays of dying sunlight.

With a movement too swift for the eye to follow, honed by years of training with the finest weapons masters in Thebes, he swung the blade in a perfect arc that caught the fading light like a falling star. It passed through Khamudi's neck with terrible efficiency, cleaving flesh and bone as though they offered no more resistance than papyrus reed. For a split second, nothing seemed to happen—the world held its breath, suspended between one age and the next.

A collective gasp rose from the assembled Hyksos soldiers, the sound like the last breath escaping a dying beast, followed by absolute silence more profound than any that had come before. Many bowed their heads, not in grief but in acknowledgment of the inevitable. A few whispered prayers to foreign gods who had failed to protect their king. The wheel had indeed turned. The dynasty that had ruled the delta for a century had ended in a single sword stroke.

Ahmose stood motionless above the corpse, blood splatter marking his kilt and chest in a warrior's baptism. For a moment, looking down at the fallen king, his expression revealed the young man beneath the mantle of leadership—a son who had lost a father, a brother who had lost a brother, a prince who had been forced to become a man before his time. The weight of what he had done, what he had become, settled upon him like the heavy gold of a pharaoh's collar. Then the moment passed, and the mask of kingship settled once more upon his features.

He wiped the blade clean on a cloth of fine linen provided by an attendant, his movements deliberate, almost ritualistic, as if completing a sacred obligation rather than a political execution. The cloth came away stained crimson, the color deepening as it dried in the night air. Each fold of fabric seemed to absorb not just blood but the old world itself, leaving the blade clean for the new age to come.

"Justice is served," he proclaimed, raising the cleaned blade toward the first stars now appearing in the eastern sky. "The scales of Ma'at are balanced. Let it be known throughout the Two Lands that Egypt breathes free once more." His voice carried across the assembled crowd with the authority of divine mandate, the words seeming to echo from the very stones of the ancient city.

He descended from the platform with measured steps, leaving the body where it had fallen—a final lesson to those who would oppose Egypt's rightful rule. The drum began to beat once more, no longer the ominous rhythm of approaching judgment but the steadier cadence of order restored, accompanying Ahmose's departure through the gates of what would soon be reconsecrated as an Egyptian city with purifying fire and the blessings of a hundred priests.

Behind him, the Hyksos soldiers remained kneeling in the gathering darkness, witnesses to the end of an era. Some wept silently, not for their king but for themselves, for the knowledge that they would never again see the land they had called home. Others sat in numb silence, their minds already turning to the uncertain future that awaited them in exile. Tomorrow they would begin their own journey eastward, carrying with them the memory of this night, this moment when one world ended and another began with the fall of a bronze blade through the desert air.

Thus ended the rule of the Shepherd Kings in the land of Egypt, in fire and blood and the inexorable turning of the wheel of fate. And thus began the reign of Ahmose, first pharaoh of a new dynasty, who would drive the invaders from Egypt's soil and unite the Two Lands once more under native rule, restoring Ma'at—the divine order—after a century of foreign dominion. The stars wheeled overhead, silent witnesses to the changing of the guard, as Egypt prepared to reclaim its destiny among the nations of the ancient world.

Chapter 14 - Taskmasters Assignment

July 1526 BC - Palace of Khamudi, Avaris

In the sprawling palace that had been Khamudi's seat of power, Prince Ahmose sat at a massive desk of imported cedar, its polished surface gleaming under the slanting rays of morning sunlight that filtered through the alabaster window screens. The wood, brought at great expense from the distant forests of Lebanon, still carried the faint scent of resin that mingled with the more pungent aroma of fresh ink and beeswax candles. Before him lay a pristine sheet of the finest papyrus, its surface smooth and perfect as untouched snow, awaiting words that would announce to all Egypt that the century of humiliation had ended.

Ahmose ran his fingertips over the papyrus, feeling its supple strength. How many such proclamations had been written by usurpers in this very chamber? The thought hardened his resolve.

A scribe knelt nearby on a woven reed mat, his shaved head glistening with a sheen of perspiration despite the early hour. His reed pens and ink cakes were arranged with meticulous precision upon a wooden palette—black for ordinary text, red for emphasis and divine names—ready to transform the prince's dictation into the formal language of royal proclamation. The scribe's hands, stained permanently at the fingertips from years of his craft, remained perfectly steady despite the momentous occasion.

The chamber still bore the unmistakable marks of Hyksos occupation—wall paintings depicted foreign deities with strange, elongated faces alongside familiar Egyptian gods, creating a jarring visual cacophony. The furnishings featured motifs from distant Canaan: lotus flowers intertwined with unfamiliar blooms, traditional Egyptian symbols warped by foreign sensibilities. Golden bowls embossed with scenes of warfare in a style no Egyptian artisan would recognize were displayed prominently on shelves of imported olivewood. Yet already, the transformation had begun. Ahmose's personal standard—a falcon with wings outstretched protectively over the symbol of united Egypt—had been raised above the palace roof, its shadow falling symbolically across the chamber floor. The sacred bark of Amun-Ra—hidden for decades in a secret chamber beneath the temple floor by faithful priests who had risked torture and execution—now occupied the central shrine where the Hyksos god Seth had been worshipped. Egypt was reclaiming its own, stone by stone, ritual by ritual, prayer by prayer.

Ahmose, son of Ebana, entered the chamber after a respectful knock, bowing deeply before the prince. His bronze-scaled armor was freshly polished to a honey-gold gleam, catching the light with each movement of his powerful frame. A thin scar ran from his right temple to his jawline—a badge of honor earned during the final assault on the Hyksos fortress. His bearing was that of a man delivering good news, his chest expanded with barely contained pride, his steps measured but eager.

"All the Hyksos crossed the eastern boundary, my prince," he reported, his deep voice carrying the hoarseness of a man who had shouted many battle commands in recent days. "I have sent another two hundred soldiers, as you ordered, to join the others to make sure they reach Sharuhen. Hard men, battle-tested, who will tolerate no deviation from the exile route. They will catch up with the main column by tomorrow's nightfall."

Ahmose nodded, satisfaction evident in the set of his broad shoulders. One chapter closed, another beginning. He studied the face of his loyal commander—they had grown from boys to men together in the crucible of this long campaign. The son of Ebana had never wavered, not even when defeat seemed certain.

"And the city?" Ahmose's voice was steady, controlled, betraying none of the exultation that surged through his veins like fire.

"Secured to the last alleyway and hovel, my prince." Son of Ebana's chest swelled with evident pride. "The granaries have been inventoried—less remains than we expected. The Hyksos actually left with not much left in their stores. Enough grain to feed your army for at least three days until supplies arrive from Bubastis. The streets are quiet; the people watch us with wary eyes but no resistance."

"The temples?" Ahmose leaned forward, his dark eyes intent. For a true Egyptian, the spiritual reconciliation was as important as the military victory.

"Priests of Amun-Ra are conducting purification rituals in all major sanctuaries," Son of Ebana replied, his voice dropping to a reverent tone. "Incense burns day and night. Chants that have not been heard openly in the Delta for generations echo again from the sacred precincts. The smaller shrines will be cleansed in the coming days."

He hesitated before adding, his voice lowering further as if sharing a divine secret, "They found hidden chambers beneath the temple of Seth. Sealed with mortar and concealed behind false walls. Treasures looted from Thebes decades ago—golden statuary of the old kings, ritual vessels encrusted with lapis lazuli and carnelian, even funerary goods plundered from royal tombs. The High Priest wept when they broke through the wall, my prince. They say he fell to his knees and kissed a statuette of Osiris that had belonged to your grandfather's tomb. All will be catalogued for return to their rightful places."

The prince's eyes gleamed with fierce satisfaction. Not just military victory but cultural restoration—the gods themselves would be pleased. He felt a shiver pass through him, as if the very spirit of Egypt had acknowledged this moment. His ancestors would rest easier in their disturbed tombs knowing their grave goods would be returned, the cosmic balance restored.

He gestured to the waiting scribe, who immediately straightened, eyes alert, hands reaching for his implements with practiced precision.

"It is time to inform Thebes that Egypt is whole again."

The scribe dipped his slender reed pen into freshly mixed ink, its rich black gleam promising permanence. His hand poised above the pristine papyrus with the steady confidence of decades of training. This document would become part of Egypt's historical record—preserved, copied, remembered for generations to come. The pressure of history's gaze weighed on every word, every careful stroke of the pen.

"To my mother, Queen Ahhotep, Regent of Upper Egypt, Light of the Two Lands," Ahmose began, his voice taking on the formal cadence of royal proclamation, resonant with authority that seemed to fill the chamber like invisible incense. "And to my grandmother, Royal Mother Tetisheri, Matriarch of our dynasty, whose wisdom has guided us through the darkest nights of our struggle."

The scribe's pen moved swiftly across the papyrus with a soft scratching sound, transforming spoken words into sacred hieroglyphs, each character precise and beautiful, worthy of the gods' eyes.

"Let it be known throughout the Black Land that on this day, by the will of Amun-Ra and through the strength of Egyptian arms, the Two Lands are united once more under rightful rule. The red crown and the white crown are joined again upon a true Egyptian brow."

Ahmose rose from the desk, his tall frame casting a long shadow across the floor as he began pacing the chamber. The golden beads in his ceremonial beard clicked softly with each deliberate step. Through the open doorway, servants and soldiers glimpsed their prince in this historic moment, some falling to their knees in spontaneous homage.

"The foreign king Khamudi is dead, his blood soaked into Egyptian soil as offering for his sacrilege." Ahmose's voice hardened, remembering the moment his own sword had ended the Hyksos king's life—not in honorable combat but in ignominious capture as the foreign ruler attempted to flee disguised as a common merchant. "The scales of Ma'at are balanced. Justice has been served. The gods smile once more upon the land of the Great River."

As the scribe carefully rolled the completed papyrus and sealed it with dark amber resin, the precious substance hardened against the desert heat to protect the sacred writings within. Ahmose moved to a balcony overlooking the city. The morning breeze carried the scents of the river—fertile mud, fishing boats, water flowers—mingled with the smoke of cooking fires and the distant tang of incense from the temples.

Son of Ebana watched his prince with undisguised admiration, his scarred hand resting on the pommel of his sword. This was a moment he would recount to his children and grandchildren in years to come— the day Egypt was made whole again, the day the natural order was restored. He made a silent vow to have the scene painted in his tomb when his time came to journey to the western lands.

Ahmose turned towards Ebana, the morning light catching the gold and lapis of his royal circlet. For a moment, the commander saw not just his childhood friend and battle companion, but the living embodiment of Egypt's restoration—Horus incarnate, rightful king of the Two Lands.

"I will remain in the Delta for forty days, establishing governance and ensuring no pocket of resistance remains," Ahmose continued, his voice carrying the weight of divine authority. "Every family that collaborated with the Hyksos must be identified, every official who served them must account for his loyalty. The land must be cleansed thoroughly before we can truly begin anew." His eyes narrowed, scanning the horizon as if he could see across all of Egypt by will alone. "Then I shall journey southward to Thebes, stopping at each nome to receive the homage of the governors and confirm their loyalty to the unified crown. Those who stood with us will be rewarded; those who bent too easily to foreign will must be replaced."

Outside, the sun climbed higher in a sky of perfect Egyptian blue, bathing the palace in golden light that seemed to affirm the rightness of this moment, this restoration of proper order. Birds circled the temple complexes, their cries carrying across the morning air like divine messengers.

The circle of vengeance was complete. His father, murdered by Hyksos assassins while attempting to negotiate peace, was avenged. His brother, fallen in an early battle before his prime, was avenged. The usurpers expelled, their gods humiliated, their monuments already being dismantled stone by stone. But the greater work—the restoration of Egypt's glory after a century of foreign domination—was just beginning.

"Egypt is one again," he whispered to the brightening sky, words meant for the ears of gods rather than men. "As it was in the beginning, as it shall be for all eternity. So I swear by the breath in my body and the souls of my ancestors."

A flock of ibis passed overhead, their distinctive silhouettes stark against the blue sky—birds sacred to Thoth, god of wisdom and writing. A good omen for the message about to begin its journey south.

The messengers departed within the hour, racing south along the Nile, their boats powered by rowers who worked in shifts to maintain maximum speed. They carried the joyous proclamation to a nation hungry for the news of final victory. As they passed through villages and towns, they called out the essence of their message, voices carrying across fields and marketplaces—"Egypt is united! The Hyksos are defeated! Long live Ahmose, Lord of the Two Lands!"

And everywhere they went, people emerged from mud-brick homes and verdant fields, falling to their knees in gratitude, raising arms to heavens that had finally answered generations of prayers. Women ululated in piercing tones of joy that carried across the valley. Men wept openly, unashamed of tears that honored ancestors who had not lived to see this day. Prayers of thanksgiving rose from every shrine and temple, from the grandest stone sanctuary to the humblest household altar. Impromptu celebrations erupted in market squares, with dancing and offerings of food and beer to the gods. Mothers held children aloft, telling them to remember this day—the day Egypt became whole again—to tell their own children in decades to come.

After a hundred years of foreign domination, the Two Lands had returned to their rightful place in the cosmic order. Ma'at—the fundamental balance of all things—had been restored. The world itself seemed to breathe easier.

And in the royal palace at Thebes, when the messenger finally arrived fifteen days later, dust-covered and exhausted from his journey, Queen Ahhotep received the papyrus scroll with hands that trembled not with age but with powerful emotion. Though past fifty summers, she stood straight as a spear, her face lined with the worries of decades of resistance and struggle. Her eyes, still sharp as falcon's, scanned the hieroglyphs written by her son's scribe.

As she read the words aloud to the assembled court, her voice—trained through years of command—carried to every corner of the vast audience chamber. Tears flowed freely down her face—not tears of sorrow but of completion, of a mother's fierce pride, of a queen's ultimate triumph. Behind her stood her own mother, Royal Mother Tetisheri, nearly seventy years of age yet still regal in her bearing, a living link to Egypt's past glory now restored.

The circle was complete. The wheel of fate had turned. Egypt endured, as it always had, as it always would, until the very stars fell from the heavens and the great river ran dry.

Fate of the charioteers

The morning the sun beat down mercilessly upon the mud-brick walls of Pi-Ramses, casting long shadows across the courtyard where Pharaoh Ahmose I stood contemplating the vastness of his problem. Sweat trickled down his back beneath the royal linen, leaving dark trails against his copper skin, but he remained motionless, his hawkish gaze sweeping over the encampment that sprawled before him like an unwelcome guest at a royal feast.

The heat shimmered above the distant horizon, distorting the view of hundreds of men—Egyptian charioteers who had served in the Hyksos army—now standing in uncertain allegiance, their families huddled behind them like frightened gazelles. The defeat of their Hyksos masters had left them in a precarious position: neither fully trusted by their Egyptian kin nor welcomed among the fleeing invaders. The wind carried the scent of their fear mingled with dust and the ever-present aroma of the muddy Nile.

"How many?" Ahmose asked, his voice low and measured. His fingers absently traced the golden cobra emblem that adorned his ceremonial belt, the symbol of his divine authority—authority that now faced its first true test in peacetime.

Commander Ahmose, son of Ebana, stepped forward, his battle-scarred face grim. Sunlight gleamed off the bronze pectoral that covered his broad chest, marking him as a man of high rank. The scar that bisected his left cheek had faded to a thin white line, a permanent reminder of the first battle they had fought together against the foreign oppressors.

"Nearly six hundred men of fighting age, my Pharaoh. All trained in chariot warfare. With their families, perhaps two thousand souls." The commander's eyes, dark and shrewd like a desert falcon's, held a wariness that spoke of sleepless nights spent contemplating this very dilemma.

The Pharaoh's fingers tightened around the ceremonial flail he carried, the polished wood smooth beneath his callused grip—hands that had known both the delicacy of temple offerings and the brutal reality of close combat. "And the people that stayed behind?"

"They call themselves Israelites, clustered in the western and southern quarters of Avaris. We estimate twenty thousand, perhaps more." The commander shifted his weight, the leather of his battle kilt creaking softly.(See notes on Israel migration)

Ahmose I turned to face his most trusted commander, the man who had fought beside him through the long years of bitter warfare against the Hyksos oppressors. The soft court living of recent months had not yet erased the hardness from either man's face or the deadly grace with which they moved.

"I have won Egypt only to find myself with two groups of people, families of charioteers and a group of Israelites, neither fully mine, while my own soldiers march the Hyksos to Sharuhen." His voice carried a bitterness that he allowed few to hear, revealing the burden that weighed upon him like the massive stones of the temples he planned to build.

"It is... problematic," admitted the commander, his under-statement hanging in the air between them like an unsheathed blade.

Ahmose I laughed without humor, the sound harsh in the still morning air. Nearby, a pair of ibises took startled flight, their white wings flashing against the cloudless blue sky. "Problematic? It is a viper coiled at my feet. These charioteers know our tactics now. They have learned our ways of war. And the Israelites—they build, they multiply. Neither group has reason to love an Egyptian king."

The commander's hand instinctively moved to his sword hilt, fingers wrapping around the familiar grip worn smooth from years of use. His eyes hardened with the cold pragmatism of a lifetime soldier. "We could—"

"No," Ahmose cut him off sharply, raising a hand adorned with the royal signet of Upper and Lower Egypt united once more. "I will not begin my reign over a united Egypt with a slaughter. There has been enough blood spilled to turn the Nile red twice over." He paused, remembering fields littered with the bodies of the fallen, the screams of the dying, the smell of blood and fear that had accompanied their long march to victory. "My name will be remembered for restoration, not massacre."

He paced the length of the balcony, his sandaled feet silent on the polished limestone, his shadow stretching before him like a dark harbinger. His mind worked furiously, weighing possibilities against dangers, immediate solutions against future consequences. The charioteers presented both opportunity and threat—men trained in the newest warfare techniques of the age, men whose very presence had transformed the nature of battle in the known world, yet men whose loyalty was questionable as a desert mirage. The Israelites were skilled builders, craftsmen whose labor had already transformed parts of the Delta into prosperous settlements under Hyksos rule, their hands capable of creating wonders or wielding weapons should they choose.

Both could strengthen Egypt—or tear it apart from within.

A high-pitched cry drew his attention skyward, where a falcon circled lazily on thermal currents, its keen eyes no doubt fixed on some unfortunate prey below. Ahmose watched the bird with sudden interest, seeing in its patient circling a reflection of his own position. Like the falcon, he must wait for the perfect moment to strike—not in violence, but in cunning.

As the sun climbed higher, bathing the landscape in harsh golden light that bounced off the distant waters of the Delta marshes, Ahmose I felt the weight of the double crown that awaited him in Thebes. Its physical burden was nothing compared to the responsibility it represented. He had won the war through blood and sacrifice. Now he must secure the peace through wisdom and calculation.

That evening, as torches flickered against the approaching darkness, casting dancing shadows across walls adorned with paintings of gods and ancestors, Ahmose I summoned his war council. The commanders of his army sat in a semi-circle before him, their expressions grave, their bodies still bearing the marks of recent battles—a missing finger here, a fresh scar there, eyes that had seen too much death to ever be truly at peace again.

"I have decided the fate of the charioteers," Ahmose announced without preamble, his voice filling the chamber with the authority that had driven men to follow him into the jaws of death itself. "They will not be slaughtered, nor will they be driven out."

A murmur ran through the assembly; the sound of surprise mingled with curiosity. The Pharaoh raised a hand for silence, and the room immediately stilled, the only sound the soft hissing of oil lamps and the distant call of night birds from the gardens beyond.

"Instead, they will work for us. The Hyksos dwellings stand empty, monuments to our victory. Let the charioteers and their families occupy them." His voice hardened, his eyes glinting in the torchlight like obsidian blades. "They will be taskmasters over the Israelites."

"Taskmaster," murmured his war council as they shifted uncomfortably on their cushioned seats. The word hung in the air like the scent of incense, strange and potent. It sounded to them like an unconventional solution, one that neither tradition nor precedent had prepared them for.

Pharaoh's expression darkened, shadows playing across his features, accentuating the hawkish nose and strong jaw that marked him as a descendant of the ancient line of kings. "The Israelite men are skilled builders. We need cities—strong cities—to guard our borders. Pi-Ramses must become a fortress that no army can penetrate. Pithom must be expanded to store grain against famine."

He rose to his feet in one fluid motion, towering over the seated council. The gold and lapis lazuli of his pectoral caught the firelight, sending shards of colored light dancing across the painted walls where the gods of Egypt watched in silent judgment. "The Israelites will build them. They will have these taskmasters over them. Let the two peoples watch each other while we watch them both."

The oldest of his advisors, a grizzled veteran of many campaigns whose face was a road map of wrinkles and battle scars, spoke up. His voice quavered slightly with age but still carried the authority of one who had survived when younger, stronger men had fallen. "My king, is it wise to place one conquered people over another? What if they should unite against us?"

Ahmose I smiled, a cold expression that did not reach his eyes, which remained calculating and distant. "The charioteers will seek to prove their loyalty by driving the Israelites hard. The Israelites will resent them for it. Between hatred and ambition, they will keep each other in check." He paused, letting his gaze sweep over each man present, meeting their eyes one by one, challenging any to question his wisdom further. "When a cobra and a mongoose share a pit, neither has time to trouble the master of the house."

The metaphor hung in the air, as vivid as if the deadly creatures themselves had been cast into their midst. None dared speak against the royal will now, seeing in their king's eyes the same implacable determination that had carried him through years of bitter warfare.

As the council concluded, Ahmose gazed out across the darkened landscape of the Delta, toward the distant sea that had brought so many invaders to Egypt's shores. The night air carried the scents of river water, blooming lotus, and the ever-present dust of the desert beyond—the eternal tension between life and death that defined Egypt itself. His eyes narrowed as he envisioned the future—a Egypt strengthened by the labor of its conquered peoples, its borders secured by mighty fortresses, its armies equipped with swift chariots that could strike like lightning against any foe, its temples rising to heights never before imagined, all proclaiming the glory of his reign.

"Let it be done," he commanded, his voice soft yet carrying the weight of divine authority. "Tomorrow, I ride for Thebes."

Chapter 15 - Triumphant Return

September 1526 - Thebes

The journey south along the Nile was a triumphant procession, the royal barges gliding over the sacred waters like massive water birds, their gilded prows gleaming in the sunlight, colored pennants fluttering in the gentle breeze. At every settlement, crowds gathered to honor the king who had freed Egypt from foreign domination. Children threw lotus blossoms before his chariot when he rode ashore; priests offered blessings, wafting incense toward him in great clouds of fragrant smoke; old men wept openly at the sight of a true Egyptian pharaoh passing by, their withered hands reaching out as if to touch divinity itself.

Ahmose I accepted their homage with the stern dignity expected of a warrior-king, his face impassive beneath the royal headdress despite the fierce pride that burned within his breast. The cheers of his people washed over him like a healing balm, easing the memories of friends lost in battle, of desperate moments when victory had seemed impossible. Yet even as he acknowledged the adulation of the crowds, his mind was already racing ahead to the challenges that awaited him in the ancient capital of his ancestors—the priests whose power had grown unchecked during the years of division, the noble families whose loyalty must be secured, the treasury that had been depleted by generations of war.

After twenty-two days of travel, the royal fleet rounded the final bend in the river, and the great temples of Thebes came into view, their massive pylons thrusting skyward like the fingers of gods reaching for the heavens. The limestone and sandstone structures gleamed gold in the afternoon sun, and atop the highest terrace of Deir el-Bahri, he could see two figures waiting—his grandmother Tetisheri and his mother Ahhotep, the women whose indomitable will had sustained the royal line through its darkest hours when all had seemed lost.

The sight of them—one bent with age but unbowed in spirit, the other still regal and commanding despite the silver threads now prominent in her dark hair—filled Ahmose with a sudden rush of emotion that he quickly mastered, schooling his features to reveal nothing of the almost childlike need to run to them, to be simply a grandson and son rather than Pharaoh of the Two Lands.

As he disembarked, walking with measured steps down the gangplank while nobles and officials prostrated themselves on either side, Ahmose I approached the two royal women. With a grace that belied his warrior's frame, he knelt before the elderly Tetisheri, whose dream of a united Egypt had finally been realized through his blood and sweat and tears.

"Rise, my grandson," she said, her voice trembling with emotion yet still carrying the authority that had once commanded armies when men had faltered. The elaborate wig she wore framed a face time had mapped with wrinkles but failed to diminish, her eyes still sharp as flint knives. "Rise, Pharaoh of Upper and Lower Egypt."

He stood and embraced her, feeling the fragility of her bones beneath his arms, like a bird's hollow skeleton encased in papery skin. She smelled of myrrh and age and the peculiar sharp scent of the herbal concoctions the physicians prepared to ease her joint pain. Then he turned to his mother, the woman who had commanded armies and held a fractured kingdom together while her sons fought to reclaim their birthright.

"Mother," he said simply, taking her hands in his. The calluses on her palms matched his own—she was no pampered royal who had spent the war years sheltered behind palace walls.

Ahhotep's eyes shone with unshed tears, the kohl around them making the emotion all the more striking against her still-beautiful face. "My son. My king." Her voice nearly broke on the words, the only hint of weakness she would ever allow herself to show in public.

Later, in the royal chambers where incense sweetened the air and fine linen curtains billowed in the evening breeze, surrounded by his family, Ahmose I felt the tension of the past years begin to ease from his shoulders like a heavy cloak removed after a long journey. His three children swarmed around him—Mutnofret, a serious seven-year-old girl with her grandmother's regal bearing, already conscious of her position as royal daughter; Ahmose Ankh, his six-year-old son and heir, already showing a warrior's temperament in the way he brandished a wooden toy sword; and little Princess Ahmose, barely four, who climbed fearlessly onto her father's lap, her tiny hands exploring the unfamiliar ceremonial beard he now wore.

For a few precious hours, he was not Pharaoh but simply a father returned from war. He listened to his children's chatter, marveling at how much they had grown during his long absences, noting with pride how Ankh already mimicked his stance and command presence, how Mutnofret watched everything with the calculating eyes of a future queen, how little Ahmose's laughter could dispel the clouds of worry from her mother's brow.

As the sun began its descent toward the western horizon, the palace servants moved with practiced efficiency, preparing for the grand feast that would officially celebrate Ahmose I's triumphant return. The Pharaoh retired briefly to his chambers where attendants bathed him in water perfumed with lotus and myrrh, scraping away the dust of travel from his bronze skin. They dressed him in the finest linen, so sheer it seemed to capture light itself, draping his powerful shoulders with a broad collar of gold and lapis lazuli, each bead intricately worked by master craftsmen. Around his muscular forearms, they placed bands of hammered gold inlaid with carnelian and turquoise, symbols of his divine authority.

When he emerged into the vast columned hall, a hush fell over the assembled nobility. The double crown of Upper and Lower Egypt— the red and white Pschent—sat majestically upon his head, its weight familiar yet never insignificant. In his right hand, he gripped the crook and flail, ancient symbols of the shepherd who protects his flock and the disciplinarian who punishes wrongdoers. The golden staff in his left hand caught the light from a thousand oil lamps, sending shards of brilliance dancing across the painted ceiling where Nut, goddess of the sky, stretched her star-spangled body across the heavens.

"Behold the Living Horus!" announced the High Priest of Amun, his shaven head gleaming with sacred oils. "Ahmose, Strong Bull, Beloved of Ma'at, King of Upper and Lower Egypt, Son of Ra, who has driven the vile Asiatics from our sacred soil!"

The gathered courtiers fell to their knees, foreheads touching the polished stone floor. Only the royal women remained standing—Tetisheri, her ancient eyes gleaming with satisfaction; Ahhotep, regal in her royal regalia; and Ahmose-Nefertari, the king's principal wife, adorned with the vulture headdress that marked her as queen, her slender body sheathed in pleated linen so fine it seemed to flow like water around her limbs.

At a gesture from the Pharaoh, the feast began. Servants streamed into the hall bearing platters of roasted waterfowl stuffed with herbs and spices, haunches of gazelle and oryx dripping with rich juices, fresh fish from the Nile prepared in a dozen different ways. Loaves of bread shaped like animals and humans were piled high on golden trays, while bowls of fruits—dates, figs, pomegranates—provided sweet counterpoints to the savory dishes. Wine flowed from alabaster jars into golden cups, its ruby depths holding the concentrated essence of vineyards tended by generations of careful hands.

Musicians played on harps, flutes, and sistrum, their melodies weaving through the hall like invisible threads binding the company together. Dancers moved with sinuous grace, their oiled bodies glistening in the lamplight, telling stories of battles won and enemies vanquished through the ancient language of movement that needed no words.

Ahmose watched it all from his elevated throne, his face an inscrutable mask that revealed nothing of his thoughts to the ambitious nobles who studied him with calculating eyes. These were men who had bent the knee to foreign kings when it suited them, who had collaborated with the Hyksos when resistance seemed futile. Now they competed for his favor, offering lavish gifts and honeyed words, their daughters and sisters displayed like prized cattle in hopes of securing royal marriages.

The Pharaoh accepted their homage with the cool detachment of a crocodile watching fish swim past its snout, knowing that true loyalty would be proven not by feast-day declarations but by blood and sacrifice in the campaigns to come. He nodded graciously at each tribute, his eyes missing nothing—the sweat that beaded on one nobleman's brow as he presented his gift, the slight tremor in another's hand as he raised his cup in toast, the sidelong glances exchanged between two officials who had grown fat on corruption during the chaotic years.

"You take their measure well, my son," murmured Ahhotep, who had approached the throne with the silent grace of a hunting cat. Though she had surrendered the reins of power to her son, none doubted that her influence remained profound. "The jackals fawn and bow, but their teeth are still sharp."

"As are mine, Mother," replied Ahmose, his voice pitched low for her ears alone. "And unlike them, I strike from the front, not the back."

A burst of laughter rose from a nearby table where the royal children had been permitted to join the celebration for a time. Young Ahmose Ankh was mimicking a Hyksos prisoner begging for mercy, his childish voice capturing the strange accent with uncanny precision while his sisters giggled behind their hands. The boy had never seen a Hyksos warrior, being too young to have witnessed the brutal fighting, yet he had absorbed the stories told by veterans with a warrior's instinct that made Ahmose's chest swell with pride.

As the evening progressed, the High Priest of Amun rose to perform the ritual offering to the gods. Silence fell as he approached the small altar where a statue of Amun-Ra stood, its gold and ivory features catching the lamplight like a living being. The priest's voice rose in the ancient chants, words that had been spoken since time immemorial, binding the present king to his divine ancestors.

"Great Amun, hidden one, creator of all things, look with favor upon your son Ahmose, who has restored the proper order to the Two Lands! Accept our offerings and continue to strengthen his arm against all enemies of Egypt!"

The scent of burning incense filled the hall, sweet and heavy, carrying the prayers of the assembled company upward to the painted stars. The priest approached the throne, bearing a small golden statuette of the goddess Ma'at, her feather of truth held high.

"Divine one," he intoned, presenting the statuette to Ahmose, "may Truth be your companion and Justice your guide, as it was for your forefathers. May the scales of your judgment always balance perfectly."

Ahmose accepted the sacred image, feeling its weight—physical and symbolic—in his palm. "Truth before all things," he responded, the ritual words falling from his lips with practiced ease. "Justice for all who dwell beneath Horus's wings."

Later, when the dancers had retired and the musicians played softer melodies, when many of the courtiers had succumbed to wine and rich food, Ahmose found himself standing on a balcony overlooking the Nile. The river gleamed like a ribbon of silver in the moonlight, its eternal waters flowing northward just as they had since the first morning of creation.

Ahmose-Nefertari joined him, her perfume of lotus and myrrh preceding her. She placed a cool hand on his forearm, her eyes searching his face in the moonlight.

"You are troubled, my husband," she said, not a question but a statement of fact. She knew the rhythms of his moods as well as she knew the rising and setting of the sun.

"The feast was necessary," he replied, gazing out at the dark waters. "The nobility must see strength and certainty. They must believe that Egypt stands whole and invincible once more."

"But you do not believe it," she observed.

He turned to her, his eyes softening as they always did when they rested on her face. "Not yet. The body of Egypt has been stitched together, but the wounds are still fresh. The Hyksos poison still flows in some veins. And beyond our borders, vultures circle, watching for any sign of weakness."

She nodded, understanding without need for further explanation. This was the burden of kingship—to show confidence when doubt gnawed at the heart, to project strength when weariness threatened to overwhelm, to think always three steps ahead while appearing to dance effortlessly through the present moment.

"Come," she said at last, taking his hand. "Even Pharaoh must rest before tomorrow's councils. The gods themselves sleep when Nut swallows the sun."

He allowed her to lead him back toward their chambers, passing through corridors where servants bowed low, their eyes averted from the divine couple. In their private quarters, the lamps burned low, casting warm pools of light across the painted floors where hunting scenes and battles played out in timeless tableaux.

But as night fell, casting the room into shadow relieved only by the soft glow of oil lamps, a messenger arrived, dusty from hard riding. The man's face was drawn with exhaustion, his eyes wide with the urgency of his news.

"My king," the man gasped, prostrating himself on the floor, his forehead touching the cool tiles. "Word from our spies in Canaan. The Hyksos who fled to Sharuhen are rearming. They gather chariots and weapons. They speak openly of returning to reclaim the Delta."

The brief peace shattered like a clay vessel dropped on stone. Ahmose I set his daughter gently aside and rose to his full height, once again the implacable warrior who had driven the invaders from Egyptian soil. The transformation was immediate and complete—the softness fled from his eyes, replaced by the cold calculation of a predator; his shoulders squared; his jaw set in a hard line beneath the ceremonial beard.

"Then we shall give them no chance to grow strong again," he declared, his voice resonating with the same authority that had commanded men to march into the teeth of enemy arrows. "Send word to Commander Ahmose, son of Ebana. We march onto Sharuhen in three days."

He turned to gaze out at the starlit Nile, the sacred river that had witnessed the rise and fall of dynasties, the eternal pulse of Egypt's heart. Its dark waters reflected the myriad stars overhead, a mirror of the celestial realm where the gods watched and judged the actions of men and kings alike. His jaw set in grim determination, eyes narrowed as he contemplated the final extermination of the threat that had plagued Egypt for generations. "This time, we will end the Hyksos threat forever."

The children watched wide-eyed as their father transformed before them from gentle parent to avenging pharaoh, the change as complete as if Horus himself had descended to inhabit mortal flesh. In the shadows, old Tetisheri nodded in approval, her withered hands gripping her ebony walking staff, her eyes gleaming with fierce satisfaction. The blood of conquerors ran true in her grandson, just as she had always known it would.

Egypt would be secure at last. The dynasty she had fought so hard to preserve would rise again to its former glory, perhaps surpassing it. And these children—these royal offspring with the blood of warriors and kings in their veins—would ensure that the line continued unbroken into a future bright with promise and power.

As Ahmose strode from the chamber, already calling for his armor and weapons, servants scurrying to do his bidding, the old woman permitted herself a rare smile. The future was secure. Egypt would rise again, greater than before.

Or so she believed, not knowing that within years, the seeds of future conflict were already being sown in the bitter soil of conquest and subjugation—a conflict that would eventually challenge the very foundations of Egyptian power in ways that not even the wisest seers could predict.

Chapter 16 - Suppressing the Israelites

1524 BC - Renewed Pi-Ramesses

The golden disc of Ra climbed higher into the cloudless Egyptian sky, casting rippling reflections across the waters of the eastern Delta like scattered coins of the gods themselves. Ahmose I stood at the prow of his gilded barge, the warm breeze caressing his face as they approached what had once been the festering wound of Hyksos occupation. His body had changed since the days when he led armies across the burning sands to reclaim Egypt's glory—a slight paunch now betrayed his increasing fondness for the finest beer and the rich foods that graced his table, his once-lean warrior's frame grown heavier with the golden trappings of absolute power.

Two years had passed since the last Hyksos dogs had fled Avaris like whipped curs, and where Egypt's righteous armies had pursued the hated invaders beyond the sacred borders of the Black Land to distant Sharuhen, crushing their remaining forces like grain beneath the winnowing stone. He had fulfilled the dream that had consumed three generations of his bloodline—to drive every last foreign jackal from the sacred soil of his ancestors.

Beside him stood Nakht, his chief architect, a thin man with ink-stained fingers and eyes that perpetually squinted from years of studying fine drawings under flickering lamplight. The man's hands trembled slightly—not from fear, but from the barely contained excitement of an artist about to unveil his masterpiece.

"Divine One," Nakht said, his voice quivering with the pride of a craftsman who has exceeded even his own ambitions, "you will hardly recognize what we have wrought. The foreign taint has been burned away like dross from pure gold."

"Show me," Ahmose commanded, his knuckles whitening as he gripped the polished cedar rail. "Show me how Egyptian hands have cleansed what Asiatic dogs defiled."

As they drew closer, the scent of the Delta filled his nostrils—that intoxicating blend of rich black mud, blooming lotus, and the eternal life-giving waters of blessed Horus's river. But beneath these familiar perfumes lingered another odor that made his jaw tighten: the acrid smell of sweat from thousands of laborers toiling under Ra's merciless eye, the distinctive musk of a people working beyond the limits of ordinary endurance.

The barge docked at a newly constructed quay of dressed stone so perfectly fitted that even a papyrus leaf could find no purchase between the joints. A contingent of officials awaited their living god, their bodies prostrating themselves as he disembarked, foreheads pressed to the warm stone in the ancient gesture of submission to divine authority.

"Rise, my servants," Ahmose commanded, his deep voice carrying the weight of the gods themselves. His kohl-rimmed eyes swept the transformed cityscape like a falcon surveying its domain. "Now show me what Egyptian genius has accomplished."

The procession wound through broad avenues lined with sphinx guardians whose enigmatic smiles had been carved from granite torn from the very heart of the southern quarries. They passed temples whose construction continued like some vast, eternal prayer made manifest in stone—the rhythmic song of copper chisels on limestone creating a percussion that echoed from the towering walls like the heartbeat of the gods themselves.

"Magnificent," Ahmose murmured, watching thousands of workers swarm over the rising structures like purposeful ants. "But tell me, Pashedu—" He turned to his overseer of works, a man whose broad shoulders spoke of years wielding tools before his elevation to command. "How do our... guests... fare under Egyptian discipline?"

Pashedu's weathered face creased into something that might have been a smile if it had contained any warmth. "They multiply like rabbits in the season of flood, Divine One. It is... troubling."

"Troubling?" Ahmose's voice dropped to that silky tone his enemies had learned to fear. "Explain this to your Pharaoh."

"Their numbers have nearly doubled since you commanded them put to the work gangs, Divine One." Pashedu gestured toward the Hebrew quarter with a hand adorned by a single copper ring—the mark of his office. "The more burdens we heap upon their backs, the more their women's bellies swell with new life. Their children thrive where Egyptian infants might perish."

Ahmose followed his overseer's gaze to where Israelite children played in narrow streets despite their circumstances, their laughter carrying on the evening breeze like some cruel mockery of their parents' bondage. Women heavy with child moved between communal wells, and men, though bent by the day's labor, still possessed eyes that burned with an inner fire when they thought no Egyptian was watching.

"And our overseers? The Egyptians who... collaborated... during the occupation?"

Pashedu's expression grew calculating. "They serve with the fervor of the converted, Divine One. Perhaps too much fervor. They compete to prove their loyalty through harshness, each trying to outdo his fellows in breaking Hebrew backs."

The Pharaoh nodded slowly, understanding the delicate game he had set in motion. By placing former Hyksos sympathizers as taskmasters over the Israelites, he had created a perfect test of loyalty—and they had passed it by becoming the cruelest masters imaginable. Yet still the Hebrew stock multiplied and flourished.

At the eastern edge of the city, where the storage complex rose like a small mountain, hundreds of Israelite workers toiled under the brass hammer of Ra's fury. Their bronze bodies gleamed with sweat as they mixed mud and straw for bricks, hauled massive stones with ropes and wooden rollers, the veins standing out like rivers on their straining necks and forearms.

"Move, you Hebrew dogs!" bellowed a taskmaster mounted on a prancing stallion, his whip uncoiling like a striking cobra. The leather sang through the air before biting deep into the shoulders of an old man who had paused to wipe sweat from his eyes. Blood welled like a crimson flower against sun-darkened skin, but the worker made no sound—only that flash of hatred burning in his deep-set eyes before he bent his neck in submission.

From his shaded pavilion, Ahmose watched with the detachment of a god observing the struggles of mortals. This was the natural order—the strong commanded, the weak obeyed. Had not his own divine ancestors used Nubian captives to raise their eternal monuments? Yet something in that old Hebrew's eyes unsettled him more than he cared to admit.

1522 BC - The Royal Family's Inspection

The royal barge cut through the sacred waters like a golden blade through the finest linen, its prow catching Ra's morning glory as Ahmose returned to Pi-Ramses with his family in tow. He was determined that his heirs should witness the transformation of Egypt's northeastern fortress, should understand the price of security and the cost of mercy.

Prince Ankh, nine summers old but already carrying himself with the unconscious arrogance of royal blood, strutted beside his father with a ceremonial dagger at his hip—its hilt inlaid with lapis lazuli blue as the sacred Nile and ivory white as the desert bones. His dark eyes missed nothing, cataloguing details with the intensity of a born hunter.

"Father," the boy said, his voice carrying the confidence of one who had never known want or fear, "the workers look different from when we came before."

"How so, my son?" Ahmose asked, studying his heir with the attention a master craftsman might give to his finest work.

"Harder. Angrier. Like caged lions I've seen in the royal menagerie." Ankh's observation was delivered with the casual cruelty of childhood. "Their eyes burn even when they prostrate themselves."

"And what lesson does this teach you about the art of kingship?"

The boy considered this with the gravity of a miniature pharaoh. "That submission of the body does not always mean submission of the spirit?"

"Excellent. And such spirits are...?"

"Dangerous, Divine Father. They must be broken completely or..." Young Ankh's voice trailed off as he glimpsed the implications.

Seven-year-old Amenhotep, gentler by nature and bearing a scroll case instead of a weapon, walked more hesitantly behind his brother. His thoughtful eyes took in every detail of the transformed city, but his questions came from a different place entirely.

"Must they suffer so greatly, Father?" he asked quietly, watching an Israelite woman cross the street with a young child balanced on her hip and another growing visibly beneath her simple dress. "Could they not serve Egypt without such... harshness?"

Ahmose's expression softened slightly as he looked upon his younger son. "Suffering builds character, my gentle boy. It separates the wheat from the chaff, the gold from the dross. These people must learn their place in the great design of Ma'at."

"But if they grow stronger under hardship rather than weaker...?"

The Pharaoh's eyes sharpened with approval. Even at seven, Amenhotep possessed the kind of strategic mind that would serve Egypt well. "Then we must find other methods to achieve our ends."

Princess Mutnofret, twelve summers old and already showing the budding grace that would make her a jewel of the royal court, observed the scene with the calculating eyes of royal womanhood. "The Hebrew women birth many children, Divine Father. More than Egyptian wives of similar station."

Queen Ahmose Nefertari, walking with the serene dignity of one who had shared a god's bed and borne his heirs, nodded thoughtfully. "It troubles your father, daughter. Numbers can become power, and power in the wrong hands..."

"Becomes rebellion," Mutnofret finished with understanding beyond her years.

That evening, as they dined in the new palace's central hall—where columns painted in royal blues and sacred reds rose to support a ceiling adorned with golden stars against the deep blue of night—troubling reports reached the Pharaoh's ears. The hall itself was a masterpiece worthy of the gods, its walls depicting Ahmose in glorious battle against cowering Asiatic enemies, his figure rendered larger than life while his foes groveled like insects beneath his sandaled feet.

"Divine One," reported Harnakhte, the chief administrator whose nervous temperament seemed at odds with his exalted position, "the Hebrew women continue to multiply at an alarming rate. Our attempts to control their breeding through increased labor have... failed."

Ahmose set down his golden wine cup with enough force to splash the precious vintage across the polished table like spilled blood. "Failed? Explain this failure to your Pharaoh."

"They are unnaturally resilient, Great Horus," the administrator continued, sweat beading on his upper lip despite the pleasant temperature maintained by servants wielding ostrich-feather fans. "Disease that would decimate other populations barely touches them. Hardships that should reduce their fertility instead seem to... encourage it."

"And their midwives?" the Pharaoh demanded, his voice dropping to that dangerous purr his courtiers had learned to fear.

"Skilled beyond any rational measure, Divine One. They attend births with knowledge that our own physicians' envy. Hebrew women rarely die in childbirth, and their infants thrive where others might perish."

The weight of the problem settled on Ahmose's shoulders like a stone mantle. He glanced at his children—Ankh demonstrating some military technique with a piece of bread while Amenhotep watched with reluctant admiration, young Ahmose sitting with the perfect poise already expected of royal daughters. These were his legacy, his gift to eternity. He would not see them threatened by a subject people who bred like animals and grew strong under oppression.

"Summon the chief midwives of the Hebrews to my presence tomorrow," he commanded, his decision crystallizing like salt from evaporated seawater. "The senior women who oversee their birthing chambers."

"It shall be done immediately, Divine One," Harnakhte replied, bowing until his forehead nearly kissed his knees.

The Command of Death

The following day found two Hebrew midwives standing before the living incarnation of Horus like lambs awaiting the sacrificial knife. The audience chamber's oppressive grandeur seemed designed to crush the spirits of petitioners—massive columns rising like the trunks of stone forests to support a ceiling painted with protective vultures, their wings spread in eternal guardianship over the golden throne where earthly divinity held court.

Shiphrah, her face mapped with the lines of seven decades spent bringing life into the world, kept her eyes fixed on the polished granite floor where flecks of gold caught the dancing light of smoking oil lamps. Her hands—hands that had guided countless souls from the dark warmth of the womb into the harsh light of existence—were gnarled like olive wood but still possessed of their ancient strength.

Beside her, Puah's olive skin had taken on the gray pallor of unbaked clay. Younger than her companion but equally skilled in the sacred mysteries of birth, she stood with shoulders slightly hunched as though attempting to make herself invisible before the terrible majesty of absolute power.

"You are the chief midwives of the Hebrew women?" Ahmose's voice sliced through the incense-heavy air like a blade through silk, each word carrying the weight of divine authority.

"Yes, Divine One," Shiphrah answered, her throat as dry as the desert beyond the Black Land's blessed borders. "We oversee all who serve our women in their time of greatest need."

The Pharaoh leaned forward on his golden throne, the sacred uraeus serpent upon his brow seeming to coil with malevolent life as lamplight played across its scales. Around the vast chamber, guards stood at attention like statues carved from flesh and bronze, their ceremonial spears gleaming with the promise of swift death for any who would dare raise hand or voice against their god-king.

"Listen well to the words of Pharaoh," he commanded, his voice dropping to that silky whisper that somehow carried more menace than any shout. "When you attend the Hebrew women in their birthing chambers, you will watch carefully for the moment when new life emerges from the sacred portal of the womb."

He paused, letting the weight of anticipation settle over them like a burial shroud.

"If the child that emerges is male—" His hand moved in a sharp, slashing gesture that needed no explanation. "—you will send his spirit to Osiris before he draws his first breath of earthly air. Female children may be permitted to live and serve Egypt as their mothers do."

The words hung in the perfumed air like invisible serpents, their poison seeping into every corner of the vast chamber. Puah's head snapped up before she could stop herself, horror flooding her features like water rushing through a broken dam. The full meaning of the command crashed over her like the flood waters of an angry Nile—infant boys, helpless and innocent, to be murdered by the very hands sworn to guide them safely into the world.

Shiphrah's elbow dug sharply into her younger companion's ribs—a warning that might mean the difference between life and death for both of them. The older woman's face remained as blank as uncarved stone, though a muscle twitched near her jaw like a caged bird beating against the bars of its prison.

"You find fault with the will of Pharaoh?" Ahmose asked, his voice carrying the deadly softness of a cobra's hiss. The guards flanking his throne shifted almost imperceptibly, bronze spear points catching the light like the fangs of waiting predators.

"Never, Divine One," Puah whispered, prostrating herself until her forehead pressed against the cool stone and the mingled scents of incense and human sweat filled her nostrils. "We are less than dust beneath the sandals of the living god. We hear your divine words and will obey."

"Excellent," Ahmose nodded, his ringed fingers drumming a slow rhythm against the gold-inlaid armrest of his throne—a sound like distant thunder promising a storm to come. "You will instruct every midwife under your authority in this sacred duty. Remember always that the eyes of Pharaoh see all things, in all places, at all times. Those who fail in this service will feed the sacred crocodiles of the Nile, and their families will join them in that honor."

The threat was delivered without heat or passion, a simple statement of natural law rather than an expression of anger. This very lack of emotion made it infinitely more terrifying than rage would have been. Pharaoh's word was the foundation upon which the world itself rested—absolute, eternal, unquestionable.

With a casual flick of his fingers, he dismissed them from his divine presence, turning his attention to a papyrus scroll held by a waiting scribe as though the fate of an entire generation had been no more significant than deciding the menu for his evening meal. Such was the terrible arithmetic of absolute power—lives weighed and measured in moments, destinies sealed with gestures, then filed away in the endless bureaucracy of empire.

The midwives backed away from the throne with bent bodies and lowered eyes until the massive cedar doors, bound with bronze and carved with protective hieroglyphs, closed behind them with the finality of a tomb being sealed. Only when they had passed beyond the towering pylon gates, beyond the reach of the painted ears that adorned every wall, did they dare exchange glances heavy with the weight of impossible choices.

"What will we do?" Puah whispered as they walked through streets lit by guttering torches, their shadows dancing like demons on the painted walls.

Shiphrah's weathered face was granite in the flickering light. "We will do what we must to preserve the sons of our people, and let Pharaoh believe what his divine wisdom tells him to believe."

"But if he discovers our deception—"

"Then we will die with honor rather than live as murderers of innocents," the old woman replied, her voice carrying the steel of tempered bronze beneath its whispered softness. "The God of our fathers sees all things, even the secret chambers where life begins. He will provide a way, as He has always provided."

The Pharaoh's Final Resolve

Later that night, alone on the broad balcony of his private chambers, Ahmose stood overlooking his transformed city like a god surveying his creation. The moon hung in the star-scattered sky like a silver coin thrown by the gods, casting its cold light over the sleeping metropolis and transforming familiar streets into a landscape of sharp shadows and luminous surfaces carved from solid silver.

Below him, beyond the gleaming government buildings and soaring temples that proclaimed Egypt's eternal glory, the mud-brick districts of the workers sprawled in darkness—a vast honeycomb of humanity teeming with lives not bound to his will by blood or birth. The night breeze from the sacred Nile carried its familiar perfume of water and night-blooming flowers, but underneath ran that ever-present current of humanity—cooking fires, human sweat, and the indefinable scent of thousands of souls breathing, dreaming, hoping in the darkness.

His dynasty's grip on the throne remained new enough to feel fragile in the dark hours when sleep eluded him. Barely thirty years had passed since his mother Ahhotep had rallied the scattered Theban forces after his father's death, keeping the flame of resistance burning through the darkest period of foreign domination until her son was old enough to lead armies and reclaim his birthright. The memories remained fresh as yesterday's wounds—Egyptian nobles forced to prostrate themselves before Hyksos kings, sacred temples defiled by foreign hands, the resources of the Black Land flowing like tribute to alien masters.

Never again. Not while breath remained in his body or divine blood flowed in his veins would he permit another non-Egyptian people to grow powerful within Egypt's borders. The Israelites had once been few, welcomed during the time of Hyksos rule because of their distant kinship with those foreign overlords. Now they multiplied like locusts in a grain field, filling the land with their alien presence and strange customs.

His path stretched before him as straight and clear as the road to the underworld. The midwives would obey his divine command or face the consequences. Hebrew boys would die in their first moments of life, their numbers would dwindle like water in the desert sun, and eventually the threat they represented would diminish to nothing more than a troublesome memory.

History would judge him not by the gentleness of his mercy but by the security he bequeathed to his sons and his sons' sons. Let future scribes record that Ahmose I had been a pharaoh who understood the hard arithmetic of survival, who had made the choices necessary to ensure that Egypt remained Egyptian for all the generations yet to come.

The living god turned back toward his chamber where Queen Ahmose Nefertari slept beneath sheets of the finest linen, her breathing soft and regular in the darkness. His decision had been made with the cold clarity that divine wisdom demanded. Power required such choices. Egypt's eternal security demanded such sacrifices.

Even if the blood to be spilled would not be his own.

Chapter 17 - Grief beyond words

1520 BC Respite at Avaris

The journey from Thebes had been long and arduous, but Pharaoh Ahmose felt his spirits lift as the royal barge rounded the final bend of the great river and the walls of Avaris came into view. The ancient Hyksos stronghold, now firmly under Egyptian control, had been transformed into a glittering jewel of the empire—its massive fortifications rebuilt with gleaming limestone blocks, its towers flying the sacred banners of the Two Lands. This respite from the endless councils of war and matters of state was exactly what his family needed.

His son, Prince Ahmose Ankh, had been restless in the capital, his young warrior's blood crying out for action and adventure. Here at Avaris, away from the suffocating protocols of the royal court, the boy could test himself against the finest charioteers in the kingdom, honing the skills that would one day make him a pharaoh worthy of his bloodline.

As the servants made fast the mooring ropes and the gangplank was lowered, Ahmose smiled to see his son's eyes already fixed on the distant training grounds where horses stamped and harness leather gleamed in the morning sun.

Tragedy strikes

The chariot grounds at Pi-Ramesses, north of Avaris, shimmered in the fierce midday heat, waves of superheated air rising from the hard-packed earth to create wavering mirages on the horizon. The vast expanse had been specially prepared for military training—stones removed, soil tamped down, perimeter marked with painted poles topped with fluttering streamers of dyed linen.

Dust clouds rose from prancing horses as Prince Ahmose Ankh, now twelve years old, prepared to demonstrate his newly acquired skills to his father. The boy had grown tall for his age, his body beginning to shed its childish softness in favour of the lean strength that would one day make him a formidable warrior. His chest was bare beneath the bright sun, already showing the muscular development that would mark him as a man of action.

The prince wore a simple linen kilt, its pleats crisp and white against his sun-darkened skin. A leather helmet protected his head—a concession to his mother's concerns that the proud boy had accepted only reluctantly, his desire to appear fearless warring with his duty to obey the queen. Around his upper arms gleamed golden bands inscribed with protective hieroglyphs, gifts from his grandmother Tetisheri before her death the previous year.

Nearby, nine-year-old Amenhotep watched from the shade of a sycamore tree, his slight frame dwarfed by the hulking royal guardsman assigned to protect him. Unlike his brother, Amenhotep showed little interest in weapons or warfare. His delicate hands—already stained with ink from his morning studies—were more suited to holding papyrus scrolls than chariot reins. He sat cross-legged on a cushion, a scroll partially unrolled on his lap despite the occasion, his mind divided between brotherly concern and scholarly fascination with the text before him.

"Watch carefully, little brother!" Ankh called out, grinning widely to reveal teeth white against his tanned face. His voice had begun to change, occasionally breaking from boyish treble to deeper tones that presaged the man he would become. "One day you'll need to know how to do this too, even if you'd rather be counting grain stores!"

Amenhotep managed a weak smile in return, raising a hand in acknowledgment. But his eyes betrayed his anxiety, darting between his brother and the powerful horses that stomped and snorted nearby, their coats gleaming with sweat, muscles rippling beneath sleek hides.

Ahmose sat upon a portable throne at the edge of the practice grounds, his massive form creating a substantial shadow despite the high position of the sun. Though no longer actively leading troops into battle, he maintained the powerful physique of his warrior days, his shoulders broad beneath his royal regalia. He nodded approvingly as his heir climbed confidently into the lightweight war chariot, pride evident in the slight upward curve of his lips.

The vehicle was smaller than standard, specially crafted for the young prince, but otherwise identical to those used by Egypt's elite forces. Its body was fashioned from bent wood covered with tightly stretched leather, painted with scenes of royal victories. The wheels—technological marvels brought to Egypt by the very Hyksos they had expelled—had six spokes radiating from the hub like sunrays, rimmed with leather-wrapped wood for durability.

Behind the king stood Queen Ahmose Nefertari, her face a carefully composed mask that belied the tempest raging in her heart. At thirty-two, she retained the striking beauty that had captivated Ahmose in their youth, but motherhood and queenship had etched new depths into her character. Her dark eyes, lined with kohl that emphasized their almond shape, tracked every movement of her eldest son with the intensity of a falcon watching its prey. She had argued vehemently against this demonstration, her maternal instincts screaming warnings that her royal duties forced her to suppress.

"He is too young still," she had pleaded with her husband in the privacy of their chambers the night before. "Another year, perhaps two, and he will be ready for such advanced maneuvers. Why risk—"

But Ahmose had been adamant, his own memories of boyhood training driving his decision. "I was younger than he when I first stood in a war chariot," he had replied, his voice brooking no argument. "Egypt's king must be forged in steel, not coddled like a temple cat."

Now, watching her son's youthful confidence as he gripped the chariot's rail, Nefertari felt her throat constrict with a premonition she dared not voice. Her hands, adorned with rings bearing the cartouches of Egypt's gods, clenched unconsciously at her sides, the gold cutting into her flesh as she struggled to maintain royal composure.

"Begin!" Ahmose commanded, raising his hand in a gesture that brooked no hesitation.

The driver, an experienced charioteer assigned to train the prince, flicked the reins with practiced precision. The two horses—matched bays chosen for their even temperaments as much as their speed—surged forward as one, their muscles rippling beneath gleaming coats.

Prince Ankh stood proud in the swaying vehicle, his young face alight with excitement and determination. One hand gripped the rail that curved around the front of the chariot, his knuckles white with tension despite his outward confidence. The other held a practice javelin, its point blunted for safety but still weighted to simulate the real weapon he would one day wield in battle.

The chariot picked up speed, circling the training grounds once, twice, each time faster than before. The prince's body instinctively adjusted to the rhythm of the racing chariot, bending slightly at the knees to absorb the shocks as the wheels bounced over the uneven ground.

"Now the targets!" Ahmose called out, his deep voice carrying across the training ground. Though his face remained composed, his eyes shone with unmistakable pride as he watched his son master the vehicle that had transformed warfare throughout the known world.

At his command, servants pushed straw targets into position along the perimeter of the grounds. Each was roughly man-shaped, mounted on wooden frames and dressed in scraps of foreign clothing to simulate the enemies of Egypt. The chariot wheeled sharply, heading toward the first target, the horses responding instantly to the driver's subtle cues.

Prince Ankh raised his javelin, his young face a mask of concentration as he sighted along the shaft. With a grunt of effort, he hurled the spear, putting the full weight of his body behind the throw.

It struck the target dead center, piercing the foreign-styled headdress and driving deep into the straw body. The impact toppled the figure backward, sending up a small cloud of dust as it hit the ground. Appreciative murmurs rose from the watching courtiers.

"Again!" Ahmose cried, his voice betraying his pride, his massive fist punching the air in triumph.

The chariot raced toward the second target, wheels throwing up dust that lingered in the still air. The prince was given another javelin by the driver, their hands meeting in a smooth exchange practiced countless times. He raised it, poised to throw—

And then it happened.

One of the horses, perhaps startled by a bee or simply overexcited by the speed and noise, swerved unexpectedly to the left. The movement, coming without warning, sent the chariot lurching violently to one side. The driver fought the reins, muscle standing out on his forearms as he struggled to regain control, but the sudden movement threw the prince off balance.

For a heartbeat, Ankh teetered on the edge of the racing vehicle, his javelin dropping forgotten from nerveless fingers as both hands clawed desperately for purchase on the rail. His eyes widened with sudden fear, his mouth opening in a shout that was lost in the thunder of hooves.

Then he fell, tumbling beneath the wheels of the chariot itself.

The sound—a sickening crack that seemed to echo across the training ground—carried clearly in the sudden silence that fell over the assembled crowd. It was the unmistakable sound of bone giving way, of a young life ending in an instant of violence and pain.

"ANKH!" The scream that tore from Nefertari's throat was pure animal anguish; a sound no human throat should make. The careful composure of thirty-two years, the rigid training of queenship, the practiced dignity of royal bearing—all of it shattered in an instant like pottery struck by a mace. She was running before conscious thought could stop her, her elaborate wig flying loose, her jeweled collar bouncing against her throat as her long legs carried her across the training ground with desperate speed.

Behind her, Ahmose's roar joined hers—primal, the cry of a wounded animal rather than a king. He was on his feet and running before the chariot had even come to a stop, his royal regalia fluttering behind him like the wings of a falcon in descent.

The dust settled in the merciless heat of the afternoon. Prince Ankh lay motionless on the hard-packed earth, his neck bent at an impossible angle, a crimson pool spreading beneath his head like an offering to some cruel deity. His eyes—those eyes that had sparkled with mischief and ambition only moments before—stared sightlessly at the brilliant blue sky, already dulling as his ka prepared for its journey to the Field of Reeds.

Nefertari reached him first, falling to her knees beside her son's broken body with such force that her kneecaps struck the hard earth with audible cracks. But physical pain was nothing compared to the agony that consumed her as she gathered the still-warm body into her arms, heedless of the blood that immediately began to stain her finest linen.

"My son, my beautiful son," she keened, her voice breaking on each word as she cradled his head against her breast. Her tears fell like rain upon his cooling face, mixing with the dust and blood. "My warrior prince, my bright star—"

Ahmose fell to his knees beside her, the fine linen of his royal kilt soaking up the blood of his firstborn. His hands hovered uselessly above the broken body, trembling with a mixture of disbelief and mounting rage.

"Healers!" he bellowed, his voice cracking with desperation. "Bring the healers! NOW!"

But the royal physician, reaching them moments later with chest heaving from his sprint across the grounds, needed only one glance to know the truth that their hearts refused to accept. The elderly man dropped to his knees beside the royal couple, his gnarled fingers touching the prince's throat, feeling for a pulse that no longer beat.

He looked up at his king and queen, his own eyes brimming with tears. "Divine Ones... he is gone," he whispered, the words hanging in the air like poison. "His ka has already departed for the Field of Reeds. Not even the magic of Thoth could call him back now."

Nefertari's wail rose again, a sound so raw and terrible that it seemed to tear the very fabric of the air. She clutched her dead son closer, her body rocking back and forth in the ancient rhythm of grief, her queen's crown askew, her kohl running in black streams down her cheeks.

Across the training ground, little Amenhotep stood frozen in horror, his slight frame quivering like a reed in the wind. His face had drained of all color, leaving his features ghostly against the kohl that rimmed his wide, disbelieving eyes. The scroll had fallen unheeded from his lap as he stared at his invincible older brother lying broken upon the earth. His mouth moved soundlessly, as if trying to recite a prayer, but no words came.

Mutnofret stood motionless at the edge of the training ground, her kohl-rimmed eyes wide with shock, but her mind already racing beyond the immediate tragedy to calculate its implications. Though only fourteen summers had passed since her birth, the royal blood flowing through her veins had taught her to think like a queen even in moments of crisis.

Her gaze moved from the broken prince to young Amenhotep, trembling in the shade of his sycamore tree. The boy who was to have been her husband lay dead in the dust, but more importantly, the dynasty now rested upon the shoulders of a child who had never shown the slightest interest in the arts of war or rulership. Her intended marriage, arranged to preserve the purity of the royal bloodline, was now meaningless—but perhaps that was not entirely unwelcome.

Her eyes drifted across the assembled courtiers until they found the figure she sought—General Thutmose, standing among the military advisors. Even in this moment of tragedy, she could not help but notice the way his broad shoulders filled his leather armor, the controlled strength in his bearing as he watched the unfolding disaster with professional concern rather than personal grief. He was perhaps ten years her senior, a man rather than a boy, with the weathered hands of a true soldier and eyes that held depths that scholarly young Amenhotep would never possess.

Thutmose caught her gaze across the training ground, and for a moment their eyes held. In that brief exchange, Mutnofret saw recognition—not just of her beauty, which many men had noted, but of her intelligence, her strength, her potential as something more than a decorative royal bride. Here was a man who might value a woman's mind as well as her bloodline, who might offer partnership rather than mere duty.

The sounds of royal grief filled the air around them, but Mutnofret felt a strange sense of liberation settling over her like a cool breeze. The gods, it seemed, had freed her from a future she had never truly wanted, opening a path toward something that might prove far more interesting than a traditional royal marriage to a boy-king. She lowered her eyes demurely, but not before letting the general see the slight curve of her lips—not a smile of joy at the prince's death, but acknowledgment of possibilities that had not existed moments before.

Ahmose did not weep. Something had crystallized within him, turning his grief into something hard and dangerous. His face hardened into a mask of stone, his eyes burning with a terrible, cold fury that made even his closest guards step back involuntarily. He rose slowly to his feet, his hands clenched into fists so tight that his knuckles showed white against his sun-darkened skin.

"Who was driving?" he asked, his voice terrifyingly quiet, like the moment of stillness before a desert storm breaks.

The charioteer, himself injured from the crash, was dragged forward by the guards. Blood streamed from a gash on his forehead, and his left arm hung at an awkward angle that spoke of broken bones. He could barely stand, swaying between the soldiers who held him upright.

"Divine One," he gasped, terror evident in his voice. "The horse—it was not—I tried to—please—"

"Take him," Ahmose said flatly, each syllable precise and final as a death sentence. "He will be buried with my son. He has failed in his duty to protect the heir of Egypt."

The man's scream of terror cut through the afternoon heat like a knife, but Ahmose had already turned away, deaf to the charioteer's pleas as the man was dragged toward the dungeons to await his grisly fate.

Nefertari looked up from her son's body, her tear-streaked face contorting with fresh anguish. "My lord," she whispered, her voice hoarse from screaming. "Please—the man did not will this tragedy. The gods—"

"The gods?" Ahmose's voice rose to a roar, spittle flying from his lips as thirty years of controlled royal bearing finally shattered. "The gods took my son! My heir! They have left me with—" His gaze fell upon Amenhotep, trembling beneath his tree, and something in his expression made the boy shrink back in terror.

Nefertari struggled to her feet, her son's blood staining her robes, her face a mask of grief and growing horror at her husband's transformation. "Ahmose, please—grief clouds your judgment. This is not—"

"Do not presume to counsel me, woman!" The blow came without warning, the back of his hand striking her cheek with enough force to send her stumbling backward. The assembled courtiers gasped in shock—never before had Pharaoh raised his hand against his queen, no matter the provocation.

Nefertari straightened slowly, one hand pressed to her reddening cheek, her dark eyes blazing with fury that matched his own. "I am not 'woman' to you, Ahmose," she said, her voice deadly quiet. "I am your queen, your wife, the mother of your children—including the son who lies dead at your feet. Strike me again and you will find that grief can make queens as dangerous as kings."

For a moment, husband and wife stared at each other across their son's body, two apex predators circling, testing each other's strength. Then Ahmose's shoulders sagged slightly, some of the rage bleeding out of him at the sight of his wife's magnificent fury.

"Forgive me," he said, but his voice held no true remorse, only exhaustion. "I... the gods test me sorely this day."

Nefertari said nothing, merely knelt again beside their son's body, but her eyes promised that this moment would not be forgotten, that accounts would be settled when the time came.

For seven days, Ahmose shut himself away in his chambers, the heavy cedar doors barred against all but the most essential servants. He refused food, pushing away even the finest delicacies. He refused comfort, even from his wife, whose own grief left her prostrate upon her bed, attended by hollow-eyed handmaidens who dared not speak above whispers.

But Nefertari's grief was different from her husband's. Where his turned inward, becoming a festering wound that poisoned his judgment, hers burned bright and clean, tempering her resolve like fire tempers steel. She emerged from her mourning chamber on the third day, her face pale but composed, her eyes holding a new hardness that made even veteran courtiers step aside.

She threw herself into the funeral preparations with fierce devotion, overseeing every detail of her son's mummification and burial. She consulted with the most learned priests, ensuring that every ritual was performed perfectly, every prayer recited without flaw. If her son was to be denied his destined throne, he would at least enter the afterlife with all the honors due a prince of Egypt.

More importantly, she began to pay attention to conversations in corners, to the whispered concerns of nobles and priests about the king's state of mind. Power in Egypt flowed through multiple channels—not just through Pharaoh's absolute authority, but through the complex web of family relationships, priestly hierarchies, and military loyalties that actually governed the Two Lands. A queen who understood these currents could wield considerable influence, especially when the king's judgment was clouded by grief and rage.

In the suffocating darkness of his grief, sleep had finally claimed Ahmose on the seventh night—and with it came a vision that burned itself into his soul. He had seen Egypt's children withering like grain beneath a merciless sun, their small bodies carried away by invisible hands while the Israelite offspring flourished like weeds in fertile soil.

In the dream, he watched his kingdom's future drain away drop by drop, each Egyptian child lost while Hebrew mothers birthed sons by the thousands. The vision showed him an Egypt grown old and feeble, its throne rooms empty, its armies led by foreign hands, its gods forgotten while the Hebrew deity grew fat on the worship of countless descendants. When he woke, the taste of ash filled his mouth and a terrible clarity had settled over him like a shroud.

On the eighth day, Ahmose emerged from his seclusion, his face gaunt but his eyes burning with cold determination. The soft living of recent years had fallen away from his frame, revealing once more the hard, ruthless warrior who had clawed his way to power.

His first act was to order the preparation of an exquisite tomb for his fallen son. His second was to summon his advisors to the throne room, where massive granite columns soared toward a ceiling painted with stars.

"The Israelites continue to multiply," Ahmose said without preamble, his voice hoarse but edged with steel. "They grow stronger while we have grown weaker. This cannot continue."

The council members exchanged uneasy glances but remained silent, none daring to meet the gaze of their king when grief and rage had transformed him into something terrible and unpredictable.

"The midwives have failed in their duty," Ahmose continued, each word precise and cold. "They were ordered to kill the male infants at birth, yet the Israelite boys continue to fill the streets. Their mothers laugh and sing while Egyptian mothers weep."

He rose from his throne, the movement stiff and deliberate. "I will not allow Egypt to face another foreign threat within our borders. Not now. Not when my dynasty hangs by so slender a thread."

His gaze fell upon young Amenhotep, who had been brought to the council meeting despite his tender age. The boy sat rigid with fear upon a smaller chair beside the throne, his eyes enormous in his pale face, his thin shoulders bent beneath the weight of the heavy necklace of office he now wore as heir to Egypt.

"Every son born to the Hebrews shall be cast into the river," Ahmose proclaimed, his voice rising to fill the vast chamber. "Every daughter shall be permitted to live. Send soldiers house to house, village to village. None shall be spared."

At the back of the throne room, Nefertari stood among the queen's retinue, her face carefully composed despite the horror growing in her heart. She had feared this moment, had seen it building in her husband's increasingly erratic behavior over the past week. But to hear the words spoken aloud, to witness the birth of what would surely become a slaughter of innocents, filled her with a revulsion that threatened to overwhelm her careful control.

She caught the eye of the high priest of Amon-Ra, seeing her own concern reflected in his weathered features. Around the room, she noted similar expressions of unease among the older, more experienced counselors. Her husband might be Pharaoh, divine ruler of Egypt, but even gods could make mistakes—and it fell to their servants to guide them back to wisdom when grief led them astray.

"My lord," ventured the eldest councilor hesitantly, "such a measure is... extreme. Perhaps a less severe approach might—"

"Do you question my will?" Ahmose snarled, rounding on the old man with cobra-like speed. His face contorted with fury that made the elderly advisor shrink back in terror. "Did I question when the gods saw fit to take my son? My heir?"

The councilor prostrated himself immediately. "Never, Divine One. Your will is Egypt's law. I spoke only out of concern for the practical implementation of your divine command."

Nefertari watched the exchange with growing alarm. This was not the man she had married, not the careful, thoughtful ruler who had guided Egypt through years of prosperity. This was grief made manifest, rage given divine authority—and the results would be catastrophic not just for the Hebrews, but for Egypt itself.

She began to plan, even as her husband's voice continued to echo off the painted walls, decreeing death for countless innocents. There were channels of influence beyond the throne room, networks of power that even Pharaoh could not completely control. If Ahmose would not listen to reason, perhaps others could be persuaded to moderate the worst excesses of his grief-maddened decree.

The next dawn saw Ahmose's royal barge cutting through the Nile's waters toward Thebes, its black sails heavy with mourning. Beside him sat his queen, her face etched with exhaustion, while behind them lay the small sarcophagus of their son.

What had begun as a peaceful family respite now ended in tragedy, the royal family's return to the capital marked not by joy but by the weight of unimaginable loss. The oarsmen rowed in solemn rhythm, carrying them back to a throne room that would forever echo with the absence of small footsteps.

In the days that followed, the screams of mothers echoed through the Israelite quarter as Egyptian soldiers tore newborn boys from their mothers' arms and carried them to the Nile's waiting waters. The narrow streets ran not with blood but with tears, as families were torn apart by the decree of a king whose grief had hardened into something monstrous.

Nefertari watched from her window as the horror unfolded, her hands clenched so tightly that her nails drew blood from her palms. She had tried everything—subtle pressure through the priests, appeals to the military commanders, even direct confrontation with her husband in the privacy of their chambers. Nothing had swayed him from his chosen course.

"You speak of mercy," Ahmose had said during one of their increasingly bitter arguments, "but where was mercy when the gods took our son? Where was justice when they left us with..." His gaze had drifted toward Amenhotep's chamber, and the contempt in his voice had chilled her blood.

Some families managed to hide their sons, concealing them in root cellars or behind false walls, passing them to childless couples in villages beyond the immediate scrutiny of Egyptian patrols. But many could not. The soldiers were thorough, driven by fear of their king's wrath.

The Nile, lifeblood of Egypt, became a grave for the innocent, it sacred waters stained with the blood of children sacrificed to a Pharaoh's fear and grief. The crocodiles grew fat and lazy, no longer needing to hunt. Birds of prey circled overhead, their harsh cries a counterpoint to the wailing of bereaved mothers.

Back in Thebes, at night, alone in his vast bedchamber, Ahmose would sometimes wake from nightmares of his son's broken body, the image of Ankh's sightless eyes and twisted neck burning in his mind like a brand. On such nights, he would find his face wet with tears he could not shed in daylight.

Other nights, he dreamed of drowning Hebrew infants, their tiny hands reaching accusingly toward him from the dark waters of the underworld. In these dreams, the faces of the children would sometimes transform, becoming the face of Ankh, his beloved firstborn, calling to him from the depths while Ahmose stood paralyzed on the shore, unable to reach him.

On such nights, when sleep became an enemy rather than a refuge, he would rise and make his way through torch-lit corridors to Amenhotep's chamber. The guards would straighten as he passed, averting their eyes from the sight of their king in his night robe.

In Amenhotep's chamber, he would stand over the sleeping boy, studying his delicate features in the gentle glow of the oil lamp. The child slept peacefully, one hand curled beneath his cheek, untroubled by the nightmares that plagued his father. Ahmose would watch him, wondering if this gentle child could ever bear the weight of Egypt's double crown—if these slender shoulders could support the burden that had been thrust upon them by fate's cruel hand.

The dynasty would continue through him now—this thoughtful, scholarly boy who flinched at the sound of clashing weapons, who preferred the company of scribes to soldiers. This child who now carried the future of Egypt in his fragile hands.

Perhaps, Ahmose thought in his darkest moments, the gods had punished him for his pride by taking his warrior son and leaving him this gentle one instead. Perhaps this was their way of showing that even Pharaoh must bend to divine will. Or perhaps it was a test—a challenge to shape this unlikely heir into a ruler worthy of the Two Lands.

Whatever the gods' purpose, Ahmose vowed that Egypt would remain strong, its borders secure, its monuments rising ever higher through the labor of a subjugated people who would never again pose a threat. He would build a legacy that would stand for eternity, a kingdom so mighty that even a scholarly king could not diminish its glory.

Or so he believed, not knowing that within months, the waters that had claimed so many Hebrew sons would deliver one child safely into the arms of destiny—a child who would one day challenge the very foundations of Egyptian power.

But that was a story yet to unfold, a future that not even the greatest seers in Egypt's temples could foresee as Ahmose turned away from his sleeping son and walked back through the silent palace, alone with his grief and his terrible resolve.

Chapter 18 - Basket Among the Reeds

March 1519 BC - Son of Jochebed

The evening air hung heavy with humidity as Amram stood at the threshold of their modest mud-brick dwelling, the weight of seventy years etched into the deep furrows of his weathered face. Sweat beaded on his brow despite the falling darkness, glistening in the amber light of oil lamps that cast long, tremulous shadows across the packed-earth floor. Outside, the distant sounds of Hebrew laborers returning from the day's brutal work in Pharaoh's brick pits mingled with the mournful braying of donkeys and the constant, reassuring murmur of the nearby Nile.

Behind him, his wife Jochebed's muffled cries pierced the heavy silence as she labored to bring forth their child. Her knuckles whitened as she gripped the birthing rope suspended from the ceiling beam, each contraction drawing a primal groan from deep within her. Despite her forty years and the pregnancies she had already endured, this birth seemed harder, as though the child sensed the peril awaiting it in this world dominated by Egyptian cruelty.

"Push, my sister," the midwife urged, her voice steady despite the turmoil roiling in her breast. "Once more, and your child will come forth."

Puah knelt at the foot of the birthing mat, a woman whose hands had welcomed hundreds of Hebrew babies into the world. In the flickering lamplight, her dark eyes betrayed a fear she dared not speak aloud. Her fingers, still slick with birth blood and amniotic fluid, trembled almost imperceptibly as she prepared to receive the infant. The acrid smoke from the oil lamps mixed with the metallic scent of blood and the earthy smell of sweat-dampened mud walls.

The child's first lusty cry rent the close air of the dwelling—a sound that should have heralded joy but now carried mortal danger. A son. Puah's heart sank and soared simultaneously as she beheld the perfect male infant before her, his tiny limbs flailing in protest at his sudden entry into the world.

By Pharaoh's decree, she should now take this male child and silence him forever—pinch his nostrils shut, press her thumb against his windpipe, or snap his delicate neck with a practiced twist. Quick. Merciful. Final. The image made her stomach heave, but it was the fate that awaited all Hebrew boys in this land of oppression.

For months, she had navigated this murderous edict with cunning deception, arriving deliberately late to Hebrew births, claiming to Egyptian officials who interrogated her that these foreign women delivered with unusual speed. "Like wild gazelles," she had told them with downcast eyes that concealed her fierce defiance, "dropping their young almost before they feel the pains." The officials, men who recoiled at the mere mention of birthing blood, had accepted her explanation with disgusted waves of dismissal, their gold rings flashing in the sunlight as they turned away from matters, they considered beneath their dignity.

But tonight, fate had conspired against her. She had been nearby when Jochebed's waters broke, unable to pretend ignorance or delay. And now this perfect male infant lay before her, his skin still mottled and wrinkled from his journey into the world, his tiny chest rising and falling with each precious breath that defied Pharaoh's will.

Puah reached for the linen cloth she used to clean newborns, her mind racing through desperate calculations. She had witnessed the consequences of resistance—watched Egyptian soldiers smash infants against doorposts when mothers refused to relinquish them, heard the heart-rending screams of women whose babies were torn from their breasts and carried to the Nile for drowning. The memory of those sounds still echoed in her nightmares, mixing with the taste of bile that rose in her throat. Perhaps one quick moment of pain now would spare this child and his family greater suffering? The thought sickened her even as she entertained it.

The infant's eyes flickered open suddenly—dark, solemn eyes that seemed to hold the wisdom of generations, eyes that pierced through Puah's professional detachment to touch something ancient and sacred within her. In that moment, the fear that had clutched her heart loosened its grip, replaced by a determination that burned like fire in her veins.

"He is beautiful," Amram whispered, his voice rough with emotion as he touched the infant's head with its dusting of dark hair. The raw pride mingled with terror in the father's voice—broke something in Puah's carefully constructed armor, the final barrier between duty and rebellion.

She cleaned the child with gentle, efficient movements honed by years of practice, then swaddled him tightly in a linen cloth, her fingers moving with particular care as she wrapped his tiny shoulders and chest, creating a cocoon of temporary safety. The baby's skin felt warm and soft against her palms, so perfectly formed, so utterly innocent of the cruelty that surrounded him.

"Listen to me," she whispered, her voice so low that Amram and Jochebed had to lean forward to hear, the words barely disturbing the air between them. "This child was never born. Do you understand?" Her eyes locked with Jochebed's, seeking confirmation. "If anyone asks, you delivered a stillborn girl."

She pressed the warm bundle into Jochebed's trembling arms. The new mother's eyes widened with understanding, then filled with tears of gratitude that spilled silently down her cheeks. The women's hands overlapped on the child's swaddled form, a silent pact formed between them, sealed by desperation and hope in equal measure.

"The soldiers patrol at dawn and dusk," Puah continued, gathering her birthing tools and wrapping them in a blood-stained cloth with practiced efficiency. The familiar ritual of packing her instruments steadied her nerves. "They rarely come during the middle watches of the night. Keep him quiet—crushed poppy seed in honey water if you must."

"We won't let them take him," Jochebed said, her voice hoarse but resolute as she clutched her son to her breast. The milk was already letting down, staining her simple linen shift. "I won't surrender another child to the Nile." The words held all the fierce protective power of a mother lioness, tempered by the haunted knowledge of past losses.

Puah nodded once, sharply, her expression grim. She had made the same vow months ago, though she had never spoken it aloud. She had delivered eight baby boys since Pharaoh's decree, and all eight still suckled at their mothers' breasts, hidden away in root cellars, behind false walls, or passed temporarily to childless couples in villages beyond Egyptian scrutiny. Each birth was an act of rebellion, each saved child a silent victory against tyranny.

"May the God who sees all things protect him," she murmured, placing her hand briefly on the infant's head before slipping toward the door. The simple blessing carried the weight of generations of faith, passed down from Abraham through Isaac and Jacob to this moment of crisis. "And may He forgive us all for what these times force us to become."

As she disappeared into the night, Puah knew she had sealed her own fate should her deception be discovered. The penalty for defying Pharaoh was death—often slow and agonizing, a public spectacle designed to discourage further resistance. But with each boy she saved, something fierce and righteous grew stronger within her—a certainty that though Pharaoh might command the power of Egypt, a greater power commanded her loyalty, one that would not abandon His people in their hour of need.

Inside the humble dwelling, Jochebed sat propped against the wall, her newborn son nestled against her breast. Her fingers traced the perfect curve of his ear, the soft swell of his cheek, memorizing every detail as if she might lose him at any moment. Exhaustion pulled at her, but fear kept her alert, her senses attuned to every sound outside their door—the shuffle of sandaled feet, the distant laughter of night guards, the rustle of palm fronds in the evening breeze.

"Look at him," Amram whispered again, sinking down beside his wife. His hand, scarred from decades of labor making bricks without straw, trembled as he touched the infant's head. In that tender gesture lay all his pride, all his terror, all his desperate hope that somehow this child might survive Pharaoh's murderous decree.

In the corner, their daughter Miriam, barely ten years old, watched with solemn eyes that had witnessed too much for her tender age. The childhood innocence that should have been her birthright had been stolen by Egyptian cruelty, replaced by a precocious understanding of life's harshness. The flickering lamplight cast shadows across her small face, making her appear older than her years. Their son Aaron, three years older than his sister, slept unaware of the new life that had entered their home—and the danger that came with it. His breathing was deep and even, untouched by the anxiety that gripped the others.

"What do we call him?" Jochebed asked, her voice barely audible above the baby's soft breathing.

Amram was silent for a long moment, studying his son's face in the dim lamplight. The child's features were already distinct—a strong chin, a straight nose, lips that curved in the slightest suggestion of a smile even in sleep. "Let's wait," he finally said. "Names have power. Let's keep that power hidden until we know God's plan for him."

Jochebed nodded, understanding. No name meant no official existence. A shadow child was harder to find, harder to kill.

For three months, they concealed the child in their humble dwelling, a feat that grew more difficult with each passing day. When neighbors approached, Jochebed pressed a herb-soaked cloth to the baby's mouth to quiet his cries, her heart racing at each close call. The pungent smell of crushed herbs became a familiar scent in their home, mixed with the sweeter fragrance of the oils she rubbed on his skin. They took turns keeping watch, sleeping in shifts, jumping at every sound of Pharaoh's guards patrolling the Hebrew quarter south of Pi-Ramses. The strain etched new lines into their faces, added silver to their hair, but strengthened their resolve to save their son at any cost.

As the weeks passed, their son grew stronger, his cries more insistent, his lungs more powerful. The neighbors began to cast suspicious glances their way, their eyes lingering on Jochebed's milk-stained garments, their ears alert to sounds that shouldn't exist. Questions were asked in hushed tones at the well, whispers circulated that perhaps the midwife had lied about the stillbirth. Each day brought new dangers, new possibilities for discovery and destruction.

"We can't hide him any longer," Amram said one night, his voice breaking as he stroked his son's cheek. In the three months since the birth, he had grown to love this child with a fierceness that frightened him. The boy's personality was already emerging—alert, curious, seeming to study the world with those dark, intelligent eyes. "The soldiers will come soon. They suspect."

The old couple had already endured the unthinkable, taking in the children of Amram's brother after the Egyptians had claimed him for their building projects, watching as friends and relatives disappeared into Pharaoh's labor camps, never to return. Now, with their own son's life at stake, they faced an impossible choice that no parent should ever have to make.

June 1519 BC - Avaris

Jochebed sat hunched over in the corner of their dwelling, her fingers working deftly with the papyrus reeds she had collected from the marshes under cover of darkness. The sharp green scent of the plants filled the small space, mingling with the earthy smell of mud and the pungent odor of bitumen. The reeds felt smooth and pliable in her hands, still damp with river water and morning dew. For days she had labored, weaving the plants into a small ark, just large enough to hold her infant son.

The final product of her desperate industry sat before her now—a basket woven tight as fabric, its seams sealed with pitch, a vessel hovering between hope and despair. It was both cradle and potential coffin, salvation and surrender. Her heart revolted at the thought of placing her child in this fragile craft and entrusting him to the Nile's unpredictable currents, but she could see no other path to safety. The Egyptians had closed every other avenue of escape.

"The bitumen," she said, extending her hand toward Amram, her voice steady despite the trembling of her heart. "We must seal every crack."

Amram passed her the sticky black substance, its acrid smell sharp in his nostrils. They had traded their last valuable possessions for it—a copper bracelet passed down through generations, now surrendered to save their child. The transaction had been conducted in whispers at the edge of the marketplace, the precious metal exchanged for a small clay pot of the waterproofing pitch, a bargain that might purchase their son's life.

"Will it hold?" Amram asked, watching as she smeared the pitch over the woven basket with careful precision. His voice betrayed the doubt that had plagued him since they had conceived this desperate plan.

"It has to," Jochebed replied, her voice little more than a whisper. Her fingers worked methodically, covering every potential leak, every weakness in the woven structure. The pitch felt warm and sticky under her fingertips, clinging to the reeds like hope itself. "The reeds are strong, and the pitch will keep the water out." She spoke with a confidence she did not entirely feel, but doubt was a luxury they could not afford. The basket was their son's only chance.

As she worked, Miriam sat quietly beside her, watching her mother's hands with an intensity beyond her years. The girl had appointed herself guardian of her baby brother, singing softly to him when he fussed, distracting him when hiding was necessary. Her voice, though young, carried melodies passed down through generations of Hebrew mothers. Now she would play an even more crucial role in their desperate gambit.

"I won't fail," she promised, her young voice steady with purpose. "I'll watch over him until he's safe."

That night, as their son slept peacefully, unaware of his parents' anguish, Amram and Jochebed held each other and wept silently in the darkness. Their tears fell for the child they would place in the hands of an unpredictable river and a more unpredictable God, for the cruelty of a world that forced such choices upon them, for the uncertain future that awaited them all. The baby stirred between them, making soft sounds of contentment that broke their hearts anew.

"Yahweh hasn't forgotten us," Amram murmured into his wife's hair, though doubt edged his words. His faith, once robust as a cedar of Lebanon, had been whittled down by years of unanswered prayers and unrelieved suffering. "He won't forget our son."

Jochebed pressed her face against her husband's chest, drawing strength from his heartbeat, from the familiar scent of his skin mixed with brick dust and honest sweat. "If He parted the waters for Noah, surely He can guide one small basket to safety," she whispered, clinging to this slender thread of hope in the darkness of their circumstances.

Dawn had barely broken, the eastern sky just beginning to blush with the first light of day, when Jochebed wrapped her son in a linen cloth embroidered with the symbols of their ancestors. Into every stitch she had poured her prayers, her hopes, her fierce maternal love. She had worked on it by night while the child slept, her fingers flying by lamplight, creating a tangible expression of her devotion to wrap around him when her arms no longer could. The fabric smelled of the precious oils she had rubbed into the threads, a fragrance that would carry her love with him wherever the river might take him.

Their dwelling, a humble structure nestled among dozens like it in the Hebrew settlement, lay just south of the magnificent Pi-Ramses. From their door, they could see the gleaming white limestone of Pharaoh Ahmose I's palace looming a mere kilometer to the north—so close, yet separated by an unbridgeable gulf of power and privilege. The palace's towering obelisks and massive statues of the god-king stood as constant reminders of the Egyptians' absolute authority and the Hebrews' absolute subjugation. In the early morning light, the monuments seemed to glow with divine fire, mocking the humble mud-brick homes that crouched in their shadow.

"The princess bathes in the river at sunrise," Miriam reported, returning from her scouting mission with flushed cheeks and bright eyes. The scent of river grass clung to her clothes, and her feet were damp with morning dew. The girl had been watching the royal family's habits for weeks, noting the precise time when Pharaoh's daughter Mutnofret and her attendants walked to their private bathing area along the Nile. Each morning, the young princess descended to the river with her handmaidens, following a ritual of purification and beauty that never varied in its timing or execution.

"You're certain of this plan?" Amram asked, his voice thick with doubt as he paced the small confines of their dwelling. The scheme seemed too fragile, too dependent on coincidence and the capricious mercy of their oppressors. "To place our son in the hands of Egyptians— the very people who'd see him dead?"

"What choice do we have?" Jochebed replied, kissing her baby's forehead one last time before placing him in the waterproofed basket.

Her lips lingered on his warm skin, memorizing the feel of him, the sweet baby scent that rose from his tiny body. "If he stays here, he dies. If by some miracle the princess finds him..."

She couldn't finish the thought. The possibility seemed too tenuous, too dependent on the whims of their oppressors. And yet, the alternative was certain death. At least this way, their son had a chance, however slight.

"Miriam will watch from the reeds," Jochebed continued, gathering her courage from some deep, untapped reservoir within her soul. The plan had come to her three nights ago as she lay sleepless, listening to her son's gentle breathing beside her. Whether divine inspiration or desperate maternal imagination, it offered the only path forward she could see. "If the basket is found, she'll approach and offer to find a Hebrew nurse."

"And if they discover she's the child's sister?" Amram's brow furrowed with concern for his daughter as well as his son. One rash word from Miriam could doom them all to a death more terrible than anything they had yet imagined.

"They won't. Our daughter is clever." Jochebed placed her hands on Miriam's shoulders, feeling the girl's slight frame trembling with the weight of responsibility being placed upon it. The child's bones felt fragile under her palms, yet she sensed the steel that ran through her daughter's spirit. "You must be careful, my heart. Stay hidden until the basket is discovered. Speak only if spoken to. Remember your story."

The girl nodded, her young face set with determination beyond her years. In her eyes shone a mixture of fear and resolve that squeezed Jochebed's heart. So much burden to place on one so young—and yet, what choice did they have? In this world shaped by Egyptian cruelty, childhood itself was a luxury few Hebrew children could afford.

As the first light of dawn touched the eastern horizon, painting the sky in shades of gold and amber, Jochebed carried the precious cargo toward the river, her husband and daughter trailing behind. They moved silently through the sleeping settlement, past mud-brick dwellings indistinguishable from their own, each housing families living under the same cloud of oppression and fear. The air was cool and sweet with the fragrance of night-blooming jasmine, a deceptive peace that belied the desperate mission they undertook.

The palace guards were changing shifts—the perfect moment to slip unnoticed toward the bathing place frequented by the royal women. The air was cool and damp with morning mist rising from the river, providing additional cover for their furtive journey. The sounds of their sandaled feet were muffled by the soft earth, and the gentle lapping of water against the reeds created a natural rhythm that masked their approach. The mighty Nile flowed before them, its waters glinting in the early light, promising both life and death in its inexorable current.

With trembling hands, Jochebed placed the basket among the reeds growing thick along the riverbank, just upstream from where the princess would bathe. The water lapped gently at the vessel's sides, testing its buoyancy, its waterproofing. The sound was soft, almost musical, as if the river were singing a lullaby to the child, it now sheltered. Jochebed's heart lurched as the basket dipped slightly before finding its equilibrium, floating securely among the swaying green stalks.

She whispered a final blessing over her son, words ancient as the hills of Canaan, passed down through generations since Abraham first heard the divine call. The prayer—part plea, part surrender—rose from her lips to mingle with the morning mist, carrying with it all the love and hope and terror of a mother's heart. Then she stepped back as the current caught the tiny ark, carrying it gently into the flowing waters of the Nile, the very river that had claimed so many Hebrew sons now becoming her own child's uncertain salvation.

"Go," she whispered to Miriam, her voice breaking despite her resolve to remain strong. "Watch over your brother."

As the girl disappeared into the reeds, her slight form moving with the natural stealth of youth, Jochebed turned away, her husband's arm the only thing keeping her from collapsing under the weight of her grief. Together they walked back toward their home, each step an agony of separation, each breath a silent prayer to the God who had seemed so distant in these dark days of bondage. The morning air carried the scent of river water and growing things, innocent fragrances that would forever remind her of this moment when she surrendered her child to providence.

"Now," Amram said, his voice steady despite the tremor in his limbs, "we wait, and we trust."

The words were simple, but they encompassed all the faith, all the hope, all the desperate longing that sustained them in this moment of supreme sacrifice. They had done what they could. The rest was in hands greater than their own.

The summer heat pressed down upon Pi-Ramses like a physical weight, the air thick and still beneath a cloudless sky of burnished bronze. Even the palace gardens, with their carefully tended pools and shaded walkways, offered little relief from the oppressive temperature that made breathing feel like swallowing liquid fire. In the royal retreat, Queen Mother Ahhotep sat beneath a canopy of woven palm leaves, her aging beauty enhanced by kohl-rimmed eyes and hennaed hair arranged in intricate braids. Gold and lapis lazuli adorned her neck and wrists, glinting in the dappled light that filtered through the palm fronds above. The precious metals felt warm against her skin, heated by the relentless sun. She watched with regal detachment as her grandchildren splashed in a shallow pool, their young voices rising in laughter that echoed across the carefully tended garden.

The youngest among them, Prince Amenhotep, showed his royal blood in the imperious way he commanded his sisters to fetch him floating lotus blossoms. Though barely five, he already carried himself with the confident bearing of one born to rule, secure in the knowledge that his every whim would be indulged, his every command obeyed without question. The water around him sparkled with droplets that caught the light like liquid diamonds.

"He has his father's temperament," Ahhotep observed to her granddaughter Mutnofret, who sat beside her, fanning herself languidly with an ostrich feather fan. The soft whisper of air from the fan brought little relief but provided the familiar rhythm of royal leisure. The observation carried both pride and warning—Pharaoh Ahmose's iron will have united Egypt, but his impatience had also created unnecessary enemies.

"Indeed," Mutnofret agreed, though her thoughts seemed elsewhere, her gaze drifting toward the Nile that flowed beyond the garden walls. At fifteen, she embodied the ideal of Egyptian beauty—slender yet curvaceous, with almond-shaped eyes enhanced by green eye paint and full lips touched with the red of crushed pomegranates. Her linen dress, so fine as to be nearly transparent, revealed the perfect form beneath while its pleats created an elegance befitting her station. The fabric rustled softly with each movement, a whisper of wealth and privilege.

"I shall bathe in the river this morning," she announced, setting aside her fan with a decisive gesture. "The pool is too warm to offer any relief." The royal swimming pool, for all its elaborate design and aesthetic beauty, could not compare to the cool, flowing waters of the Nile when the heat pressed down like a smith's forge.

"Take guards," Ahhotep cautioned, her eyes narrowing slightly. Decades in the royal court had taught her that danger lurked everywhere, especially for women of royal blood. The sound of her jewelry clinked softly as she leaned forward, emphasizing her words. "The Hebrew slaves grow more numerous and more restless each day. Their eyes watch our every move, their hearts harbor resentments we cannot fathom."

Mutnofret waved a dismissive hand, the gesture elegant despite its impatience. Her gold bracelets caught the light as she moved. "My bathing place is well-protected, grandmother. No Hebrew would dare approach." Her confidence was that of youth and privilege combined— a belief in her own inviolability that came from a lifetime of absolute power.

An hour later, surrounded by her handmaidens, Mutnofret descended the stone steps to her private bathing enclosure. The cool stone felt blessed relief under her bare feet after the heated pathways above. The architects had diverted a portion of the Nile's flow into a secluded pool, screened by papyrus reeds and guarded by her father's most trusted soldiers. The morning air had already begun to thicken with heat, promising another scorching day, and the prospect of cool water against her skin beckoned irresistibly. The sound of flowing water created a peaceful melody that drowned out the distant sounds of the palace.

Her handmaidens helped her disrobe, removing the sheath dress of fine linen, the elaborate beaded collar, the golden armlets and anklets that marked her royal status. Each piece was handled with reverent care, placed on soft cloths to protect them from dust and damage. As she stood naked, waiting for her attendant to bring the scented oils that would protect her skin from the water's drying effects, one of the younger girls gasped suddenly, her hand flying to her mouth.

"My lady, look! There, among the reeds!" The girl's voice trembled with excitement or fear—perhaps both. Her finger pointed toward something that bobbed among the green stalks at the pool's edge.

Mutnofret followed the girl's pointing finger and saw a small basket, bobbing gently in the water, caught in the reeds at the edge of her bathing pool. It seemed out of place in this carefully controlled environment— an intrusion of chaos into perfect order. The woven reeds were darkened with water, and something about its purposeful construction suggested human hands rather than random debris.

"Fetch it," she commanded, curiosity piqued by the unexpected object. Perhaps it contained offerings from some ambitious noble seeking favour, or messages from a secret admirer too timid to approach directly.

The servant waded into the water, her intake of breath sharp as the cool liquid touched her warm skin. She retrieved the basket with careful hands, bringing it to her mistress with water streaming from its base, droplets falling like tears onto the stone platform. The girl's eyes were wide with apprehension as she placed it at Mutnofret's feet and stepped back hastily, as if the object might contain some danger.

With hesitant fingers, Mutnofret lifted the woven lid. The cry that escaped her lips brought her guards rushing forward, spears ready, their bodies tensed for threat. But the princess raised a hand to stay them, her eyes never leaving the basket's contents.

"A child," she whispered, staring at the infant who gazed back at her with dark, solemn eyes that seemed to hold knowledge beyond his few months of life. "A Hebrew child."

The baby let out a cry, tiny fists waving in the air as if to announce his presence, to demand recognition of his precarious existence. The sound, so vulnerable and yet so insistent, pierced something in Mutnofret's heart that she had not known existed. His skin was perfect, unmarked by the harsh conditions that plagued the Hebrew quarter, and his limbs moved with the healthy vigor of a well-cared-for infant.

"Drown it," her chief handmaiden suggested with casual cruelty, her lip curling in distaste. "It is only a Hebrew boy. Your father has decreed all Hebrew males should die in the river." The woman's tone was matter-of-fact, as if suggesting the disposal of a troublesome insect rather than a human child.

But something in the child's face stirred Mutnofret's heart. Perhaps it was the way he quieted when she reached to touch his cheek, his tiny hand grasping her finger with surprising strength. Perhaps it was the perfect bow of his lips, or the intelligence that seemed to shine from his dark eyes. His skin felt impossibly soft against her palm, warm with life and innocent trust. Or perhaps it was the gods themselves who moved her to compassion, using this moment to set in motion events that would echo through centuries to come.

"No," she said firmly, lifting the child from his basket with careful hands. The baby's weight was solid and reassuring in her arms, and she felt his tiny heartbeat against her chest. "I shall keep him." The decision, made in an instant, carried the weight of royal authority that brooked no opposition. Even as she spoke the words, Mutnofret felt their significance, as if she stood at a crossroads of fate, choosing a path that would alter not just her life but the course of empires.

From the concealment of the dense reeds just beyond the bathing enclosure, Miriam watched the scene unfold with her heart hammering against her ribs. The sound of her pulse seemed loud in her ears, nearly drowning out the princess's words. She had followed the basket's journey downstream, darting through the reeds like a small animal, keeping the precious cargo in sight while remaining hidden from Egyptian eyes. When she saw the princess lift her brother from the basket with tender hands rather than the disgust she had feared, Miriam knew the moment had come to take the greatest risk of her young life. Her throat felt dry as dust, but she swallowed her fear and stepped forward.

Gathering courage that belied her years, she stepped from her hiding place into the open, where she could be seen by the royal party. Her simple dress was dusty from her journey through the reeds, her feet bare and muddy, but she held herself with a dignity born of desperate purpose. The morning sun felt warm on her face as she emerged from the cool shadows of her hiding place.

"Princess," she called, bowing low to hide her face and the fear that surely showed there. Her voice carried clearly across the water, steady despite the terror that threatened to choke her. "Shall I find a Hebrew woman to nurse the child for you?" The words emerged steadier than she had dared hope, carrying across the water with clear purpose.

The princess's guards moved to seize the girl, their faces dark with suspicion and irritation at this interruption of royal privacy. Their bronze spear points gleamed in the morning light as they advanced. But Mutnofret raised a hand to stop them, her gaze still fixed on the child in her arms, who had begun to fuss hungrily. The infant's cries were becoming more insistent, and she could feel his small body tensing with need.

"You would do this?" she asked, studying the infant whose needs she was suddenly, acutely aware she could not meet herself. Despite her royal power, she could not command milk to flow from her maiden breasts.

"I know of a woman, good and gentle, who has milk," Miriam replied, keeping her eyes downcast as befitted a slave addressing royalty. Her heart pounded so violently she feared the Egyptians might hear it, might somehow divine her connection to the child through the force of her desperate hope. The scent of river water and growing reeds filled her nostrils as she waited for the princess's response.

Mutnofret hesitated only a moment before nodding, her decision swift and decisive as all royal commands must be. "Go then. Bring this woman to the palace by midday. She will be paid to nurse the child until he is weaned." The practicality of the arrangement appealed to her—a solution that addressed the immediate need while maintaining the distance appropriate between royalty and Hebrew slaves.

Miriam ran, her feet barely touching the ground, tears of joy and relief streaming down her face as she raced back through the settlement toward home. The burden of responsibility that had weighed on her young shoulders lifted with each step, replaced by elation that their desperate gamble had succeeded beyond all reasonable hope. The morning air rushed past her face, carrying the promise of salvation.

By noon, Jochebed stood before the princess in a palace antechamber, her head bowed in submission while her heart soared with gratitude to the God who had worked this miracle. She had hastily washed and changed into her best dress—which was still little more than a poor woman's garment—but she carried herself with the quiet dignity of a mother reunited with her child. The palace's marble floors felt cold beneath her bare feet, and the walls towered above her with their painted scenes of Egyptian gods and pharaohs.

Mutnofret studied the Hebrew woman carefully, noting the gentleness with which she received the fussing infant, the immediate way the child quieted at her touch. Something passed between woman and child—a recognition, a bond—that confirmed her choice. The baby's cries ceased the moment he felt his mother's familiar embrace, and Jochebed's milk began to flow in response to his need.

"You will care for him until he is of age to join my household," Mutnofret instructed, her tone leaving no room for negotiation. "I shall call him Moses, for I drew him out of the water." The naming was an act of possession, of claiming, that established her authority over the child's destiny.

Jochebed bowed lower, hiding the flash of triumph in her eyes. "As you command, my lady. I shall nurse him well and teach him to honor his benefactress." The words were perfectly subservient, betraying nothing of the joy that threatened to burst from her breast.

As Jochebed carried her son back to their home—now as his nurse rather than his mother—her mind raced with possibilities. She had been granted what no other Hebrew mother had received: time with her son, legitimate time that need not be hidden or denied. She had three precious years, perhaps four, before the boy would be claimed by the palace.

That night, as Moses suckled at her breast in the privacy of their dwelling, Jochebed whispered to her husband, her voice hushed with wonder: "Do you see how God has worked? Not only is our son alive, but I am paid to raise him as my own."

Amram nodded, his face solemn in the lamplight that cast long shadows across the walls of their humble home. The day's events had restored something of his faith, but caution still tempered his joy. "And when he goes to the palace? What then?"

Jochebed's eyes gleamed with a mother's fierce hope. "I will teach him who he is—that he is Hebrew, that he is ours. Perhaps when he walks in the halls of power, he will remember his people's suffering." She gazed down at the child in her arms, her voice dropping to barely a whisper. "The Almighty has preserved him for a purpose we cannot yet see, but I will ensure he knows from whence he came."

The thought hung between them, fragile yet persistent. A Hebrew child raised in Pharaoh's house, but carrying the knowledge of his true heritage. What God intended, they could not fathom, but they had witnessed His hand at work this day.

Outside their window, the Nile flowed on beneath a canopy of stars, indifferent to the momentous events it had witnessed that day—events that would alter the course of nations and echo through the centuries to come. The river that had been decreed as the grave of Hebrew sons had instead become the cradle of their people's greatest hope.

Chapter 19 - Rise and Death of a Prince

1515 BC Avaris

The morning sun blazed across the eastern horizon, casting long, spear-like shadows across the dirt-packed streets of Avaris. Golden light illuminated dust clouds beneath ornamented horses' hooves as the royal envoy arrived, their bridles jingling with small golden bells that announced power and authority long before they came into view. The procession moved with fate's inexorable purpose through the Hebrew quarter, guards clearing paths with polished spear butts, sending barefoot children scattering like startled quail and mothers hurrying indoors, eyes downcast but watchful.

At the modest mud-brick dwelling of Jochebed and Amram, four-year-old Moses played in the packed-earth courtyard, small fingers tracing patterns in the dirt. His dark, intelligent eyes focused on his creation, oblivious to the approaching delegation that would cleave his life into before and after. The boy's skin had darkened under the harsh Egyptian sun, his lean frame already showing promise of the man he would become.

Inside the cool shadows of their home, Jochebed worked at her loom, skilled hands moving with practiced precision. The rhythmic clack-clack of the shuttle momentarily masked the growing commotion outside. Familiar patterns of thread coming together beneath her fingers offered comfort that would soon be torn away.

When the pounding came at their door—not a neighbor's respectful knock but authority's imperious demand—Amram rose with the weary resignation of a man who had long anticipated this moment. His shoulders, bent from years of labor beneath the Egyptian whip, straightened as if preparing to bear one final burden.

He opened the door to an imperial official dressed in pristine white linen, flanked by four of Pharaoh's guard. Their polished bronze breastplates gleamed like giant scarab carapaces in the morning light. The royal house insignia marked them as elite palace guard, men who had earned their position through blood and loyalty.

"We come for the boy Moses," the official announced, his voice carrying flat certainty that expected no resistance. "His time with the Hebrew nurse is ended. He is summoned to Thebes to join the royal household."

Jochebed appeared at her husband's shoulder, fingers digging into the weathered doorframe until her knuckles whitened. Blood had drained from her face, leaving her complexion ashen beneath olive skin.

"He is just a child," she whispered, though she knew her words were futile as tears in the desert.

The official's tone softened slightly, surprising humanity flickering in eyes that had witnessed both empire's grandeur and cruelty. "The princess has been generous. Four years you have kept him when the agreement was for three. Now his education in Egypt's ways must begin. The future beckons, and Egypt will not wait."

Moses abandoned his game and ran to his mother, clutching at her rough linen skirts. His dark eyes, large and luminous, filled with curiosity as he regarded the strangers in gleaming armor. Unlike other Hebrew children who had learned to fear Egyptian soldiers from birth, Moses showed no fear—only youth's natural inquisitiveness.

"You will prepare him for travel," the official continued, his gaze softening as it fell upon the boy. "We depart for Thebes with the noon tide."

As the officials waited beneath a lone acacia's shade, Jochebed knelt before her son, strong hands trembling as they framed his small face. She struggled to maintain composure, biting her lower lip to still its quivering. How does one prepare a child for such parting? How does one compress a lifetime of maternal wisdom into hurried moments that must sustain across years of separation?

"My son," she whispered fiercely, taking his small hands in hers, feeling delicate bones beneath warm skin. "You go now to live in Pharaoh's house, but never forget who you are. You are a child of

Abraham, Isaac, and Jacob. Our people's blood flows in your veins like the Nile's waters—deep and eternal."

Moses nodded solemnly, his expression grave beyond his years. Too young to fully comprehend her words' weight but sensing their importance, he committed them to his heart's depths.

Amram pressed a small wooden amulet into the boy's palm—a simple carving of their tribal emblem, worn smooth by anxious fingers during weeks since they had received word of the princess's summons. "Keep this hidden," he murmured, closing the boy's fingers around it. "Let it remind you of your true family when you dwell among strangers. Even in foreign gods' shadow, remember the God of our fathers watches over you."

Too soon, departure arrived. Miriam, now fourteen and beginning her transformation from girl to woman, wept openly as she embraced her brother. Her tears left damp trails in the dust on Moses' cheeks.

"I will pray for you every day," she whispered, her voice breaking. "Every single day until we meet again."

Aaron, at seven, watched with wide, uncomprehending eyes as his baby brother was carried toward Thebes. His small frame trembled, dusty feet rooted where he stood. Unlike the adults who understood the moment's gravity, Aaron's young mind could only grasp that something precious was being taken from their family. His soft childhood hands clutched nervously at his simple garment's edge.

When he finally moved forward, it was with a child's hesitant steps, torn between obedience and the instinct to follow his brother.

"Remember us," was all he said, the words emerging rough-edged from his throat.

As the royal procession departed, Moses seated in a cushioned litter between two guards, his small figure diminishing with distance, Jochebed stood in the street long after dust had settled. Her outstretched hand still reached for what she could no longer touch, fingers grasping empty air. The sun climbed higher, casting her elongated shadow behind her like grief's physical manifestation stretching into an uncertain future.

Journey to Thebes

The twenty-day journey to Thebes followed the Nile's life-giving artery southward through a landscape that unfolded like a living scroll of Egyptian life. For Moses, each league traveled was a league further from all he had known, each river bend revealing new wonders that expanded his world beyond the Hebrew quarter's narrow confines.

Yet with childhood's remarkable adaptability, he soon found fascination in the passing panorama: verdant barley and emmer wheat fields giving way to tawny desert stretches, fishing villages where bronze-skinned men cast nets with practiced precision, and temple complexes rising majestically from the sacred river's banks, their pylons and obelisks reaching toward heaven like the gods' fingers themselves.

The royal barge cut through waters with stately grace, its cedar planks polished to honey-gold sheen, its sail emblazoned with the royal cartouche billowing in the north wind. By night, they moored along shore, and Moses would lie awake beneath a star ceiling more numerous than he had ever imagined, listening to the river's mysterious sounds—hunting crocodiles' splash, hippopotami's grunting, water's soft slap against the hull.

Arrival at Thebes

The royal barge docked at the palace quay amid fanfare and ceremony that bewildered Moses with its color and cacophony. Trumpets blared, announcing their arrival, and incense filled the air with sweet smoke curling like spectral fingers toward the cloudless sky.

Standing at the marble steps' top, resplendent in gold and lapis lazuli that caught the sun in blinding flashes, stood Princess Mutnofret, her belly swollen with child, her face serene beneath an elaborate headdress marking her royal status.

At nineteen, Mutnofret had blossomed into a woman of remarkable beauty and poise, delicate features set in studied dignity. The years had added calculating depth to her gaze—a woman accustomed to navigating court politics' treacherous currents. Her marriage to Thutmose I, a commander of common birth but uncommon valor who had distinguished himself in Ahmose's Nubian campaigns, had already produced one son. Now a second child quickened in her womb, moving beneath her heart like continued power's promise.

As Moses was led up the steps, his small hand engulfed in that of the official who had become his reluctant guardian during their journey, Mutnofret felt an unexpected surge of emotion. In the four years since she had pulled the infant from the Nile, saving him from certain death on a whim she could not fully explain, she had visited him only twice, seeing in him a curiosity, perhaps even a pet.

But now, facing the solemn-eyed boy with his intelligent gaze and straight shoulders, she recognized something more—a presence, a potential that stirred something protective within her.

"Welcome, Moses," she said, extending her hand adorned with rings that gleamed like captive stars. "Do you remember me?"

Moses bowed as he had been hastily instructed during their journey, bending at the waist with grace that seemed innate rather than learned.

"Yes, Great Lady," he replied, his voice clear and steady, betraying none of the trepidation he must surely feel.

Mutnofret smiled, pleased at his composure. "And do you know what your name means, child?"

"Yes, Great Lady," Moses replied, not understanding her words, his Hebrew accent still evident in his Egyptian speech, giving the words a musical quality not unpleasing to the ear.

"I called you Moses because I drew you from the river myself." Mutnofret placed a jeweled hand on his shoulder, feeling the slight frame beneath the new linen tunic he had been given for this presentation. "And now I have drawn you into Pharaoh's house. From this day forward, you shall be educated alongside the royal children. You shall learn Egypt's greatest scholars' wisdom and our finest warriors' skills."

Moses nodded, his expression serious beyond his years, absorbing this pronouncement with gravity that impressed even the cynical courtiers watching from discreet distance.

"Yes, Great Lady," he said simply—a response containing neither the fawning gratitude expected of one so elevated from lowly beginnings, nor any hint of resentment that might naturally arise in a child torn from his family.

Before the Throne

The throne room of Pharaoh Ahmose I hummed with power's quiet energy, like air before a desert storm. Massive columns soared overhead, their capitals carved into papyrus bloom likenesses, painted in vibrant blues and golds that caught light streaming through high clerestory windows. Incense burned in gold braziers, filling the vast chamber with myrrh and frankincense's heady scent.

Courtiers and officials lined the approach to the dais in their finest linens and jewels—a human corridor of wealth and influence through which the newly arrived Moses must pass.

At the hall's far end, elevated on polished black granite, sat Ahmose upon Egypt's seat, the crook and flail of kingship crossed upon his chest. At thirty-four, the pharaoh's once-powerful frame had begun to diminish, shoulders slightly stooped beneath the double crown's weight. Years of warfare and rule had etched weariness lines around his mouth and eyes. Yet those eyes remained sharp as a falcon's, taking in everything, missing nothing—the eyes of a man who had driven foreign invaders from his land through sheer will as much as military might.

When Moses was presented—a small figure in newly made royal linen, his hair freshly oiled and cut in Egyptian fashion—the court fell silent, watching for the pharaoh's reaction to this Hebrew child brought into their midst.

Ahmose beckoned the boy forward with a gnarled finger, gold bands around his wrists clinking softly.

"So," he said, his voice carrying easily in the hushed chamber despite its age-roughened edges, "this is the foundling my daughter plucked from the river."

"Yes, Great Pharaoh," Moses replied, executing a flawless prostration he had been coached in repeatedly during the hours before his presentation.

The pharaoh studied him for a long moment, his expression inscrutable. Then, to the court's surprise, he chuckled—the sound like pebbles shifting in a dry riverbed.

"Well spoken. There is fire in you, Hebrew. Perhaps my daughter was wise to see potential where others saw only a slave child."

Moses remained prostrate, as instructed, until specifically commanded to rise, but his ears burned at the words "slave child"—a reminder of origins that even royal garments could not disguise.

Mutnofret stepped forward, her jewels catching light, her pregnant belly preceding her like a statement of her value to the dynasty.

"Father," she said, her voice musical yet carrying authority's weight, "I ask that Moses be incorporated into the royal household, to be educated with your grandchildren, to serve Egypt as his gratitude dictates."

Ahmose considered, fingers tapping thoughtfully on his throne's arm, the sound of rings against gold a soft counterpoint to whispers that had begun rippling through assembled courtiers. The court held its collective breath. To elevate a Hebrew to such status was unprecedented, potentially dangerous in a kingdom where Hyksos rule's memory—rule by foreigners—still burned like an unhealed wound.

Yet to deny his beloved daughter, especially in her condition...

"So be it," Ahmose declared at last, his voice filling the chamber with divine decree's weight. "Let the boy be taught our ways. Let him learn Egypt's traditions, our priests' wisdom, our commanders' strategies. In time, we shall see if your river gift proves worthy of the investment."

"Rise, Hebrew," Ahmose commanded, and Moses obeyed, standing straight-backed before the most powerful man in the known world. "Look upon me, that I may see your eyes."

Moses raised his gaze to meet the pharaoh's—an act that would have been punishable by death for most commoners. In the boy's dark eyes, Ahmose saw not fear, not awe, but clear intelligence and something else—a sense of separate self-unusual in one so young.

This was not a boy who would be easily shaped, despite his tender years.

"You may go," Ahmose said after a moment of silent assessment. "Remember that your life was forfeit before my daughter found you. Every breath you take is by her grace and my permission."

"Yes, Great Pharaoh," Moses replied, the formal Egyptian phrase flowing from his lips with surprising ease.

Night Reflections

That night, in his new chambers adjoining the royal nursery, Moses stood at the window looking out over vast Thebes, its temples and palaces bathed in moonlight that turned limestone to silver. The wooden amulet his father had given him was hidden beneath his mattress—the only physical reminder of his true origins in this strange new world of luxury and intrigue.

The boy's eyes filled with tears as the day's events' enormity finally overwhelmed him. He wept silently; one small hand pressed against his mouth to stifle any sound that might bring servants running. He wept for his mother's embrace, for his father's quiet strength, for his sister's songs and his brother's rough affection. He wept for familiar scents and sounds of the only home he had known, now replaced by alien perfumes and echoing grandeur.

Yet even as tears tracked down his cheeks, Moses found his gaze drawn to the wonders spread before him. The moonlit city gleamed like a jewel—mighty temples with soaring pylons, gardens with exotic flowers releasing perfume into night air, the distant Nile's shimmer like a silver ribbon winding through darkness.

Already the palace's comforts and wonders pulled at him, tempting him to embrace this new identity, to release memory of dusty streets and humble dwellings.

In that moment, balanced between two worlds, Moses felt the first stirrings of the conflict that would define his life—a prince of Egypt with slaves' blood running through his veins. A boy with two mothers, two peoples, two destinies.

As he finally turned from the window and climbed onto his new bed's soft linen sheets, exhaustion claiming him at last, he could not know that greater forces than even Pharaoh were at work in his life—forces that would one day bring him back full circle to the people from whom he had been taken.

1514 BC Thebes - Another Prince is Born

The cries of a newborn echoed through the royal birthing chamber, cutting through heavy air like a desert hawk's keening. Mutnofret lay exhausted upon the birthing stool, her body slick with labor's sweat, as she delivered her second son into the royal midwife's waiting hands.

The chamber smelled of blood and incense, of female exertion and new life.

Thutmose, waiting anxiously in the antechamber, paced the floor like a caged lion. Each cry from within sent his heart racing anew, memories of his first wife's death in childbirth still raw despite years' passage.

When at last the midwife emerged, her linen apron stained with her work's evidence but her face wreathed in smiles, he froze mid-stride.

"Another son, my lord!" she announced, her voice carrying the joy that only those who usher new life into the world can truly know. "Strong and healthy, with his mother's beauty and his father's vigor!"

Relief and joy washed over Thutmose's weathered face, softening hard lines carved by years of campaigning under the merciless sun. At forty, he had risen from common soldier to pharaoh's son-in-law and crown prince—a meteoric ascension that had earned him as many enemies as allies within the royal court's labyrinthine politics.

A second son strengthened his position immeasurably, giving him an heir and a spare in a world where infant mortality stalked even the most privileged households.

Inside the opulently appointed chamber, Mutnofret reclined against a mountain of cushions, her face flushed but triumphant as she cradled her newborn son. The infant's skin was still red from birth's trauma, tiny fists waving in protest at the bright new world into which he had been thrust.

"My wife," Thutmose said, kneeling beside her and taking her free hand in his. His voice, accustomed to issuing commands that sent men into battle, softened to a reverent whisper. "Once again you honor me beyond measure."

Mutnofret smiled wearily, exhaustion lines around her eyes doing nothing to diminish her beauty. "Egypt needs strong princes, husband. I am merely doing my duty to the Two Lands."

Her gaze shifted to the infant at her breast, his mouth working eagerly at her milk-swollen nipple. "He has your chin," she observed, "and perhaps your temperament as well, given how fiercely he fought his way into the world."

Thutmose laughed, the sound rich with pride. "Then he will be a warrior indeed." He reached out to touch the downy head of his newest son, calloused fingers incongruously gentle against delicate skin. "What shall we call him?"

Mutnofret considered, her political mind never ceasing its calculations, even in this intimate moment. "Amenmose," she decided. "For he is truly a gift from Amun-Ra, and his birth strengthens the divine blood of your line."

May 1514 BC Thebes - Death of the Liberator

The palace gardens bloomed with lotus and papyrus, their colors vibrant against lush greenery that thrived in the Nile Valley's fertile soil. Golden carp darted beneath ornamental pools' surfaces, their scales flashing like coins in a merchant's purse.

In this paradise created by human hands, Pharaoh Ahmose I walked slowly along shaded paths, leaning heavily on his most trusted commander's arm—Ebana.

War had withered the once-mighty pharaoh, leaving his limbs thin and his breathing labored, the sound rough as sand shifting in wind. Yet his mind remained sharp as an obsidian blade, his will undiminished by physical frailties that had overtaken his body.

The double crown had been left behind in his chambers—too heavy now for his neck to support for long periods—but his authority remained as absolute as when he had driven the Hyksos from Egyptian soil decades before.

"Do you remember the taking of Avaris, my friend?" Ahmose asked, pausing to rest on a stone bench overlooking a tranquil pool where lotus blossoms opened their pink and white petals to the sun. "How the Hyksos fled before us like chaff before the wind?"

Ebana, himself battle-scarred but still standing straight as a spear, nodded, his eyes distant with memory. Years had etched deep lines around his mouth and eyes, but had done nothing to diminish the warrior's presence that surrounded him like an invisible cloak.

"I remember, Divine One. The sky was dark with their arrows, the air thick with dust and the dying's screams. It was there you earned your name as the Liberator, the one who drove foreign oppressors from our sacred soil."

"Those were days of glory," Ahmose sighed, his gaze fixed on something only he could see—perhaps the young warrior he had once been, fearless and vital, leading his troops into enemy territory's heart. "We were young then, believing ourselves immortal, our bodies responsive to our will as a fine chariot to its driver."

"You achieved what your brother and father could not," Ebana reminded him, his voice rough with emotion. "You reunited the Two Lands. Your name will live for eternity, inscribed in stone and in Egypt's people's hearts."

Ahmose smiled faintly, the expression bringing momentary youth to his time-ravaged features. "And what of the Hebrew boy my daughter favors? What do you make of him, Ebana? You who have always spoken truth to me, even when it pained my ears to hear it."

Ebana considered his words carefully, knowing the weight they would carry with his king. "The boy is exceptional, my king. Quick to learn, respectful of our ways, yet... there is something in him that remains apart. A quality I cannot name—a fire that burns behind his eyes when he thinks himself unobserved."

"Destiny, perhaps," Ahmose murmured, his bony fingers plucking absently at a loose thread on his linen robe. "I have watched him when he thinks himself unobserved. There is a purpose in him, Ebana. A purpose yet unrevealed."

"Do you regret allowing him into the royal household?" Ebana asked—the question many at court had whispered but none had dared voice to the pharaoh himself.

Ahmose shook his head slowly, the movement deliberate, as though his thoughts were heavy things requiring careful balancing. "No. Whatever the gods intend for him; it is woven into Egypt's fate as well. Better we shape that purpose than leave it to chance or, worse, allow it to grow wild among his own people."

As they continued their slow garden circuit, Ahmose's breathing grew more labored, air whistling through constricted chest passages. Ebana noticed with growing concern the blue tinge to his king's lips, the tremor in the hand that gripped his arm with surprising strength.

"Divine One, perhaps we should return to your chambers. The physician—"

"No," Ahmose interrupted firmly, decades of absolute rule's authority still evident in his voice despite its weakened state. "I would stay in the sun a while longer. The warmth eases my joints, and I have spent too many days confined to darkness of late."

He paused, his eyes growing distant. "Tell me of your campaigns in Nubia. Remind me of the days when we rode side by side into battle, when our blood ran hot with youth and conquest."

Ebana recognized the request for what it was—a dying man's desire to relive his moments of glory, to feel once more youth's vigor through shared memories. And so, he spoke, his soldier's voice softening as he recounted their victories, their narrow escapes, the bonds forged in blood and triumph that had connected them across decades.

As he described their famous crossing of the cataracts, where they had lost three boats and a dozen men but secured a passage thought impossible, Ahmose's grip on his arm suddenly tightened, fingers digging into Ebana's flesh with surprising strength—then went slack, tension flowing out of them like water from an overturned vessel.

The pharaoh's head drooped forward, a last breath escaping his lips in a soft sigh, barely audible above the gentle splash of water in the nearby fountain.

"My king?" Ebana whispered, though he already knew.

The body beside him still held Ahmose's form, but the essence of the man—the fierce intelligence, the indomitable will that had reunited Egypt—had departed, journeying now toward the western horizon and whatever awaited beyond.

Ahmose I, liberator of Egypt, vanquisher of the Hyksos, restorer of the Two Lands, had completed his journey to the western horizon. The barge of Ra would carry him now to judgment before Osiris, his heart to be weighed against Ma'at's feather.

Ebana lowered his old friend gently to the bench, arranging his limbs with dignity before summoning the palace guards. The great wheel of Egyptian history had turned once more, and a new pharaoh would soon ascend to the throne of the Two Lands.

Chapter 20 - Shadows of Succession

1494 BC Thebes Reign of Amenhotep

The Nile flowed eternal, a ribbon of life-giving blue cutting through the golden sands, indifferent to the machinations of men who claimed dominion over its banks. Its waters carried the whispered secrets of a thousand generations, the blood and tears of an empire that had stood since time immemorial. Amenhotep I sat upon the throne of Egypt, a man of thirty-five summers whose face already bore the weight of two decades of rule—his eyes holding the wisdom and weariness of one who had seen twice that many seasons pass.

In the grand throne room of Thebes, the golden light of Ra streamed through high windows of alabaster, catching the burnished gold of his regalia and setting the lapis lazuli of his ceremonial collar ablaze with celestial fire. The air hung heavy with the scent of frankincense and myrrh, the sacred smoke curling upward to the painted heavens that adorned the ceiling. The great pharaoh's face was placid, contemplative, as his wife Merytamun sat beside him, her slender fingers adorned with rings of lapis and gold, her eyes, outlined in perfect kohl, watching the nobles with quiet assessment.

Peace had settled over Egypt like the fertile silt that the great river deposited each season—a peace bought with blood and maintained with unwavering authority.

"Twenty-one years since my father's death," Amenhotep said, his voice carrying the authority that came from divine bloodlines, resonating across the polished floors of the audience chamber. "Twenty-one years since I, a mere boy of ten, assumed the throne of the Two Lands."

Merytamun nodded, her kohled eyes reflecting wisdom beyond her years, the corner of her mouth lifting in a smile that spoke of shared memories. "And Egypt has prospered under your steady hand, my husband. The granaries overflow, the temples rise ever higher, and our enemies bow their heads in submission."

The assembled court murmured their agreement; heads bowed in deference to their god-king. Yet beneath the veneer of unity, currents of ambition swirled like hidden whirlpools in the seemingly placid waters of the Nile. For the gods are fickle in their favor, and the peace of Egypt would soon know upheaval.

Commander Thutmose strode into the royal palace, his bronzed body bearing the scars of countless battles like hieroglyphs telling the story of his valor. His muscled frame moved with the fluid grace of a desert predator, each step calculated and confident. The royal guards stiffened as he passed, recognizing in him a natural authority that commanded respect beyond his station. Though merely a military leader, he carried himself with the quiet confidence of a man destined for greater things—a destiny written in the stars long before his birth.

Fresh from the southern campaigns, the dust of Nubian gold mines still clung to his sandals, and the screams of conquered chieftains still echoed in his dreams. He had seen the fury in their eyes as Egyptian chains bound their wrists—a fury that would burn across generations, waiting for the right moment to consume everything Thutmose held dear. The commander dismissed such concerns; after all, what could broken slaves do against the might of Egypt? But destiny has a way of using the broken to humble the mighty.

Behind him trailed his two wives, as different as the desert from the delta, yet each formidable in her own right.

Mutnofret, now his secondary wife, moved with calculated grace, her obsidian eyes ever watchful, ever scheming. Her beauty had not faded with the years but had instead transformed into something more dangerous—a weapon honed by experience and ambition. The gold beads in her elaborate wig clicked softly with each step, a sound like the warning rattle of a cobra preparing to strike. Beside her walked their sons, Wadjmose and Amenmose, twenty-seven and twenty-five respectively, both bearing their father's strong features and warrior's physique. They moved with the assurance of men who had never known want, their eyes hungrily absorbing the opulence of the palace they might one day rule.

But it was not her legitimate sons who occupied Mutnofret's thoughts as she entered the throne room. Hidden among the temple workers, disguised as just another Egyptian architect, was the child she had pulled from the river reeds twenty-nine years ago. The Hebrew infant whose very existence defied every prophecy and threatened every throne in Egypt. She had raised him as her own, loved him as fiercely as any mother, and now she must protect him from the very man who shared her bed. For Mutnofret knew something that would chill the blood of every Egyptian noble: the child of prophecy was not coming to destroy Egypt—he was already here, building temples to honor gods who had marked him for an entirely different purpose.

His chief wife, Queen Ahmose, possessed a delicate beauty that belied her ambition. Where Mutnofret was fire, Ahmose was water—seemingly yielding yet ultimately reshaping everything she touched. Her face, heart-shaped and serene, revealed nothing of her thoughts as she walked half a step behind her husband, her linen gown whispering against the stone floor. At her side was their daughter, Hatshepsut, barely twenty, yet with eyes that revealed an intelligence that would one day challenge the very foundations of Egyptian rule. The girl's slender frame carried itself with unusual dignity, her gaze direct and assessing, noting everything while seeming to note nothing.

The rivalry between the two branches of Thutmose's family crackled in the air like lightning before a desert storm. Ahmose's pale beauty had won her the position of Great Royal Wife, relegating Mutnofret to secondary status—a humiliation that burned in the older woman's breast like molten gold. But Mutnofret possessed something Ahmose did not: sons who could inherit the throne, and a secret that could destroy Egypt itself. The game between them was played with smiles and courtesies, but the stakes were measured in royal blood and the survival of dynasties.

Thutmose bowed before Pharaoh, his military bearing evident even in this gesture of subservience. The movement was precise, respectful yet somehow conveying that this was a man unaccustomed to bending his neck to anyone. "My king," he said, his voice deep and resonant in the hushed chamber, "I bring news from the eastern frontier."

Amenhotep leaned forward slightly, the weight of the double crown momentarily evident in the tightening around his eyes. "Speak, Commander. What word from our borders?"

"The Mitanni grow restless, Divine One. Their raiders test our defenses, probing for weakness. They have yet to find any." A ghost of a smile crossed Thutmose's weathered face, pride in his men evident in his stance.

The Pharaoh nodded slowly, fingers tapping thoughtfully against the arm of his throne. "And what would you suggest, Commander?"

"A show of force, Majesty. Nothing more is needed. The sight of Egyptian standards on their horizon will remind them of their place." Thutmose's words carried the confidence of a man who had never known defeat, whose tactical brilliance had expanded Egypt's borders farther than any commander before him.

From her position beside the throne, Merytamun watched the exchange with keen interest, noting the subtle shift in the court's attention—how the nobles' eyes had moved from Pharaoh to Commander, drawn like iron filings to a lodestone. Her slender fingers tightened imperceptibly on the armrest of her chair.

In the shadow of the Temple of Karnak, where massive stone columns rose like the trunks of primeval trees to support a roof that seemed to touch the very heavens themselves, Moses walked with purpose, his stride that of a man comfortable in his own authority. The sandals on his feet, crafted from the finest leather, made little sound on the sacred flagstones. At twenty-nine, his body had been honed by rigorous training, muscles moving fluidly beneath skin bronzed by the Egyptian sun. His mind had been equally sharpened by years of study under the chief architect Ineni, learning the ancient principles of construction that had raised monuments to challenge eternity.

Yet for all his Egyptian education and bearing, something indefinable marked him as different. Perhaps it was the way he paused before certain hieroglyphs, as if ancestral memories stirred in his blood. Perhaps it was how his eyes lingered on the depictions of Hebrew slaves in the temple friezes, seeing not just decoration but the faces of his true people. He walked as an Egyptian prince, but his soul carried the weight of four hundred years of bondage, and destiny waited in the shadows like a patient hunter.

The priests and acolytes bowed slightly as he passed, acknowledging his position while their eyes held the reservation always shown to one not fully of Egyptian blood. Moses had learned to ignore such looks, focusing instead on the work that gave his life meaning—the creation of beauty that would outlast all who beheld it.

But tonight was different. Tonight, the High Priest of Amun-Ra had cast the sacred lots, and the bone tablets had fallen in a pattern that made the old man's hands tremble. The signs spoke of transformation and destruction, of a deliverer who would rise from among the Egyptians themselves to lead their slaves to freedom. As Moses passed beneath the painted gaze of Pharaoh's portrait, the priest clutched his amulets and whispered prayers to gods who might already have chosen their champion.

Mutnofret found him there, her approach silent as a desert serpent, perfumed oils announcing her presence a moment before her voice. "You have grown strong, Moses," she said, her tone carrying both approval and calculation. The late afternoon light caught the gold thread in her gown, setting it ablaze against the rich blue linen.

Her heart constricted as she looked upon him—this young man who had been more son to her than her own flesh and blood. She remembered the morning twenty-nine years ago when her servant had brought her a basket from the reeds, how the infant within had looked up at her with eyes that seemed to hold ancient wisdom. She had known then, in the way that mothers know things that cannot be explained, that this child would reshape the world. Now, seeing him grown into a man of power and intelligence, she felt the bitter joy of a woman who had raised a lion cub only to watch it become a creature too wild and dangerous for captivity.

He turned, his eyes narrowing slightly at her presence. The woman had always unsettled him, though he had never been able to articulate precisely why. Perhaps it was the way her smile never quite reached her eyes, or how she seemed to assess everyone as either tool or obstacle. "Lady Mutnofret. What brings you to Karnak this day? Surely not devotion to the gods."

A laugh escaped her, genuine amusement sparking in her eyes at his boldness. "You still lack the proper Egyptian reverence, Hebrew. Perhaps that is why I find your company refreshing." She moved closer, the scent of lotus and myrrh enveloping him. "Change is coming," she said, her gaze sweeping over the massive columns reaching toward the heavens. "Amenhotep's health wanes. The physicians whisper of shadows in his water, darkness growing in his liver. My husband will soon rise to power."

The words hung between them like an executioner's blade. Mutnofret had spent sleepless nights pacing her chambers, torn between loyalty to her husband and love for her foster son. She knew Thutmose's suspicious nature, how he saw threats in every shadow and enemies behind every smile. When he became pharaoh, his paranoia would grow tenfold, and Moses—foreign-born, beloved by the people, touched by prophecy— would become a target too tempting to ignore. She had to make Moses understand the danger without revealing the full truth: that she had saved him once from the waters of the Nile, and now she must save him from the man who shared her bed.

Moses remained silent, sensing the unspoken warning beneath her words. The sun cast long shadows across the temple grounds, turning the familiar contours of stone into something alien and foreboding.

"You have found contentment under Ineni's tutelage," she continued, trailing slender fingers along the hieroglyphs carved into a nearby column. "Your designs for the new western temple complex have impressed even the high priests. But a storm approaches, Moses. When Amenhotep falls, the court will fracture like a poorly fired clay vessel. Those without clear allegiances will be swept away in the flood."

"And you suggest I declare such allegiance now?" Moses asked, watching her carefully. "Pledge myself to Thutmose before Amenhotep's body is cold?"

Mutnofret's eyes flashed with warning. "Guard your tongue, architect. Walls have ears, and Amenhotep still draws breath." She glanced around before continuing in a lower voice. "When the time comes, remain in the shadows. Make yourself useful but not essential. There are... prophecies about you that make certain powerful men uneasy."

The truth she could not speak burned in her throat like swallowed fire. The prophecies did not just make men uneasy—they spoke of plagues that would ravage Egypt, of firstborn sons dying in the night, of the Nile turning to blood. They spoke of a Hebrew deliverer who would humble pharaohs and lead multitudes into the wilderness. And every description, every divine sign, pointed to the young man standing before her—the child she had pulled from the reeds and raised as her own. She loved him too much to tell him his destiny, and she feared for Egypt too much to let that destiny unfold unchallenged.

"Prophecies?" Moses frowned. "What nonsense is this?"

"Not nonsense to those who believe." Mutnofret's gaze bore into him with sudden intensity. "Remember your origins, Moses. Not all see your adoption by the royal house as a blessing. Some see it as an ill omen—a Hebrew raised to power in the heart of Egypt."

Before Moses could respond, she turned away, the dismissal clear in her bearing. "Consider yourself warned, son of the river. The winds of change show favor to no man, regardless of how firmly he believes his feet are planted."

As she walked away, Mutnofret's composed facade cracked just enough to reveal the anguish beneath. She had done what she could—planted the seeds of caution that might keep him alive when the storm broke. But she knew, with the terrible certainty of a mother's heart, that all her warnings and machinations would prove futile. The God of the Hebrews had marked Moses for something far greater and more terrible than the comfortable life of an Egyptian architect. Soon, very soon, that God would call His servant home, and when He did, the very foundations of Egypt would tremble.

1493BC - Thebes

The year came with the fury of the khamsin winds, sweeping away the old order with invisible yet irresistible force. The desert wind howled through the streets of Thebes, sending commoners scurrying for shelter and whipping sand against the walls of palaces as if to remind even the mightiest that nature respected no borders.

Amenhotep's death followed swiftly after his beloved Merytamun passed into the afterlife. Their royal barges, laden with treasures to serve them in the next world, floated down the Nile like twin flames, visible for miles in the gathering dusk. The court whispered that his heart had simply stopped beating when hers did, unwilling to continue without her presence—a romantic notion that few truly believed but many repeated, preferring it to darker rumors of poisoned wine and political machinations.

A Commoner became King

In the golden Hall of Coronation, where light reflected from a thousand polished surfaces to create an otherworldly glow, Thutmose stood tall as the priests anointed him, transforming the soldier into Pharaoh Thutmose I. The double crown of Upper and Lower Egypt— the white crown nested within the red—settled upon his head as though it had been crafted for him alone, the weight of five thousand years of tradition resting on his brow.

"Behold the living Horus!" intoned the High Priest of Amun, his voice carrying to the farthest corners of the vast hall. "Son of Ra, Chosen of the Gods, Lord of the Two Lands! Thutmose, first of his name, Mighty Bull, Beloved of Ma'at!"

The assembled nobility prostrated themselves as one, foreheads touching the cool stone floor in submission to their new god-king. The smell of sacred oils and burnt offerings hung heavy in the air, mingling with the sweat of hundreds of bodies packed tight in ceremonial finery.

But one figure did not prostrate himself completely. Hidden among the temple architects and craftsmen, Moses bowed his head just enough to avoid notice while his mind reeled with the implications of this moment. The man being crowned pharaoh was the husband of the woman who had saved his life, raised him, loved him—and who now feared for his very existence. As the crowd chanted Thutmose's names and titles, Moses felt the weight of destiny settling on his shoulders like a mantle he could not remove.

Queen Ahmose watched with undisguised pride, her position as Great Royal Wife secured at last after years as the second, lesser spouse. Her face, carefully composed into a mask of serene dignity, could not entirely hide the triumph that shone in her eyes as she knelt behind her husband, ready to rise with him into legend.

Behind her stood Hatshepsut, her young face already showing the determination that would mark her reign. The girl's gaze was fixed not on her father but on the crown he now wore, her expression one of assessment rather than awe, as if measuring the weight she herself might one day bear.

And behind them both, Thutmose's two sons observed the ceremony, their futures seemingly assured by their father's ascension. Wadjmose, as firstborn, stood slightly forward, his chest swelling with pride and anticipation. Amenmose, ever in his brother's shadow, watched with more reserved emotions, his eyes occasionally drifting to where the court officials stood, mentally noting who showed genuine loyalty and who merely mouthed the words.

Neither son noticed their mother's absence from the front ranks of celebration. Mutnofret had positioned herself where she could watch Moses without drawing attention, her heart breaking as she saw the moment of recognition cross his features. Soon—perhaps within days— she would have to choose between the man she had married and the son she had saved. The choice would destroy her, but she had made it long ago on the banks of the Nile when she pulled a basket from the reeds and looked into the eyes of destiny itself.

Mutnofret, relegated to the position of lesser wife—a demotion that would have broken a weaker woman—maintained her composure even as her status diminished. She knelt with perfect form, her face a study in appropriate reverence. Her eyes, however, revealed calculations and schemes that would shape the destiny of the Two Lands. For Mutnofret had not raised her sons to accept second place, and the game of dynasties was only beginning.

But her schemes now served a different purpose than mere ambition. Every move she made, every alliance she forged, every secret she uncovered was directed toward a single goal: keeping Moses alive long enough to fulfill whatever destiny the gods had planned for him. She had become a player in a game whose rules she barely understood, fighting to protect a piece whose true value would only be revealed when the final moves were played.

In the quiet gardens of the royal palace, where artificially diverted channels of the Nile created a paradise of lotus blossoms and papyrus reeds, Moses found solitude to practice with his sword. The blade flashed in the sunlight as he moved through the ancient fighting forms, his body responding with the precision that came from years of disciplined training.

Each movement of the bronze blade seemed to cut through more than air—it sliced through the comfortable illusions that had sustained him throughout his privileged youth. With every thrust and parry, Moses felt the Egyptian identity he had worn like fine linen beginning to fray at the edges, revealing something darker and more primal underneath. He was no longer simply practicing sword forms; he was preparing for a war he couldn't yet see, against enemies he couldn't yet name.

Sweat gleamed on his muscled torso, running in rivulets down skin darkened by the sun to nearly the same shade as any native Egyptian. Only the slight curl of his black hair and certain angles of his face hinted at foreign origins—features that had grown more pronounced as childhood softness gave way to adult definition.

"You strike like a true Egyptian warrior," Mutnofret commented, watching him from beneath the shade of a sycamore tree. She had approached without sound, a skill she had perfected through years of navigating court intrigues.

Moses lowered his blade, using a linen cloth to wipe the sweat from his brow. His breathing, barely elevated by the exertion, returned to normal as he regarded her with cautious eyes. "Yet I am not truly one of you, am I? The priests have never let me forget my Hebrew blood."

The words struck Mutnofret like physical blows. She had spent twenty-nine years trying to make him forget those very origins, weaving him so thoroughly into Egyptian society that no one—including Moses himself—would ever question his place among them. But blood calls to blood, and the God of his fathers was stronger than all her careful preparations.

A sad smile played across Mutnofret's lips, an expression that might have seemed genuine to one who knew her less well. "Blood matters less than loyalty," she replied, her voice dropping to ensure no servants overheard their conversation. The gentle splash of water from a nearby fountain provided cover for their words. "But I did not seek you out to discuss philosophy."

Moses sheathed his sword, the bronze blade sliding home with a metallic whisper. He waited, knowing that Mutnofret never spoke without purpose, never sought anyone out unless she stood to gain something from the encounter.

"Thutmose I sees threats in every shadow since taking the throne," she said, moving closer, her eyes scanning the garden for any unwelcome observers. "It is the way of new kings, especially those who have risen from common stock. The priests still whisper of prophecies regarding you—that you will bring destruction to Egypt."

"I have shown nothing but loyalty to this land," Moses protested, indignation flaring in his chest. "I have designed temples to honor its gods, trained with its armies, learned its history and laws—"

Even as he spoke the words, Moses felt their hollow ring. Loyalty? To gods who accepted the blood of Hebrew slaves as sacrifice? To laws that condemned his birth people to endless bondage? To an army that had crushed the freedom of a dozen nations? The loyalty he claimed felt suddenly like chains around his soul, and for the first time in his adult life, he wondered what he truly owed to Egypt.

"Nevertheless," Mutnofret continued, cutting him off with a raised hand, "you would be wise to make yourself scarce. Keep to the temples, to your studies. Become invisible until Thutmose's paranoia subsides." Her voice softened, taking on an almost maternal tone that sat strangely on her lips. "You may have been raised in the palace, Moses, but you are not of royal blood. You have no powerful family to protect you if accusations are made."

The lie burned her throat as she spoke it. He did have powerful family—she was his family; had been since the moment she chose to save him rather than let the Nile claim him. But that protection came at a price she was no longer sure she could pay. Protecting Moses might mean betraying Thutmose, and betraying Thutmose would mean death—not just for her, but for her sons as well. The mathematics of survival had become too complex for easy solutions.

Moses's jaw tightened, the muscles clenching visibly beneath his skin. "You're telling me to hide."

"I'm telling you to survive," Mutnofret replied, her eyes reflecting genuine concern that surprised him. "For all our sakes." She reached out, placing a hand on his arm—a gesture so uncharacteristic that it gave her words added weight. "There are storms coming, Moses. Even I cannot see their full shape, but I know they approach. When they break, only those firmly anchored will withstand the deluge."

As she departed, her linen gown whispering across the manicured grass, Moses stood in the fading light, a man caught between worlds. The sword at his hip and the architectural plans in his chambers represented the duality of his existence—warrior and builder, destroyer and creator, Egyptian and Hebrew. Unaware that the gods had already set his feet upon a path that would change the course of history, he watched the sun sink toward the western horizon, casting long shadows across the garden like the fingers of fate reaching out to claim him.

The game of gods and pharaohs was about to begin in earnest, and the fate of nations hung in the balance.

Chapter 21 - Double Tragedy

1492 BC Tragedy in Nubia

The blood-red sun hung low over the churning waters of the Nile, casting long, ominous shadows across the rippling surface as Pharaoh Thutmose I's war fleet sliced through the current, heading south toward Nubia. The year 1492 BC marked the beginning of a campaign that would cement his legend—and herald his greatest sorrows.

The air was thick with the scent of river water mingled with the sweat of oarsmen, their muscled backs glistening as they drove the vessels forward with metronomic precision. Standing at the prow of the lead vessel, a magnificent cedar-wood craft adorned with gilded hieroglyphs proclaiming the glory of Egypt, Thutmose cut an imposing figure despite his advancing years. His weathered face, like leather tanned in the desert sun and lined by decades of military campaigns, was set in grim determination. The golden cobra on his war helm caught the dying light, throwing sinister, dancing shadows across the polished deck.

"The Nubians grow bold again," he said to his son Wadjmose, who stood beside him, eager for his first taste of true battle. The Pharaoh's voice carried across the water like a lion's rumble, commanding even the river birds to silence.

"They mistake change for weakness," Wadjmose replied, his hand resting on the hilt of his bronze sword. At twenty-eight, he had grown into a formidable warrior with broad shoulders and keen eyes that missed nothing. His polished bronze breastplate gleamed in the fading light, etched with scenes of hunting lions. Yet battlefield experience eluded him still—a fact that gnawed at his pride like hunger. "Today we correct their error."

Thutmose nodded, studying his firstborn with a mixture of pride and concern. The boy had his mother's high cheekbones but his father's fierce brow. "Egypt's enemies are eternal, my son. Each generation must teach them anew the price of defiance." He clasped Wadjmose's shoulder, feeling solid muscle beneath the ceremonial cloak. "Blood-written lessons endure longest."

Behind them, twenty vessels stretched across the breadth of the Nile, their sails furled as oarsmen took over for the journey upriver. Egypt's finest warriors filled the ships—men trained since boyhood in war's harsh arts, their bodies hardened by desert campaigns and their loyalty unwavering. Spears and shields gleamed in neat rows along the decks, while archers protected their bowstrings from the river's humidity with practiced care.

The rhythmic beat of war drums pulsed through the air, keeping time for the oarsmen and announcing to all that Egypt's might was on the move. As night fell, torches blazed along each gunwale, transforming the fleet into a river of fire snaking through the darkness.

In his private cabin, Thutmose pored over papyrus maps, marking known Nubian strongholds with small obsidian markers. "Their main force will be here," he told his commanders, tapping a spot near the second cataract. "But we must guard against ambush in these narrow passages." His finger traced the river's contours where it squeezed between towering cliffs.

Ahmose, his grizzled veteran commander whose body bore scars from a dozen campaigns, nodded gravely. "Scouts report they've gathered warriors from as far south as Kush. They mean to make a stand, my Pharaoh."

"Let them," Thutmose replied, his eyes glittering like polished jet in the lamplight. "It saves us hunting them down one by one."

The Nubian campaign began with desert storm fury. Egyptian forces swept through the borderlands, meeting fierce resistance at every turn. The Nubians fought with desperate homeland fervor—tall, ebony warriors whose spears found gaps in Egyptian armor and whose terrain knowledge gave them fleeting advantages. But Egyptian discipline and superior weaponry gradually turned the tide.

Villages burned, their smoke rising like black serpents into the cloudless sky. The screams of the defeated mingled with victorious battle cries, a cacophony that followed the advancing army like an invisible shadow.

On the third day, as Egyptian forces pressed toward the Nubian stronghold—a fortress of mud brick and stone perched on a hill overlooking a river bend—disaster struck. Wadjmose, burning to prove himself worthy of royal blood, led a charge against the enemy's right flank. His war chariot thundered across rocky ground, the prince standing tall and fearless as he releases arrows with deadly accuracy. His personal guard followed, their battle cries rising above combat's din.

The initial assault shattered the Nubian lines, driving them back in disarray. Warriors scattered before the prince's advance, their formations crumbling under Egyptian precision. Victory seemed assured—until hidden Nubian archers rose from concealment among the rocks and sparse vegetation dotting the hillside.

"Shields!" Wadjmose shouted, but his warning came too late.

The air darkened with arrows, obsidian tips glinting briefly before finding their marks. Before Egyptian shields could rise, three shafts struck Wadjmose's chest, the impact hurling him backward from his chariot. His body hit the ground with terrible finality, blood blooming like crimson flowers across his ornamented breastplate.

From his command position atop a nearby rise, Thutmose watched in horror. The world slowed as his son fell, the prince's gold-inlaid armor gleaming in harsh sunlight. A roar tore from the Pharaoh's throat— primal, scarcely human in its anguish.

"To me!" he bellowed, his voice carrying like thunder across the battlefield. "To your Pharaoh!"

Egyptian forces rallied to his cry, ranks closing around their leader as he led a counterattack so ferocious the Nubians broke and fled. Thutmose himself claimed seven lives with his bronze khopesh, its curved edge becoming slick with blood as he carved a path of vengeance through enemy ranks. Where his sword fell, death followed, and surviving Nubians would later speak of how his eyes had glowed with Sekhmet's wrath.

By nightfall, the battle was won, but at a cost beyond measure. Thutmose knelt beside his son's body, now washed clean of blood and battle grime. The prince's wounds had been packed with fragrant herbs, his eyes closed and hands placed carefully on his chest. Around them, his army's victory celebrations seemed distant, hollow mockery.

"He died a warrior's death," Ahmose offered, standing at respectful distance despite his own bandaged wounds.

"He died before his time," Thutmose replied, his voice like granite grinding against granite. He touched his son's cold forehead with surprising gentleness, brushing away a strand of hair. "The Nubians will pay for each drop of his blood."

Night winds carried death's scent and distant jackal howls. In his tent, Thutmose sat alone with untouched wine, staring into darkness as he contemplated his loss. The pharaoh's mantle had never felt heavier.

Thutmose's vengeance was swift and terrible. The captured Nubian ruler, brought before him in chains, stood proud despite his wounds, dark eyes defiant as he faced his conqueror.

"You fought well," Thutmose acknowledged, studying the enemy who had cost him so dearly. "But you chose the wrong foe."

"Egypt has always been our enemy," the Nubian replied steadily. "Our fathers fought yours, and our sons would have fought your sons. Such is the way of things."

"Not anymore," Thutmose said coldly. "Your sons will remember this day and tremble at the thought of crossing our border."

The execution came at dawn, without ceremony. By Thutmose's command, the body was bound to his flagship's prow—a grim trophy and warning to all who would challenge Egypt's might. The dead ruler's unseeing eyes stared back at the land he had failed to defend as the fleet began its journey north.

As the ships turned downriver toward Thebes, Thutmose stood silent at the helm, victory turned to ashes. The Nile, indifferent to human sorrows, carried them homeward, its waters reflecting the harsh blue of cloudless sky. Behind him, in the hold, lay his son's body, prepared with preservation's first rites—beginning the elaborate rituals that would guide him to the afterlife.

In night's silent watches, when only helmsman and sentries remained awake, Thutmose would stand at the rail, watching stars wheel overhead and wondering if his son's ka now walked among them. The ache in his chest was physical—a hollowness no victory could fill.

1491 BC - Thebes

With Wadjmose gone, royal succession's burden fell heavily upon Amenmose's shoulders. The younger son, now twenty-six, found his responsibilities multiplied overnight. Where once he had enjoyed a second prince's freedom—hunting in the marshes or studying with priests—he now faced the intense scrutiny reserved for the heir to the Two Lands.

In the palace at Thebes, Amenmose stood before empire maps, studying territories his father had recently subjugated. Lamplight cast long shadows across the papyri, making Egypt's boundaries seem to pulse and shift before his eyes. His mother Mutnofret watched from the shadows, her dark eyes missing nothing.

"Your father expects the Nubian tribute reports reviewed by morning," she said, moving to stand beside him. Her voice was soft but carried command's unmistakable steel. Though she wore mourning's simple white linen, her bearing remained regal, her posture straight as a spear.

Amenmose nodded, weariness etched on his handsome features. Unlike his brother, who had inherited their father's solid build, Amenmose was slender and scholarly, with sensitive hands better suited to writing instruments than weapons. "And the Karnak temple plans require approval, as does appointing a new overseer for the gold mines." He sighed, running a hand through his short-cropped hair. "I never sought this, mother. Not at such a price."

Mutnofret placed a hand on his arm, her touch gentle but her eyes calculating as a merchant weighing gold. "Few men worthy of power actively seek it, my son. The gods thrust it upon them, recognizing strength even when we ourselves cannot." She turned his face toward hers, studying him as if seeing him anew. "You possess gifts your brother lacked—a quick mind, understanding of the people. Egypt needs these qualities as much as it needs warriors."

Amenmose wanted to believe her, but doubt gnawed at him like desert wind eroding stone. His father had always favored Wadjmose, the son who shared his passion for war and conquest. How would he view this scholarly second son who preferred debate to battle?

"The priests say omens favor us," Mutnofret continued, sensing his unease. "The Nile will flood abundantly this year, bringing rich soil for planting. Take it as a sign your rule will bring prosperity."

"If I live to rule at all," Amenmose murmured, his eyes returning to the map and the vast territory his father had conquered—territory that must now be managed, administered, kept loyal to the crown.

His mother's calculating gaze sharpened. "You doubt your father's protection?"

"I doubt my worthiness of it." The admission came quietly, barely audible above the oil lamps' flickering flames.

"Then prove it to yourself," she said simply. "And to him."

1489 BC - Tragedy in Syria

Two years passed, and fate had not finished testing Pharaoh Thutmose I. Grief's scars had begun healing, but the wound remained— a constant ache beneath rule's daily business. Thutmose had thrown himself into work, personally overseeing monuments to commemorate his victories and ensure his immortality. But in quiet moments, his firstborn's ghost would return to haunt him.

The Syrian expedition had been organized to distract the pharaoh from lingering grief—a chance to enjoy pursuits of his younger days before the Double Crown's weight had settled on his brow. Amenmose had insisted on joining, driven by his need to prove himself worthy in his father's eyes, despite his scholarly nature making him better suited to administration than adventure.

The Syrian desert bloomed in rare beauty that spring, wildflowers carpeting valleys between rugged hills, their colors vibrant against the tawny backdrop of sand and stone. Game was plentiful—gazelle, ibex, and the prized Syrian elephant, larger than its African counterpart and highly valued for its ivory.

The Syrian elephant was magnificent, its tusks gleaming ivory in morning light as it crashed through undergrowth, sending birds scattering into cloudless sky. Thutmose, despite his fifty years, led the hunting party with vigor of a man half his age, determined to claim the trophy himself. He carried a specially designed spear with a bronze head broad enough to penetrate the elephant's thick hide.

"There, my Pharaoh!" called one of the beaters, pointing where vegetation swayed with the great beast's passage.

Thutmose urged his horse forward, the hunt's excitement burning through his veins like fire. For these brief moments, rule's burdens fell away, and he was simply a man pitting courage and skill against a worthy opponent. The elephant crashed through a thicket ahead, momentarily visible as it crossed a small clearing.

But as they burst into the clearing, the elephant, instead of continuing its flight, turned to face its pursuers. With a trumpeting cry that shook the very air, it charged.

Amenmose spurred his mount forward, spear raised high, determination etched on his young face. Here, finally, was his chance to prove himself worthy of royal blood—to show his warrior father that a scholar could also be brave.

"Fall back!" Thutmose screamed, but his words were lost in the elephant's furious trumpeting.

The massive beast's charge was impossibly swift. Amenmose's spear found its mark in the elephant's shoulder but did nothing to slow its advance. In one terrible moment, the prince's horse reared in panic, throwing its rider directly into the elephant's path.

Thutmose's bodyguards surged forward with shields and spears, but they were too late. The elephant's massive foot came down upon Amenmose's chest with sickening force. Then its trunk wrapped around the prince's broken body, flinging him through the air like a discarded doll.

When Thutmose reached his son, Amenmose's eyes were still open, staring sightlessly at the azure sky. Blood trickled from his mouth; his limbs splayed at unnatural angles. The pharaoh fell to his knees, clutching his son's shattered body to his chest, a wail of anguish tearing from his throat.

The royal hunt, meant to bring glory, had instead delivered devastation. As the elephant was finally brought down by a hail of spears, Thutmose cared nothing for the trophy. This hunt's price had been far too high.

When Thutmose returned to Thebes, he was a man transformed. Grief had hollowed his once-robust frame, turning his hair white and etching deep lines into his face. In a span of two years, he had lost both sons—his bloodline's future. The dynasty he had fought to establish now balanced on the slenderest thread. As his litter bearers carried him through Thebes' streets, crowds that gathered to welcome their Pharaoh home fell silent at the sight of him, their jubilation turning to whispered concerns.

Thutmose knew, with a battlefield veteran's certainty, that his own time grew short. The succession question, once settled so comfortably with two strong sons in line for the throne, now loomed before him like a chasm.

In the great hall of the palace, Hatshepsut stood alone before her father's throne. At twenty-two, she possessed regal bearing that belied her years, her slender figure draped in finest linen, her dark eyes reflecting an intelligence that had only grown sharper with time. Though she wore youth's simple side-lock, there was nothing childlike in her posture or expression as she awaited her father's arrival.

The hall fell silent as Thutmose entered, leaning heavily on a cedar staff inlaid with gold. His chamberlain began announcing him with the traditional litany of titles, but the Pharaoh waved the man to silence before he could finish.

"My daughter," Thutmose said, his voice rough with emotion. "You alone remain to me now."

Hatshepsut approached and knelt before him, taking his weathered hands in hers. The contrast was stark—her smooth, youthful skin against his age-spotted flesh, her strength against his newfound frailty. Yet there was similarity too, in the set of their jaws, the keen assessment in their eyes.

"I am here, father. I am of your blood. Thutmose's line will not end while I draw breath." Her voice carried clearly in the vast chamber, confident and measured.

For a long moment, father and daughter regarded each other, silent understanding passing between them. In her face, Thutmose saw echoes of his mother—a woman of uncommon courage who had guided Egypt through troubled times before his own reign began. Perhaps the gods, in their mysterious wisdom, had been preparing this moment all along.

In that moment, destiny's seeds were sown—seeds that would one day flower into one of Egypt's most remarkable reigns. But such revelations belonged to the future. For now, Egypt mourned with its pharaoh, and the great river flowed on, indifferent to mortal triumphs and tragedies, carrying the Two Lands' hopes and sorrows toward an uncertain horizon.

As the sun set over Thebes, painting limestone temples in shades of fire and gold, Thutmose I placed his hand on his daughter's head in blessing. The gesture was witnessed by court officials who had gathered at discreet distance, their faces carefully neutral as they contemplated the implications of what they saw.

"You are your grandfather's daughter," Thutmose said quietly, for her ears alone. "He would be proud to see you now, as I am."

Hatshepsut bowed her head, accepting the weight of his words and all they implied. "I will not fail you," she promised. "Nor Egypt."

As stars began appearing in the darkening sky, visible through the audience chamber's high windows, the ancient cycle of death and renewal continued its eternal dance. Egypt endured, as it had for thousands of years, through flood and drought, through war and peace, through the reigns of pharaohs both mighty and weak. The Two Lands had survived worse crises than losing two princes, and would survive this one as well.

But that night, in the royal palace's private chambers, a father grieved for his sons, and a daughter contemplated a future none had prepared her for. And somewhere in Egypt's vastness, unknown to either of them, a man called Moses pursued his quiet studies, unaware that fate would soon draw him back into the world of power and conflict he had left behind.

Chapter 22 - The Nubian Deception

June 1483 BC - Nubia, 5th Cataract

The year dawned hot and merciless over the southern lands beyond the fifth cataract. The sun rose like a ball of molten copper, its fierce rays striking the parched earth with malevolent intensity. In a mud-brick stronghold nestled among the arid hills, the Nubian chieftains gathered in council, their faces etched with the bitter memory of defeat—not just any defeat, but a humiliation that had festered in their souls for nine long years.

The council chamber, hewn partially into living rock and partially built of mud-brick baked hard as iron under the relentless southern sun, offered little relief from the heat. Sweat glistened on dark skin as the chieftains arranged themselves on woven reed mats around a central fire pit where flames danced low despite the day's heat—a sacred tradition never abandoned, regardless of discomfort.

Nine years had passed since Pharaoh Thutmose I had crushed their forces, slaying their leader with his own hand and binding his corpse to the prow of an Egyptian warship. The defeated king's body had been displayed as a grim trophy all the way down the Nile, his skin blackening in the sun, his open eyes pecked empty by carrion birds—a deliberate desecration that denied him proper passage to the afterlife. Nine years of nursing hatred, of rebuilding strength, of bitter prayers to dark gods, of waiting for the perfect moment to strike. Nine years of watching their children grow up as refugees in their own land, their women weeping over graves that held no bodies because their men had been fed to the crocodiles of the sacred river.

That moment, they believed, had finally arrived.

"The reports from our spies cannot be disputed," said Zagwe, the eldest of the chieftains, his body lean and scarred from countless battles. His chest, bare above a leopard-skin kilt, bore the ritualistic markings of forty campaigns, each scar a testament to survival. A heavy gold collar rested on his collarbone; the only symbol of his status he deemed worthy to wear. "The great Thutmose grows frail. His limbs tremble when he thinks none are watching. The strength that once flowed through him like the Nile at flood has begun to ebb. But more importantly, his pride remains as fierce as ever."

Around the fire pit, faces darkened with anticipation gleamed in the flickering light. Men nodded, some fingering the hilts of their daggers, others clutching amulets blessed by tribal shamans to grant them victory in the coming conflict. The air grew thick with the scent of bodies and ambition.

"And both his sons lie in the House of Death," added Makeda, the only woman among them. Unlike the warriors with their naked torsos and battle scars, she wore a simple linen robe dyed with indigo, her wrists heavy with copper bracelets that clinked softly when she moved her hands in emphasis. Her skin was the color of polished ebony, stretched taut over high cheekbones. Her authority came not from physical strength but from the keen insights that had saved their people more than once. "Egypt is vulnerable as it has not been in a generation. The Hebrew slaves grow restless in their bondage, and whispers of rebellion drift through the workers' quarters like smoke through reed huts."

Her dark eyes, lined with kohl in the Egyptian fashion—a deliberate choice that reminded them all of who their enemy was—swept the assembled warriors. Some avoided her gaze, unsettled by a woman's presence in war council, but none dared challenge her right to speak. She had earned that right with a wisdom that had proven true too often to ignore.

The youngest chieftain, Piankhi, leaned forward, his muscular frame tense with eagerness. Unlike the others who bore the marks of age and experience, his body was unmarred except for the ritual scarification that swirled across his chest and back in intricate patterns signifying his royal lineage. At twenty-five, he had never known defeat in battle, never tasted the bitterness of subjugation that had been his father's final meal.

"Then the time for vengeance has come," he declared, his voice rich and melodic despite the harshness of his words. "Let us gather our warriors and strike at the heart of Egypt! The blood of my father cries out from the muddy banks of the Nile where his spirit wanders, denied proper burial. I have dreamed of him every night for nine years, and always he points northward, toward the land of our enemies."

"Patience, young one," Zagwe cautioned, raising a weathered hand. The gold rings on his fingers caught the firelight as he gestured for calm. "Egypt is never truly vulnerable unless we make it so. We must be cunning as well as bold. The snake strikes not when it is hungry, but when its prey looks elsewhere."

He gestured to a man standing in the shadows, a figure so still and silent that some had forgotten his presence entirely. Nesuto stepped forward, the dim light revealing a face half-hidden behind an elaborate mask of woven reeds and feathers—the disguise that had allowed him to move undetected through Egyptian territory for months. He unrolled a papyrus stolen from an Egyptian courier, the material itself a luxury that few Nubians had ever touched. On it was drawn a detailed map of the Nile Valley from the first cataract to the delta, each fortress marked in red ochre, each town and temple noted with hieroglyphs that Nesuto had painstakingly learned to decipher.

"We have studied the old lion well," Zagwe declared, his finger tracing their planned route of attack. The nail was stained blue-black from a poison he had once survived—another mark of his indomitable will. "Thutmose values his throne above all else—above strategy, above wisdom, above the safety of his own kingdom. We will use this pride against him like a spear thrust through his ribs."

The plan unfolded with brutal simplicity, born from years of careful observation and intimate knowledge of their enemy's character. One force would push through the western desert to the Red Sea. When they reached the hidden cove, they would board four seaworthy vessels in that sheltered inlet. From there, they would sail north along the coast and strike at Memphis itself—not to conquer, but to threaten. To make enough noise, spill enough blood, burn enough granaries that word would race south to Thebes like wildfire before the wind.

"The beauty of striking Memphis," Zagwe continued, his eyes gleaming with satisfaction, "is that the old pharaoh cannot ignore it. He will not delegate such a threat to subordinates. His pride will demand that he will lead Egypt's finest warriors north to crush us personally, leaving Thebes with only a token guard—old men and boys playing at being soldiers."

"And the second blow?" asked Piankhi, studying the map with gleaming eyes, his fingers hovering over the parchment as if he could already feel the conquest beneath them. A single drop of sweat fell from his chin onto the map, marking a spot that Zagwe quickly wiped away.

Zagwe smiled, a predator's grin in the firelight that revealed teeth filed to points in the warrior tradition of his youth. "While Thutmose marches his armies six hundred miles north to Memphis—a journey of thirty days through desert heat that will exhaust even his strongest men—our main force will wait at Elephantine. When our spies confirm that Thebes lies undefended, we will strike like lightning at the true prize. Not Memphis with its mud-brick walls and sweating merchants, but Thebes with its temples full of gold, its treasuries bulging with tribute from a dozen conquered lands."

The council murmured approval, already imagining the glory and plunder that awaited them. Fingers traced the hilts of daggers, lips moved in silent prayers to ancestors and gods, eyes gleamed with visions of Egyptian women and gold.

Only Makeda remained silent, her dark eyes thoughtful, one hand absently caressing the amulet of ivory and obsidian that hung between her breasts—a talisman said to grant its wearer visions of what might come.

"Speak, wise one," Zagwe prompted, noticing her silence. His tone softened slightly, betraying the respect he held for her despite their occasional differences. "What troubles you about our plan?"

"I fear the unknown," she said simply, her voice carrying the weight of genuine concern rather than mere caution. "Thutmose has ruled long and is cunning despite his age. The lion may grow old, but it remembers how to kill. What weapons might he hold in reserve? What commanders may rise to meet us?"

She rose to her feet in a single fluid motion and moved to the map, her fingers tracing the hieroglyphs that marked Thebes. "My dreams have been troubled of late. I see a man I do not recognize standing between our people and victory. Not Thutmose, but someone younger, someone who carries Egypt in his blood but is not of Egypt. In my visions, he stands before the gates of Thebes with authority that comes not from birth but from something deeper—from the gods themselves, perhaps."

"His best commanders will march with him to Memphis," Piankhi scoffed, dismissing her concerns with a wave of his hand. The golden armband on his bicep gleamed as muscles flexed beneath his skin. "And his own sons are long dead. The old lion has lost his teeth. As for your dreams—perhaps they are merely the anxieties of one who has never held a spear in battle."

Makeda's eyes flashed dangerously, but she controlled her temper with practiced ease. "Perhaps," she conceded, her tone revealing nothing of the anger that briefly tightened her features. "But even toothless lions can be dangerous when cornered. And the gods sometimes raise up champions from the most unexpected places. I have seen this defender in my dreams standing beside me, his hand in mine, as if fate itself seeks to bind our destinies together."

Zagwe waved her concerns aside, though with more respect than Piankhi had shown. "Our plan is sound, and the time is now. The Egyptians have grown soft in their prosperity, while we have honed our strength in adversity. Their bodies are pampered with oils and perfumes, while ours are hardened by sun and wind and honest labor. Most importantly, we have learned to think as our enemy thinks, to use his strengths against him."

He rose to his feet, a signal that the council was concluded. Around his neck hung the severed thumb of the Egyptian commander who had once captured him—a grisly talisman that he would touch for luck before every battle. "In three days, we march. Let the Egyptians learn what it means to face the wrath of a patient enemy who has had nine years to plan their downfall."

As the chieftains dispersed, Makeda lingered before the map, her fingers tracing and retracing the route to Memphis. Something troubled her still—something beyond what she had revealed to the council. In her dreams, she had seen not just the unknown defender of Egypt, but herself standing beside him, her hand in his. More disturbing still, she had seen their peoples not as eternal enemies, but as allies against a darkness she could not yet name. It was this vision, more than any fear of defeat, that disturbed her waking thoughts.

What strange fate awaited them all on the banks of the distant Nile?

Two-pronged attack

The Nubian force designated to sail down the Red Sea departed first, their departure timed with the precision of a leopard's strike. Each man knew the stakes—failure meant not just death, but the obliteration of their people. Thutmose had been merciful after the last war only by the standards of absolute tyrants. Another rebellion would be met with genocide. It was victory or extinction now; there could be no middle ground. The road to Memphis laid before them like a path through the underworld, fraught with perils but leading to either glory or oblivion.

The main force, consisting of the most battle-hardened veterans under Zagwe's personal command, would wait twenty days before beginning their movement south to Elephantine. This delay was calculated with the cold precision of a chess master—long enough for the Memphis assault to fully commit the Egyptian response, but not so long that their enemies might suspect the deception.

From his command position at Elephantine, a hundred miles south of Thebes, Zagwe waited for the first phase of their campaign to unfold exactly as planned. The ancient trading post, with its granite quarries and strategic position at the first cataract, provided the perfect staging ground. Close enough to strike swiftly at Thebes once the trap was sprung, far enough south to avoid detection by Egyptian patrols, and positioned along trade routes that would provide early intelligence of any Egyptian troop movements.

Two of his most trusted spies had been dispatched northward with orders to observe and report on every movement in and around Thebes.

They carried with them trained hawks capable of covering the distance to Elephantine in a single day—a communication network that would give Zagwe the intelligence he needed to time his strike with devastating precision.

Zagwe lifted his gaze to the stars, finding the constellation that his people believed represented the Great Spear. Tonight, it hung directly over Egypt—an omen he took as favorable. At his side stood Makeda, summoned to his tent after the initial movements were set in motion.

"Are your dreams troubled still?" he asked her, not turning from his contemplation of the night sky.

"They are," she admitted, her voice low. "I see victory and defeat intertwined, like serpents mating. I cannot tell which will devour the other. But I also see something else—a convergence of destinies that will reshape both our peoples."

Zagwe finally looked at her, his face solemn in the lamplight. "Then we must ensure that our serpent strikes first and true. The old pharaoh's pride will be his undoing, and Egypt's gold will buy us a new future for our children."

In the distance, a night bird called—the same cry that would signal the beginning of their final assault on the jewel of Upper Egypt.

Chapter 23 - Hidden Prince Arise

July 1483 BC Thebes

Ten days passed before news of the Nubian attack reached Pharaoh Thutmose I in Thebes. The city lay drowsing in midday heat, its white walls gleaming under the merciless sun, its temples and palaces rising like the dreams of gods made manifest in stone. Within the royal palace, couriers and officials moved with practiced efficiency through columned halls where the air hung heavy with incense and perfume.

The messenger arrived at dusk, when the day's heat had begun to relent and the Pharaoh was concluding his audiences. The man staggered into the throne room, his clothing torn and dusty from running, his face drawn with exhaustion, collapsing to his knees before the raised dais where Thutmose sat in divine splendor.

"Great Pharaoh, living forever," the man gasped, prostrating himself before the throne. His voice rasped from a throat parched by days of desperate travel. "The black dogs of Nubia have attacked Memphis."

A ripple of shock passed through the assembled courtiers. Fans stilled in the hands of slaves, conversations died mid-sentence, and all eyes turned to their ruler, awaiting his response.

Thutmose sat very still, only the tightening of his grip on the armrests of his throne betraying his shock. At sixty-five, he remained imposing— a tall figure draped in the finest linen, his chest adorned with a pectoral of gold and lapis lazuli, his head crowned with the double crown that signified his rule over both Upper and Lower Egypt. But the years had taken their toll. His once-powerful frame had thinned, and lines of pain around his eyes spoke of ailments he refused to acknowledge publicly.

"Memphis?" he repeated, his voice steady despite the gravity of the news. That single word held volumes of disbelief and concern. Memphis was the ancient capital, still the commercial and cultural heart of Lower Egypt. An attack there struck at the very roots of his power. "You are certain?"

"Yes, divine one. The district burns, and the governor has sealed the city gates against the attackers. He begs for reinforcements." The messenger's voice broke with emotion—fear, exhaustion, perhaps simple relief at having delivered his burden before collapsing. "They came from the desert, divine one, like demons riding the khamsin wind. No one saw them until the killing had begun."

Thutmose rose to his feet in a single fluid motion that belied his years, his decision already made. The gold beads in his ceremonial beard clicked softly with the movement, a sound that in the sudden silence seemed unnaturally loud. "Summon Commander Pennekh and my war council. We march at first light."

As courtiers scurried to obey, their sandals slapping against polished stone floors, Thutmose turned to his daughter Hatshepsut, who had been present for the audience. Now thirty, she had grown into a woman of remarkable beauty and even more remarkable intellect, serving as her father's closest advisor since the death of his sons. Her face, perfectly composed despite the shocking news, revealed nothing of her thoughts, but her eyes—so like her father's—were calculating, measuring, assessing.

"Father, you cannot personally lead this expedition," she protested once the messengers had been dismissed, keeping her voice low enough that only he could hear. Her hand rested lightly on his arm, feeling the tremor that ran through his muscles even as he fought to control it. "The journey alone would exhaust your strength before you ever faced the enemy."

Thutmose's eyes flashed with momentary anger, then softened as he recognized the genuine concern behind her words. He patted her hand, then gently removed it from his arm—a subtle reminder that despite her position, he remained Pharaoh, answerable to none but the gods.

"What would you have me do?" he asked, his voice carrying genuine inquiry beneath its edge. "Send commanders without their leader against a threat to the very heart of our kingdom? The people must see their Pharaoh leading the defense, not hiding behind palace walls while enemies sack our cities."

One of the commanders raised a question that hung in the air like incense smoke. "What if this attack is a feint, designed to draw you from the safety of Thebes? What if Memphis is not their true target? What if they seek not plunder but your life?"

Thutmose considered the words, his hand absently stroking his ceremonial beard—a gesture that those who knew him recognized as a sign of deep thought. The silence stretched, broken only by the distant sound of temple drums and the soft whisper of evening wind through the palace corridors.

"I will send my full army to Memphis immediately," Thutmose finally replied, ignoring the commander's deeper concern. "They can reach the city before more damage is done. I will keep my personal guard here to protect Thebes."

The decision was made. As dawn broke over Thebes, bathing the limestone temples in soft golden light, two Nubian Medjay crouched among the jagged rocks overlooking the city, their dark bodies glistening with oil, muscles tensed beneath their leopard-skin cloaks. Through narrowed eyes accustomed to reading the desert's secrets, they watched the Egyptian forces depart in disciplined columns, bronze spearheads glinting in the morning sun, war chariots raising clouds of dust along the northern road. A smile of triumph crossed the face of the older spy, Bakari, revealing teeth filed to points in the ancient warrior tradition of his ancestors.

"The trap is sprung," he whispered to his companion, his voice carrying the satisfaction of a hunter who has successfully baited his prey. "The cobra has left its nest unguarded."

They had realized what the Egyptians had not—Thebes, jewel of Upper Egypt, repository of unimaginable wealth, was now vulnerable. Without wasting precious moments, they slipped away like shadows retreating before the sun, moving with the silent efficiency of men who had navigated these lands since childhood. They travelled south along hidden trails toward Elephantine, avoiding Egyptian patrols, surviving on dried meat and water from hidden oases, their powerful legs covering distances that would exhaust ordinary men.

Eight days later, sweat-streaked and dust-covered, they reached the Second Cataract where a thousand Nubian warriors waited in a hidden wadi, restless men with ebony spears and curved swords who hungered for Egyptian blood and the treasures of the north. The Nubian chief Zagwe, a giant whose chest bore the scars of twenty battles, listened to their report with growing excitement, his fingers tightening around his war club of black ironwood.

August 1483 BC - Thebes

Fifteen days after the Egyptian army had marched north, a breathless messenger reached Thutmose at Thebes, bringing the alarming news that the Nubians were advancing from the south—a dark tide of vengeance sweeping toward an undefended city.

The situation grew more dire with each passing hour. Reports confirmed that the Nubians had attacked the Egyptian forts and strongholds to the south with unexpected ferocity. One by one, the carefully constructed defenses that had protected Egypt's southern frontier for decades were falling. Messengers arrived daily with news worse than the last—this outpost overwhelmed, that garrison put to the sword, another commander's head sent floating down the Nile as a grim warning of what awaited resistance.

In his war chamber within the palace of Thebes, Thutmose studied the reports with growing desperation. Maps spread before him showed the advancing Nubian forces marked in red ochre—a stain spreading northward with each new dispatch. His best commanders were either already engaged in fighting or too old for field command. The army he had dispatched to Memphis had indeed stemmed the tide there, driving the Nubian raiders back toward the sea, but the southern front continued to crumble.

"Is there truly no one else we can send?" he demanded of his personal guard, his voice sharp with frustration. The chamber, lit by oil lamps that cast flickering shadows on walls adorned with battle scenes from more glorious days, had grown stifling with the heat of too many bodies and too much anxiety.

The men exchanged uneasy glances, none willing to state the obvious: they lacked the experienced leadership needed for a crisis of this magnitude. All the senior commanders who had proven themselves had gone on the northern campaign. They had fallen into the Nubian trap perfectly.

It was Mutnofret, Thutmose's wife of many years, who finally broke the uncomfortable silence. She had entered the chamber unannounced, her quiet dignity commanding immediate attention despite her lack of formal authority in military matters. Unlike Hatshepsut, who often dressed in the style of a male royal to emphasize her political role, Mutnofret embraced the traditional regalia of a queen—an elaborate wig adorned with gold ornaments, a sheath dress of finest linen, jewelry that emphasized her status without being ostentatious.

"There is one," she said, her voice carrying the weight of absolute certainty. In the silence that followed her pronouncement, the distant sound of temple drums could be heard—priests performing rituals to ensure divine favor in the coming conflict.

All eyes turned to her, including Hatshepsut's, who regarded her stepmother with surprise. Mutnofret rarely involved herself in matters of war or state, preferring to focus on the traditional duties of managing the royal household and overseeing religious observances. Yet now she stood before the war council with the confidence of one who holds a key other have forgotten.

"One who?" Thutmose asked, his patience clearly wearing thin. His hand tapped a restless rhythm on the arm of his chair—a sign those close to him recognized as dangerous.

"Moses," Mutnofret replied simply, the name falling into the chamber like a stone into still water, creating ripples of confusion and disbelief.

A ripple of confusion passed through the room. The soldiers frowned, trying to place the name. Scribes shuffled through papyri, seeking records. Hatshepsut's brow furrowed; the name was unfamiliar despite her extensive knowledge of Egypt's military leadership.

"Moses is dead," Thutmose said flatly, his tone suggesting the matter was closed. But Hatshepsut, watching closely, saw something flicker in her father's eyes—not surprise, but a flash of what might have been hope quickly suppressed.

A ghost of a smile touched Mutnofret's lips, a subtle expression that held both triumph and vindication. "Is he? How strange then, that I should know exactly where to find him."

The silence that followed her statement was profound, broken only by the distant cry of a night bird somewhere in the palace gardens. Finally, Thutmose rose from his chair, dismissing his council with a gesture as imperious as it was abrupt.

When only Thutmose, Mutnofret, and Hatshepsut remained, the pharaoh faced his wife with narrowed eyes, his body tense with controlled anger. "If you have kept such knowledge from me all these years, the offense is grave."

"Not as grave as the offense you planned against him," Mutnofret countered calmly, meeting his gaze without flinching. There was steel beneath her gentle exterior—a strength that had allowed her to survive decades in the treacherous environment of the royal court. "I will tell you where Moses can be found, but only if you swear by the name of Amun-Ra that no harm will come to him by your command."

"Who is this, Moses?" Hatshepsut interjected, unable to contain her curiosity any longer. She moved between them, her gaze shifting from one to the other, sensing undercurrents of an old conflict she had never been privy to. "A commander I have not heard of? A man whose existence has been kept from me despite my position?"

Mutnofret turned to her, something like sadness crossing her features. In the lamplight, the lines around her eyes seemed deeper, speaking of burdens carried too long in silence. The flickering flames caught the silver threads in her hair, once as black as Nubian obsidian, now bearing witness to decades of palace intrigues and heartaches.

"More than that, princess," she said, her voice carrying the weight of hidden histories. "Though he may never have marched into battle as a general, he was trained by the greatest military minds in Egypt—men who had bathed in the blood of crushed Kushite rebellions. The high commanders themselves taught him every stratagem and tactic in the sacred military scrolls, knowledge usually reserved for pharaoh's own bloodline."

Her fingers, gnarled now but still elegant, traced an invisible pattern on the limestone table between them. "I watched him in the training grounds, princess. The sword in his hand became like the tail of Sobek himself—swift, deadly, and inevitable. He could defeat five of the royal guard in succession, his movements like water flowing around stone. And all this knowledge, all this skill, lies dormant within him now." Her eyes, dark as the silty depths of the Nile, fixed on the princess with sudden intensity. "And before all that, before his legend was even whispered, he was a child I helped save from certain death."

Thutmose's face darkened with anger, the skin around his mouth growing tight. "You presume much, wife."

"I presume nothing," Mutnofret replied with dignity. "I merely state facts. Egypt stands on the brink of disaster. You need Moses now as you have never needed him before. The only question is whether your pride is worth more to you than your kingdom."

For a long moment, Thutmose stood silent, the conflict within him visible in the rigid set of his shoulders, the tight clenching of his jaw. Then, finally, desperation won out over pride. "You have my oath. Now speak."

"He serves in the Temple of Amun here in Thebes," Mutnofret revealed, her voice softening now that her point was won. "He has lived quietly there for years, devoting himself to study and prayer, keeping well away from court affairs."

"Here? In Thebes?" Thutmose's surprise was evident, a rare break in the careful composure he maintained as Pharaoh. "All this time, he has been within reach?"

"A wise precaution," Mutnofret replied calmly, her gaze unwavering. "Given what you had planned for him."

"Father, what is this mystery?" Hatshepsut demanded, her frustration finally breaking through her usual control. She moved to stand directly before Thutmose, forcing him to meet her gaze. "Who is this man that lives so close yet remains unknown to me? Why have I never heard his name in all my years at court?"

Thutmose exchanged a long look with Mutnofret before answering, a silent communication passing between them—the understanding of two people who had shared a life and its burdens for decades. Finally, he sighed, some of the regal stiffness leaving his frame as he resigned himself to revealing long-buried truths.

"He was a foundling, a Hebrew child rescued from the river when my predecessor ordered the death of all male Hebrew infants to prevent the fulfillment of a prophecy." Thutmose's voice grew distant, as if he spoke of events witnessed by another man in another lifetime. "Your step-mother, before we got married, found him floating in a basket among the reeds and took him as her own. He grew up alongside your half-brothers, trained in all the arts of war and governance."

"I hid him from your father when the priests demanded his death," Mutnofret continued, her eyes briefly clouding with old sorrows. "The official story was that he died in the eastern desert, but with my help, he found sanctuary in the priesthood, where his considerable intellect could still serve Egypt, if in a different capacity."

Hatshepsut absorbed this information in stunned silence, her mind racing to reconcile this hidden history with what she knew of Egypt's past. The implications were staggering—a Hebrew foundling raised as royal, a commander whose very existence had been erased from official records, a conspiracy of silence maintained for years at the highest levels of power.

"If he was so valuable," she finally asked, her voice carefully neutral despite the turmoil of her thoughts, "why let him go? Why create the fiction of his death?"

"Because the priesthood feared him," Thutmose replied grimly, moving to a nearby table where wine waited in a golden pitcher. He poured himself a cup with hands that trembled slightly, whether from age or emotion impossible to tell. "They believed old prophecies that claimed he would bring destruction to Egypt. I was... persuaded... that he had become a threat."

He drank deeply, then set the cup down with more force than necessary. "They came to me with dreams and portents, with scrolls written in languages so ancient even they could barely decipher them. They spoke of a deliverer who would rise from among the enslaved Hebrews, a man raised as Egyptian who would turn against us and lead his people to freedom."

"And you believed them?" Hatshepsut's disbelief was evident in her tone.

"I believed in protecting Egypt," Thutmose replied sharply. "The priests swore that Moses was this deliverer. They demanded his execution."

"And now?" Hatshepsut pressed, her analytical mind already moving beyond the revelations to their practical implications for the current crisis.

"Now Egypt needs him," Mutnofret said simply, her gaze moving between husband and daughter. "And perhaps, after all these years, he needs Egypt as well. The wheel of fate turns, bringing us back to moments we thought long past."

Thutmose made his decision with the swiftness that had served him well in his younger years as a military commander. "Go to the Temple of Amun," he instructed Hatshepsut, his voice regaining its accustomed authority. "Find Moses and bring him to me. Tell him that Egypt has need of him."

Hatshepsut nodded, her mind already turning to the strange task ahead. But one question remained, too important to leave unasked. "And if he refuses?"

"He won't," Mutnofret said with quiet certainty, her hands folded calmly before her. "Not once he understands what is at stake. Moses may have left the palace, but Egypt has never left his heart. He will come."

The Meeting at the Temple

The Temple of Amun stood majestic in the heart of Thebes, its towering pylons casting long shadows across the sacred precinct. The morning sun gilded the tops of obelisks while leaving the sprawling courtyards below in cool shadow. Priests moved in solemn procession through colonnaded halls, their bald heads gleaming, their white linen robes immaculate despite the ever-present dust of the desert city.

Hatshepsut approached with a mixture of curiosity and trepidation, her royal litter carried by twelve servants up the paved avenue of sphinxes that led to the temple's main entrance. Though she visited the temple regularly in her official capacity, today's mission filled her with an unfamiliar uncertainty. What manner of man was this Moses, that he could inspire such conflicting emotions in her father and stepmother?

As the royal daughter of Pharaoh, no door remained closed to her. The high priest himself hurried forward to greet her, bowing low, his ceremonial leopard skin draped over pristine white linen. With minimal explanation—for the less said about Moses, the better—she was led through increasingly restricted areas of the temple complex, into sections where ordinary worshippers never ventured.

She found him in a secluded courtyard, instructing a small group of novice priests in the ancient texts. The space was simple but beautiful— a square of open sky surrounded by painted columns, with a small pool at its center reflecting the deep blue of the Egyptian heaven. Papyrus and lotus grew in carefully tended beds, their green vitality a stark contrast to the stone and sand that dominated most of Thebes.

At thirty-six, Moses possessed a powerful frame that spoke of regular physical training despite his priestly surroundings. Hatshepsut noted with surprise that unlike the other priests, he had not shaved his head— instead, thick black hair was pulled back in a simple queue at the nape of his neck. His face was handsome in a severe way, with high cheekbones and penetrating eyes that suggested both intelligence and intensity. Old battle scars marked his muscular torso, speaking of a past that no amount of temple life could erase.

He looked up as she entered, and for a moment their eyes met across the courtyard. Something passed between them—recognition, not of faces but of souls, of two people bound by destiny they had yet to understand. Surprise registered briefly in his expression before he composed himself and bowed deeply, though not with the full prostration protocol demanded.

The novices, recognizing the royal princess, prostrated themselves immediately, pressing their foreheads against the cool stone pavement in perfect unison, like reeds bending before a strong wind.

"Leave us," Hatshepsut commanded, her voice carrying the natural authority of one born to rule. The young priests scattered like birds before a hawk, their sandaled feet making soft slapping sounds against the stone as they retreated.

"Princess Hatshepsut," Moses greeted her, rising from his bow. His voice was deep and measured, carrying a resonance that seemed to vibrate in the quiet courtyard. He remained standing, not prostrating himself as protocol demanded—a subtle defiance that did not go unnoticed. "This is an... unexpected honor."

Hatshepsut studied him carefully, taking in every detail. Around his neck hung not the ceremonial pectoral of a high priest, but a simple amulet carved from lapis lazuli—a symbol of truth and heaven. In his bearing, she sensed something that set him apart from other priests: an alertness, a coiled readiness that spoke of a warrior's instincts never fully dormant.

"You know me," she observed, moving deeper into the courtyard. A shaft of sunlight caught the gold beads woven into her elaborate wig, setting them ablaze with reflected fire.

"All of Thebes knows the daughter of Pharaoh," he replied carefully, his eyes never leaving hers. In them, she saw a sharpness, an awareness that belied his apparent removal from court politics. This was not a man who had spent nine years in blissful scholarly isolation.

"Yet I had never heard of you until today," she countered, circling the pool at the center of the courtyard, trailing her fingers through the water, disrupting its perfect reflection. "My stepmother concealed your very existence, even from me. A man whose name causes both fear and hope when spoken aloud."

Moses watched her movement with the intensity of a hawk tracking prey, though his expression remained carefully neutral. "The past is a buried treasure, princess. Sometimes it is best left undisturbed."

"Egypt cannot afford such luxury now," Hatshepsut said, her voice hardening. She stopped beside him, close enough to detect the faint scent of incense that clung to his skin and the underlying scent that spoke of a man who still trained his body despite his peaceful surroundings. "Our enemies strike from the south. The forts fall one by one. My father needs a commander who knows how to fight the Nubians."

Something shifted in Moses's expression—a tightening around his eyes that suggested old memories surfacing. His hands flexed at his sides, powerful fingers forming fists before deliberately relaxing. "And he sends you to retrieve his discarded weapon. How desperate he must be."

The bitterness in his voice was unmistakable, and Hatshepsut realized this would be more difficult than she had anticipated. The man before her carried wounds that time had not healed—wounds that ran deeper than mere political disagreement.

"You were never discarded," she said, her voice softening slightly. "Hidden, perhaps. Protected. But never discarded."

Moses turned away from her, his gaze fixing on the temple walls where ancient battles were depicted in vivid colors—pharaohs in their war chariots, trampling enemies beneath the hooves of their horses. "Protected," he repeated, and there was something like a laugh in his voice, though without humor. "Is that what they call exile now?"

"You could have been executed," Hatshepsut pointed out bluntly. "The priests demanded it. My father was... convinced... that you represented a threat. Yet here you stand, alive, learned, still serving Egypt in your own way."

"Serving Egypt," Moses mused, his voice dropping to barely above a whisper. He moved to the wall, his hand tracing the painted figure of a warrior-king. "I have served Egypt all my life, princess. In the training yards, learning the arts of war. In the libraries, studying the tactics of our enemies. Even here, in the temple, preserving the wisdom of our ancestors. And what has it gained me? What has it gained Egypt?"

For the first time, Hatshepsut heard genuine pain in his voice—not just the bitterness of exile, but the deeper ache of a man who had given everything to a cause that had ultimately rejected him.

"It has gained you this moment," she said quietly, moving to stand beside him. "The moment when Egypt needs you most. When all your training, all your knowledge, all your sacrifice can serve its greatest purpose."

Moses was silent for a long moment, his hand still resting on the painted wall. When he spoke again, his voice was different—thoughtful rather than bitter. "The Nubians are not like other enemies. They fight differently, think differently. They understand the desert in ways that most Egyptians do not."

"But you do," Hatshepsut said, sensing an opening. "You were trained to fight them. You understand their tactics."

"I was trained to fight everyone," Moses replied, turning to face her again. In his eyes, she saw something awakening—not eagerness, exactly, but the stirring of abilities long suppressed. "The Nubians, the Canaanites, the Sea Peoples. Your father's generals made sure I knew how to counter every threat Egypt might face."

"And now Egypt faces the greatest threat of all," Hatshepsut pressed. "Not just an enemy army, but the collapse of our entire southern frontier. Without those forts, without control of the gold mines and trade routes, Egypt will weaken. Other enemies will see our vulnerability and strike. The kingdom itself is at stake."

Moses began to pace, his movements suddenly sharp and focused. She could see the transformation beginning—the scholar-priest giving way to something harder, more dangerous. "How many men does my father have left in Thebes?"

"Your father?" Hatshepsut caught the slip, but chose not to comment on it directly. "Perhaps three hundred guards, mostly ceremonial troops. The rest went north to Memphis."

"Three hundred." Moses stopped pacing, his mind clearly racing through calculations. "Against how many Nubians?"

"A thousand, perhaps more. They've united several tribes under one war chief—Zagwe, they call him. A giant who has never lost a battle."

For the first time since she'd entered the courtyard, Moses smiled. It was not a pleasant expression, but rather the grin of a predator contemplating prey. "I know of Zagwe. He relies on terror and overwhelming force. His tactics are... predictable."

"You'll come then?" Hatshepsut asked, hope rising in her chest.

Moses glanced at the senior priests who had gathered at a respectful distance, watching the exchange with obvious anxiety. Their presence was a silent reminder of the forces that had once aligned against him—forces that might do so again if they felt threatened.

"These men once prophesied that I would bring destruction to Egypt," he said quietly, his voice dropping so that only she could hear. "They whispered poison in your father's ear until he believed I was a greater threat than any foreign enemy. Perhaps they fear that prophecy is finally at hand."

Hatshepsut sensed this was the crucial moment—the point where Moses would either commit himself to Egypt's cause or retreat forever into the safety of scholarly obscurity. She thought of her father, aging and desperate, facing the collapse of everything he had built. She thought of the people of Thebes, unaware that death was marching toward them from the south. She thought of Egypt itself, the eternal kingdom that had endured for millennia but now faced its greatest trial.

"Or perhaps," she said, stepping closer, close enough that she had to tilt her head back to meet his gaze, "you are the instrument chosen by the gods to prevent that destruction. Perhaps the prophecy speaks not of you bringing ruin, but of your absence allowing it to flourish."

Moses stared at her for a long moment, weighing forces and possibilities she could only guess at. The courtyard seemed to hold its breath; the very air suspended between heartbeats. Finally, he looked past her to address the priests directly.

"You who feared me," he called out, his voice echoing in the vast courtyard, bouncing off stone columns to return with otherworldly resonance. "You who saw my death as necessary for Egypt's survival. What say you now? Shall I return to the sword, or remain here in contemplation while Egypt burns?"

The high priest of Amun stepped forward, his face grave beneath his ceremonial headdress. He had been young when Moses first came to the temple—a junior priest witnessing history unfold. Now, nine years later, he found himself the vessel of ancient wisdom, caught between prophecy and immediate threat.

"The omens are... complex, great one," he intoned, his voice carrying the practiced gravity of one who speaks for the gods. "But the gods send trials to test the faithful. Perhaps this is yours." He paused, stroking the ceremonial beard that hung from his chin. "Nine years ago, the signs spoke of danger should you remain in the palace. Now, perhaps, they speak of danger should you remain in the temple. The gods move in patterns beyond mortal understanding."

Moses nodded slowly, as if the cryptic answer had confirmed something he already knew. When he turned back to Hatshepsut, she saw that his decision had been made. The transformation was complete—the priest had become the general, the exile had become Egypt's salvation.

"I will come," he said simply, his voice carrying new resolve. "For Egypt, if not for Pharaoh."

Relief flooded through Hatshepsut, though she kept her expression neutral. "You will need armor, weapons—"

"No," Moses interrupted, his hand moving to touch the lapis amulet at his throat. "What I need cannot be found in an armory. I will bring only what I have learned here, and this—to remind me of truth when lies surround me like vultures."

As they prepared to leave the temple, Hatshepsut noticed the priests watching Moses with a mixture of fear and something like relief. Some made subtle protective gestures as he passed, while others bowed deeper than protocol required—acknowledgment not of his rank, but of something more profound. She realized then that there was far more to this story than either her father or Mutnofret had revealed. This man was no ordinary adopted son of the royal household. In the way the priests watched him, in the reverence and fear that followed in his wake, she sensed a destiny that extended far beyond Egypt's current crisis.

The walk through the streets of Thebes became a procession of whispers and wonder. The common people seemed to sense something significant in their passage. Merchants paused in their haggling, laborers rested on their tools, women drawing water from public wells grew still—all watching as the royal princess and the tall, austere stranger moved through the narrow streets toward the palace.

Few recognized Moses, for his years in the temple had changed him from the public figure he once was. His hair had grown long, his face had been marked by years of study and contemplation, and his body had been shaped by different disciplines than those of his youth. Yet something in his bearing, in the purpose of his stride, spoke of importance, of destiny awakening.

"They sense it too," Moses observed as they walked, his voice thoughtful. "The change that comes with crisis. Egypt stands at a crossroads, and the people know it, even if they cannot name it."

"What do you sense?" Hatshepsut asked, genuinely curious. "You who have lived apart from the world, studying its patterns—what do you see that others miss?"

Moses was quiet for several steps, his gaze taking in the familiar sights of the city where he had been raised. Finally, he spoke. "I see an Egypt that has forgotten the lessons of its enemies. We have grown comfortable in our power, certain in our superiority. But the world changes, princess. New powers rise; new alliances forms. If Egypt does not adapt, it will fall."

"And you can prevent that?" Hatshepsut enquires.

"I can try," Moses replied simply. "I have spent nine years studying not just the military arts, but the deeper patterns of conflict—why empires rise and why they fall, what makes peoples strong and what makes them weak. The Nubians are not just raiders seeking plunder. They are a people displaced, desperate, driven by forces we do not fully understand. To defeat them, we must understand them."

By the time they reached the palace gates, rumors were already spreading through the markets and workshops of Thebes—whispers of a savior returned from the dead, of an ancient prophecy finally coming to fruition. By sunset, the whole city would be alive with speculation. By dawn, when Moses would stand before Pharaoh once more, the tale would have grown to mythic proportions.

Hatshepsut glanced at the man walking beside her, wondering if he was aware of the ripples his mere presence was creating. If he was, he gave no sign, his face set in lines of grim determination, his mind clearly focused on the challenges ahead rather than the speculation behind.

One thing was certain—the wheel of fate had indeed turned full circle, bringing Egypt's past rushing into its present. What remained to be seen was whether that confluence would save the Two Lands, or destroy them utterly. But as she looked at Moses, seeing the quiet confidence in his bearing, the controlled power in his movements, Hatshepsut felt something she had not experienced in weeks: hope.

The hidden prince had arisen. Now it remained to be seen what he would make of his second chance to serve the land that had both raised and rejected him.

Chapter 24 - The Lion of Egypt

August 1483 BC, - Thebes

The morning sun cast long shadows across the assembly ground, its golden rays catching the bronze spearheads of Egypt's finest warriors like fire. Moses stood beside Pharaoh Thutmose I, his muscular frame tense under the weight of expectation. Before them, three hundred of Egypt's royal guard—not the seasoned soldiers who had departed for Memphis, but men accustomed to the comfort of palace walls—stood in rigid formation, their eyes fixed upon the man who would lead them into battle.

Moses had long hair the night before. Now he was standing in front of his new recruits, watching them as they watched him. He had shaved his head and rubbed oil into his scalp to look like a commander, the gleaming surface reflecting the harsh desert sun above the training grounds. Moses felt their stares penetrate him like arrows—some filled with curiosity, others with skepticism—and a few with undisguised hostility. He had proven himself in the royal court and in the sacred temples, mastering the intricacies of diplomacy and divine ritual, but never had he faced the chaos of war where men's lives hung by threads of bronze and courage.

Thutmose, despite his increasingly frail appearance, stepped forward with the regal dignity that only a Pharaoh could command. His body might be failing him, ravaged by the weight of years and responsibility, but his spirit remained as indomitable as the great pyramids themselves. His voice, though thin as papyrus, carried across the silent ranks with surprising power, each word weighted with divine authority that seemed to emanate from the very throne of Amun-Ra.

"Men of Egypt," the Pharaoh began, raising a jeweled arm that seemed almost too delicate for the gold adorning it, "behold your commander." His gesture encompassed Moses, who stood tall despite the churning uncertainty in his gut. "You will follow him as you would follow me, for in him flows the wisdom of the gods and the strength of the Nile itself."

A senior officer stepped forward from the ranks, his weather-beaten face creased with doubt and the harsh lines that only years of campaign could carve into a man's features. The scars crisscrossing his arms told of battles fought and survived, of experiences Moses had yet to face, of brothers lost to enemy spears. His eyes, narrowed with suspicion earned through blood and sand, locked with Moses' as he addressed the Pharaoh with the careful deference of one who had learned when to speak and when to hold his tongue.

"My Pharaoh, with the deepest respect," the officer said, his voice rough as desert sand grinding against stone, "this man has never faced the Nubians in battle. He has never felt an enemy spear thrust at his heart or watched his brothers die beside him in the dust. The men need a commander who understands the weight of their lives, who—"

"Silence!" Thutmose snapped, his frailty momentarily eclipsed by royal fury that flashed like lightning across his gaunt features. The transformation was startling—for a moment, the young warrior-king who had expanded Egypt's borders seemed to inhabit his aging frame once more. "The gods have guided my choice, and their wisdom surpasses mortal understanding. You question not just your Pharaoh but Amun-Ra himself." The divine name hung in the air between them like incense, heavy with power and consequence. "Moses shall lead, or you will answer to me with your life—a price I will collect without hesitation."

The threat was not idle; all present knew that Thutmose I had not earned his throne through weakness, and even in his declining years, his word remained absolute as the rising sun.

Moses surveyed the men who would now place their lives in his hands, feeling the weight of their souls pressing against his conscience. His dark eyes, sharp and piercing beneath strong brows, moved methodically over each face, reading the stories written in scars and weathered skin. Though he had never led men into actual battle, Egypt's greatest military minds had forged him into a weapon of strategy and tactics—generals who had conquered Nubia, Libya, and the Levant had personally instructed him in every aspect of warfare, from siege craft to cavalry charges, from desert fighting to naval combat. What he lacked in battlefield experience, he more than compensated for with knowledge that few commanders could match—wisdom gleaned not just from ancient texts but from the living masters of war themselves. His mind was already calculating, assessing, planning how best to use these warriors against the Nubian threat that awaited them beyond the southern borders.

"Pharaoh honors me beyond measure," Moses said, his voice deeper and steadier than Thutmose's, resonating with a confidence he did not entirely feel but knew he must project. "And by the strength of my arm and the guidance of the gods, I shall honor Egypt with victory or die in the attempt."

The officer bowed deeply, pressing his forehead almost to the dust in submission, and retreated to his position among the ranks. But the damage was done—Moses could feel the ripple of uncertainty passing through the formation like wind through a field of barley, bending but not breaking the stalks of discipline that held them together.

Without hesitation, Moses moved among the men with the fluid grace of a warrior trained by Egypt's finest military masters, examining their weapons with the practiced eye of one schooled in every form of combat known to the civilized world. He tested the weight of their bronze-tipped spears with the knowledge of a man who had trained with veteran spearmen from a dozen conquered lands, checked the leather bindings of their shields with the attention to detail that Egypt's greatest tacticians had drilled into him through countless hours of instruction. He asked pointed questions about their experience in previous campaigns, their knowledge of Nubian tactics, their strengths and weaknesses—cataloging every detail that might mean the difference between victory and catastrophe. Each man represented a piece on the great board of war, and he needed to understand how to move them to maximum effect.

He paused before a young soldier whose hands betrayed a slight tremor that spoke of nerves wound tight as bowstrings. The youth's armor, though well-maintained, bore none of the dents and scratches that marked a veteran's gear—a telling detail that confirmed Moses' suspicions.

"Your first campaign?" Moses asked quietly, his voice pitched so that only those nearby could hear, understanding that a man's fear need not become public shame.

"Yes, my lord," the young man answered, eyes fixed straight ahead.

Moses placed a hand on the soldier's shoulder, feeling the tension there. "What is your name?"

"Emhat, my lord."

"Emhat, the first battle tests every man," Moses said, his voice carrying just far enough for the surrounding men to hear. "But remember this—no Egyptian soldier fights alone. You stand with your brothers, with Egypt, with the gods themselves." He squeezed the young man's shoulder. "And with me."

The tension in Emhat's body eased slightly, and Moses continued through the ranks, taking the measure of the men who would follow him into the unknown reaches of Nubia. By midday, they were marching southward, toward a conflict that would change everything—for Egypt, for Nubia, and for Moses himself.

Marching by land

The traditional approach would have been by water, using the Nile's current to carry them swiftly into Nubian territory. The boats had been prepared, their decks stacked with supplies, their sails ready to catch the north wind. But Moses had spent the night studying the patterns of the river and their enemies' expectations, tracing papyrus maps until his eyes burned from the strain.

"We march by land," he announced to his captains when they gathered to discuss the campaign. The men exchanged glances, their surprise evident. Moses continued, pointing to the swollen waterways on the map spread before them. "The Nubians expect us by river, as Egyptian forces have always come." Moses said, his voice low enough that only his commanders could hear. "They prepare for boats and men showing our strength in the time-honored manner of warfare."

He turned, placing a hand on his lieutenant's shoulder, the calluses of a lifetime of training rough against the worn leather. "But I have conceived something they will never expect." Despite the commander's questioning gaze and pointed inquiries about these plans, Moses revealed nothing more, knowing that secrecy now would prove as vital as sharp bronze when they struck.

Late August 1483 BC - Buhen

The Nubian forces moved like a dark river of muscle and bronze, slipping past Sai Island with the precision of seasoned warriors who knew both terrain and purpose. Dust rose in columns behind them as their leather sandals beat against the cracked earth, and the sun glinted off polished obsidian blades strapped to their backs. Their war paint, smeared with ochre and ash, shimmered under the heat of the late afternoon, giving them an otherworldly air—like avenging spirits summoned from the dunes. The rhythmic slap of feet against stone mixed with the soft chanting that accompanied their march, voices rising and falling like the desert wind.

The Nile flowed beside them, calm and indifferent, its waters thick with silt and secrets. To the Nubians, it was both guide and guardian, carrying them downstream toward Buhen—a fortress of stone and legend nestled at the lip of the Second Cataract. The fortress loomed ahead, its sandstone walls already warming with the last golden rays of the sun, casting long shadows like fingers across the arid plain.

Far to the north, Moses walked at the head of his column, his linen cloak streaked with desert dust, his eyes scanning the narrowing path along the Nile's edge. He had left Thebes at dawn, his army moving with deliberate haste, the silence between them broken only by the occasional call of a heron or the clank of bronze shields. The river widened as they moved south, its surface broken by reeds and crocodile trails, while granite boulders jutted from the water like the bones of ancient gods. Moses bore the weight of command with outward calm, but beneath that stillness simmered a storm of uncertainty. As Buhen's spires came into view, carved into the cliffside like a scar, Moses raised a hand, signaling his men to halt. There, on the far bank, the enemy appeared at last: a long procession of warriors silhouetted against the copper sky, unaware they were being watched.

Hidden within the sandstone ridges, Moses crouched beside a wind-smoothed boulder, its surface warm beneath his calloused hand. The air smelled of sunbaked reeds and the faint tang of sweat and iron. He could see the Nubian chieftain now—a tall figure with a leopard pelt slung across his shoulder and a curved blade at his hip. They marched with the easy confidence of men who believed themselves unchallenged, their war chants echoing off the canyon walls. Moses narrowed his eyes. The element of surprise was his. But the timing had to be perfect. One misstep, and the desert would drink the blood of his soldiers. He drew a slow breath, his mind turning like the Nile's current—deep, relentless, and full of unseen depths.

Nubian Encampment

The Nile was swollen with the beginning of the annual inundation, its waters gleaming like polished bronze beneath the setting sun. Moses stood at a distance, his keen eyes narrowed as he studied the distant Nubian encampment across the surging waters. Below him, three hundred men waited in silence—palace guards with burnished breastplates that had never seen battle, mingled with raw recruits whose hands still bore the calluses of farmers' tools rather than sword hilts.

"They outnumber us three to one," whispered the commander, a grizzled veteran with a scar that twisted from his temple to his jaw.

Moses turned to him; his face carved from granite in the fading light. "The river shall be their undoing," he said, his voice carrying the weight of absolute conviction. "Tonight, we become an army of thousands."

As darkness fell across the ancient land, Moses moved among his men, his presence commanding absolute attention. "Each man carries two torches," he ordered. "Space yourselves widely. Move constantly. Let the night itself become alive with our numbers."

Moses' plan unfurled with the precision of a desert falcon's strike. Soon, the eastern bank blazed with hundreds of moving lights, spread across the shoreline. The flames danced and multiplied in the night, creating the illusion of a vast host gathered on the riverbank. The acrid smell of burning pitch mixed with the muddy scent of the flooding Nile.

Across the churning waters, in the Nubian camp, Commander Zagwe emerged from his tent, his massive frame silhouetted against the firelight. The gold torque around his muscular neck glinted as he stared in disbelief at the constellation of flames that had appeared on the opposite shore. His weathered hands, scarred from countless battles, gripped the tent flap as he tried to comprehend what he witnessed.

"By the gods," he breathed, as his captains gathered around him. "How many are they?"

"Thousands," replied his scout, voice trembling. "They must have marched from Memphis itself. The Pharaoh has sent his entire army."

Zagwe's hand closed around the hilt of his curved sword, his knuckles whitening. Years of warfare had taught him to read the signs of enemy strength, but this display confounded him. "Impossible. Our spies reported no such movement."

As dawn broke, painting the sky in shades of amber and gold, Moses had already withdrawn his men to a hidden position behind the eastern dunes. The torches were extinguished, leaving behind a vast area of disturbed sand and manufactured tracks of a phantom army.

Zagwe, emboldened by the light of day, dispatched his swiftest warriors across the river on reed boats. They moved with the silent grace of predators, wary of ambush, but found only an abandoned campsite stretching far beyond what their eyes could encompass.

The leader of the scouts returned to Zagwe, his expression troubled. "Commander, they have vanished. But they left behind evidence of a force greater than anything we have faced. The ground is trampled by thousands."

Standing at Zagwe's shoulder was Makeda, her ebony skin weathered by eight decades of life along the Nile. Her blind eyes stared sightlessly toward the eastern shore, but her voice carried the weight of prophecy. The old woman's gnarled fingers clutched at bone amulets around her neck, and those who knew her recognized the signs of her visions.

"I have dreamed it," she whispered, her bony fingers clutching Zagwe's massive forearm. "The Savior of Egypt rises from the ashes. Death awaits us at the river's edge. He comes not as many, but as one man with the strength of thousands."

Zagwe's face darkened. In all his campaigns, Makeda's dreams had never led him astray. Her visions had saved his forces from ambush at the Third Cataract and warned him of the treacherous alliance with the Blemmyes. "We withdraw to the Fourth Cataract," he commanded. "The forts shall protect us until we can gather our full strength."

On the eastern bank, a scout raced back to Moses with the news. The young commander's lips curved into a rare smile. "They retreat southward."

"They run to their doom," Moses said, already calculating. "By land, we can reach the forts before them. Gather the men. We march to the fourth cataract without rest."

The most senior captain, Paheri—the same man who had questioned Moses before Pharaoh—frowned deeply. "The desert route shall be brutal, Commander. Men will die before we even reach the cataract."

"Some may," Moses acknowledged, meeting the captain's gaze without flinching. "But fewer than would die facing the Nubians head-on. I would rather battle the desert than meet the enemy where he expects us."

Paheri held Moses' gaze for a long moment, then nodded slowly. "As you command," he said, and Moses heard the first note of respect in the veteran's voice.

The journey proved punishing beyond even Moses' expectations. The desert heat blistered their skin, and the weight of their armor and supplies drained their strength with each step across the merciless sands. Men collapsed from exhaustion, their lips cracked and bleeding, their water skins emptying faster than planned. But Moses was always there, moving tirelessly among the ranks, helping fallen soldiers to their feet, sharing his own water ration, leading by example rather than command alone.

September 1483 BC - Nubia 4th Cataract

Ten days of hard marching brought them at last to the ancient forts that had guarded the Fourth Cataract since the time of the pharaohs. They made camp in the shadow of a weathered outcropping, where crackling flames threw dancing shadows across the captain's weathered features. That night brought welcome tidings from his scouts—dust-covered runners who spoke in hushed tones of lightly manned garrisons, mostly Nubian auxiliaries under a handful of officers.

Dawn brought opportunity. Moses dispatched soldiers to the scattered settlements that dotted the riverbank, and by the sun's zenith he had assembled a curious army. Farmers abandoned their fields, merchants left their stalls, and herders drove their flocks to safety before taking up makeshift arms. These common folk stood shoulder to shoulder with his trained fighters, their crude spears and farming tools transformed by distance and flickering torchlight into the weapons of a fearsome host.

The deception proved masterful. When this motley force approached the ancient stones, the Nubian defenders took one look at the approaching multitude and abandoned their posts, fleeing south along the Nile with scarcely a backward glance. Moses wasted no time in positioning his civilian conscripts along the ramparts, where they created the convincing illusion of fortresses bristling with seasoned warriors.

Four days passed before Zagwe's flotilla rounded the river's bend, their vessels heavy with fighting men and provisions while foot soldiers marched in disciplined columns along the southern embankment. The Nubian commander stood proud at his lead vessel's prow, but his expression shifted from confidence to stunned disbelief as he beheld the impossible sight before him—the very forts he had counted upon for refuge now flew Egypt's standards, their walls apparently thick with thousands of defenders where he had expected to find sanctuary.

Makeda clutched her amulets, trembling. The ancient woman's voice cracked like dry papyrus. "The dream comes true. The one who commands the impossible stands before us."

Zagwe, for the first time in his storied career, gave the order to retreat without engaging the enemy. His flotilla on the opposite side of the Nile turned southward, seeking the safety of the Fifth Cataract, leaving behind the strategic forts that had guarded the frontier for generations.

From the highest tower, Moses watched the Nubian withdrawal, his face impassive despite the triumph. Beside him, Paheri shook his head in wonder.

The grizzled captain's weathered hands trembled as he clasped Moses' shoulder, his voice thick with awe that bordered on reverence. "By the gods, what I witnessed today defies all reason—palace guards, green recruits, farmers, merchants routing a thousand Nubian warriors without spilling so much as a single drop of their blood." His eyes, clouded by decades of war, now blazed with the fervor of one who had glimpsed something beyond mortal understanding. "Mark my words— this victory will echo through the ages like thunder across the desert, and your name will be whispered in the same breath as the ancient heroes, for you have proven that true conquest lies not in the strength of the sword, but in the wisdom to turn enemies into allies and battles into legends." Moses turned from the parapet, his eyes already focused on the next campaign, the next victory. "Tales are for elders by the fire," he said. "We have only begun to fight."

The fort buzzed with excitement as the Nubian forces retreat southward, their boats becoming mere specks on the vast expanse of the Nile. The taste of bloodless victory was sweet, and the men's confidence in their young commander had transformed into something approaching reverence.

"Commander!" called out Senbi, a palace guard with shoulders like granite blocks. "Let us pursue them! We can strike while they're scattered and demoralized." A chorus of approving shouts rose from the gathered warriors, their blood heated by success.

Moses raised a hand, and silence fell instantly. What had begun as a force of three hundred was now four hundred strong, bolstered by frontier garrisons who had rallied to his banner and local men eager to fight under the commander who outwitted the feared Nubian warlord.

"Your courage does you credit," Moses replied, his voice carrying across the courtyard. "But courage without cunning is merely sacrifice." He gestured toward the supplies they had captured. "The Nubians expect pursuit. They will be prepared for it, lying in wait to transform their retreat into an ambush."

"Tonight, we rest. Tomorrow, we hunt—but not as the Nubians expect." His voice dropped, becoming almost seductive in its confidence. "They believe they know the mind of an Egyptian commander. I intend to prove them wrong."

The men dispersed, some still grumbling about delayed vengeance, but none willing to directly challenge Moses. As the night deepened, Paheri found his commander alone on the battlements, studying maps by moonlight.

"They trust you," the lieutenant said. "But that trust must be fed with victory."

Moses nodded without looking up. "And they shall have it. But not through the doorway the Nubians have left invitingly open."

September 1483 BC - Atbara River, Nubia

The Nubians withdrew to their stronghold positioned at the strategic fork where the Nile and Atbara rivers met. From a distant ridge, Moses surveyed it with narrowed eyes, taking in every detail of the formidable position. Steep banks on two sides provided natural defenses, while fortified walls of stone and timber protected the others. Small figures moved along the battlements—sentries watching for the Egyptian approach. The sound of hammering drifted across the water as the defenders strengthened their walls.

The moon cast silver light across the rushing waters of the Atbara River as Moses led his force westward along its northern bank. They had marched for nearly an hour, far past the point where the Nubian stronghold stood. Here, the river narrowed significantly, cutting through a rocky gorge before widening again on its journey to join the Nile.

"The crossing looks treacherous," Paheri observed, watching the churning waters below. The roar of water over stone filled the night air.

"For an army, yes," Moses agreed. "For men moving in small groups, with ropes and determination—it is merely difficult."

Through the night they worked, establishing a rope system anchored to the massive boulders on either side. The current was fierce, threatening to sweep away even the strongest swimmers, but Moses had chosen his crossing point well. A series of submerged rocks created a natural, if dangerous, pathway.

By dawn, the entire force had crossed, wet and exhausted but intact. Moses allowed them only brief rest before beginning the march back toward the Nubian stronghold, now on the southern bank of the Atbara, approaching from the direction they least expected.

The terrain proved their ally, offering forest cover that thickened as they neared the Nubian stronghold. By midday, the Egyptian force was positioned in the dense tree line less than four hundred meters from the western wall.

"Now," Moses whispered to Paheri, "we wait. Let them grow complacent. Let them believe we approach from the river or the northern road." His eyes gleamed in the dappled forest light. "And when they are convinced of our intentions, we shall show them how completely they have been deceived."

Paheri reported five days later after his latest scouting mission. "They still watch for northern approaches. Their boats patrol the main channel of the Nile, and they've posted sentries along the eastern bank of the Atbara. But this western approach? Nothing."

Moses nodded, satisfied. "They believe the western bank secure due to the difficulty of crossing upstream. A reasonable assumption—for a conventional commander."

Paheri's voice came from just behind his shoulder. "We cannot storm those walls without heavy losses," the captain observed, his tone grim.

Moses nodded slowly, his mind working through the possibilities. "Then we shall not storm them," he decided, straightening up. "We'll make them come to us, or starve behind their walls."

Night fell over the land like a black cloak studded with silver stars. Moses moved silently among his men, speaking orders in hushed tones that carried with them the expectation of immediate obedience. The air was filled with the scent of the river and the distinctive smell of the acacia forests that provided their cover. Night birds called from the darkness, their cries mixing with the distant sound of Nubian sentries calling the watch.

"Begin," Moses commanded, and at once hundreds of bronze digging implements flashed in the moonlight.

The earth was hard, baked by the relentless African sun, but the Egyptian soldiers attacked it with disciplined fury. Trenches began to materialize along the western approach to the fortress, just beyond arrow range of the Nubian defenses. Moses had calculated the distance precisely, having watched the Nubian archers during their practice sessions days before.

"Deeper," he instructed as he walked the line. "A man must be able to walk on his knees without his head showing." The soldiers redoubled their efforts, sweat gleaming on their bodies despite the cool night air. The sound of bronze striking stone created a steady rhythm in the darkness.

Nubian stronghold

Inside the Nubian stronghold, a sentry cocked his head, his ears catching the faint sounds of digging carried on the night breeze. The rhythmic scraping and the soft curses of laboring men penetrated even the stone walls.

"Commander," he called softly to his superior. "Listen."

Teferi, the Nubian captain of the western wall, frowned as he registered the unmistakable sound of bronze striking stone, the grunts of men laboring. His own hands bore the calluses of years spent fortifying positions—he knew the sounds of siege preparation. "Wake the men," he ordered. "Quietly. But do not sound the alarm yet."

The Nubians assembled along the wall, peering into the darkness, unable to see the source of the sounds but knowing with growing certainty that the Egyptians had somehow materialized on their supposedly secure flank.

"Should we send a sortie?" asked one of Teferi's guards, his hand already moving to his sword hilt.

"No," the captain replied, his jaw tight. "That's what they want—to draw us out in the darkness when we cannot gauge their numbers. We wait for dawn."

The night proceeded with this strange symphony—the rhythmic sounds of digging from the darkness, the tense silence of the Nubians on their walls. When Zagwe himself was informed, the great commander's face showed none of the uncertainty that gnawed at his gut. "Let us see what faces us before we reveal our hand," the warlord commanded.

As the first light of dawn crept across the eastern sky, the Nubians lined their battlements, straining to see what the night had concealed. What they witnessed sent a chill through their ranks.

A vast network of trenches now scarred the approach to their western wall, and in these earthworks were positioned what appeared to be hundreds of Egyptian soldiers. Sunlight glinted off spear points and helmets as men moved within the zigzagging network of defenses. The morning breeze carried the scent of disturbed earth and the oil used to preserve their weapons.

"By the gods," whispered Teferi. "How did they cross the Atbara? How did they bring so many without our knowledge?"

Zagwe's face was a mask of stone as he surveyed the new threat. What had been his strongest, most secure flank was now facing a siege force of unknown size, already entrenched and positioned beyond effective bow shot. The careful plans he had made, the defensive positions that had served him for years—all suddenly worthless.

"They dig in like desert foxes," he said finally. "This changes everything." He turned to his captains. "Double the western wall guard. Move the women and children to the eastern compound. Prepare for a long siege."

In his command trench, Moses smiled as he watched the frantic activity along the Nubian battlements. The alarm trumpets were sounding, orders were being shouted, and most importantly, the defenders were rushing to reinforce the western approaches—exactly as he had planned.

What the Nubians could not see was that many of the "soldiers" in the furthest trenches were nothing more than spears and shields positioned to give the appearance of men, while the actual fighting force remained hidden in the forest, resting for what was to come.

"The deception is complete," Paheri said with admiration. "They believe we've committed our entire force to a western siege."

Moses nodded, his eyes never leaving the fortress. "Fear multiplies numbers, old friend. They see what their fears tell them to see." He pointed to the eastern wall where guards were being withdrawn to reinforce the west. "And now they weaken the very place where our true strength shall strike."

That night the soldiers again dug the trenches even deeper, the sound of their labor carrying clearly to the Nubian defenders, a constant reminder that their enemies grew stronger with each passing hour.

Chapter 25 - The Princess of Nubia

October 1483 BC - Atbara River, Nubia

A week passed, the sun rising and setting over a strange standoff. The Nubians remained secure in their fortress, but the psychological pressure of the Egyptian presence grew with each passing day. The women and children, now confined to the cramped northern compounds, added to the strain on resources and morale. Water remained plentiful thanks to the fortress well, but tensions rose as the siege continued.

On the eighth day, as the midday sun stood at its highest point, Moses emerged from the trenches into the open ground between the Egyptian positions and the Nubian walls. What followed became a spectacle that drew every eye from the battlements.

Moses stood bareheaded in the punishing sunlight, his bronzed torso gleaming with oil. In his hands, he held his khopesh, the curved sword of Egyptian nobility, its polished surface catching the light like liquid fire.

"Bring me the new recruits," he called to Paheri.

A dozen young Egyptian soldiers advanced toward their commander, their movements betraying their inexperience despite weeks of training. These were not hardened veterans but farm boys and craftsmen's sons, conscripted for this campaign and still learning the warrior's trade.

The Nubian defenders crowded the western wall to watch, momentarily forgetting their duties. Even Zagwe came to observe, his face impassive but his eyes missing nothing.

Moses began with sword work, positioning the recruits in a semicircle around him. "Hold your khopesh like this," he demonstrated, his grip firm yet relaxed. "The weapon should feel like an extension of your arm, not a burden dragging it down."

He moved among them, adjusting stances with patient precision. When one boy—barely eighteen summers—fumbled his grip, Moses guided his hands to the correct position without rebuke. "Better," he said simply. "Now watch."

What followed was a methodical demonstration of swordplay fundamentals. Moses moved through basic cuts and parries with fluid economy, each movement precise and controlled. There was nothing flashy about his technique—just the quiet mastery of a man who had spent years perfecting his craft.

"The blade follows your eyes," he instructed, demonstrating a simple diagonal cut in slow motion. "See your target first, then let the sword find it." He had them practice the movement repeatedly, correcting errors with the patience of a master craftsman teaching his trade.

After an hour of sword work, Moses called for bows. The archery training that followed was equally methodical. He demonstrated proper stance, draw, and release with consistent accuracy, his arrows finding their marks on distant targets with mechanical precision.

"Breathe in as you draw," he told a nervous recruit whose arrows were flying wide. "Hold at full draw, exhale half, then release on the pause." He stood behind the young man, guiding his form. "Your bow is only as steady as your breathing."

When the recruit's next arrow struck the target's edge, Moses nodded approvingly. "Progress. Do it again."

The javelin training that followed showcased Moses' natural athleticism. His throws were long and straight, delivered with an effortless motion that made the heavy spears seem weightless in his hands. But it was his teaching that held the Nubians' attention—the way he broke down the throwing motion into manageable steps, how he remembered each recruit's particular weaknesses and worked to correct them.

On the walls, a Nubian captain spat into the dust. "Theatrics," he growled. "Training boys to impress us."

Zagwe's eyes narrowed as he studied the Egyptian commander instructing his recruits. "No," he said slowly. "Look closer. Those are green troops, barely trained. Yet see how they respond to him—how their fear transforms into confidence under his guidance. That is leadership." He turned to his lieutenant. "A commander who can turn farm boys into warriors in the field is far more dangerous than one who merely swings a sword well."

Day after day, this ritual continued. Moses worked with different groups—swordplay one day, archery the next, sometimes hand-to-hand combat where his controlled demonstrations of holds and throws revealed both strength and restraint. The weapons and skills varied, but the outcome remained constant—a steady transformation of raw conscripts into disciplined soldiers.

Within the fortress, whispers spread among the Nubian warriors. Some noted how the Egyptian recruits moved with increasing confidence. Others observed the growing respect in the young soldiers' eyes when they looked at their commander. The women told their children to watch and learn, for this was how a true leader shaped men.

Zagwe watched his enemy's daily training sessions and recognized the deeper strategy at work. Moses was not just maintaining his siege— he was forging an army in full view of his enemies, transforming weakness into strength through patient instruction and personal example.

"He shows us our future," Zagwe told his assembled captains in the privacy of his command tent. "Every day his men grow stronger while ours grow more demoralized. And he does it openly, letting us see exactly how outmatched we will be if this continues."

The Nubian commander understood the psychological game being played. Moses was winning the battle without striking a blow, demonstrating not just his own competence but his ability to multiply that competence in others. It was leadership of the most unsettling kind—the sort that created loyalty through earned respect rather than fear.

At the northern side of the Nubian fortress where the Atbara River joined with the mighty Nile, Princess Tharbus stood alone in her quarters, a three by four-meter square area for her and two of her siblings and also her grandmother.

She was twenty summers old, born to privilege as the daughter of Zagwe, Lion of Kush and Warlord of the Upper Nile. Unlike most royal women of her bloodline, Tharbus had been educated by her father's captured Egyptian scribe, learning not only the graceful hieratic script of the northern kingdom but also their history, their gods, and their ways of war. Knowledge, her father had once told her, was a weapon sharper than any spear—though he had never imagined his daughter might one day wield that weapon against him.

The cool night breeze caressed her face, carrying with it the scent of tamarisk and the distant musk of the river. For fourteen nights, she had observed the Egyptian commander, watching as he systematically built loyalty and competence in his forces through patient instruction and personal example. There was something in his teaching style that spoke to her—a controlled strength that never descended to cruelty, a strategic mind that understood that true power came not from intimidation but from earning respect.

"He builds warriors from nothing," she whispered to herself, the words carried away by the night wind. "And they would follow him into the underworld itself."

Behind her, the door to her chambers opened silently. Makeda, her maternal grandmother and spiritual advisor to the royal house of Kush, entered with the aid of a gnarled walking stick carved from acacia wood and inlaid with ivory fetishes of protection.

"You watch the Egyptian again, today," the old woman said. It was not a question.

Makeda moved to stand beside her granddaughter, her rheumy eyes somehow still sharp enough to pick out the distant campfires. "I have dreamed of him," she said, her voice dropping to the tone she used when speaking of her visions. "Three nights in succession, the same dream. A man with the head of a lion and the wings of a falcon, standing astride the Nile as it turns to blood."

Now Tharbus turned, studying her grandmother's weathered face in the moonlight. "What does it mean?"

"Death," Makeda said simply. "Death for our people if we continue this path." She reached out with fingers twisted by age, grasping Tharbus's wrist with surprising strength. "The gods have shown me the future, child. This fortress will fall. Your father's blood will soak the earth. Our women will be taken as slaves; our children scattered like chaff in the wind."

Tharbus felt ice form in her veins despite the warm night air. Makeda's visions had guided the royal house for three generations, never once leading them astray.

"Unless..." the old woman continued, her voice dropping to a whisper.

"Unless what?" Tharbus demanded.

Makeda's eyes seemed to look beyond the physical world, seeing paths and possibilities hidden from mortal sight. "Unless you become the bridge between two worlds. The blood price must be paid, but not with the lives of our people." Her gaze sharpened, focusing on her granddaughter with sudden intensity. "You must go to him. Offer him what he desires most."

"The fortress," Tharbus breathed, understanding dawning. "But Father would rather die than surrender."

"That is precisely what he will do," Makeda confirmed. "Unless you act. The Egyptian does not desire wholesale slaughter—I have watched him as you have. He seeks victory, not vengeance. But he will do what he must."

Tharbus turned back to the view of the distant camp, her mind racing. "What you ask is betrayal."

"What I ask is salvation," Makeda corrected. "Sometimes the greatest loyalty requires the appearance of treachery. Your father built this fortress to protect our people. Would you let his pride destroy what his wisdom created?"

Long into the night they talked, grandmother and granddaughter, weighing consequences against possibilities, duty against survival. When the first hint of dawn lightened the eastern sky, Tharbus had made her decision.

With hands that trembled only slightly, she unclasped the golden amulet from around her neck—a protective charm blessed by seven high priests of Amun—and placed it on her writing table. In its place, she fastened a simple pendant of lapis lazuli, the stone of truth and judgment. Then she took up her reed pen and a fresh sheet of papyrus.

"I am Princess Tharbus, daughter of the Nubian chieftain," she began, the hieratic script flowing from her pen with practiced elegance. Each word felt like both a betrayal and a salvation.

The water boy, Amesse, was the son of her father's Egyptian body servant—a child with quick eyes and quicker feet who had been trusted to fetch fresh water each morning despite the siege. She summoned him as the sun crested the eastern hills, pressing the tightly rolled scroll into his small hand.

"You know what to do," she said softly, kneeling to meet his eyes. "Speak to no one. If you succeed, your mother will be granted her freedom when this is over, as will you."

The boy nodded solemnly, understanding far more than his twelve years would suggest. He slipped the scroll into his loincloth and took up his water skin, moving with practiced casualness toward the hidden postern gate.

Moses completed his inspection of the night guard when the waterboy emerged into the faint starlight, with the lean, almost skeletal frame of those born to hardship in the borderlands. His eyes were enormous in his thin face, darting nervously from Moses to the nearby sentries. By some miracle of stealth or desperation, he had slipped through both the Nubian defenses and the Egyptian lines—a feat that would have challenged Moses' best scouts.

Moses studied the boy for a long moment, noting the quality of his simple loincloth—not the garb of a peasant—and the distinctive blue-beaded bracelet on his wrist that marked him as a servant in a noble house.

"You risk much to be here," Moses said in a neutral tone, his hand relaxing but not moving far from his weapon.

The boy swallowed visibly, his throat working with the effort. Fear emanated from him in almost palpable waves, yet something else burned in those large, dark eyes—purpose, and perhaps awe at finding himself face to face with the commander whose name was spoken in whispers throughout the fortress.

"For you," the boy whispered, glancing over his shoulder as though expecting pursuit. From within the folds of his garment he withdrew a small object—a tightly rolled papyrus scroll bound with a thread of deep purple, the royal color of Nubian nobility.

"I am Princess Tharbus, daughter of the Nubian chieftain. For two weeks I have watched you from our walls. The gods have touched my heart. I offer you what no Egyptian commander has ever been granted—the keys to our fortress. One condition only: that you take me as your wife under Egyptian law, protecting me and my family from execution. If you agree, send a token of acceptance with the water boy."

Moses stared at the papyrus message in his hands, the carefully written hieroglyphs dancing in the flickering light of the oil lamp. The parchment carried the scent of myrrh—a royal fragrance. His weathered fingers traced the elegant symbols as he contemplated what accepting this proposal might mean. After weeks of siege beneath the merciless Ethiopian sun, his men were growing restless, their shields and spirits equally battered.

Moses presented the waterboy with the precious lapis lazuli amulet that had hung against his chest. The stone caught the first rays of sunlight, its deep blue surface reminiscent of the Nile's waters at dusk—a piece of Egypt he carried into foreign lands.

"Take this to her," Moses instructed, the weight of the amulet leaving his palm feeling strangely light and vulnerable. The boy received it with reverence, dark eyes widening at being entrusted with such a treasure.

Then, with unexpected boldness, the child gestured emphatically, pointing to Moses and holding up two fingers. He pantomimed soldiers walking alongside him, repeating the motion with increasing urgency.

Moses noticed a small tattoo on the boy's wrist—the mark of a royal servant. This was no ordinary water carrier; he belonged to the household of Princess Tharbus herself.

"You wish for my men to accompany you?" Moses questioned, knowing his words were not understood but hoping his tone conveyed the meaning.

The boy nodded vigorously, relief washing over his face.

Moses stroked his beard, considering this unexpected request. Was it a trap? Yet something in the boy's earnest expression suggested otherwise. After weighing his options—as he had done countless times since leading the Egyptian forces into this foreign campaign—he nodded and summoned the two soldiers who had stood beside him since the early days in Pharaoh's palace.

"Follow the boy," Moses instructed, his voice low enough that the sleeping camp would not be disturbed. "Keep your daggers close but hidden. If you do not return by midday, we expect the worst."

The two soldiers clasped forearms with their commander, a silent pledge to return or perish with honor. As the three figures disappeared into the morning haze, Moses felt the weight of his decision settle upon his shoulders like a stone tablet. If his men did not return, the price of his misjudgment would be measured in blood.

A tense half hour crawled by like an eternity. Moses paced the perimeter of the camp, watching the eastern horizon where the sun climbed higher, casting long shadows across the parched landscape. The distant fortress walls shimmered in the heat, seemingly impenetrable. Just as he was preparing to send a search party, he spotted two silhouettes approaching through the rippling air.

The two soldiers were returning, their normally stoic faces transformed by excitement rather than etched with fear. Moses felt the knot in his stomach loosen slightly, though years of military command had taught him that good news could turn to ash in an instant.

"Commander!" one named Bassa called out, his voice carrying across the camp. "The gods favor us today!"

The men arrived, dust-covered but unharmed, their eyes bright with what they had witnessed.

"Speak," Moses commanded, leading them to the privacy of his tent.

"We followed the boy along the winding banks of the Atbara River," Bassa began, his voice still hushed with amazement. "There is a path beneath the overhanging reeds that concealed our approach."

"At the north wall of the fortress," Bassa continued, "hidden behind a cluster of acacia and thornbush, there stands a small door built into the wooden wall—nearly invisible to unknowing eyes."

"The water boy knocked three times on the door, then once," Bassa added. "Then the door opened from the inside."

"She speaks our tongue," Bassa added with amazement. "Perfect Egyptian, as though raised on the banks of the Nile itself."

"Then she showed us the chamber," Bassa continued. "She explained that it could easily hide fifty of our best warriors. She proposes we bring our select fighters before dawn tomorrow and wait in the chamber. We can open the main gates from within while she ensures the guards at that position are... occupied elsewhere."

Moses listened intently, hope rising in his chest like the Nile during inundation season. The fact that his men had entered the enemy stronghold and returned unharmed was indeed a promising sign.

As the sun reached its zenith, Moses began making preparations, selecting his most disciplined warriors for the dawn mission. Risk remained substantial, but now there was cause for cautious optimism—perhaps even something more. The blue stone amulet, his most cherished possession, might soon become not only a symbol of military victory but of an alliance that would echo through the corridors of history.

As midnight approached, Tharbus dismissed her handmaidens, keeping only her two siblings and her most trusted companions—her father's cousin Nomti, who had opposed the war from its inception, and three senior women of her household who had raised her since her mother's death in childbirth. Together, they waited in tense silence in her private chambers, listening for the soft knock that would signal the arrival of the Egyptian force at the hidden door.

When it came—three gentle taps followed by one—Tharbus felt a strange calm descend upon her. The die was cast. Whatever happened now was in the hands of the gods.

She opened the door herself, admitting not just Moses but fifty of his most skilled guards, now trained in warfare, who moved with the silent precision of desert predators. In the dim lamplight, the Egyptian commander was even more imposing than he had appeared from the distant walls—tall and broad-shouldered, with the muscular build of a man who led from the front rather than the rear. His face was all sharp planes and angles, like a statue carved by a master craftsman, dominated by eyes that missed nothing and revealed little.

Those eyes locked with hers now, studying her with an intensity that made her feel as though he could see through flesh to the thoughts beneath. She forced herself to meet his gaze without flinching, chin raised in the proud manner of her royal lineage.

"We must move quickly," Moses said. "Explain how we reach the main gate."

As Tharbus unrolled the fortress plans and outlined their route, she was struck by the cool efficiency with which Moses absorbed the information. There was no wasted motion in his body or mind—every gesture, every question served a purpose. Yet beneath that martial discipline, she sensed something else—an intelligence that went beyond mere military calculation, hints of a man whose complexity matched her own.

When she finished her explanation, he divided his men with quick commands, then fixed her with that penetrating gaze once more. "You make sure you stay in your quarters with your family."

"As you command..." she replied while Moses moved to the door.

"Now!" Moses commanded, his voice echoing through the stone chamber where he and his fifty chosen warriors had positioned themselves after infiltrating the stronghold under cover of darkness.

The Egyptian soldiers moved with practiced precision, unbarring the massive western gate—the fortress's only entrance—and forcing it open. The ancient hinges groaned in protest as morning light spilled into the courtyard, illuminating the scene for what was to come.

Outside, the main body of the Egyptian army waited. At Moses' signal, they poured through the opening like a flood of bronze and leather, weapons gleaming in the early sun. Above them, Egyptian bowmen took position along the fortress walls, arrows nocked and trained on the courtyard below. Their faces were masks of grim determination as they secured the high ground, cutting off any possibility of escape.

Inside the fortress, confusion erupted into panic as Nubian warriors realized they had been betrayed from within. Some rushed toward the now-open gate, only to meet the advancing Egyptian forces head-on. Others looked desperately for escape routes that did not exist, finding instead the silhouettes of bowmen ready to strike down any who attempted to scale the walls.

"Close ranks!" Moses called to his men as they moved from their position near the gate toward the central hall. "Leave none behind you!"

The battle that followed was less a contest of arms than a methodical culling. The Nubians fought with the desperate courage of trapped men, but their disorganized resistance was no match for Egyptian discipline. Those who surrendered were bound; those who continued to resist met swift ends at spearpoint or beneath Egyptian blades.

Moses cut his way through the chaos, his sword rising and falling in practiced arcs. His years of military training had honed his body into a weapon as deadly as any blade, and he moved with the fluid grace of a predator among prey. Two Nubian warriors rushed him simultaneously—he sidestepped the first, parried the second, then dispatched both with economical strikes that wasted neither energy nor time.

"The chieftain is in the central hall," reported one of Moses' captains, blood streaming from a shallow cut above his eye.

Moses nodded, gathering a dozen of his best men with a gesture. Together they fought their way deeper into the fortress, leaving behind them a courtyard now carpeted with Nubian dead and dying. The bowmen above tracked their movement, shifting position to maintain their deadly coverage of any potential escape route.

They found Chieftain Zagwe in the central hall as expected, surrounded by the last of his captains—proud men who stood with weapons drawn, knowing what fate awaited them but refusing to submit without a final stand.

The chieftain raised his sword and charged at Moses with a roar of defiance. His remaining captains followed, their war cries filling the chamber as they launched themselves at the Egyptian force.

Moses met the attack, blade ringing against blade as they fought across the stone floor of the hall. The older man's strength was surprising, his technique honed by decades of warfare. For a moment, Moses found himself driven back by the ferocity of the assault, his sandals slipping on the blood-slick stones.

Then his training reasserted itself. He parried a wild swing, stepped inside the chieftain's guard, and struck him with the pommel of his sword—not to kill but to subdue. The Nubian leader crumpled to the floor, blood streaming from his temple.

Around them, the battle for the hall concluded with brutal efficiency. The Nubian captains fought to the last man, preferring death to capture. Only Zagwe and three of his most valued captains were deliberately spared, subdued rather than slain by Moses' explicit orders.

From the courtyard came only silence now. The bowmen remained at their posts, arrows trained on the few surviving Nubians who had been forced to their knees in surrender.

"Bind him," Moses ordered his men, pointing to the unconscious form of Zagwe. "He and these captains. They are to be taken to Thebes alive."

As the prisoners were secured, Moses stepped to the hall's entrance and surveyed the fortress that had been, until this morning, the heart of

Nubian resistance. The courtyard was a tableau of conquest—Egyptian soldiers moving methodically among Nubian bodies, ensuring none would rise again. The western gate stood open to the desert beyond, a path that would soon bear the survivors to judgment before Pharaoh's throne.

Victory was complete. Another piece of Egypt's empire secured. Yet as Moses watched his men drag the bound chieftain away, he could not help but wonder if, in another life, their positions might have been reversed—if he might have been the one defending his people against a conqueror's sword rather than wielding it in a foreign king's name.

Two days later, Moses led a procession from the captured fortress— his soldiers marching in disciplined formation, the captured chieftains walking in chains, and his new wife riding beside him, her head held high despite the hostile stares of many Egyptians and the accusatory glances of her own people. Behind them came her family and attendants, now under Moses' protection as promised.

The journey back to Thebes took sixteen days, each one bringing them closer to the moment of truth—would Pharaoh honor Moses' promise to his Nubian bride, or would royal prerogative supersede a commander's oath?

As they approached the great city, its white walls gleaming in the distance like a mirage, a royal procession emerged to meet them. Thutmose I, too weak to stand for long, was carried on a litter of gold and ivory, his frail body nearly lost among the opulent cushions. Courtiers and priests followed in his wake, and at his side walked Princess Hatshepsut, her face an unreadable mask as she watched Moses approach with his Nubian bride.

"You have saved Egypt," Thutmose proclaimed when Moses knelt before him, triumph and exhaustion etched in equal measure on the young commander's face. "As I knew you would."

The Pharaoh's eyes moved past Moses to the line of captives, focusing on the proud figure of the Nubian chieftain who still glared defiance despite his chains and wounds.

"Bring him to me," Thutmose ordered, his voice suddenly cold.

Guards dragged the chieftain forward and forced him to his knees before the royal litter. With surprising strength for one so frail, Thutmose I took a ceremonial dagger from a cushion beside him, its blade glinting in the harsh sun. Without ceremony, he personally slit the throat of the elder—Tharbus's father. Blood sprayed across the sand as the chieftain collapsed, his final expression one of grim satisfaction that he had at least died by a pharaoh's hand rather than a common executioner's.

Moses felt Tharbus grip his arm with fingers that would surely leave bruises, but her face revealed nothing as she watched her father die. She had known the price of her choice from the beginning.

"The others will be executed at the temple of Amun," Thutmose announced, his voice carrying to all assembled. "Their blood will feed the gods who protected Egypt in its hour of need."

Then, surprising everyone present, he turned to Moses and said, "But I will honor your promise. The princess and her immediate family may live as Egyptians, under your protection." His eyes, sunken in his wasted face yet still sharp with intelligence, shifted to Tharbus. "In gratitude for what you have done for my men, I shall call you Isis from now on. Consider this Pharaoh's wedding gift to you both." Isis, the revered goddess of protection and healing was a name spoken with reverence, and now, it belonged to the woman who had saved many from death.

Back at Thebes

As the royal procession turned back toward the city, Hatshepsut remained behind momentarily, her tall figure silhouetted against the sky. She approached Moses with measured steps, her eyes—outlined heavily with kohl—taking in every detail of his appearance and that of his new wife.

"So, the hero returns with exotic spoils," she said, her voice pitched for his ears alone. "A fortress conquered and a foreign princess claimed. The court will speak of little else for months." Her gaze locked with his. "You've changed, Moses. Something in your eyes..."

"War changes all men, Princess," he replied carefully.

"Indeed." She studied Isis for a moment longer, assessing the Nubian woman as one might evaluate a potential rival—or ally. "Welcome home, Commander," she said finally, her voice carrying a note that only Moses seemed to detect—a mixture of respect and something more complex, more personal. Then she turned, following her father, her back straight, her head high.

As the royal procession disappeared into the swirling dust, Moses stood with his new wife at his side, contemplating all that had transpired since he had left Thebes as an untested commander. He had proven himself in battle, conquered the unconquerable, and returned with a wife whose courage matched his own. Yet something told him that the greatest challenges still lay ahead.

Behind them, the other captive chieftains were being dragged to Thebes and their eventual execution. Before them lay the gleaming city, its temples and palaces promising a return to civilization after weeks in the wilderness of war. And beside him stood Isis, her hand still on his arm, her presence a reminder of how quickly life could change course.

"Are you ready?" he asked her, nodding toward the city that would now be her home.

"I was ready the moment I sent you that message," she replied, her voice steady despite all she had witnessed. "The gods have set us on this path together. Let us see where it leads."

With that, they moved forward toward Thebes, toward the future that awaited them both—a future neither could have imagined when the Nubian war began. Moses, once a prince of Egypt raised in luxury and trained in temples, had become a commander of men, a conqueror of fortresses, and husband to a woman who had sacrificed everything for her people's survival.

The gods, it seemed, were not finished with him yet.

Chapter 26 - Pharaoh Moses

1482 BC Thebes

The air in the small chamber hung heavy with incense and intrigue. Tendrils of aromatic smoke curled upward from alabaster burners, casting shifting shadows across walls adorned with painted scenes of gods and kings. Five men sat in a semicircle; their faces partially obscured by the wavering light of oil lamps made of hammered gold. They were not the kind of men who typically gathered in secret—each held power openly in the courts of Thebes—yet tonight they spoke in hushed tones, their eyes darting occasionally to the sealed doorway where two trusted guards stood with spears crossed.

"Thutmose is dead," said Hapuseneb, the High Priest of Amun, his jeweled fingers steepled before his thin lips. The lamplight caught in the lapis lazuli and carnelian of his broad collar, sending splashes of color across his imperious face. "The question before us is not one of mourning, but of Egypt's future." His voice, accustomed to resonating through the vast halls of temples, was now deliberately subdued, almost a whisper.

Ahmose Pennekh, the aging Commander of the Royal Guards who had served two pharaohs, nodded gravely. Deep lines carved his weathered face like the dry riverbeds of the desert, testaments to battles fought and secrets kept. The gold rings on his gnarled fingers clinked softly as he stroked his grizzled beard. "The succession must be immediate," he growled. "The Nubians have only just been subdued. Any sign of weakness and they will rise again. I've seen what happens when power passes uncertainly—blood flows like the Nile in flood season."

"Hatshepsut cannot rule as king," declared Ineni, the Master Architect whose genius had transformed Thebes into a city of wonder. Though his body had begun to bow with age, his eyes remained sharp as a falcon's, accustomed to measuring and judging with precision. "It is against Ma'at—against the very order of creation. A woman on the throne would invite chaos from both gods and men."

The fourth man, Userhat, the vizier, remained silent, his calculating eyes moving from face to face. His robes were the simplest among them, belying the vast wealth he controlled. The rings on his fingers were few but of extraordinary quality, speaking of a man who understood true value over mere ostentation.

The fifth man sat apart from the others, his build more muscular, his skin burnished by recent warfare and desert sun. Unlike the others, he wore no elaborate wig, his head shaved clean in the style of a warrior. The light caught the planes of his face—strong, determined, with a prominent nose and jaw that had been immortalized in victory stelae throughout Nubia. His eyes, deep-set and penetrating, had seen both the opulence of the palace and the hardship of battle. This was Moses, recently returned from his Nubian campaign, husband to the Nubian princess now called Isis, and—in the room all knew it—Moses is a Hebrew by birth.

"There is another option," said Hapuseneb finally, breaking the silence. His voice was smooth as oil, practiced in the arts of persuasion that had elevated him from provincial nobility to one of the most powerful positions in Egypt. "One that preserves the stability of Egypt while adhering to tradition."

All eyes turned to Moses.

"Moses is Thutmose's adopted son," Hapuseneb continued, leaning forward so that his gold pectoral caught the lamplight. "He has proven himself in battle. The soldiers worship him—the defeat of Nubia has made him a living legend. The people already revere him as the conqueror. The priests respect his piety." A slight smile played at his lips. "And most importantly, he has no competing claim to the throne that might divide the kingdom."

Moses felt a tightening in his chest, as if a vice had closed around his heart. Since returning from Nubia with his bride, her belly already beginning to swell with their first child, he had expected to return to the relative peace of the priesthood, or perhaps a military command. Not this. Never this. The weight of the proposal seemed to press the air from his lungs.

"Impossible," he said, his voice low but firm as granite. "I cannot be Pharaoh. I am not of royal blood." In the silence that followed his words, he could hear the distant call of a nightjar from the palace gardens, a mournful sound that seemed to echo his own disquiet.

Userhat leaned forward, the gold of his broad collar catching the lamplight, his eyes narrowing like a cat preparing to pounce. "Blood can be... redefined. Stories can be told, and with enough power behind them, they become truth." His thin lips curled into a smile that did not reach his eyes. "We are the makers of truth in Egypt, my friend. The scribes write what we tell them to write. The people believe what we tell them to believe."

Ineni, who had known Moses since he was a boy rescued from the Nile, spoke next. His voice carried the gravitas of decades spent building Egypt's greatest monuments. "You would not be the first pharaoh with humble origins. Many dynasties began with men who had no right to rule—until they took it." He gestured with hands calloused despite his high station, hands that had shaped the future of Egypt in stone. "Power creates its own legitimacy."

"And what of Hatshepsut?" Moses asked. "The daughter of Thutmose. Would she accept such an arrangement?" The question hung in the air, heavy as the incense smoke.

A knowing look passed between the four officials, a silent communication born of years plotting the course of the Two Lands together.

"She would," Hapuseneb confirmed, his voice smooth as freshly oiled papyrus, "if she were to become your Great Royal Wife." He spread his hands, rings glinting. "A perfect solution—she maintains her dignity as daughter of Thutmose and gains the power of queenship, while you gain the legitimacy of marriage into the royal line. Egypt gains stability."

The room fell silent as Moses absorbed the enormity of what was being proposed. Outside, the gentle lapping of the Nile against the palace quay provided a rhythmic counterpoint to his racing thoughts. Through the small window, he could see stars scattered across the night sky like jewels on Isis's dark skin.

"And the child?" he asked finally, thinking of Tharbus—now called Isis—heavy with his child. The memory of her smile that morning flashed through his mind, the way she had guided his hand to feel the kick of their unborn child.

"Your Nubian wife will be recognized as a secondary royal wife," Userhat assured him, his tone suggesting this was a generous concession. "Her children will be princes of Egypt. But Egypt needs this union with Hatshepsut to heal old wounds and secure your legitimacy." His eyes hardened slightly. "The nobility will accept no less."

Moses stood and walked to a small window that overlooked the Nile, silver in the moonlight. The river flowed eternal, unchanging in its changing, while the lives of men—even pharaohs—were as brief as the morning mist upon its surface. He thought of the Israelites and of the God they worshipped, so different from the pantheon of Egypt. And he thought of his people, laboring under Egyptian taskmasters, their backs scarred by whips, their spirits crushed by generations of servitude.

Perhaps as Pharaoh, he could ease their burden. Perhaps this was why he had been spared as an infant, why he had been raised in this house of power. The thought took root in his mind like a seed finding fertile soil—a purpose that might justify the deception he was about to embrace.

"I will do it," he said finally, turning back to face the men who had just made him king. His voice was steady now, filled with a new resolve. "For Egypt. And for peace."

As the words left his lips, Moses felt as though he stood at a crossroads, the path ahead shrouded in mist. But there was no turning back now. The die was cast, and with it, the fate of two peoples— Egyptian and Hebrew—now rested on his shoulders.

Coronation of Moses

The Great Courtyard of Amun-Ra blazed with the light of a thousand torches, their flames dancing in the gentle evening breeze like golden leaves. The scent of myrrh and frankincense hung in the air, mingling with the perfumes of the assembled nobility. Nobles from throughout the Two Lands had assembled, their finest linens gleaming white against their oiled skin, jewelery glinting at throats and wrists—wealth enough to ransom kingdoms displayed on their bodies. Women's eyes rimmed with kohl gazed admiringly at the spectacle, their lips reddened with ochre, their wigs adorned with lotus flowers and gold beads that tinkled softly with each movement of their heads.

The common people pressed against the outer walls, straining for a glimpse of the spectacle within, their excited murmurs rising like the hum of bees. Soldiers stood at rigid attention, their polished spears catching the torchlight, their leather armor creaking as they maintained their positions.

Moses stood before the altar, adorned in the regalia of pharaoh—the double crown of Upper and Lower Egypt heavy upon his brow, pressing into his flesh as if to remind him of the burden he now carried. The false beard, symbol of divine kingship, had been affixed to his chin with scented wax, its weight pulling at his skin. The crook and flail, symbols of the shepherd and the disciplinarian, were crossed upon his chest. His body had been anointed with sacred oils that made his skin glisten in the torchlight, purified in the waters of the Nile brought in ceremonial vessels, and blessed by the priests of every major deity.

He had spent the morning in ritual purification, priests chanting over him as they prepared his body for transformation from mortal to divine. Now, as the sun set and the stars emerged in the darkening sky, he would complete the journey from man to god-king.

Beside him stood Hatshepsut, regal and composed in a gown of finest linen so sheer it seemed to capture light rather than cloth. Gold adorned her neck, arms, and ankles, and a ceremonial uraeus—the royal cobra—adorned her brow. If she harbored any resentment at this arrangement, she concealed it perfectly behind a mask of serene dignity. Her kohl-lined eyes met his briefly—not with love, but with understanding. This was a marriage of state, a union to preserve a dynasty, a pact between two people raised to prioritize duty above all else.

Behind them both stood Isis, formerly Tharbus, Princess of Nubia. Her belly now swelled visibly with Moses' child, and her dark beauty drew many admiring glances. Unlike the Egyptians around her, her skin was the deep, rich color of the fertile soil of Upper Nubia, marked with the ritual scars of her people—thin, precise lines that curved across her cheekbones like the phases of the moon. She had adapted quickly to Egyptian customs, learning the language and the intricate court etiquette with remarkable speed. Yet in her eyes, Moses could still see the fierce spirit of the woman who had first watched him from the battlements of her father's fortress. Where Hatshepsut's gaze held calculation, Isis's held genuine affection—and something more, a quiet strength that had drawn him to her from their first meeting.

Userhat stepped forward, resplendent in his leopard skin mantle and elaborate headdress. His voice, trained through decades of temple rituals, carried across the hushed courtyard like the call of a god. "Behold Son of Ra, Lord of the Two Lands, Strong Bull of Ma'at, chosen of Amun, Moses!"

The crowd erupted in acclamation, thousands of voices joining in a roar of approval that shook the very stones of the courtyard. The sound washed over Moses like a physical force, nearly staggering him with its intensity. These people—his people now—believed in him, trusted him to lead them into prosperity and security, to maintain the balance between chaos and order, to stand as intermediary between them and the gods.

But as he raised his hands to acknowledge their adoration, the heavy gold bracelets sliding against his wrists, Moses felt the weight of his deception. He was not the son of Thutmose, not even Egyptian by birth. He was Hebrew, born to slaves, saved by a princess's whim and now elevated to godhood in the eyes of the very people who oppressed his true kin. The irony was sharp as a ceremonial knife, cutting through the glory of the moment.

Later, as the celebration continued around him—nobles feasting on roasted gazelle and duck, musicians playing upon harps and sistrums, dancers twirling with rings of fire—Moses found himself momentarily alone with Hatshepsut on a balcony overlooking the festivities. The moon hung low and full over the Nile, turning the river to a ribbon of silver that wound through the darkened land.

"You seem troubled." she said, the last word tinged with irony. Her perfume, an exotic blend of lotus and cassia, wafted between them, marking her territory as surely as a boundary stone.

"I am contemplating the weight of responsibility," he replied carefully, watching a heron wing its way across the face of the moon, solitary and free as he would never be again.

Hatshepsut laughed, a sound like the chiming of small bells, practiced and precise. "Do not deceive yourself, Moses. We both know who rules Egypt now." Her voice was low enough that only he could hear, her painted lips barely moving.

Moses turned to look at her fully. In the moonlight, her profile was sharp, determined, beautiful in the way of a finely crafted dagger. The royal uraeus gleamed at her brow, the cobra poised to strike.

"You have the crown," she continued, running a slender finger along the rim of her golden wine cup, "but I have the knowledge. I have been raised from birth to rule. I know every noble family's weakness, every priest's secret ambition, every foreign court's vulnerability." Her eyes, rimmed with kohl, narrowed slightly. "You have been raised to serve—first as a prince, then as a priest, then as a commander. Now you will serve as Pharaoh, but make no mistake: I am the power behind that throne."

Her words were delivered without heat, a simple statement of fact rather than a threat. And in that moment, Moses realized that Hatshepsut had accepted this arrangement not as a defeat but as an opportunity—a way to exercise the power that tradition denied her.

Before he could respond, she glided away, her linen gown whispering against the polished stone floor as she returned to the celebration with a radiant smile that revealed nothing of their exchange. Moses watched as she moved through the crowd, stopping to speak with a priestess here, a commander there, weaving the invisible threads of influence with practiced skill.

Across the courtyard, Moses saw Isis seated upon a cushioned chair, receiving the blessings of nobility. Though she wore Egyptian finery—a beaded collar of turquoise and gold, armlets shaped like protective serpents—she maintained the dignity of her Nubian heritage in her posture, her head held high as befitted a princess of the south. Her hand rested protectively over her belly, a silent communion with the life growing within. She caught his eye and smiled—a genuine smile, untainted by the political machinations surrounding them, a private moment in the midst of public spectacle.

At least in her, Moses thought, he had found something real amidst the illusions of power. A harbor in the storm that was surely coming.

The morning sun streamed through the high windows of the royal audience chamber, casting long rectangles of light across the polished limestone floor, its golden warmth belying the tense atmosphere within. Moses sat upon the throne of Egypt, a massive chair of cedarwood overlaid with gold leaf and inlaid with ivory and precious stones. The tall back of the throne was adorned with images of the gods bestowing life upon the pharaoh, while its arms ended in carved lion heads, symbols of royal might.

Moses wore the red crown of Lower Egypt today, its weight less physically taxing than the double crown but no less symbolically burdensome. His body had been oiled and painted for the occasion, golden dust highlighting his cheekbones, kohl extending his eyes in the sacred manner. He was hearing petitions from nobles and commoners alike, the steady stream of supplicants having begun at dawn and showing no signs of abating as midday approached.

At his right hand stood a scribe, a slight man with quick eyes who recorded each decision in meticulous hieroglyphs on a fresh roll of papyrus, his reed pen moving with practiced precision. At his left stood Hatshepsut, ostensibly as his supportive queen, but in reality, providing guidance through subtle gestures and whispered advice. She wore a gown of pleated linen so fine it seemed to float around her like mist, and her jewelery clinked softly with each small movement—a constant reminder of her presence.

A delegation from the Delta approached, bowing low before the dais, their foreheads touching the cool stone floor in prostration. Their spokesman, a thin man with the shaved head of a priest and eyes reddened from the dust of travel, spoke of poor harvests and the need for grain from the royal storehouses. His voice trembled slightly as he described children with swollen bellies and elders too weak to leave their pallets.

As he concluded his plea, Moses glanced at Hatshepsut, who gave an almost imperceptible nod, her eyes calculating—weighing political advantage against cost to the treasury.

"Let it be done," Moses decreed, his voice resonating through the chamber with the authority he was still learning to wield. "The storehouses at Memphis shall be opened to provide relief." He paused, then added, "And send physicians to assess the cause of this famine. If the canals need dredging or the irrigation systems repair, it shall be attended to before the next planting season."

Hatshepsut's eyebrow raised slightly at this addition—a small sign of surprise or perhaps approval. The delegation withdrew, showering blessings upon the new pharaoh's name, their faces alight with relief and gratitude.

When the last petitioner had departed, the sun's angle indicating late afternoon, Moses rose, feeling the stiffness in his back from hours of sitting in formal posture. Servants immediately approached with refreshments—cool water scented with mint, dates stuffed with honey and nuts, thin wafers of bread that melted on the tongue.

"You did well," Hatshepsut said, surprising him with what sounded like genuine approval. She accepted a silver cup of wine from a servant, taking a small sip before continuing. "The people are pleased with their new pharaoh. They find you approachable yet decisive." A slight smile played at her lips. "A welcome change after my father's... stricter approach."

"They are pleased because I granted them what they asked for," Moses replied, stretching subtly to ease his cramped muscles. The weight of the crown had left an indentation around his temples that throbbed dully. "That is an easy path to popularity, but not always to good governance."

A flicker of respect showed in Hatshepsut's eyes. "Perhaps you will make a pharaoh after all." She tilted her head, studying him with new interest. "You surprise me, Moses. I had expected to guide your every decision, yet you show wisdom of your own."

Later that night, as Moses lay beside Isis in their royal chambers, listening to her soft breathing in sleep, he contemplated the strange turn his life had taken. The chamber was spacious and luxurious; its walls painted with scenes of plentiful harvests and successful hunts—images of abundance meant to ensure the same in life. Silver lamps burned sweet-scented oil, casting a gentle glow over the polished cedar furniture inlaid with ivory and gold. Through the open balcony doors, a cool breeze carried the scent of night-blooming jasmine from the gardens below, along with the distant sound of water being drawn from the sacred pool.

From foundling to pharaoh, from adopted prince to ruler of the mightiest kingdom on earth. And soon to be a father. The child Isis carried would be raised as Egyptian royalty, never knowing the hardship of his father's true people. Would that be a blessing or a curse? Moses wasn't certain.

Perhaps this was his destiny—to use his position to bridge the divide between Egyptian and Hebrew, to end the suffering of his people without bloodshed or conflict. Perhaps in time, he could even reveal his true heritage and be accepted nonetheless. The throne gave him power; wisdom would teach him how to use it.

With these hopeful thoughts, Moses drifted into sleep, his hand resting protectively over Isis's belly, unaware that the God of his ancestors had plans far different from his own—plans that would shake the very foundations of Egypt and change the course of history forever.

Chapter 27 - Life in the Palace

1481 BC Thebes Pharaoh Thutmose II

The heat of the day had begun to subside as Moses, now Thutmose II, Pharaoh of all Egypt, Lord of the Two Lands, descended the alabaster steps of the royal palace. His sandaled feet whispered against the polished stone, each step carrying the weight of dual identities that threatened to tear his soul asunder.

"You have matters in the northern quarter to attend this evening, Divine One?" Sennefer, his most trusted vizier, matched his stride, keeping his voice low enough that the palace guards could not overhear.

Moses flicked his eyes toward the man. "I do. Until the moon reaches its zenith, I am not to be disturbed."

The Pharaoh's guards remained at the palace entrance as he strode toward the small chamber concealed behind the temple of Amun-Ra. Here, in this sanctuary unknown to all but Sennefer, the transformation began. Strong fingers removed the heavy gold pectoral from his chest, the uraeus serpent crown from his brow. Layer by layer, Pharaoh Thutmose II disappeared, and in his place emerged a figure still royal but lacking the divine trappings—Moses, adopted prince of Egypt, openly Hebrew by birth, but secretly the very Pharaoh who ruled the empire.

The gold-threaded robes were exchanged for simpler garments—fine enough for a prince, humble enough to create an atmosphere of scholarship rather than royal dictate. Only a single gold armband remained, marking his station as a prince of Egypt. His eyes—deep-set and questioning—reflected the burden of his dual existence.

The chamber glowed with the warm light of oil lamps, but tonight the familiar space held additional aromas that stirred something deep within Moses's memory—the scent of unleavened barley bread, olives crushed with wild herbs, and dates sweetened with honey in the Hebrew manner. Seven elders sat in a semicircle upon woven reed mats, their weathered faces animated in discussion that fell silent as Moses entered.

Their bodies bore the unmistakable signs of hard labor—calloused hands, sun-leathered skin, shoulders slightly stooped from years under burdens no Egyptian noble would ever bear.

"I trust you have been treated with proper hospitality?" Moses asked, settling himself on a simple wooden chair before them.

Ammiel, eldest among them, inclined his head respectfully, his silver beard catching the lamplight. The old man's eyes held a warmth that reminded Moses achingly of something he could not quite place—a feeling of safety, of being cherished. "Indeed, Prince Moses. Such comforts are foreign to us. We are grateful that you, born of our blood but raised in Pharaoh's house, have not forgotten your origins." He gestured to the simple meal spread between them. "Tonight we hoped you might share bread with us, as your father Abraham did with strangers, never knowing they were angels of the Most High."

Moses felt his chest tighten as the familiar scent of the bread reached him more fully. Unbidden, a fragment of memory flickered—small hands breaking bread while a woman's voice hummed softly, words he had not understood then but which now seemed to hover at the edge of recognition. His mother Jochebed, blessing bread in their humble dwelling beside the Nile, her work-roughened hands gentle as she placed morsels in his eager mouth.

"How could I forget?" he replied carefully, his voice catching slightly. "The blood of Jacob runs in my veins, though fate placed me in the house of Pharaoh." He spoke the words with conviction, for they were true, if incomplete.

Nun, a younger man whose weathered face spoke of years hauling stone blocks under the merciless sun, studied Moses with eyes that held both respect and desperate hope. His calloused hands bore fresh cuts from rope and stone—marks Moses recognized from inspecting construction sites as Pharaoh. "It gives our people hope, my Prince, that one of our own sits so close to power. My wife birthed our third son last month, and when I held him..." Nun's voice broke slightly. "I wondered if he might live to see freedom, if perhaps through your influence, our suffering may ease."

The bitter irony of these words was not lost on Moses. The very suffering Nun spoke of was, by law and tradition, mandated by him in his role as Pharaoh Thutmose II. Yet each week, as he learned more of the Hebrew ways, the contradiction tore at his conscience like vultures at carrion. As he looked at Nun's scarred hands—hands that had likely helped build the very palace where Moses now held court—the weight of his deception felt crushing.

"Show me again the sacred text you brought," Moses gestured toward the scrolls beside Ammiel, his voice rougher than intended. "The Shema, was it not?"

Eleazar, a man of middle years whose gentle manner spoke of learning despite his lowly station, smiled as he reached for the precious scroll. "Ah yes, the prayer every Hebrew child learns at his mother's knee. My own grandmother taught it to me when I was but three summers old, as it was taught to her, and her grandmother before." His eyes softened with memory. "She would hold me close and whisper the words, making me repeat them until they lived in my heart rather than merely my mind."

Ammiel unrolled the parchment with reverent hands. The Hebrew characters—so different from the hieroglyphs Moses commanded as Pharaoh—seemed to pulse with life in the flickering light. As Moses stared at them, something stirred in the deepest recesses of memory— not the shapes of the letters, but the rhythm, the cadence, the way the words wanted to be spoken.

"Shema Yisrael, Adonai Eloheinu, Adonai Echad," Eleazar intoned, his voice dropping to a melodic chant that seemed to wrap around Moses like warm linen on a cold night.

Moses closed his eyes, and suddenly he was four years old again, small fingers pressed against a woman's throat as she sang these very words, feeling the vibration of her voice, the steady beat of her heart beneath his palm. The memory hit him with such force that his breath caught. Jochebed—his birth mother—rocking him as darkness fell over their humble dwelling, her voice carrying both love and desperate prayer as she prepared to surrender him to the Nile and to the God she trusted to preserve him.

"Mama," he whispered in Hebrew, the word slipping out unbidden, his childhood voice breaking through decades of Egyptian training.

The elders exchanged glances, not understanding the significance of what they had witnessed, but recognizing the profound emotion that had swept over their princely student.

"Hear, O Israel, the Lord our God, the Lord is One," Ammiel translated gently, his own voice thick with unexpected emotion. "These words are the foundation of our faith, Prince Moses. They remind us that despite our bondage in Egypt, we serve but one God—the God who sees our suffering and remembers His promises."

Moses repeated the Hebrew phrase, his tongue finding the unfamiliar syllables with surprising ease, as though his body remembered what his mind had forgotten. The melody came back to him unbidden—not just the tune, but the way his mother had swayed as she sang, the protective circle of her arms, the scent of her hair as she bent over him. His pronunciation was nearly perfect, startling even himself.

"Your tongue knows these words, though your mind has forgotten them," observed Jephunneh, the youngest, barely past thirty but already bearing the marks of hard labor. His insight came not from learning but from a shepherd's wisdom, earned watching over flocks in the wilderness. "The Most High planted them deep, where Pharaoh's tutors could not reach."

Moses nodded, unable to speak past the tightness in his throat. The chamber suddenly felt charged with presence, as though the God they spoke of hovered near, drawing him back to a faith he had barely known he possessed.

"The blessing over bread now," Moses requested, his voice hoarse with emotion. "That I might honor the God of our fathers when I break bread." As he spoke, his hands moved of their own accord, cupped slightly as though holding something precious—the way Jochebed had taught him to hold the bread while she blessed it, reverent and expectant.

"Baruch atah Adonai, Eloheinu Melech ha'olam, hamotzi lechem min ha'aretz," Ammiel pronounced slowly, his gnarled hands making the same gentle gesture Moses remembered, raising the bread toward heaven before breaking it.

Moses repeated the words, his pronunciation improving with each attempt. The guttural "ch" sound that had once caught in his throat now flowed naturally, as though some barrier had dissolved. When Ammiel broke the bread and offered him a piece, Moses found himself kissing it softly before eating—another gesture that came from memory deeper than thought.

Eleazar leaned forward, his eyes bright with understanding. "You honor the bread as my grandmother did, as all Hebrew mothers teach their sons. The kiss acknowledges God's gift, shows gratitude for sustenance." He paused, studying Moses with new curiosity. "How long were you with your birth mother before the princess found you?"

"Four years," Moses replied without thinking, then caught himself. He had never spoken of this to the elders before, had maintained the fiction that he had been found as an infant. The admission hung in the air like incense, heavy with implication.

"Four years," Ammiel repeated thoughtfully, stroking his beard. "Old enough to walk, to speak, to learn the Shema and the blessings. Old enough to remember, even if the memories were buried deep." His weathered face creased with something approaching awe. "The Most High preserved not just your life, Prince Moses, but your soul. He hid His truth within you, waiting for this time to resurrect it."

"Not just preserved," added Jamin, an elder who had remained mostly silent, a man whose scarred hands spoke of decades working metal in Pharaoh's foundries. His voice carried the weight of hard-won wisdom. "My son was taken to work the copper mines when he was twelve. Ten years he labored there, speaking only Egyptian, eating only Egyptian food, living by Egyptian ways. When he finally returned to us, we feared we had lost him to their culture." Jamin's eyes brightened. "But when we sang the evening prayers, his voice joined ours as if he had never left. The deep places of the heart remember what the mind forgets."

Moses felt tears threatening—tears that a pharaoh could never shed, but which a son returning to his heritage might be forgiven. The simple act of sharing bread with these men felt more significant than any royal banquet, more nourishing than the elaborate feasts of the palace. This was communion not just with food, but with a people, a faith, an identity he had thought lost forever.

As the evening deepened and the oil in the lamps burned lower, Moses found himself asking questions that revealed the depth of his hunger—not for knowledge, but for belonging. He learned how Hebrew fathers blessed their sons, how mothers taught their daughters the songs of their people, how families gathered on the Sabbath to remember that they were more than slaves, that they carried within them the promise of something greater.

When the moon reached its apex, Moses rose from his chair with reluctance that surprised him. The evening had passed like a moment, yet felt like a lifetime. "I must take my leave of you now, my teachers. The palace has many eyes, and questions would arise if a prince, even one of Hebrew birth, spent too many hours with—" He caught himself before saying 'slaves,' the word suddenly seeming too harsh, too distant. "—with my people," he finished instead.

Ammiel clasped his arm in a gesture of respect that no Egyptian would ever offer a Pharaoh, but which felt natural, right, familial. "Until next week then, Prince Moses. May the God of our fathers continue to awaken what He has planted within you." The old man's eyes held depths of compassion that made Moses feel truly seen for the first time in years. "And may He give you strength for the path He is preparing."

"And may He give you all strength for your labors," Moses replied, the blessing feeling more significant than he had intended. The weight of his gold armband seemed to burn against his skin—the only physical reminder of the deception that separated him from complete honesty with these men who had become his teachers, his anchors to a heritage he was only beginning to reclaim.

He left them then, these men who knew him as Moses the Hebrew, rescued from death by water, raised in Pharaoh's house but still connected to his birth people. They watched him go with reverence and hope, never suspecting that when next they prostrated themselves before the Great House of Pharaoh, it would be their student to whom they bowed.

In the privacy of his innermost chamber later that night, Moses stood before a polished copper mirror, the weight of the double crown once again upon his head. His reflection stared back, adorned with all the trappings of godhood that his Hebrew teachers would consider blasphemous idolatry. But behind the painted eyes and artificial beard, something had changed. The face looking back at him held echoes of the child who had learned the Shema at his mother's knee, who had kissed bread in gratitude, who had belonged somewhere before he belonged everywhere.

1480 BC Hatshepsut's Criticism

Since giving birth to young Menkhe—now a toddler of one year with his father's intensity and his mother's regal bearing—Isis had gained status at court.

Hatshepsut, Moses' royal sister-wife from their arranged marriage to continue the bloodline of Thutmose I, had responded to Isis's rising influence by asserting her authority wherever possible. Today she wore the regalia of the God's Wife of Amun, a powerful religious position she had maintained even after becoming queen, the elaborate headdress framing her face like the disk of the sun.

"I fail to see the purpose of this exercise," she said coldly when the elders had been dismissed with gifts of food and fine linen—tokens that would change their families' fortunes for months to come. The reception hall seemed larger now, emptied of its temporary guests, the silence between Moses and Hatshepsut expanding to fill the space. "And why do you return from these meetings changed? You carry their scent, their manner of speaking. Tonight, you even blessed our evening meal in their barbarous tongue."

Moses turned to her, choosing his words carefully. A misstep here could undo months of diplomatic effort. But the memory of bread shared in fellowship, of prayers that awakened his deepest self, gave him unexpected strength. "Knowledge of all peoples under our rule strengthens Egypt. The Israelites are numerous in the Delta;

understanding their ways brings them closer to our governance." He kept his tone reasonable, but there was new conviction beneath the diplomacy.

"Brings them closer?" Hatshepsut's laugh was brittle as sun-baked clay. "You bring them into the very heart of Egypt's power, treat them as honored guests rather than the laborers they are." She gestured toward Moses, her rings catching the lamplight like trapped fire. "I saw how you looked at them—not as subjects, but as family. As if their simple shepherd-god and crude customs were worthy of Pharaoh's attention."

The word 'family' hit Moses like a physical blow, because it was true in ways Hatshepsut could never understand. Those weathered faces, those calloused hands, that gentle way of breaking bread—they were his people in blood and spirit, connections that ran deeper than political expediency. "They are people, Hatshepsut. Not beasts of burden." His voice remained level, but there was steel beneath the calm, tempered by newfound certainty about who he was beneath the crown.

"They are tools, like any other," she countered, moving closer, the scent of her expensive perfume momentarily overwhelming the lingering smell of honest bread and olives that still clung to his robes. "Tools to build Egypt's glory. My father understood this. Ahmose understood this. Only you seem to question it."

The sun had shifted, casting Hatshepsut's shadow long across the polished floor, reaching toward Moses like an accusing finger. Outside, the sounds of palace life continued—servants calling to one another, the distant clatter of kitchens preparing the midday meal, a priest singing a hymn to Ra as he made his rounds. But Moses heard beneath these familiar sounds something new—the rhythm of Hebrew prayers, the cadence of ancient songs, the heartbeat of a people who remembered they were more than their bondage.

Their argument was interrupted by the arrival of Ineni, the elderly architect who had served the royal house for decades. He entered with the shuffling gait of extreme age, his once-powerful body now bent like a reed in the wind, but his eyes remained bright with intelligence. He bowed deeply, then straightened with the aid of a walking staff carved with scenes from his greatest architectural achievements.

"Forgive the intrusion, Divine One," he said to Moses, his voice thin but clear, "but the plans for the new temple at Karnak require your approval." He cast a respectful nod toward Hatshepsut, acknowledging her presence while tactfully providing an escape from the tense conversation.

Moses welcomed the interruption and followed Ineni to a side chamber where papyrus scrolls were laid out on a cedar table inlaid with ivory. Sunlight poured through a high window, illuminating the plans with golden clarity. The architect unrolled the largest scroll with hands spotted by age but still remarkably steady, revealing intricate designs for a massive hypostyle hall.

"It will be the grandest temple in all Egypt," Ineni said, his old eyes alight with creative fire despite his advanced years. "Twenty-two columns in the central nave, each tall enough to contain an entire obelisk." His finger traced the precisely drawn lines. "Here, the processional way for the sacred bark of Amun. Here, the sanctuary where only the highest priests may enter. And here," he tapped a spot on the papyrus with particular emphasis, "a chamber for Pharaoh's private communion with the god."

Moses studied the plans, but as he looked at the magnificent design, his mind's eye saw something else—Hebrew children grown to men, their backs bent under massive stone blocks, their hands raw from ropes and chisels, their families watching anxiously each evening for their return. The evening, he had just spent, sharing simple bread with gentle men whose sons would build this monument to foreign gods, gave the architectural drawings a different meaning entirely.

"The expense will be considerable," he observed, mentally calculating not just the gold and cedar, but the human cost—the lives that would be shortened, the families that would be separated, the spirits that would be broken in service to this glory.

"Indeed, Divine One. But is that not the purpose of the royal treasury? To glorify the gods and ensure Egypt's place in eternity?" Ineni's enthusiasm was palpable, the passion of an artist seeing his greatest work take shape, even knowing he might not live to see its completion.

"And how many laborers will this require?" Moses asked, though he dreaded the answer.

"Four thousand at minimum," Ineni replied promptly, seemingly pleased by the pharaoh's attention to detail. "Primarily from the Israelite settlements. They have become quite skilled after generations of such work. Jamin the metalworker has three sons who have shown particular aptitude for stone carving—they could train others, speed the work considerably." He said this with the casual indifference of one discussing the qualities of different types of stone, not human lives, not the sons of a man who had shared bread with Moses just hours before.

Four thousand men taken from their families, working under the desert sun, hauling massive stone blocks to satisfy the glory of gods Moses increasingly doubted existed. Among them would be Jamin's sons, boys who had probably learned the Shema at their father's knee, who blessed bread with the same gentle gestures Moses had remembered tonight. The irony of his position struck him anew—an Israelite commanding the forced labor of his own people, his true brothers building monuments to foreign deities while their backs bent and broke under the weight.

The chamber suddenly felt airless, the walls pressing in despite its spacious dimensions. Through the window, Moses could see a corner of the palace garden where young Menkhe played under the watchful eye of his Nubian nurse, carefree and secure in his royal future. What a contrast to Jamin's grandsons, who would grow up watching their fathers return home each night exhausted and scarred, their childhood measured not in games but in the slow destruction of their families' bodies and spirits.

"I am complicit, am I not, Ineni?" Moses said quietly, the words coming from a place deeper than policy or politics.

The old architect looked up, surprised by the question and the raw honesty in the pharaoh's voice. "Divine One?"

"I was raised in comfort, educated by the finest minds, given command of my troops. And now I sit in judgment over all Egypt." Moses gestured to the opulent chamber around them, its walls painted with scenes of the pharaoh smiting Egypt's enemies, its ceiling adorned with stars to mimic the night sky. "I have never known hunger, or fear, or the lash of a taskmaster's whip. Yet I learned that the man who taught me to bless bread has three sons who will build this temple. I will never know their names, but they will know the weight of every stone we demand they carry."

Ineni studied him with eyes made wise by decades of observing the powerful. The architect had seen pharaohs come and go, had witnessed the rise and fall of court favorites, had designed tombs for those whose ambitions exceeded their lifespan. Something in Moses's manner tonight was different—more troubled, more human than divine. "Few pharaohs reflect upon such matters, Divine One. It is... unusual." He paused, choosing his words carefully. "In all my years of service, I have never heard a ruler speak of knowing the builders' names."

"Is it wrong to consider the cost of our glory? Not in gold or cedar, but in human suffering?" Moses ran his fingers over the papyrus, tracing the outline of what would be built with the sweat and blood of men who had taught him to pray, who had welcomed him as family despite the vast gulf between their stations. "These Israelites—they are not merely laborers. They have names, families, hopes. They remember being free."

The old architect was silent for a long moment, weighing his response carefully. Moses could almost see the thoughts moving behind those ancient eyes, calculating the risk of honest speech against the safety of platitudes. Then he said, "I have served two pharaohs before you, Divine One. Each believed absolutely in their divine right to command, to build, to war. None questioned the foundations upon which their power rested." He paused, his gnarled hand resting on the plans for what might be his final masterpiece. "Perhaps that is why the gods chose you for this time. Perhaps Egypt needs a pharaoh who sees with different eyes—who knows that even the greatest monuments are built by men with beating hearts."

Healing of Menkhe

Their conversation was interrupted by the sound of rapid footsteps. A guard appeared at the doorway, his face tense with urgency.

"Divine One, forgive the intrusion, but Queen Isis requests your presence urgently. Your son is ill."

Fear gripped Moses' heart like a physical hand, squeezing until he could barely breathe. The architectural plans, the weight of governance, the complexity of his divided loyalties—all fell away in the face of a father's terror. He hurried through the palace corridors, his sandals slapping against the stone floors, servants and nobles flattening themselves against walls to allow their pharaoh passage. The weight of the crown was forgotten, the concerns of governance momentarily set aside—he was simply a father fearing for his child.

He found Isis in the royal nursery, a spacious chamber with walls painted with protective symbols and scenes of childish delight—birds in flight, fish swimming in the Nile, children playing at games. The usual sounds of laughter and play were absent, replaced by the terrifying silence of serious illness. Isis cradled their son, whose small face was flushed with fever, his normally active body limp in her arms. Her eyes, usually bright with intelligence and humor, were now dark with fear, her composed features strained with worry.

"He burns like fire," she said, her own face streaked with tears that had carved tracks through her ceremonial face paint. She had clearly rushed from some court function at the first news of their child's illness. "The physicians have given him herbs, but the fever does not break." Her voice cracked on the last word, the composed royal wife giving way to the terrified mother.

Moses took the child from her arms, feeling the unnatural heat radiating from his small body. Young Menkhe's eyes, usually bright and curious like his father's, were glazed and unfocused, staring at something beyond the painted ceiling. His tiny chest rose and fell with rapid, shallow breaths, each one a labor. The boy's normally lustrous black curls lay damp and matted against his scalp, and his skin—usually a perfect blend of his father's bronzed complexion and his mother's deeper tone—had taken on a frightening pallor beneath the flush of fever.

"Have the priests been summoned?" Moses asked, his voice steady despite the panic threatening to overtake him. Years of military training had taught him to remain calm in crisis, though never had a crisis felt so personal, so visceral.

Isis nodded, the gold beads in her braids catching the light with the movement. "They prepare offerings to Sekhmet even now. Incense burns in every temple in Thebes. The chief physician has consulted the sacred texts and prepared potions of honey, herbs, and minerals." She stroked their son's cheek with trembling fingers. "But..." She hesitated, her eyes darting to the nursery entrance where servants and guards might overhear.

"What is it?" Moses asked, moving to sit on a cedar bench near the window, still cradling his son. The weight of the child in his arms seemed simultaneously too light and unbearably heavy—this small life that had become the center of his world.

"I wondered if perhaps... your people's God might help him." The words came out as barely more than a whisper, treasonous in a palace dedicated to the gods of Egypt. "Tonight, when you returned from your studies, you were different. Peaceful, but also... powerful. As if you had touched something the Egyptian gods cannot reach."

Moses looked at her in surprise. The nursery suddenly seemed very quiet, as if even the air held its breath. Outside, an ibis called, its voice carrying clearly in the stillness. Isis had adopted the worship of Egyptian deities readily upon their marriage—an arrangement made to continue the royal bloodline of Thutmose I—showing particular devotion to Hathor, goddess of motherhood and love. She had never before shown interest in the Hebrew God, had never questioned the elaborate pantheon that governed Egyptian life.

"The God of Abraham, Isaac, and Jacob," he said, not as a question but as recognition of something that had been building within him all evening. The memory of Ammiel's blessing, the taste of bread shared in faith, the ancient words that had awakened in his heart—perhaps this was why the God of his fathers had preserved him, raised him to this position, allowed him to rediscover his heritage precisely when his son's life hung in the balance.

"Would He hear a mother's plea for her child?" Isis asked, moving closer, placing her hand on their son's forehead, her wedding rings—one bearing the royal seal of Egypt, the other the carved jasper of Nubian royalty—glinting in the late afternoon light. "You speak His name differently than you speak the names of our gods. With... recognition. As if He knows you."

Moses gazed down at his son, then back at his wife. The question hung between them, charged with implications neither fully understood. In that moment, he felt the three parts of his identity—Egyptian pharaoh, Hebrew by birth, and father desperate to save his child—converging into something he had never been before: a man prepared to stake everything on faith.

The nursery, with its painted Egyptian deities watching from every wall—Taweret the protector of children, Bes the ward against evil spirits, Isis the divine mother—suddenly seemed insufficient. These gods of wood and stone and paint had failed to protect his son. Perhaps it was time to turn to the God who had preserved him as an infant floating on the Nile, who had guided him through battle and brought him to this moment of choice.

"I will pray," he said simply, the decision feeling like stepping off a cliff into unknown space.

As Isis watched, Moses closed his eyes and began to speak in Hebrew—not the formal prayers he had learned from the elders, but words that came from the deepest part of his heart, in the language his mother had used to bless him as a child. His voice started as a whisper but grew stronger, more confident, as though the God he addressed was not distant but present, not foreign but familiar.

"Adonai, Eloheinu, Elohei Avraham, Yitzchak v'Yaakov"—Lord, our God, God of Abraham, Isaac, and Jacob—he began, the Hebrew flowing more naturally than it ever had. "Rofeh cholim"—Healer of the sick—have mercy on this child. He is innocent of the divisions between Egypt and Israel. Let him live, and I will serve You as You direct."

The words surprised him even as he spoke them, for they were not planned but emerged from a place deeper than thought. As he prayed, holding his fevered son, Moses felt something shift within himself—a yielding, a surrender of the careful control he had maintained over his divided life. The Hebrew prince and the Egyptian pharaoh were no longer in conflict but united in this moment of desperate faith.

Hours passed. Moses continued to pray while Isis sat beside him, sometimes placing her hand on his shoulder, sometimes adding her own whispered pleas in Nubian and Egyptian. The palace grew quiet around them, the normal sounds of evening fading into the deep stillness of night. Oil lamps were replenished by silent servants, and food was brought and left untouched.

Near dawn, as Moses's voice had grown hoarse from hours of prayer, young Menkhe stirred in his arms. The child's eyes, clear for the first time in days, focused on his father's face. The fever had broken, leaving his skin cool and damp with healthy perspiration. He reached up with a tiny hand and touched Moses's beard, then smiled—the first smile they had seen since the illness began.

"Baruch Hashem," Moses whispered—Blessed be the Name— words that came to him as naturally as breathing, though he had never learned them from any teacher.

Isis burst into tears of relief, but as she reached for their son, she paused, studying Moses with new understanding. "You prayed in your heart's language," she said softly. "Not as a prince learning Hebrew customs, but as a son speaking to his Father."

Moses nodded, unable to deny what had become undeniably true. The God of his ancestors had heard, had answered, had claimed him in a way that could not be reversed or ignored. Whatever else he was— pharaoh, husband, commander—he was first and always a Hebrew, called by the God of Abraham to purposes he was only beginning to understand.

That night, as young Menkhe slept peacefully between his relieved parents, Moses contemplated the path his life had taken. The royal bedchamber was bathed in moonlight that streamed through the high windows, casting everything in silver and shadow. The normal sounds of palace life had quieted to the occasional footstep of a guard or the distant call of a night bird from the gardens.

Pharaoh of Egypt, husband to his royal sister-wife Hatshepsut and to Isis, father to the future ruler of the world's greatest empire. Yet increasingly, he felt like a stranger in his own palace, drawn to a heritage and a God he was finally beginning to understand. The Hebrew elders had spoken of a promise—that their God would deliver them from bondage in Egypt. How could Moses reconcile this with his position as Egypt's ruler? How could he be both deliverer and oppressor?

The answer came to him not as words but as certainty, deep and unshakeable as bedrock. The God who had preserved him as an infant, who had awakened his memory tonight, who had healed his son, had plans that transcended human understanding. Moses's dual identity was not an accident or a burden, but preparation for something greater than he had ever imagined.

He watched Isis sleeping, one protective arm curled around their son even in slumber. Her face in repose had shed the careful court mask, revealing the young woman he had first met in Nubia—fierce, intelligent, capable of both tenderness and strength. Their marriage, arranged to preserve the royal bloodline of Thutmose I, had grown into something neither of them had anticipated—a partnership built on mutual respect and genuine affection. She had crossed boundaries of nation and culture to be with him; tonight, she had crossed the boundary of faith as well, witnessing the power of the Hebrew God and accepting it without question.

Something was changing within him, a shifting of loyalties as profound as the changing course of the Nile itself. He did not yet understand where this current would take him, but he felt its pull, inexorable as the tide. The Hebrew elders who had welcomed him as family, the ancient prayers that awakened memories deeper than thought, the God who answered desperate fathers' pleas—these were not merely academic interests but the foundation of his true identity, finally acknowledged and embraced.

As he drifted toward sleep, Moses felt both fear and exhilaration at the thought of what might lie ahead—a journey into unknown territories of the soul as challenging as any military campaign he had ever undertaken. The boy who had learned the Shema at his mother's knee was awakening within the man who wore Pharaoh's crown, and that awakening would change more than just his own life.

Outside, the stars wheeled overhead, the same stars that had watched over Abraham as he journeyed to a promised land, the same stars that would guide generations yet unborn. In their timeless light, the concerns of pharaohs and empires seemed fleeting as morning mist on the Nile, but the promises whispered in Hebrew prayers seemed eternal as the constellations themselves.

Chapter 28 - Exile of the Heart

March 1479 BC - Thebes

The palace gardens of Thebes blazed with torchlight, a thousand flames dancing in the soft evening breeze, illuminating tables that groaned under the weight of Egypt's finest delicacies. The scent of roasted meats mingled with the heady perfume of lotus blossoms and imported myrrh, creating an intoxicating aroma that hung like an invisible cloud over the celebration. Dancers moved sinuously through the crowd, their lithe bodies painted with gold dust that caught and reflected the light with each undulation, creating living statues that seemed to flicker between flesh and metal as they moved to the hypnotic rhythm of flutes and harps.

Nobles from throughout the Two Lands had gathered, their bodies adorned with jewels and fine linen, their eyes sharp with ambition as they watched their divine ruler. They had brought gifts of extraordinary value—pure gold from the mines of Nubia that gleamed with untold wealth, lapis lazuli from beyond the eastern deserts that captured the very essence of the night sky, fragrant cedarwood from the distant forests of Lebanon, and spices from lands so far away that their names existed only as whispers among the merchant caravans that dared to travel beyond the empire's borders.

Moses moved among his guests with the practiced ease of a man who had worn power like a second skin for nearly three years. He accepted their lavish gifts and honeyed words with the grace expected of Egypt's divine ruler, though each compliment seemed to weigh upon him more heavily than the golden collar that encircled his neck. He wore the blue war crown, its distinctive shape marking him as supreme commander though Egypt enjoyed an era of unprecedented peace. His muscular body, still powerful despite his forty years, was adorned with the finest jewelery created by the royal workshops—broad pectoral plates of gold inlaid with precious stones, armlets shaped like coiled serpents with ruby eyes, and rings that flashed with every gesture of his long-fingered hands.

To all observers, he appeared every inch the pharaoh, comfortable in his power and divine status, the living embodiment of Horus on earth. Yet beneath the practiced smile, Moses found himself silently reciting the words Ammiel had taught him months before: "Shema Yisrael, Adonai Eloheinu, Adonai Echad." The Hebrew prayer ran through his mind like an undercurrent, a reminder of another identity that grew stronger with each passing day.

Only those closest to him might have noticed the distance in his eyes—a remoteness that suggested his spirit wandered far from the celebrations that honored his earthly form. Behind the practiced smile and measured words, Moses' thoughts drifted like a papyrus boat on the current of the great Nile, pulled inexorably toward questions that had haunted him with increasing urgency since that night when his son's fever had broken under the Hebrew God's healing touch.

Hatshepsut presided over the feast from a raised dais, her kohl-rimmed eyes missing nothing as she watched Moses navigate the crowd. Her slim body was draped in sheer linen so fine it seemed to capture light rather than block it, and around her throat lay a collar of gold and carnelian that had once belonged to Queen Ahmose herself. Over the years, their relationship had evolved into one of mutual respect tempered by wariness, like two cobras that share the same basket without striking—for now.

She had come to appreciate his intelligence and fairness in governance, the even hand with which he dispensed justice and the strategic mind that had expanded Egypt's borders without unnecessary bloodshed. He, in turn, had learned to value her cunning and deep understanding of Egyptian politics, the subtle ways she manipulated the nobility and the priesthood to maintain stability in the Two Lands. Yet there remained a gulf between them that no amount of shared rule could bridge—a fundamental difference in values that had grown more pronounced since Moses began his Hebrew studies, creating a tension that crackled between them like summer lightning.

Across the garden, Isis chased after their son, her ebony curls bouncing against her shoulders, laughter spilling from her lips as the child darted between startled nobles with the innocent disregard of youth.

Menkhe was a sturdy toddler of two years, his skin the rich copper tone that spoke of his mixed heritage, his mother's dark curls framing a face that already showed the intensity of his father's gaze. He darted like a fish through the river of humanity, oblivious to his status as a prince of Egypt, finding joy in the simple freedom of movement and the game of pursuit.

Watching his son's carefree laughter, Moses remembered the terror of that fever-wracked night, the desperate Hebrew prayers that had poured from his heart, the moment when the God of his fathers had answered and healed the child. That night had changed everything—not just Menkhe's recovery, but Moses's understanding of where his true allegiance lay. The memory of his son's fever breaking under Hebrew prayers now made every Egyptian ritual feel hollow, every claim of divine pharaonic power ring false.

"He grows strong," observed a voice at Moses' side, the words carrying the weight of years.

He turned to find Mutnofret, now an elderly woman whose influence at court remained considerable despite her advancing age. She had been one of the few to know Moses' true origins, having been there when he was pulled from the Nile as an infant, a secret she had guarded as carefully as the royal seal.

"Too strong for his mother to control, it seems," Moses replied with a smile, watching Isis finally capture their squirming son and swing him into her arms, covering his face with kisses that made the boy giggle with delight.

"Children need freedom to discover their strength," Mutnofret said, her voice carrying decades of wisdom. She paused, her gaze becoming more penetrating. "As do men."

Moses looked at her sharply, hearing something significant beneath the surface of her words, like the current that runs deep below the calm face of the Nile. "What troubles you, Mother-of-Egypt?"

The old title—one he had used since childhood—softened her expression. Mutnofret had been like a mother to him after his adoption into the royal household, a steady presence when the politics of the court threatened to overwhelm the boy who had never asked to be prince.

"I am old, Moses," she said quietly, her voice carrying no self-pity, merely stating a truth as immutable as the rising of the sun. "My time draws near. Before I join my ancestors in the Field of Reeds, there are truths that must be spoken."

She led him to a quiet corner of the garden, away from the festivities, where the music became a distant melody carried on the night breeze and the laughter of the courtiers faded to a murmur. In the shadows of a sycamore tree, its ancient branches reaching toward the star-filled sky like supplicants before a god, she took his hands in her wrinkled ones. Her skin felt like papyrus against his palms, fragile yet somehow enduring.

"You have been a good pharaoh," she said, her eyes reflecting the distant torchlight. "Just and merciful, strong when needed, generous in victory. Egypt has prospered under your rule. The granaries are full, the borders secure, the people content."

"With Hatshepsut's guidance," Moses acknowledged, giving credit where it was due. For all their differences, he could not deny the woman's skill at governance.

"Yes," Mutnofret agreed with a slight nod. "She was born to rule. But you..." She paused, searching his face with the intensity of a scribe studying a complex hieroglyph. "You were born for another purpose."

Moses felt a chill despite the warm evening, as though a cloud had passed over the face of Ra himself. The words echoed something Ammiel had said during one of their secret meetings—that the Most High had preserved Moses not for Egypt's glory, but for His own purposes. "What purpose?"

"That is for you to discover." Her fingers tightened around his, surprising in their strength. "But I fear you will not find it while you sit upon Egypt's throne." She released one hand to gesture at the celebration beyond them. "I have watched you these past years. You perform your duties flawlessly, like a well-trained dancer who knows every step but finds no joy in the music. Yet your heart is elsewhere. You study Hebrew texts when you think no one notices, speak with Israelite elders under the guise of administrative matters, question the labor practices that have built Egypt's greatness for generations."

"Is it wrong to seek knowledge?" Moses challenged, his voice low but intense. "To question suffering? Is that not also the duty of Pharaoh—to ensure justice for all who dwell within the Two Lands?"

"For an ordinary man, no," Mutnofret replied, her expression softening with something like pity. "For a wise and compassionate ruler, such questions are natural. But for Pharaoh, son of Ra, divine ruler of the Two Lands?" She shook her head slowly, the gold beads in her headdress catching the torchlight. "You cannot serve two masters, Moses. Either you are Pharaoh, with all that entails—the divine right, the sacred duty, the unquestioned authority—or you are..."

"Or I am what?" Moses pressed when she fell silent, something in him already knowing the answer yet needing to hear it spoken aloud.

"Or you are a Hebrew," she finished simply, the words falling between them like stones dropped into still water. "A son of slaves, whose God is not one of ours. A man caught between two worlds, belonging fully to neither."

The words hung in the warm night air, a truth both had known but neither had spoken aloud in decades. Moses felt their weight settle on his shoulders; heavier than any crown he had ever worn. In the distance, he could hear the laughter of his guests, but it sounded hollow now, like the echo of voices in an empty tomb.

Later that night, as the celebration continued around him, Moses found himself increasingly withdrawn from the revelry. The music that had earlier seemed pleasant now grated on his ears; the laughter of the nobles rang hollow, their flattery as substantial as the morning mist that rises from the Nile only to be burned away by the sun. He observed the excesses of the feast with new eyes—the mountains of food that would feed an Israelite family for months, the rivers of wine flowing freely while labourers died of thirst in the quarries, the casual displays of wealth that represented the toil and sweat of thousands.

As he watched a particularly elaborate dance performance, Moses found himself thinking of Benjamin, the metalworker who had shared bread with him, whose scarred hands had blessed the simple meal with such reverence. That same Jamin whose three sons were now conscripted to work on the new temple at Karnak, their young backs bent under stones meant to honor gods they did not worship. The irony was not lost on him—he was celebrating Egypt's prosperity while the very men who had taught him to pray worked themselves to death building monuments to Egyptian deities.

He watched his nobles competing to praise his divinity, their words as empty as the desert wind. Priests performed elaborate rituals to gods he no longer believed in with his whole heart, their chants rising to heavens that suddenly seemed indifferent. Dancers contorted their perfect bodies for the pleasure of the elite, their beauty a mask for the ugly truth of how such splendor was maintained—through the broken backs of his own people, his true brothers in blood and faith.

And suddenly, he could bear it no longer.

The weight of thirty-six years of compromise pressed down upon him like the massive stones of a pyramid, threatening to crush his very soul. Every laugh, every flattering word, every self-satisfied smile from his nobles now seemed an accusation—a reminder of his complicity in a system built upon the broken backs of his own people. The Hebrew prayers that had once brought him comfort now felt like indictments, the God who had healed his son now seemed to demand an accounting of his stewardship.

Moses slipped away from the feast, moving through the palace corridors with the silent grace of a man who had spent a lifetime navigating the dangers of court. Servants bowed as he passed, their eyes downcast in the presence of divinity, unaware of the turmoil that raged within the heart of their god-king. He made his way to the highest terrace of the palace, a private space where he had often come to think when the burdens of rule grew heavy.

From this vantage point, he could see all of Thebes, the greatest city in the world spread before him like a jeweled tapestry. The full moon bathed the city in silver light, turning the limestone temples and palaces into structures that seemed carved from pure light. In the distance, he could see the massive construction site of Karnak temple, torches marking where work continued even at night, tiny points of fire that represented uncounted lives spent in service to gods who demanded ever-grander monuments to their glory.

How many of his people—his true people—labored there even now, their backs breaking under stones meant to honor gods they did not worship? Among them were Benjamin's sons, young men who had learned the Shema at their father's knee, who had been taught to bless bread with the same gentle gestures Moses now remembered from his own childhood. How many would die before the great temple was complete, their names unremembered, their bodies cast aside like broken tools?

The sight of those distant torches brought back the memory of another night—oil lamps burning in a secret chamber, Hebrew elders sharing simple bread, the taste of unleavened barley and honey that had awakened memories deeper than thought. That night, Moses had been a student discovering his heritage. Tonight, he was a pharaoh confronting the cost of his power.

"Something has changed in you."

The soft voice startled him from his reverie. He turned to find Isis standing behind him, their son asleep in her arms, his small face peaceful in slumber. The moonlight silvered her dark skin and cast her eyes into shadow, yet Moses could feel the weight of her gaze as surely as a physical touch.

"Tonight?" he asked, his voice barely above a whisper.

"No," she said, stepping closer until she stood beside him at the parapet. "It has been happening slowly, for years. Like water wearing away stone—imperceptible day by day, yet undeniable when one looks back across the seasons." She shifted Menkhe to her other arm, his small head lolling against her shoulder in perfect trust. "But tonight, I see it clearly, as though a veil has been lifted."

"What do you see?" Moses asked, unsure if he wanted to hear her answer.

"I see a man who stands at a crossroads," she replied, her eyes reflecting the distant fires of the city. "A man divided against himself. You are no longer the warrior I married in Nubia, whose eyes burned with certainty and whose heart beat with the rhythm of Egypt." She paused, her voice growing softer. "Ever since that night when our son's fever broke under your Hebrew prayers, I have watched you struggle with the knowledge of which god truly answered your plea."

The observation struck him like a physical blow. She had seen what he had barely admitted to himself—that the healing of their son had been a turning point, the moment when the God of Abraham had proven more real, more present, than all the golden idols of Egypt combined.

"I'm sorry," he said, though he wasn't sure what he was apologizing for—the man he had been, or the man he was becoming.

"Do not be," she replied, surprising him with the gentle understanding in her voice. "Change is the way of life. The Nile rises and falls, the seasons turn, men grow and transform. This is the natural order of things." She shifted Menkhe to her other arm, his small weight seemingly no burden to her. "But know this—whatever path you choose, I will honor the man you were, the man who gave me our son, and the man who showed me that there are gods beyond Egypt's borders who hear a mother's desperate prayers."

Moses reached out to touch his son's cheek, soft with sleep, warm with the innocent trust of childhood. His chest tightened with a love so fierce it was almost painful. "I love him more than life itself."

"I know," Isis said, her voice soft with her own love. "And he will know it too, whatever happens. I will tell him that his father was a man who chose truth over comfort, righteousness over power." She paused, her eyes bright with unshed tears. "That is a legacy any son would be proud to inherit."

Something in her tone made Moses look up sharply. "You speak as though you expect me to leave."

Isis smiled sadly, the expression transforming her face into a mask of ancient wisdom that reminded him forcefully of her years as a temple priestess before she became his wife. "I have seen the look in your eyes when you speak with the Hebrew elders. I have heard the passion in your voice when you argue against the treatment of their people in council meetings. I have felt the distance grow between us as your thoughts turn inward, wrestling with questions I cannot answer." She shifted their son against her shoulder. "Your body may be here in Thebes, draped in the regalia of Pharaoh, but your soul has already begun its journey elsewhere. The God who healed our son has claimed you, and I am not fool enough to compete with the divine."

The truth of her words struck him like a physical blow. She saw him with a clarity he had not even granted himself, recognizing the inevitable path before him when he had been afraid to acknowledge it. Her acceptance of the Hebrew God's power, her recognition that Moses belonged to a larger purpose than Egypt could contain, filled him with both gratitude and overwhelming sadness.

That night, Moses could not sleep. He paced his chambers, the polished limestone floor cool beneath his bare feet, his mind a tempest of conflicting thoughts and emotions. The frescoes that adorned his walls—scenes of hunting in the marshes, of victory in battle, of offerings to the gods—now seemed like images from another man's life, a stranger whose face he wore but whose heart he could no longer understand.

He was Pharaoh of Egypt, ruler of the mightiest empire on earth. He had wealth beyond counting, power beyond measure, a beautiful wife and son, and the adoration of millions. His name would live forever, inscribed in stone and spoken in reverence for generations to come.

Yet his people—his true people—labored under Egyptian whips, their backs scarred, their spirits nearly broken. They built monuments to gods they did not worship, lived in poverty while he dwelled in opulence, and called upon a God who seemed to have forgotten them. But had He forgotten them? Or was He preparing deliverance through the most unlikely vessel—a Hebrew raised as Pharaoh, positioned to understand both the power of Egypt and the pain of Israel?

The question that had haunted him for months returned with new urgency: How could he serve both Egypt and the God of Abraham? How could he continue to enforce the very bondage that his Hebrew teachers said their God would end? The contradiction had become unbearable, a wound that refused to heal.

As he wrestled with these thoughts, Moses found himself whispering the Hebrew prayers Eleazar had taught him, the words flowing more naturally now than any Egyptian incantation. "Baruch atah Adonai, Eloheinu Melech ha'olam"—the blessing over bread that had awakened such powerful memories. The simple words carried more weight than all the elaborate rituals of the Egyptian priesthood, connecting him to a faith that demanded justice, not merely worship.

As dawn approached, painting the eastern sky with bands of gold and crimson, Moses made his decision. The first light of Ra touched the alabaster pillars of his chamber as he went to his private sanctuary and removed the royal regalia—the heavy gold collars that marked his divine status, the embossed armbands depicting his victories in Nubia, the jeweled belt that symbolized his control over the Two Lands. In their place, he put on a simple linen kilt and a plain cloak such as might be worn by any common Egyptian official on a journey through the provinces.

But even as he prepared to leave, Moses knew this was no temporary journey of discovery. The path before him led away from everything he had known, toward a future as uncertain as the horizon itself. He was abandoning not just power, but the safety of the only life he had ever known.

Then he went to Isis, who woke as he entered their bedchamber, her eyes immediately alert as though she had been waiting for this moment.

"You are leaving," she said. It was not a question.

"I must see for myself how my people live," he replied, his voice steady though his heart raced like a chariot team at full gallop. "Not as Pharaoh on a ceremonial visit, with everything cleaned and prepared for divine inspection, but as one of them." He paused, the weight of what he was about to say pressing down upon him. "I must discover what the God who healed our son requires of me."

Isis rose from the bed like a gazelle, graceful even in the suddenness of the movement. She went to a cedar chest in the corner of the room, its wood polished by years of handling, its corners reinforced with bronze. From it, she withdrew a bundle wrapped in plain cloth.

"Then take these," she said, handing him the bundle. "The clothes of an Israelite. One of the servants brought them at my request weeks ago, after I saw the direction of your heart."

Moses looked at her in surprise, the bundle heavy in his hands not from its weight but from its significance. Her preparation for this moment revealed the depth of her understanding, her acceptance of a path that would take her husband from her. "You knew?"

"I have seen this coming for over a year," she replied, her dark eyes unreadable in the dim light. "Perhaps longer. Since you began asking questions about your origins that had no comfortable answers. Since you started slipping away to the Hebrew quarter in disguise, thinking I did not notice your absences. Since that night when you prayed in Hebrew over our son's fever and I realized which god had truly answered." She reached up to touch his face, her fingers tracing the line of his jaw as though memorizing its contours. "I do not understand it fully, but I respect your need to find your own truth. The God who saved our child has a claim on you that Egypt cannot match."

Moses unwrapped the bundle to find the simple garments worn by Israelite men—a rough-woven tunic the color of dust, a cloak of undyed wool that would protect against the cool desert nights, sandals made of reed and leather that would mark him as a laborer rather than a noble. The coarse fabric felt foreign against his hands, accustomed as they were to the finest linen and silk, yet somehow it felt more honest than all the royal regalia he was leaving behind.

He looked at Isis, overwhelmed by her understanding, by the depth of love that allowed her to help him leave. "Will you return?" she asked, her voice steady despite the pain that shadowed her eyes.

"I don't know," he answered honestly, unwilling to offer false comfort. The path ahead was shrouded in uncertainty, guided only by a growing conviction that the God of Abraham had purposes for him that Egypt could not fulfill.

She nodded, accepting his uncertainty with the same grace with which she accepted everything life had brought her—both the exalted position as Pharaoh's wife and now, perhaps, its loss. "Then go with the blessing of your gods and mine. And know that your son will hear stories of his father's greatness, whatever path you choose." She paused, her voice catching slightly. "I will tell him that his father was called by a god so powerful that even Pharaoh had to obey."

As the first light of dawn broke over Thebes, setting the Nile aflame with golden reflections, Moses—dressed now as an Israelite, his royal finery left behind—slipped out of the palace through servants' passages he had known since childhood. The guards, accustomed to obeying rather than questioning, let him pass with barely a glance, their eyes sliding over him as though he were invisible. The transformation was complete—the god-king had become just another Hebrew laborer, indistinguishable from thousands of others.

At the palace gates, he paused and looked back at the magnificent structure that had been his home for thirty-six years. The rising sun turned its limestone walls to gold, its columns casting long shadows across the courtyard like the bars of an exquisite cage. From an upper balcony, two figures watched him—Hatshepsut, her tall, slim form unmistakable even at this distance, her posture rigid as a temple obelisk. Beside her stood a palace scribe, no doubt summoned to witness this unprecedented abdication.

As their eyes met across the distance, Hatshepsut called out, her voice carrying clearly in the still morning air: "You'll be back, Moses! When the desert has scoured the idealism from your bones, when you've tasted the reality of your precious Hebrews' lives, you'll return! Power is not so easily abandoned!"

Moses paused, considering her words. The woman who had been both his partner in rule and his subtle adversary understood power but not purpose. She could not imagine willingly relinquishing the throne of Egypt for anything—least of all for a heritage among slaves. Her voice rang with the certainty of one who had never questioned the foundations of her own identity.

"Power is not abandoned, sister," he called back, using the formal address that acknowledged their shared rule. "It is redirected. The question is not whether one has power, but how one uses it."

Hatshepsut's laugh was sharp as flint against stone. "Noble words from a man walking away from the greatest power on earth! We shall see how noble they sound when you are hauling stone under the overseer's whip!"

Moses made no further reply. The woman who had been his partner in rule could not understand that some things mattered more than comfort, more than safety, more than power itself. The God who had preserved him as an infant, who had awakened his memories through simple bread and ancient prayers, who had healed his son when Egyptian magic failed—that God had a claim on him that transcended earthly authority.

Turning away from the palace, from power, from divine kingship, he set his face toward the Hebrew settlements in the Delta and the unknown future that awaited him there. Behind him lay certainty, power, and glory. Before him lay doubt, danger, and the possibility of discovering his true purpose in the vast plan of the God who had called Abraham from Ur, who had preserved Jacob in famine, who had multiplied Israel in Egypt.

The sun climbed higher as he made his way through the awakening city, its golden light illuminating the path before him—not the broad, ceremonial avenues he had travelled as Pharaoh, but the narrow, dusty lanes of common men. With each step that carried him away from the palace, he felt both the weight of what he was abandoning and the curious lightness of having chosen his own path for perhaps the first time in his life.

As he walked, Moses found himself reciting the Shema once more, the Hebrew words flowing naturally from his lips: "Hear, O Israel, the Lord our God, the Lord is One." The prayer that had awakened his deepest memories now became his declaration of faith, his acknowledgment that he served a Master greater than Pharaoh, mightier than Egypt, more enduring than the pyramids themselves.

He did not look back again.

In the distance, beyond the bustling markets and crowded streets of Thebes, lay the road to the Delta—to Avaris, to Goshen, to the land where his people dwelt in bondage. There he would learn what it meant to be truly Hebrew, to share not just their blood but their suffering, their hopes, their faith in a God who saw their affliction and remembered His promises.

The journey to his true identity was just beginning.

Chapter 29 - Slaying of an Egyptian

April 1479 BC - Avaris

The sun blazed mercilessly over Avaris, a molten copper disk suspended in a cloudless sky, casting harsh shadows across the mud-brick dwellings where the Israelites existed in cramped squalor. Moses pulled his rough woolen head covering lower, the coarse fabric scratching against his skin as he carefully concealed his baldness—the distinctive mark of Egyptian nobility that would instantly betray him among these people.

After a lifetime in the cool, spacious halls of the palace with their soaring limestone columns and polished granite floors, the heat and stench of the laborers' quarters assaulted his senses with brutal force. The acrid smell of human waste mingled with woodsmoke and the sour tang of unwashed bodies. Children with distended bellies and matchstick limbs played listlessly in the dirt, their laughter a rare counterpoint to the general misery. Hollow-eyed women carried water jars on their heads, their shoulders permanently stooped from decades of burden, skin leathered by the relentless Egyptian sun.

This was the truth he had come to witness—not the sanitized reports delivered to his throne by officials whose careers depended on telling him what they thought he wished to hear. These were his people, though they knew it not. These were the descendants of Abraham, living in bondage while he had dwelled in luxury, oblivious to their suffering. How many of those carefully worded scrolls had he approved without questioning their human cost? How many construction projects had he authorized from his golden throne while men like these collapsed under impossible quotas?

"You there! Move aside for the water carriers!"

The harsh voice cracked like a whip from behind, and Moses stepped quickly to the edge of the narrow pathway, pressing himself against a sun-baked wall. An Egyptian taskmaster strode past, his bronze-tipped whip casually draped over one well-muscled shoulder, arrogance etched into every line of his clean-shaven face. Behind him followed a line of Israelite women bearing heavy water jars, their eyes downcast, shoulders trembling with fatigue. One woman, perhaps no more than sixteen, stumbled on the uneven ground. Water sloshed over the rim of her jar, splashing onto the dusty path.

The taskmaster whirled, his face contorting with rage. "Clumsy Hebrew sow!" he snarled, his voice dripping with contempt as he raised his whip threateningly. "Spill another drop and you'll feel the kiss of leather!"

The young woman flinched, her thin shoulders hunching as if already anticipating the blow. For a heartbeat, Moses saw naked terror in her eyes before she lowered them again, steadying herself with trembling hands.

Moses felt rage building in his chest, hot and dangerous as molten metal in a founder's crucible. His hand instinctively moved toward the knife hidden beneath his robes—a reflex born of years commanding Egypt's armies. But he forced himself to remain still, fingers uncurling with conscious effort. He was not here as Pharaoh. Not here to command. He was here to understand.

"You're not from around here," said a voice at his elbow, quiet but carrying unexpected authority.

Moses turned to find a wiry, middle-aged man studying him with intelligent eyes that missed nothing. The man's beard was streaked with gray, and his hands bore the calluses of hard labor, but there was a quiet dignity in his bearing that set him apart from the broken masses shuffling through the narrow streets.

"No," Moses agreed cautiously, his mind racing to construct a plausible story. "I come from... Thebes."

"Thebes?" The man arched an eyebrow, skepticism evident in the slight tilt of his head. "That's a long journey. What brings a man from Thebes to this miserable corner of Egypt where even the gods seem to have turned their backs?"

"I seek my family," Moses replied, deciding that a partial truth was safest. "I believe they live here in the west of Avaris."

The man nodded slowly, appraising Moses with renewed interest. Despite his rough clothing, Moses knew his bearing betrayed his upbringing—the straight spine and confident gaze of one accustomed to being obeyed could not be easily disguised.

"Many of our people live here," the man said carefully. "What family do you seek?"

Moses hesitated. He had learned from the Hebrew teachers at court that he was born to Amram and Jochebed of the tribe of Levi, but would they still live? Would they even remember the infant they had set adrift on the Nile four decades ago? Would they welcome the man who had ruled over their captivity?

"I seek the house of Amram," he said finally, his throat suddenly dry. "Of the tribe of Levi."

Something shifted in the man's expression—surprise, followed by wariness that bordered on suspicion. His eyes narrowed almost imperceptibly, and he took a half-step closer, examining Moses's face with new intensity.

"Amram is my father," he said, his voice dropping to barely above a whisper. "I am Aaron, son of Amram and Jochebed."

Moses stared at the man, thunderstruck. This was his brother—his blood brother, not by adoption or political alliance, but by birth. The brother he would have grown up alongside had fate not intervened. The brother who had known hunger and the taskmaster's whip while Moses had dined from golden plates and commanded armies.

"And you are...?" Aaron prompted, his wariness now more pronounced, one hand unconsciously moving to a concealed position at his waist—protecting a hidden weapon, Moses realized.

"I am..." Moses faltered, the enormity of the moment crushing the words in his throat. How could he explain who he was? How could he bridge the vast gulf between their lives? "I am Moses," he said simply.

Aaron's eyes widened, the color draining from his sun-darkened face. "Moses," he repeated, as though tasting a foreign word, rolling it on his tongue to test its authenticity. "That is an Egyptian name."

"It is the only name I have known," Moses admitted, the truth burning like fire in his chest. "But I believe I was born to your parents. I believe I am your brother."

Aaron took a step back, suspicion plain on his face, his hand now clearly gripping whatever weapon he carried. Around them, the bustle of the street continued, but Moses felt as though they stood in a bubble of silence, the fate of both their lives balanced on the knife-edge of this moment.

"My brother Moses was taken from us when he was an infant," Aaron said, his voice tight with controlled emotion. "We believed him dead, or lost forever among the Egyptians. My mother wept for three years without cease."

"Not lost," Moses said quietly, holding Aaron's gaze despite the accusation he saw there. "Found. Raised in the house of Pharaoh's daughter. Educated as a prince of Egypt."

For a long moment, Aaron stared at him in disbelief, searching his face for traces of familial resemblance, for any thread of connection to the infant lost decades ago. Then, with a sudden decisiveness, he grasped Moses by the arm with surprising strength and pulled him into the shadows between two dwellings.

"If what you say is true," he hissed, his breath hot against Moses' ear, "this is not a conversation for the open street. The Egyptians have spies everywhere, and a claim like yours could mean death—for you and for us. There are those who would kill to prevent any Hebrew from rising above his station."

"Take me to your parents," Moses urged, gripping Aaron's forearm in return. "To our parents. They will know if I speak truth."

Aaron hesitated, conflict evident in his furrowed brow, then nodded once, a sharp, decisive movement. "Follow me. But keep your head down and do not speak to anyone. Your accent marks you as different—neither fully Egyptian nor fully Hebrew. Such men are trusted by neither side."

They moved through the warren of streets, Aaron leading with the confidence of one who had navigated these paths since childhood. The dwellings grew slightly more substantial as they progressed, suggesting a hierarchy even among the oppressed. Aaron explained in hushed tones as they approached a modest structure set slightly apart from others.

"This is the home of my father Amram," he said. "Once he was a respected elder among the Israelites, known for his wisdom in settling disputes and his knowledge of our ancient laws. That was before age had bent his back and clouded his mind."

Aaron's voice softened with both love and sorrow. "He remembers little of the present," he continued, "but the past remains clear to him. He speaks often of Egypt as it was when he was young, before the new king arose who knew not Joseph. Mother cares for him now, though she too feels the weight of her years."

He led Moses through a low doorway into the dim interior, where the air hung heavy with the scents of crushed herbs and smoldering tamarisk. An elderly woman sat cross-legged on a reed mat, grinding grain with a stone, the rhythmic scraping a counterpoint to the labored breathing that filled the small space. Her white hair was covered by a simple linen cloth, but stray locks escaped to frame a face lined by decades of hardship yet somehow unbowed. Across from her, an ancient man dozed on another reed mat, his chest rising and falling irregularly beneath a thin blanket.

"Mother," Aaron called softly, the tenderness in his voice revealing the depth of his love. "We have a visitor."

Jochebed looked up, squinting in the poor light, her hands continuing their work by memory alone. "Who comes to visit old ones like us?" she asked, her voice surprisingly strong despite her advanced years, carrying the musical cadence that Moses recognized from the Hebrew slaves at court.

Aaron drew Moses forward, one hand firmly on his shoulder as if afraid he might flee. "He claims to be... Moses. Our Moses."

The grinding stone fell from Jochebed's hands with a dull thud, sending a puff of flour into the air where it caught the single shaft of sunlight penetrating the dwelling. She rose slowly, her joints protesting audibly, disbelief and desperate hope warring in her faded eyes. She approached Moses cautiously, like one who fears a mirage might vanish if approached too quickly.

"Remove your head covering," she commanded, her voice suddenly imperious, the voice of a mother who expects to be obeyed.

Moses obeyed without hesitation, revealing his bald head, gleaming with the oil used by Egyptian nobility. The contrast between his groomed appearance and the humble surroundings could not have been starker.

Jochebed studied his face intently, her gnarled fingers reaching up to trace the line of his jaw, the arch of his brow, lingering on a small scar above his right eyebrow—an injury from childhood that he had almost forgotten. "The eyes," she murmured, her voice breaking. "You have your father's eyes. The same amber flecks in brown, like the waters of the Nile at sunset." She paused, then whispered, "And this scar—from when you were barely walking, reaching for a bronze bowl that fell and cut you. I remember cleaning the blood, fearing it would mark you for life."

Behind her, the old man stirred, disturbed by the unusual activity. "Who speaks of me?" he asked, his voice thin and quavering, like dry papyrus rustling in the breeze.

"Rest, father," Aaron said, moving to adjust the thin cushion beneath Amram's head. "We have a guest, that is all."

But Jochebed turned to her husband, tears streaming freely down her lined face, carving shining tracks through the dust of the day. "Amram," she said, her voice trembling with suppressed emotion. "It is our son. Our Moses has returned to us. The child of the river has come home at last."

The old man struggled to sit upright, bony hands pushing against the reed mat, rheumy eyes straining to see through the dim light. "Moses?"

he wheezed, his voice strengthening with excitement. "The child of the river? The one taken by Pharaoh's household?"

"Yes," Jochebed confirmed, dropping to her knees beside him, supporting his frail body with surprising strength. "He has come back to us. The prophecy speaks true—in the fullness of time, all rivers return to the sea."

Moses knelt beside the reed mat, an unfamiliar emotion constricting his throat. This frail old man was his father by blood, not the mighty Thutmose I who had commanded armies and ruled an empire. This humble dwelling, not the alabaster halls of Thebes, was his true birthright. The realization was both humbling and strangely liberating.

"Father," he said, the word strange and precious on his tongue. "I have come to know my people."

Amram's trembling hand reached out to touch Moses' face, paper-thin skin stretched over prominent bones. "My son," he whispered, his eyes suddenly clear and focused. "They said... they said you would deliver us. The midwives saw signs at your birth. A special child, they said. A deliverer."

The old man's gaze intensified, burning with unexpected clarity. "The night you were born, the Nile ran red as blood, and the stars formed a crown in the heavens. Your cry was not that of a newborn, but of a warrior calling to battle. These things I remember, though much else fades from my mind."

Moses did not know how to respond. He had not come to Avaris with any grand plan of liberation—only a desperate need to understand his own identity, to reconcile the Egyptian prince with the Hebrew slave-child. The weight of Amram's expectations pressed upon him like a physical burden.

Over the hours that followed, as shadows lengthened across the packed earth floor, Moses learned the story of his birth from his mother's lips. He heard of the Pharaoh's decree that male children should be killed, of the desperate decision to place him in a reed basket on the Nile, of his sister Miriam watching from the rushes as Pharaoh's daughter discovered him.

"She is married now, with children of her own," Aaron explained, his initial suspicion gradually softening as the day progressed. "She lives in another part of Avaris, with her husband Hur. They have been blessed with three sons, though the youngest sickens in this season's heat."

As night fell, Aaron brought a simple meal of bread, lentils, and watered wine—a pauper's feast compared to the banquets Moses had known, yet somehow more satisfying than any royal delicacy. They ate by the light of a single oil lamp, the flame casting dancing shadows on the walls as they spoke in low voices of the hardships of Israelite life under Egyptian rule.

"The burden grows heavier each year," Aaron said bitterly, breaking off a piece of the coarse bread. "More bricks, less straw. More hours under the sun, less food for our children. And always the whip, the constant threat of the whip."

His eyes hardened as he continued, "The overseers compete to see who can extract the most work for the least cost. They place impossible quotas, then punish failure with extra labor or reduced rations. When men collapse from exhaustion, they are left to die in the sun as examples to others."

Moses felt shame burning in his chest, hot and corrosive. Had not he himself approved the building projects that required this endless labor? Had he not accepted the reports of his overseers that the work proceeded on schedule, never questioning the human cost? Had he not dined in luxury while children starved mere leagues from his palace?

"And what of our numbers?" he asked, seeking to understand the scope of his people's situation. "How many of the children of Israel dwell in Egypt now?"

Aaron glanced at their parents, then back to Moses. His voice carried both pride and sorrow as he answered.

"We are numerous beyond counting—perhaps six hundred thousand, the promise made to Abraham has been fulfilled in this regard—we have become as numerous as the stars of heaven, though we remain in bondage."

He leaned forward, his voice dropping to a whisper. "Our elders calculate that nearly three hundred and nineteen years have passed since Abraham first received the promise. The years of our sojourning is approaching their completion, though many have lost hope that deliverance will ever come."

Moses felt the weight of those centuries, the accumulated suffering of generations. From his studies of Hebrew lore while serving as Pharaoh, he knew well the promises made to Abraham—that his descendants would be strangers in a land not their own, would serve and be afflicted, but would afterward come out with great substance. The timing seemed significant, though he dared not voice such thoughts aloud.

"Some still remember the old ways," Aaron continued, "gathering in secret to tell the ancient stories. We speak of Abraham's faith, of Isaac's binding, of Jacob's wrestlings with the Almighty. We remember Joseph's words before his death—that God would surely visit us and bring us up from this land to the place which He swore to our fathers."

Moses nodded thoughtfully. These were not new revelations to him—his Hebrew tutors at court had taught him these same histories, though from a different perspective. Now he was seeing them lived out in the experience of his suffering people, not as academic exercises but as sustaining hope in the midst of oppression.

"Tell me of the present leadership among our people," Moses said. "Who speaks for the tribes when disputes arise?"

Aaron's expression grew troubled. "That is one of our greatest challenges. The Egyptians deliberately prevent us from organizing under strong leaders. Any man who shows the ability to unite others finds himself assigned to the most dangerous work, or simply disappears in the night. We have elders who are respected, but none who can speak for all the people."

He gestured toward his sleeping father. "Men like Amram once provided guidance, but age and hardship have taken their toll. The younger generation grows up knowing only slavery, many losing connection to our heritage. Some even take Egyptian names and worship Egyptian gods, hoping for better treatment."

Moses felt the profound tragedy of this—a people chosen by the Almighty, inheritors of magnificent promises, reduced to scattered, frightened slaves with no unified voice or vision. Yet their very numbers suggested that God had not forgotten them, that the promise of multiplication had been faithfully kept even in bondage.

Long into the night they talked, the oil lamp burning low, until Amram and Jochebed had fallen asleep and only Moses and Aaron remained awake, their conversation occasional whispers in the darkness. Moses shared carefully selected details of his life in the palace—his education, his military campaigns, his administrative responsibilities— while Aaron spoke of the daily realities of Hebrew life under Egyptian rule.

"The work grows harder each season," Aaron murmured, his voice heavy with weariness. "It is a system designed to break us, body and spirit."

Moses listened with growing understanding of the systematic oppression that kept his people in bondage. It was not mere economic exploitation, but a deliberate policy of degradation intended to prevent any possibility of organized resistance. The Egyptians had learned well from their history with Joseph—they would not again allow Hebrews to rise to positions of influence.

When dawn approached, Aaron offered Moses a place to sleep, but he declined. "I must see more," he explained, adjusting his head covering once more. "I must understand everything if I am to know what the Almighty would have me do."

Aaron nodded, understanding. "Return this afternoon. Our home is your home, brother."

Brother. The word resonated within Moses as he slipped out into the pre-dawn darkness, adjusting his head covering once more. He had been called many things in his life—prince, priest, commander, husband, father, king—but never simply "brother." There was a warmth in it, an acceptance that all his royal titles had never conveyed.

As the sun rose over Avaris, painting the eastern sky with streaks of crimson and gold, Moses wandered among his people, observing their daily routines with new eyes. Work gangs formed at dawn, men shuffling into lines under the watchful eyes of Egyptian taskmasters whose hands rested casually on whip handles. They marched under guard to the construction sites where massive monuments to Pharaoh's glory slowly took shape, each stone cemented with the sweat and blood of Hebrew slaves.

He also saw cruelty that turned his stomach. Egyptian taskmasters quick with the lash for the slightest infraction, striking with particular viciousness when they caught a laborer praying. Soldiers who commandeered food from Israelite tables without compensation, laughing as children wept with hunger. Officials who demanded bribes for the most basic services, or worse, demanded the daughters of Israelite families for their pleasure.

And always, always the work. Endless, backbreaking work under the merciless sun. Men straining to lift stone blocks that might crush them if they faltered. Women and children mixing straw with mud to form bricks, their hands raw and bleeding. Elders collapsing from heat and exhaustion, dragged aside to recover or die while the work continued unabated.

By midday, Moses had seen enough to make his royal blood boil with outrage. He was about to return to Aaron's home when a commotion caught his attention. In a narrow alley between storehouses, where the shadows offered some relief from the punishing sun, an Egyptian overseer was berating an Israelite laborer, a man Moses recognized as one who had been working since before dawn.

"Lazy Hebrew dog!" the Egyptian shouted, his face contorted with rage, spittle flying from his lips. "You think you can slow the work and not be punished? You think I don't see your deliberate obstruction?"

The laborer, a middle-aged man with prematurely gray hair and shoulders bent from years of toil, cowered against the mudbrick wall. "Please, master," he pleaded, his voice hoarse from thirst and fear. "I did not slow the work. My strength failed for a moment, that is all. I have a fever—I've been ill—"

"Then perhaps you need motivation to find new strength!" The overseer uncoiled his whip with practiced efficiency, the leather making a sickening whisper as it sliced through the air. It struck with a wet crack, biting deep into the laborer's already scarred back, drawing a fresh line of crimson across sun-darkened skin.

Moses felt something snap within him. For thirty-six years he had lived as an Egyptian, accepting without question the right of Egyptians to rule, to command, to punish. But in this moment, watching an exhausted man beaten for the crime of human frailty, Moses ceased to be Egyptian in his heart. The accumulated weight of all he had seen in Avaris—the suffering of his people, his blood kin—crystallized into a single, clarifying moment of rage.

He looked quickly in both directions. The alley was deserted save for the three of them; everyone else was at their work or sheltering from the midday heat. Without conscious thought, Moses moved forward, grasping a thick fallen branch from a nearby acacia tree. The wood was dense and heavy in his hand, a weapon worthy of a warrior.

"Enough!" he commanded, his voice carrying the authority of decades of rule, the voice that had sent armies into battle and pronounced judgment from a throne of gold.

The overseer turned, surprised by the interruption. His eyes narrowed as he took in Moses' clothing—Israelite garb but of finer quality than most slaves could afford. Around his neck hung a simple bronze amulet, the kind favored by minor Egyptian officials. The whip hung loosely in his hand, blood dripping from its tip to stain the sandy ground.

"Who are you to interfere in Egyptian business?" he demanded, his hand tightening on the whip handle. "Get back to your work before you join this lazy one in punishment!"

"I said enough," Moses repeated, closing the distance between them with the measured stride of a man accustomed to combat. The branch hung at his side, but his grip betrayed his readiness to strike. "This man has done nothing to deserve such treatment."

The overseer laughed harshly, revealing teeth stained with wine. "Nothing? These Hebrews do nothing unless forced! Every brick, every stone must be wrung from them with threats or pain. That is their nature—lazy, deceitful, and treacherous to the bone."

"Their nature?" Moses felt cold fury rising in him, different from the hot rage of moments before—this was deeper, colder, more dangerous. "And what is the nature of a man who beats another whose only crime is exhaustion? What does that reveal about the beater's soul?"

Something in Moses' bearing must have warned the overseer that this was no ordinary Israelite. He took a step back, hand tightening on his whip, uncertainty flashing across his face for the first time.

"You speak strangely for a slave," he said, suspicion creeping into his voice. His eyes narrowed as he studied Moses more carefully, noting the straight spine, the unwavering gaze, the confidence that no amount of humble clothing could disguise. "Perhaps you need to be reminded of your place in the order of things."

He raised the whip, but before it could fall, Moses struck. The acacia branch connected with terrible force, catching the Egyptian at the juncture of neck and shoulder. There was a sickening crack as bone gave way, and the overseer stumbled, eyes wide with shock and sudden pain.

"You dare!" he gasped, fumbling for the dagger at his belt, but his arm hung useless at his side, the collarbone shattered by Moses' blow.

Moses struck again, driven by rage too long suppressed, by guilt too long ignored. The branch came down on the Egyptian's chest with such devastating force that his heart expanded violently within his ribcage, the cardiac muscle stretched beyond its ability to contract. He collapsed to the ground, blood seeping from his ears and mouth as his heart failed, eyes already glazing in death, the bronze amulet around his neck catching the harsh midday sun.

For a moment, Moses stood frozen, the branch still clutched in his hand, its smooth surface now slick with blood. He had killed before—in battle, against the enemies of Egypt, with sword and spear and chariot. But this was different. This was not war. This was murder, committed in a moment of ungovernable rage.

The Israelite laborer stared at Moses in horror and awe. "You... you have killed him," he whispered, pressing himself against the wall as if afraid Moses might turn on him next. "Jehuty was his name—he has overseen this section for five years. They will search for whoever did this."

The reality of his action crashed over Moses like a wave. He looked down at the dead overseer—Jehuty, the man had been called—noting with detached clarity that the Egyptian's build was remarkably similar to his own beneath the finer clothing and well-fed flesh. "Go," he told the laborer urgently, dropping the branch beside the corpse. "Tell no one what you have seen here. For your own safety, go!"

The man needed no further urging. He fled down the alley, clutching his wounded back, leaving Moses alone with the corpse of the Egyptian. Panic threatened to overwhelm him as the full implications of his action became clear. He was no longer Pharaoh, with the power to pardon his own crimes. He was a fugitive in his own land, a killer without the sanction of war.

Looking around frantically to ensure no witnesses remained, Moses began the grim work of concealment. He stripped the bronze amulet from Jehuty's neck—it might be useful later, or its absence might confuse identification. The Egyptian's fine linen tunic, stained now with blood and sand, bore the insignia of his rank. Moses removed it as well, bundling it with the amulet before dragging the body deeper into the alley, away from casual view.

Then, with his bare hands—hands that had wielded the scepter of Egypt, that had been kissed by nobles and priests—he began to dig in the soft soil beside a storehouse wall. The work was slow and difficult, but fear and desperation lent him strength. When the hole was deep enough, he rolled the overseer's body into it and covered it with soil, smoothing the surface as best he could. The sandy earth of Avaris was loose and forgiving, swallowing the evidence of his crime.

As he worked, Moses could not shake the image of Jehuty's face—so similar to his own in the bone structure, the set of the jaw. In death, stripped of the arrogance that had marked his living expression, the overseer looked almost... regal. It was a disturbing thought, one that Moses pushed away as he completed his burial work.

Then he left, heart hammering in his chest, hands still stained with the Egyptian's blood, the dead man's belongings hidden beneath his rough Hebrew garments. He had come to Avaris seeking identity and understanding. He had found instead a moment of clarity that would forever change the course of his life—and unknown to him, the course of history itself. Behind him, in the shallow grave beside the storehouse, lay the body that would one day be discovered, misidentified, and entombed as Pharaoh Thutmose II—the king who had died too young, whose heart had mysteriously expanded in his final moments, whose flesh bore the strange marks of a death far from the palace.

Chapter 30 - A Fugitive and a Pharaoh

April 1479 BC - Avaris

The next day dawned bright and clear over Avaris, the merciless Egyptian sun climbing a cloudless azure sky as though nature itself remained indifferent to the violence of the previous afternoon. Moses had spent a restless night in the shelter of an abandoned mud-brick shed on the outskirts of the city, its crumbling walls offering little comfort against the desert's bitter night chill. Sleep had come in fitful bursts, his dreams haunted by the Egyptian overseer's wide, disbelieving eyes as life drained from them—by the sickening crack of bone yielding to acacia wood—by the dark blood soaking into the thirsty soil, disappearing as the earth claimed its offering.

His hands, once adorned with royal rings and anointed with sacred oils, were now raw from digging in the coarse ground. The fingernails that court servants had once meticulously maintained were broken and rimmed with dried blood—not his own. Moses examined them in the harsh morning light filtering through gaps in the shed's walls, marveling at how swiftly one's fortunes could change. Yesterday, he had been discovering his heritage, meeting his blood family for the first time. Today, he was a fugitive, a murderer hiding from Egyptian justice. The thought of Aaron's weathered face, of his elderly parents who had embraced him with such joy, sent a shaft of pain through his chest. What would they think when they learned of his flight? Would they understand, or would they curse the day he had returned to bring disaster upon them all?

What had he done? In that single explosive moment of ungovernable rage, he had destroyed everything—his position, his safety, perhaps even the tentative connection with his Hebrew family. If discovered, he would face Egyptian justice, which would be swift and merciless. He knew this better than anyone, for had he not ordered such punishments himself during his reign? The penalty for killing an Egyptian overseer would be excruciating public execution, even—perhaps especially—for one who had once sat upon the throne.

Yet beneath the fear and bitter regret lay a troubling certainty that settled in his gut like a stone: he would do the same again. The Egyptian's casual cruelty had been commonplace, unremarkable in the daily life of Avaris. How many times had such scenes played out across Egypt during Moses' reign? How many Hebrew backs had been flayed open by Egyptian whips while he dined on delicacies and discussed architectural plans for monuments to his own glory? How much suffering had he tacitly permitted through his silence?

These thoughts churned in his mind as he splashed tepid water from a cracked clay pot onto his face, wiping away the grit of a sleepless night. He had discovered the vessel in a corner of the shed, its contents stale but welcome nonetheless. After drinking sparingly, Moses gathered his meager possessions—the rough garments that marked him as an Israelite, a small water skin, and a piece of bread Aaron had given him the previous day—and ventured cautiously back into Avaris.

The city was already alive with activity. Workers trudged toward construction sites, women balanced water jars on their heads with practiced grace, and merchants called out their wares in the small market squares. Moses kept to side streets and shadows, his keen eyes—those eyes that had once surveyed Egypt from a throne of gold and lapis lazuli—now darting nervously at every passing soldier or Egyptian official.

He needed to speak with Aaron, to seek counsel on what to do next. Perhaps it was time to reveal himself fully to his people—not as their former ruler, but as one of them, ready to share their fate. Or perhaps Aaron would know of some safe passage out of Egypt, some caravan heading east with which Moses might travel undetected.

As he approached a small square where several narrow alleys converged, the sounds of conflict reached his ears—angry shouts and the dull thud of fist against flesh. Rounding a corner, Moses came upon a disturbing scene. Two Israelite men were fighting viciously; their faces contorted with rage as they traded blows beneath the indifferent gaze of a small gathered crowd. The larger man, his muscled arms dusty from brick-making, had pinned the smaller against a sun-baked wall, one hand at his throat.

Moses stepped forward without thinking, the instinct to maintain order—drilled into him through decades of ruling—overriding his need for anonymity.

"Why do you strike your fellow Hebrew?" he demanded, his voice carrying the unmistakable tone of command that had once echoed through the great halls of Thebes.

Both men froze at his intervention, their heads turning slowly to stare at him with sudden wariness. The bystanders too fell silent, the usual market chatter dying away like birds before a storm. The larger man released his opponent and stepped back, his sweaty face shifting from surprise to calculation. His eyes narrowed as they took in Moses' appearance—not just the quality of his garments despite their simple style, but the way he held himself, the unconscious authority that radiated from him like heat from a furnace. This was a man who had studied the faces of nobility from below, had learned to recognize the subtle signs of rank and privilege that no amount of common clothing could disguise.

As Moses stepped forward with authority, a sudden gust of wind caught the edge of his head covering, pulling it loose from where it had been carefully arranged. The linen fell away, revealing his distinctly shaven scalp—the mark of Egyptian nobility as unmistakable as a brand. Where Hebrew men wore their hair and beards long according to their customs, Moses bore the smooth, oiled baldness of the palace, his skull gleaming in the harsh sunlight like polished bronze. A collective intake of breath rippled through the gathered crowd. Here was the proof they had only suspected moments before: this was no common Hebrew who had learned Egyptian ways, but one who had been molded by Egypt itself, shaped in the very image of their oppressors. The larger man's eyes widened with a mixture of recognition and disgust, his lips curling into a sneer that held both fear and contempt.

"Who made you a prince and judge over us?" he snarled, spitting the words like poison. Recognition dawned in his eyes like a malevolent sunrise. "I know you, don't I? I've seen you in the Egyptian quarter, walking among their nobles like one of them. You're that Hebrew they say was raised in Pharaoh's house—the one who thinks himself better than his own people." His voice dropped to a menacing whisper. "Do you intend to kill me as you killed the Egyptian yesterday?"

Moses felt the blood drain from his face, leaving him light-headed. So it was known. Someone had witnessed his crime, or the laborer he had saved had spoken despite his warning. The knowledge of his deed had spread through Avaris like fire through dry reeds.

The larger man spat contemptuously on the ground at Moses' feet. "Your secret is not safe, 'brother.'" He invested the word with mocking emphasis. "The Egyptians already search for the one who killed their overseer. By nightfall, they will have your name."

The gathered crowd began to murmur, the mood shifting palpably. Some looked at Moses with newfound fear, others with the calculating avarice of men weighing the reward that might come from turning him in to the authorities. Women pulled children closer, and one old man made a warding gesture against evil.

Moses backed away, mind racing beneath his outwardly calm demeanor. He had to leave Avaris immediately, before word reached the palace. If Hatshepsut learned what he had done—and who he had done it for—her retribution would be terrible. Not just for him, but for all Israelites.

Before he could retreat further, movement on the far side of the square caught his eye. A contingent of Egyptian soldiers in polished leather armor entered from the opposite side, led by a captain Moses recognized with a jolt of alarm—Ahmes, a stern veteran who had commanded Moses' own royal guard. They moved with military precision, separating to question people methodically, describing someone matching Moses' appearance with disturbing accuracy.

With as much calm as he could muster, Moses turned and walked—not ran—toward the nearest alley. Running would only draw attention. Once out of sight of the square, he abandoned dignity for speed, breaking into a sprint that belied his forty years. He wove through the maze-like streets of the Israelite quarter, his sandaled feet slapping against the packed earth as he headed instinctively toward the city gates. The taste of copper filled his mouth, whether from fear or exertion he could not say, and dust clung to his sweat-dampened skin like a second garment.

As he ran, Moses reached up and stripped away his head covering, revealing his completely shaved head—a distinctly Egyptian custom that few Israelites adopted. Without the covering, he looked less like a Hebrew and more like a lower-ranking Egyptian official, which might afford him precious moments of confusion among his pursuers.

The eastern gate of Avaris loomed ahead, its massive wooden doors thrown open to admit the day's commerce. A steady stream of merchants, farmers, and travelers flowed through under the watchful but bored gaze of guards more interested in collecting tolls than in security. Moses slowed his pace, forcing his breathing to steady despite the hammering of his heart against his ribs. His feet, soft from years of palace living, throbbed in their simple sandals, each step a reminder of how far he had fallen from the cushioned luxury of his former life.

Ahead of him, a group of traders led dust-covered donkeys laden with goods toward the gate. Moses fell in beside them, adopting their weathered, road-weary demeanor with the skill of a court performer. He kept his eyes downcast as they approached the checkpoint, offering a silent prayer to the God of Abraham—a God he had only recently begun to consider might be more than a Hebrew superstition.

"Papers! Show your trade permits!" barked a guard, his spear held casually across his body.

The lead trader produced a crumpled papyrus scroll, launching into a detailed complaint about excessive taxation that immediately occupied the guard's full attention. Moses shuffled past as part of the group, his shoulders hunched in feigned subservience, sweat running freely down his back beneath his rough woolen garment.

"You there! Wait!"

Moses' heart seized in his chest, but the command was directed at a merchant behind him, arguing over the value of his goods. The moment of terror passed, and then he was through the gate, beyond the city walls, walking with forced casualness into the open countryside beyond.

He did not immediately leave the road, knowing that to do so would attract unwanted attention. Instead, he maintained a steady pace alongside other travelers, occasionally nodding in silent greeting as though he were merely another trader going about his business. Only when he reached the first fork in the road, where the main thoroughfare continued north while a lesser path veered southeast toward the distant wilderness of Midian, did Moses finally break away from the bustling traffic.

The southeastern path was less travelled, used primarily by copper traders and the occasional caravan venturing to the distant lands beyond the Gulf of Suez. Moses knew the route from military maps he had studied as Egypt's ruler—knew that it would take him far from Egyptian authority if he could survive the journey.

Only when Avaris had disappeared behind him, swallowed by the shimmering heat haze that rose from the sun-baked earth, did the full weight of his situation descend upon him. The adrenaline that had carried him through his escape began to ebb, leaving a bone-deep weariness in its wake. Moses sank down beneath the meager shade of a stunted acacia tree, his legs suddenly unable to support him. The silence of the desert pressed against his ears after the constant noise of the city, broken only by the whisper of wind through thorny branches and the distant cry of a hunting hawk.

In the space of twenty-five days, he had transformed from Pharaoh of Egypt—ruler of the mightiest kingdom on earth—to fugitive murderer. He had found his birth family only to be forced to abandon them without explanation or farewell. He had sought understanding of his heritage only to commit an act that separated him irrevocably from both Egyptian and Hebrew society.

He had nowhere to go but forward, into the harsh wilderness that separated Egypt from the lands of the east—a wilderness where bandits, wild beasts, and the merciless sun claimed the lives of unwary travelers every day. The path ahead shimmered in the heat, stretching toward a horizon of rocky desolation where no green thing grew and water was more precious than gold. Already, the sun beat down on his uncovered head with relentless intensity, and he could feel the moisture being drawn from his body like offerings to some pitiless god.

Moses had survived battles against Nubian warriors and Canaanite chariot armies. He had navigated court intrigues so complex they would make a serpent dizzy. He had commanded legions and ruled a nation whose glory stretched back into the mists of time. But as he faced the vast emptiness ahead, he wondered if he would survive this journey into exile, or if the desert would claim him as payment for the blood on his hands.

Rising to his feet with effort, his soft palace-bred muscles already protesting the unaccustomed strain, Moses adjusted his water skin and looked back toward Avaris one last time. Somewhere within those distant walls, Aaron and his elderly parents would soon learn of his flight. Would they understand? Would they remember him as the son and brother who had briefly returned, or as the killer whose actions might bring even harsher treatment down upon them?

"Forgive me," he whispered, though whether to his family or to the God of his fathers or to himself, he could not say.

Then he turned his face to the east and began to walk, each step carrying him further from everything he had known, deeper into an uncertain future that stretched before him like the desert itself—vast, unforgiving, and unknown.

28 April 1479 BC - Thebes

The palace at Thebes hummed with tension like a taut bowstring. Guards stood more rigidly at their posts, servants went about their duties with downcast eyes, and officials whispered in corners, their conversations dying away when others approached. Something had shifted in the very atmosphere of the royal residence—a subtle but unmistakable change that even the lowliest water-carrier could sense.

Hatshepsut sat alone in her private chamber, a spacious room whose walls were adorned with vivid scenes of the afterlife, where Osiris judged the souls of the dead. A scroll of fine papyrus lay unfurled before her on a table of polished cedar, but her kohl-lined eyes focused on nothing, seeing instead possibilities and consequences that played out in her mind like the moves of a senet game.

There had been no word of Moses. His disappearance from the palace had caused initial panic—had the Pharaoh been kidnapped? Assassinated? Then came confusion as reports filtered in of his presence among the Israelites of Avaris, dressed as one of them. And finally, the slow, dawning realization that he might not return.

A soft knock at the door interrupted her thoughts.

"Enter," she commanded, her voice betraying none of the turmoil beneath her composed exterior.

Hapuseneb, the High Priest of Amun whose service to the crown had spanned two pharaohs, stepped into the chamber and bowed deeply. His face, already lined with age like a cracked pottery vessel, seemed to have acquired new furrows in recent weeks. His hands—once steady enough to draft the most intricate temple plans—trembled slightly as he straightened.

"Divine One," he said, using the honorific reserved for Pharaoh, though technically Hatshepsut held no such title while Moses lived. "There is news from Avaris."

Hatshepsut straightened on her ebony chair, her heart quickening despite herself. Her fingers, adorned with rings of gold and precious stones, tightened almost imperceptibly on the armrests.

"Speak," she said, her voice carefully modulated to reveal nothing of her inner thoughts.

"An Egyptian overseer was found dead, buried in shallow soil behind a storehouse. He had been killed with a single blow of great force." Hapuseneb's voice carried the weight of one who understands the gravity of his words. "The body was discovered when dogs uncovered it, drawn by the scent."

"And this concerns the royal house how?" Hatshepsut asked, her voice neutral as still water, though she suspected she already knew the answer.

Hapuseneb hesitated, his ancient eyes studying her face with the wisdom acquired through a lifetime of palace service. "Witnesses claim the killer was a Hebrew man with the bearing of nobility—a man who spoke with authority no slave should possess. A man with a shaved head beneath his Israelite garments."

For a long moment, Hatshepsut was silent, absorbing the implications like poison from a coated blade. Then she rose in a whisper of fine linen and walked to the window that overlooked the temple complex of Karnak, where the great obelisks she had commissioned— the tallest in all Egypt—pierced the sky like spears aimed at the heavens.

"So," she said finally, her voice barely louder than the breeze that stirred the papyrus reeds along the distant Nile. "Moses has chosen his side."

"Divine One?" Hapuseneb prompted when she did not continue.

She turned back to face the priest, her face a perfect mask of royal composure, though something cold and calculating lurked behind her eyes—something that made even the veteran courtier suppress a shiver.

"He went to his people—his true people—and killed an Egyptian in their defense. There can be no return from such an act." The words fell from her lips like stones into a deep well. "He has revealed his heart at last."

"What would you have us do?" Hapuseneb asked, knowing that Hatshepsut would already have formed a plan—she always did.

Hatshepsut's mind worked rapidly, calculating possibilities and outcomes with the strategic precision that had made her the power behind Egypt's throne for years. Moses' absence—and now his crime—presented not a crisis but an opportunity she had long anticipated. The pieces of Egypt's future rearranged themselves in her mind, forming a new pattern with herself at its center.

"Summon the royal council," she ordered, her voice gaining strength and purpose with each word. "Bring all the priests, the military commanders, and the nobles of high rank. We face a crisis of succession that must be addressed immediately."

Hapuseneb bowed deeply and departed to carry out her instructions, his sandaled feet silent on the polished limestone floor.

Left alone, Hatshepsut allowed herself a moment of genuine emotion—not merely frustration at political disruption, but raw, overwhelming grief for Moses. She had loved him deeply, completely, with a devotion that transcended the boundaries of duty and station. His brilliant mind had captivated her, but it was his gentle strength, his unwavering integrity, that had won her heart entirely. She had adored everything about him—the way his eyes lit when he spoke of justice, the careful tenderness of his touch, the quiet confidence that made her feel both protected and understood. Now that profound love lay shattered, and she faced not just the collapse of political plans, but the devastation of a heart that might never heal.

She moved to a small side table where a polished bronze mirror stood, examining her reflection critically. At thirty-two, her beauty remained remarkable—the high cheekbones, the proud nose, the eyes that missed nothing.

"You chose poorly, Moses," she murmured to her reflection. "But I shall make better choices in your absence."

When the council convened in the great hall hours later, Hatshepsut had composed herself fully, every aspect of her appearance and demeanor calculated for maximum effect. She sat beside the empty throne of Pharaoh—not upon it, a calculated positioning that acknowledged Moses' technical authority while emphasizing her role as the true power in his absence.

The hall itself spoke of Egypt's wealth and power—its soaring columns painted in vibrant colors, its walls adorned with scenes of Pharaoh's victories in battle and offerings to the gods. The light of the setting sun streamed through high clerestory windows, bathing the assembled dignitaries in golden radiance that seemed to confer divine blessing upon the proceedings.

"Noble ones of Egypt," Hatshepsut began when all were assembled, her voice carrying effortlessly to the farthest corners of the vast chamber. "I have summoned you on a matter of grave importance. Our divine Pharaoh Moses has met with tragedy."

A murmur ran through the gathered officials like wind through wheat, faces turning to one another in question and alarm.

"While he was visiting our loyal subjects in Avaris," she continued, her face a perfect mask of royal grief, "Pharaoh was set upon by Israelite rebels who recognized him despite his disguise. They murdered him in their cowardly fashion and concealed his body."

Gasps and exclamations of shock filled the hall. General Pennekh, scarred veteran of a dozen border campaigns, half-rose from his seat with a warrior's instinctive outrage. "Divine One, if this is true, we must march on Avaris immediately! The entire Hebrew quarter should be put to the sword!"

"Peace, General," Hatshepsut replied, her voice carrying just enough steel to remind him of his place. "Justice will be served, but Egypt's response must be measured, not rash."

Several priests made signs of warding against evil, while other military commanders exchanged glances that spoke of barely contained fury.

She raised a hand for silence, her authority absolute even in this moment of supposed personal loss. "The body believed to be Moses has been recovered," she continued when quiet had been restored. "It was identified by the royal insignia he carried always, though the rebels had disfigured his face beyond recognition in their hatred of Egypt's divine rule."

Here, Hapuseneb stirred uncomfortably in his seat, his weathered features creased with what might have been doubt. But he remained silent, as she had known he would.

"How can we be certain of this identification?" asked General Pennekh smoothly, his question seeming innocent enough but carrying undertones that made several council members shift nervously. "Surely the divine Pharaoh would not have fallen so easily to mere Hebrew slaves?"

Hatshepsut met his gaze steadily, her expression never wavering. "The identification was confirmed by Captain Kheti, who served Pharaoh's personal guard and knew his possessions intimately. The insignia were genuine—the royal cartouche ring that never left his finger, the ceremonial dagger gifted by his predecessor." She paused, allowing her voice to carry the weight of grief. "As for how he fell, even the gods may be struck down when outnumbered by treacherous cowards who attack from shadows."

General Pennekh inclined his head, apparently satisfied, though his eyes suggested otherwise. But before he could probe further, she moved swiftly to assert her authority.

"In this time of tragedy, Egypt must not falter," Hatshepsut declared, rising to her feet in a deliberate display of strength. The golden beads adorning her elaborate wig caught the light with each subtle movement of her head. "The divine blood of Ra flows through the veins of Menkhe, son of our beloved Moses. Until he reaches manhood, I shall serve as regent, guiding Egypt with the wisdom granted by the gods and continuing the glorious reign that fate has cut short."

The council received this announcement with varying degrees of enthusiasm. The priests nodded approvingly—they had long been her allies. General Pennekh looked troubled but said nothing.

"The funeral rites for our fallen Pharaoh will commence tomorrow," she continued, moving smoothly to matters of immediate practicality. "Let messengers be sent throughout the Two Lands with news of his passing and of the succession."

Here, Hatshepsut's voice hardened like clay in a kiln, her expression shifting to one of cold authority that silenced even the whispers among the council. "Since it was the treachery of the Israelites that robbed Egypt of its divine ruler, let their burden be doubled. For every brick they made before, let them now make two. For every field they tended, let them now tend two. Their punishment shall continue until the debt of royal blood is paid in full."

The council murmured approval of this harsh justice, many nodding with grim satisfaction. Even General Pennekh seemed pleased by this show of strength. Only Hapuseneb, sitting at the far end of the hall like the living embodiment of Egypt's ancient wisdom, showed any sign of disquiet, his rheumy eyes filled with sorrow for what he knew to be a calculated deception.

Later, as the council dispersed to carry out Hatshepsut's instructions—priests to prepare the funeral rites, officials to draft the royal decrees, military commanders to increase security throughout the kingdom—the High Priest of Amun approached her privately in an antechamber off the main hall.

"You have secured your position with great skill, Divine One," he said quietly, his voice carrying decades of observations he had been wise enough never to speak aloud. "But what if Moses should return?"

Hatshepsut's smile was cold and brittle as winter ice on the rare occasions it formed on the pools of the royal gardens. "I will send search parties to look for him, ostensibly to recover his body for proper burial. But their true orders will be different—if they find him alive, he will not remain so. Even if he survived his flight from Avaris—and the desert shows mercy to few fugitives—he can never reclaim his throne. The official truth has been established: Pharaoh Moses is dead, murdered by Israelite rebels. Should a man resembling him appear with claims to the contrary, he would be branded an impostor and dealt with accordingly."

The implicit threat hung in the air between them, as tangible as the scent of incense that permeated the palace.

Hapuseneb bowed his head in acknowledgment of her strategy. "As you say, Divine One. May the gods grant you wisdom in your reign."

"The gods had nothing to do with it," Hatshepsut replied with rare candor, secure in the knowledge that Hapuseneb's loyalty had been proven over too many years to doubt. "This is the work of human hands—my hands—and I will complete what I have begun."

After Hapuseneb had gone, Hatshepsut remained alone in the council chamber, her gaze fixed on the empty throne that would soon be hers in all but name. Moses had chosen his fate when he abandoned his position to embrace his Hebrew heritage. She had merely seized the opportunity his absence presented, as any skilled ruler would.

"You were wrong, Moses," she murmured to the vacant seat of power, adorned with symbols of divine authority—the crook and flail, the double crown of Upper and Lower Egypt. "I told you that you would return when you discovered your true nature. But I did not understand that your true nature was never Egyptian at all."

In her private thoughts, unwitnessed by even her closest advisors, she allowed herself to wonder where he might be now—whether he had escaped into the eastern wilderness or fallen victim to the harsh desert that had claimed so many before him. But it hardly mattered. For all intents and purposes, Moses was dead to Egypt.

Young Architect's Gambit

The morning light filtered through the alabaster screens of Hatshepsut's private chamber, casting intricate patterns across the polished limestone floor. Forty-three days had passed since the burial of the man the kingdom now mourned as Thutmose II, and the regent found herself caught between the weight of deception and the burden of grief that refused to be feigned.

She stood before a bronze mirror, studying her reflection as her servants prepared the day's attire. The face that looked back at her was that of a woman who had learned to rule through necessity, her dark eyes holding secrets that would shake the very foundations of Egypt if revealed. Seven more days of official mourning remained—seven more days of playing the grieving widow before she could fully embrace the power that circumstance had thrust upon her.

A soft knock interrupted her thoughts. "My lady," came the voice of her chief scribe, "the architect Senenmut requests an audience. He brings plans for the memorial temple you commissioned."

Hatshepsut's eyebrows lifted slightly. She had indeed commissioned such a temple—another piece in the elaborate fiction that surrounded her husband's death—but she had not expected plans so quickly. "Send him in."

Senenmut entered with measured steps, his arms bearing rolled papyri and his manner conveying both confidence and appropriate deference. In the soft morning light, Hatshepsut found herself truly noticing him for the first time since his elevation from the burial detail. He was not handsome in the classical sense that Moses had been—there was no golden radiance about him, no bearing that spoke of divine favour. Instead, he possessed something perhaps more valuable: an intensity of purpose that seemed to radiate from his very core.

"My regent," he said, bowing precisely to the degree protocol demanded—neither excessive nor insufficient. "I bring preliminary designs for Pharaoh Thutmose II's memorial temple, as you commanded."

As he unrolled the papyrus across her table, Hatshepsut moved closer, ostensibly to examine his work but finding herself studying the man himself. His hands, she noted, were strong and capable—the hands of someone who had built things, created things, rather than merely commanded others to do so. When he spoke of architectural principles and sacred geometries, his voice carried a passion that reminded her, painfully, of how Moses had spoken of his god.

"You propose to build it here?" she asked, pointing to a location marked on his carefully drawn plans. "Against the cliffs at Deir el-Bahari?"

"The site would be unprecedented," Senenmut replied, his eyes meeting hers with an intensity that made her pulse quicken unexpectedly. "Carved into the living rock itself, it would speak of permanence, of a pharaoh whose reign was so blessed by the gods that even death could not diminish his connection to the sacred landscape of Egypt."

There was something almost seductive in the way he spoke of permanence and divine connection—concepts that had been so brutally torn from her world with Moses' departure. She found herself leaning closer as he explained the terraced design, his finger tracing lines on the papyrus while his voice painted visions of columned halls and sacred chambers.

"The construction would require unprecedented organization," she said, testing him. "Thousands of workers, precise coordination of materials, absolute loyalty to ensure the work continues without... complications."

Senenmut's smile was subtle but unmistakable. "I have given considerable thought to the matter of loyalty, my lady. A project of this magnitude requires not just skilled hands, but devoted hearts. Men who understand that their fate is bound to yours, that your success is their success."

The double meaning in his words was not lost on her. As their eyes held, Hatshepsut felt something stir within her that had been dormant since Moses' departure—not love, perhaps, but something equally compelling. Where Moses had offered her passion tempered with the constant awareness of his divided loyalties, Senenmut offered something different: absolute devotion wedded to brilliant capability.

"Tell me," She said, her voice softer now, "what drives a man of common birth to dream of building monuments that will outlast kingdoms?"

For a moment, his carefully maintained composure slipped, revealing something raw and hungry beneath. "The desire to be remembered, my lady. To leave a mark upon the world that speaks of what a man can achieve when he finds a cause worthy of his complete devotion."

The words hung in the air between them, charged with implications that went far beyond architecture. Hatshepsut felt herself at a crossroads—she could retreat into the safety of formal distance, or she could acknowledge the current of attraction and ambition that crackled between them.

"Rise very early tomorrow," she said finally, her decision made. "Come to my private garden before dawn. Bring your plans, but also bring your vision for Egypt's future. If you would build monuments to permanence, Senenmut, then perhaps it is time we discussed what foundations such monuments require."

As he gathered his papyri and bowed his farewell, Hatshepsut found herself studying his retreating form with new eyes. Seven days of mourning remained, but already she could feel the stirrings of something that might, given time and careful nurturing, grow into something powerful enough to help her forget the golden-haired overseer who had awakened her heart only to abandon it.

The game of succession was far from over, and Hatshepsut was beginning to suspect that her newest piece might prove to be more valuable than even she had initially imagined.

Fate of Moses

In the deepening twilight, with only the stars as witness, the truth of Moses' fate remained unknown—a mystery that would grow into legend in the years to come. The man who had been raised as Egypt's son but had chosen his Hebrew blood had vanished into the wilderness, while behind him, the greatest civilization on earth adjusted its course like a mighty river finding a new channel to the sea.

And somewhere in that wilderness, Moses himself stumbled forward, driven by forces he did not yet understand toward a destiny that would reshape the world. The stars above—the same stars that shone over the false tomb in Thebes—guided his faltering steps toward Midian, toward the mountain where fire would speak from stone, and toward the moment when a fugitive murderer would become the instrument of divine justice.

Chapter 31 - The Flames of Luxor

February 2011, - Luxor, Egypt

The night shattered with the sound of breaking glass. Professor Arthur Maddison's head snapped up from the parchment-strewn table, his bloodshot eyes momentarily unable to focus in the dimly lit monastery room. The single oil lamp cast elongated shadows across the ancient stone walls, its flame dancing like a dying spirit with each draft that whispered through the cracks in the mortar. For three days, he had barely slept, consumed by the magnificent hieroglyphics that promised to rewrite history itself. His lean, weathered face bore the stubble of neglect, and the hollow beneath his cheekbones had deepened, giving him the haunted look of a man pursued by ghosts from the distant past.

"What in God's name—" he muttered, the half-translated text before him suddenly forgotten. His thin, scholarly fingers trembled slightly as they hovered over the papyrus fragments that had occupied his every waking moment. Age spots dotted the backs of his hands, testament to decades spent under the merciless Egyptian sun, chasing the whispers of ancient voices.

The sound came again—not glass breaking this time, but the unmistakable roar of fire taking hold, devouring ancient wood with primeval hunger. Then shouts erupted in the distance, Arabic words flying fast and furious like hornets disturbed from their nest, the consonants hard and angry in the still desert night. The smell of smoke began to seep through the monastery's thick walls, acrid and threatening.

Heavy footsteps thundered up the stone staircase outside his door, each impact like the approaching heartbeat of danger itself. Maddison's hand closed instinctively around the silver letter opener on his desk—a pathetic weapon against whatever threat approached, but the only one available. The metal felt cool against his palm, a talisman against the chaos that had suddenly invaded his scholarly sanctuary.

The door flew open with enough force to crack the weathered wood against the stone wall, sending ancient dust spiraling into the lamplight like golden galaxies. Bishop Farouk Ahmani stood framed in the doorway, his massive frame heaving with exertion, sweat gleaming on his forehead in the lamplight. The Coptic cleric's dark eyes blazed with urgency beneath his impressive brow; his normally immaculate black cassock now stained with soot. A small cut on his left cheek had left a crimson trail down his neck, soaking into his clerical collar.

"Professor! We must evacuate. Now!" The urgency in the cleric's voice left no room for questions. His deep baritone, normally so measured during their scholarly discussions, now carried the raw edge of a man who had witnessed something terrible. The wooden cross that hung around his neck caught the light as his chest heaved.

Maddison rose to his feet, his legs cramping painfully after hours of immobility, bones creaking in protest. At sixty-two, the rigors of fieldwork were increasingly punishing, though his passion for discovery remained undimmed. "My research—the photographs—" he protested, hands reaching instinctively toward the precious materials that represented months of painstaking work.

"Leave it!" Farouk commanded, his eyes blazing with the intensity of a man who had seen the face of death. His large hand gripped the doorframe, knuckles white with tension. "There is no time. Take only what you can carry in one case."

The Englishman's heart twisted with physical pain at the thought of abandoning the work that could define his career, vindicate years of academic ridicule. His eyes swept over the hundreds of photographs plastered across the monastery walls—the sacred hieroglyphics that told of Menkheperre's divine connection to Thutmose III, the reincarnation of pharaohs, the hidden truths of the 18th Dynasty. Each image represented a fragment of a puzzle he had pursued since his days as a young doctoral student at Oxford, when his theories had first been dismissed with academic disdain.

"The chamber itself—" Maddison began desperately, throat dry with sudden fear. The hidden chamber beneath the monastery had remained sealed for three millennia, protected by the shifting sands and forgotten by time until their discovery just days ago.

"Is sealed and will remain so," Farouk finished with grim certainty, his massive shoulders blocking most of the doorway. "God willing, we shall return when the danger has passed." The ancient protective prayers of his Coptic ancestors seemed to hang unspoken in the air between them.

Outside, the night air filled with the unmistakable cacophony of violence—shouts, screams, the occasional crack of gunfire that echoed off stone like the anger of ancient gods. The perfect darkness of Luxor's night sky, normally strewn with stars like diamonds on black velvet, was now marred by an ominous orange glow painting the horizon, turning the familiar silhouette of the Theban hills into something sinister and alien.

With shaking hands, Maddison swept his most critical notes into his battered leather satchel, a faithful companion through thirty years of desert expeditions, along with his passport and wallet. Everything else— his laptop with its precious photographs, his reference books, his carefully organized translation notes—would have to remain. The work of three sleepless days, abandoned in mere seconds. Each piece of paper left behind felt like abandoning a child to the flames.

Farouk grabbed the professor's arm with enough force to bruise, half-dragging him down the narrow staircase and through the monastery's winding corridors. The stone walls here had witnessed seventeen centuries of prayers, persecutions, and perseverance. Now they might witness destruction once more. The small band of Coptic monks they passed moved with the practiced efficiency of men accustomed to persecution, their ancient treasures being spirited away to hiding places known only to the faithful. Their lined faces, illuminated briefly in the lamplight, showed neither panic nor despair—only grim determination born of generations of survival.

"The Muslim Brotherhood?" Maddison gasped as they burst through the monastery's side door into the warm night air, the taste of smoke immediately coating his tongue. The heat struck him like a physical blow after the cool sanctuary of the stone building.

"Yes," Farouk confirmed grimly, his grip on Maddison's arm never loosening. "The violence has reached Luxor. I had feared this would happen." The political turmoil that had been brewing in Cairo for months had finally boiled over, spreading like wildfire through the country. They had foolishly believed themselves isolated from it in the ancient city, absorbed in their academic pursuits while the modern world burned around them.

The scene that greeted them outside stole Maddison's breath more effectively than any ancient tomb's stale air. Two houses less than a hundred yards from the monastery were engulfed in flames, the fire devouring the humble mud-brick structures with ravenous appetite. The heat reached them even at this distance, a physical wall of scorching air that made Maddison's eyes water and his skin prickle with fear-sweat. The flames reached toward the heavens like suppliant hands, casting nightmarish shadows that danced across the ancient streets in mocking parody of the ritual dances once performed for Amun-Ra.

Distant figures moved in the firelight, their silhouettes distorted by the dancing flames into demonic shapes from some pharaonic underworld. Occasional shouts in Arabic punctuated the crackling roar of the inferno, the words indecipherable to Maddison but their meaning unmistakable in their hatred and triumph.

"This way," Farouk hissed, pulling the professor away from the monastery walls. "Stay in the shadows. Do not run unless I tell you to run." The big man moved with surprising grace for his size, his years navigating the complex politics of being a Christian leader in a Muslim land having taught him how to become invisible when necessary.

"But the monastery—" Maddison protested, his academic's mind still struggling to process the violent reality that had so suddenly replaced the orderly world of scholarship.

"Has survived worse over seventeen centuries," Farouk replied, his voice steady despite the chaos surrounding them. A strange calm had settled over him now, the initial panic replaced by resolute determination. "The brothers know what to do. Our concern must be your safety." Left unspoken was the knowledge that a foreign Christian would be a prime target for the mob's fury.

They moved like ghosts through Luxor's ancient streets, the same pathways that had witnessed the tread of pharaohs and priests, warriors and slaves for millennia. Now they bore witness to two men hunched in desperate flight, clinging to the deeper shadows where the firelight could not reach. The ancient stones beneath their feet seemed to pulse with memories of other flights, other fires, other times when violence had swept through this ancient place.

As they turned a corner, Maddison caught sight of another house erupting into flames, the fire climbing its walls like a hungry beast from the Duat. A family fled the building, their silhouettes black against the inferno, carrying children and dragging elderly relatives. The screams that accompanied the conflagration would haunt his dreams for years to come, primal expressions of fear and loss that transcended language.

"Where are we going?" he whispered as they paused in the shadow of a high wall, the rough mud brick cool against his back as he fought to catch his breath. His legs ached with the unaccustomed exertion, his lungs burning from smoke and fear.

"To the center of the city," Farouk replied, his eyes constantly scanning for danger, alert as a desert jackal. Sweat gleamed on his broad forehead, carving clean channels through the soot that had settled on his dark skin. "Where other foreigners live. You will attract less attention there." His hand rested momentarily on Maddison's shoulder, a brief gesture of reassurance that conveyed both strength and comfort.

"And the discovery? The chamber?" Maddison couldn't keep the anguish from his voice. The culmination of his life's work, perhaps the most significant archaeological find since Tutankhamun's tomb, abandoned to the vagaries of mob violence and fire.

Farouk's face, usually as impassive as the ancient stone carvings they had been studying, softened momentarily. The lines around his eyes crinkled with unexpected gentleness, a flicker of the deep friendship that had developed between the unlikely pair over years of academic collaboration. "God preserved it for three thousand years, Professor. He will preserve it a little longer." His faith, so different from Maddison's academic skepticism, nevertheless provided a strange comfort in this moment of chaos.

They continued their careful progress through the labyrinthine streets, occasionally forced to backtrack when confronted by roving groups of angry young men carrying torches and makeshift weapons—iron bars, wooden clubs studded with nails, the occasional gleam of a blade. The night seemed endless, time stretching like the desert itself as they navigated the increasingly dangerous city. Each alleyway might hold salvation or death, each shadow a potential threat or haven.

The stars overhead, when occasionally visible through the smoke, seemed cold and distant, the same stars that had witnessed the glory of ancient Thebes now bearing witness to its modern suffering. The warm night air grew increasingly thick with smoke, making breathing difficult and further hampering their progress.

Finally, they reached a modest two-story building near the center of Luxor, its windows dark but intact, standing as an island of calm in the sea of chaos. Farouk produced a key from his pocket and ushered Maddison inside with an urgency that brooked no argument, his large hand pressing against the small of the professor's back.

"Second floor," the bishop directed, pushing the professor toward a narrow staircase, the wood creaking beneath their combined weight. "The flat is secure. There is food and water. Lock yourself in." His voice had regained its customary authority, though tension still lingered in the set of his powerful shoulders.

Maddison turned, suddenly alarmed as realization dawned. "You're not staying?" The thought of being left alone in this unfamiliar place while the city burned around him sent a fresh wave of fear through his tired body.

Farouk's massive shoulders straightened, his silhouette against the doorway reminiscent of the ancient warrior-priests whose deeds were carved in stone on temple walls. The wooden cross on his chest caught a stray beam of moonlight, gleaming momentarily like a talisman against the darkness. "I must return to my flock. They need me more than you do now." His voice was gentle but firm, leaving no room for argument.

"But the discovery—our work—" Maddison protested weakly, knowing even as he spoke that his words were selfish in the face of the violence consuming the city.

"Will wait," Farouk placed a heavy hand on Maddison's shoulder, his touch conveying strength and reassurance. The calluses on his palm spoke of a man who had known physical labor as well as scholarly pursuits. "Stay here until I return. Do not attempt to leave, do not answer the door for anyone but me. Do you understand?" His dark eyes bored into Maddison's, demanding a promise.

The Englishman nodded, fear and frustration warring within him, his throat suddenly tight with emotion. "How long?" he managed to ask, hating the tremor in his voice.

"As long as necessary." With that, Farouk disappeared into the night like a desert mirage, his black cassock melding with the darkness as if he had been swallowed by the very shadows they had been using for protection. The soft click of the street door closing sounded unnaturally loud in the sudden silence.

The flat was small but clean, its spartan furnishings suggesting occasional rather than permanent habitation. A narrow bed with a simple metal frame occupied one corner, covered with a faded quilt embroidered with Coptic crosses. A small kitchenette with basic utensils stood opposite, while a wooden table with two chairs dominated the center of the room. A single bookshelf held a collection of religious texts in Arabic and English. Maddison suspected it was one of many safe houses maintained by the Coptic community for emergencies exactly like this one, a sanctuary in times of persecution.

He locked the door as instructed, testing the bolt twice to reassure himself of its solidity, then moved to the window, unable to resist the human impulse to witness disaster. The glass was grimy with desert dust, but clean enough to provide a clear view of the chaos below. From this vantage point, he could see several fires burning across Luxor, their orange glow like malevolent stars fallen to earth. The ancient skyline, normally so peaceful under the moon's glow, now resembled a vision from Dante's Inferno.

Occasional bursts of gunfire punctuated the night, each one making him flinch despite the distance. The sound would be followed by shouts—of triumph or pain, he could not tell. Somewhere in the distance, a woman wailed, the sound carrying clearly through the warm night air, raising the hairs on the back of his neck with its primal grief.

Hours passed with agonizing slowness. Maddison paced the small flat like a caged leopard, his mind racing between fear for his safety, concern for Farouk, and desperate yearning for the discovery they had been forced to abandon. The chamber had remained hidden for millennia, its secrets preserved by the shifting sands and forgotten memories of ancient Thebes. Would it survive this modern conflagration?

His fingers itched for pen and paper, for the comfort of academic work to distract from the fear that threatened to overwhelm him. The photographs he had managed to take of the hieroglyphics before their hasty departure were safely stored in his camera's memory card, but without his notes, without the context, they were merely beautiful images rather than revolutionary scholarship.

As midnight approached, he stood at the window again, watching the fires that had grown more numerous. The city he had visited many times throughout his academic career—always peaceful, always welcoming despite its poverty—had transformed into a battlefield overnight. The call to prayer, normally so haunting and beautiful as it echoed across the ancient ruins, was conspicuously absent this night, replaced by the discordant symphony of destruction.

The magnitude of what they had discovered in that hidden chamber beneath the Coptic church washed over him anew. Menkheperre claiming divine connection to Thutmose III, positioning himself as the reincarnation of the great pharaoh—it was revolutionary material that could fundamentally alter understanding of dynastic Egypt. The texts spoke of rituals unknown to modern Egyptology, of spiritual practices that bridged the gap between the monotheistic tendencies of Akhenaten and the traditional pantheon—a missing link in religious evolution.

If they survived to tell the world. If the chamber remained undiscovered by the violence sweeping through Luxor. If Farouk returned.

Too many ifs.

Maddison pressed his forehead against the cool glass of the window, exhaustion finally beginning to claim him after three days of scholarly frenzy followed by terror-fueled flight. The throb of a headache pulsed behind his eyes, his body's protest against the abuse he had subjected it to in the pursuit of knowledge.

"Will I get back to complete my task?" he whispered to no one, his breath fogging the glass. "Or is this again like last time?" The words fell into the empty room, weighted with decades of academic disappointment and perseverance.

The memory of presenting his earliest theories about the 18th Dynasty to the Royal Archaeological Society rose unbidden—the barely concealed smirks, the condescending questions, the whispers that followed him out of the lecture hall. Sir James Worthington's dismissive wave of his hand as he declared Maddison's work "speculative fancy without substantive evidence" still stung after all these years, the wound to his professional pride never fully healed.

The academic world had its orthodoxies, and those who challenged them did so at their peril. His subsequent relegation to teaching undergraduate survey courses while his peers led prestigious digs had been a professional wilderness from which he had only recently emerged, thanks largely to Farouk's support and connections.

Even with photographic evidence, even with the impeccable provenance of an untouched ancient chamber, would his colleagues believe him? Or would they dismiss his findings as they had dismissed his theories—as the fantasies of a man too long in the desert sun? Would Worthington and his ilk find some way to discredit him again, to push him back into academic obscurity just as vindication seemed within reach?

A distant explosion shook the building slightly, the glass vibrating against his forehead, drawing Maddison from his reverie. Whatever the future held for his discovery, survival had to come first. He moved away from the window and settled into the small armchair, its springs protesting beneath his weight, prepared for a long vigil.

He found himself involuntarily cataloguing the sounds of violence— the distant crack of gunfire, the occasional explosion, the sounds of breaking glass and wood, the shouts that sometimes rose to a crescendo before falling silent. Each had its own character, its own signature in the orchestrated chaos of the night.

In the darkness of the flat, with only the distant glow of fires to provide illumination, Professor Arthur Maddison contemplated the cruel irony of his situation. To have touched the face of history, to have glimpsed secrets buried for millennia, only to be torn away by the violent present before those secrets could be fully revealed—it was a torment worthy of the ancient gods themselves, a modern echo of Tantalus reaching for fruit that remained forever just beyond his grasp.

His eyelids grew heavy despite his determination to remain alert. The adrenaline that had carried him through their flight was ebbing now, leaving him drained and vulnerable to the exhaustion that had been building for days. As he drifted toward uneasy sleep, images of hieroglyphics danced behind his closed eyes—the sacred symbols telling their ancient story of power, divinity, and reincarnation across the ages. The falcon of Horus seemed to take flight from stone walls, the ankh pulsed with life-giving power, the cartouche of Menkheperre glowed with royal authority.

He would return to that chamber. He would complete his translations. He would show the world what he and Farouk had discovered, regardless of the academic ridicule that might follow. The truth of the past demanded to be known, to be freed from its stone prison after three thousand years of silence.

If he survived the night.

If the chamber remained untouched.

If Farouk returned.

Too many ifs, indeed.

Sleep finally claimed him, the sounds of a city burning fading into the background of his consciousness like the dying echoes of an ancient civilization. In his dreams, he walked the corridors of a temple long fallen to dust, guided by a figure in priestly robes who bore a striking resemblance to Farouk, seeking a truth that always remained one hieroglyphic panel ahead, just beyond his reach but eternally calling him forward into the heart of mystery.

To be continued….

Author Commentary & Notes

Understanding the Real People and Events Behind the Story

This novel is a work of historical fiction — but every fictional thread has been carefully woven through the fabric of real history.

What you've just read is not merely a tale for entertainment. It is a narrative built on extensive research into the Bible, Egyptian history, and ancient Near Eastern cultures. Wherever possible, I used the real names of historical figures, their actual timelines, and the locations, inscriptions, and the Egyptian records and the scriptural references that support or hint at their existence.

But history often leaves gaps — and it is in these gaps that storytelling begins.

— *Mechiel Pentz*

Rolf Krauss Chronology

The historical framework follows the Bible as a primary reference, synchronized with the Egyptian chronology as outlined by Rolf Krauss.

Kamose	1542-1539
Ahmose I	1539-1514
Amenhotep I	1514-1493
Thutmose I	1493-1482
Thutmose II	1482-1479
Hatshepsut	1479-1458
Thutmose III	1479-1426

The works of the ancient historian Josephus have also been considered, offering valuable insights into how later traditions preserved key historical moments.

Ancient Egypt Map

This map shows the cities, landmarks, and cataracts mentioned in the book, at the end of the 17th dynasty, for the reader's reference, spanning from Tjaru in the Nile Delta of Lower Egypt in the north to Meroe in the southern region of Nubia."

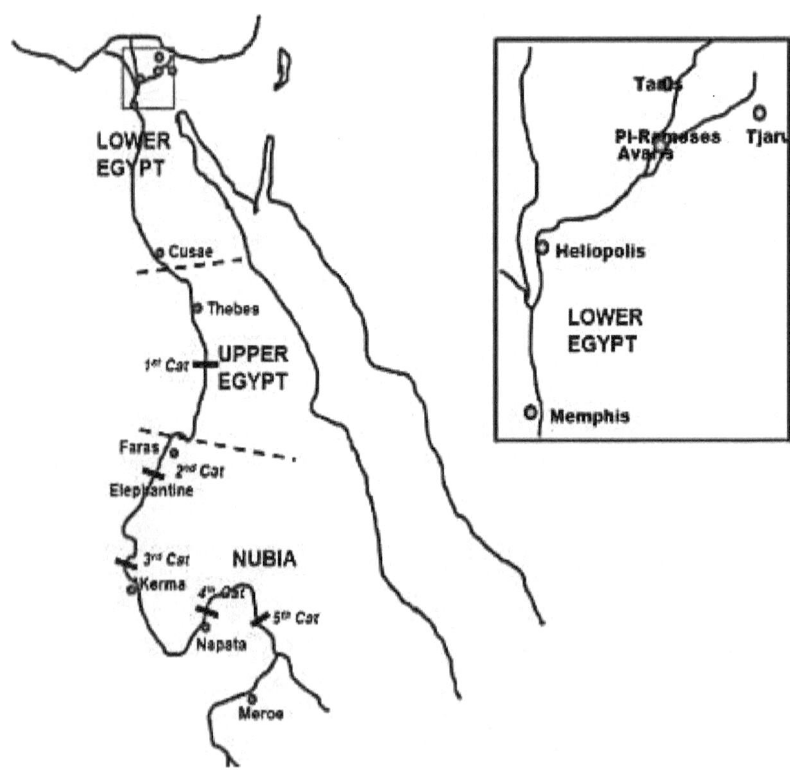

Hyksos Capital at Avaris

The Hyksos, a Semitic people who ruled Lower Egypt from 1637 BC-1529 BC (Rolf Krauss), allowed the Israelites to thrive in Goshen and their migration of non-herders and farmers towards Avaris. The Israelites and the Hyksos coexisted peacefully for over a century. This was a period of growth and stability for the Israelites,

Siege of Avaris

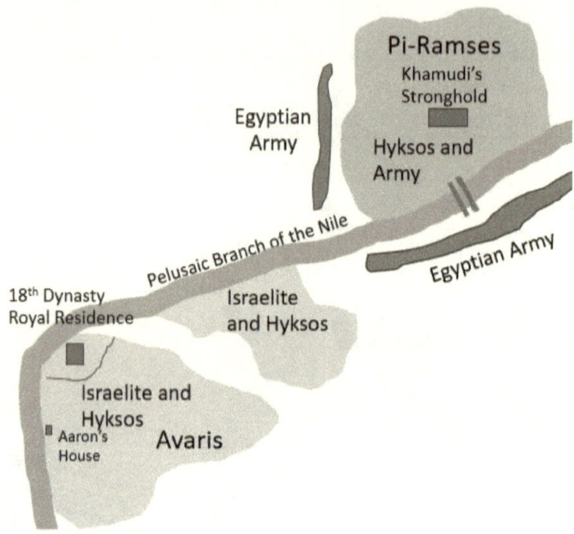

Thutmose II Nubian war and Moses Ethiopian war is the same

Ineni's inscription of Thutmose II Nubian war and Josephus' Moses Ethiopian war might actually be the same historical event through different cultural and historical lenses. Looking more closely at the parallels:

- The name connection: "Thutmose" can be broken down as "Thut-moses" - essentially containing "Moses" within it
- Both led identical first military campaigns against the same enemies (Nubians/Ethiopians)
- Both narratives share specific details like river conditions, sparing a royal woman and the fifth cataract
- Both conclude with the same outcome and Egyptian response
- Even the supporting characters have parallels as they both were still alive at this time (Mutnofret/Thermuthi)

Ethiopian war of Moses according to Josephus

Here is a theory explaining Josephus' account of Moses' Ethiopian

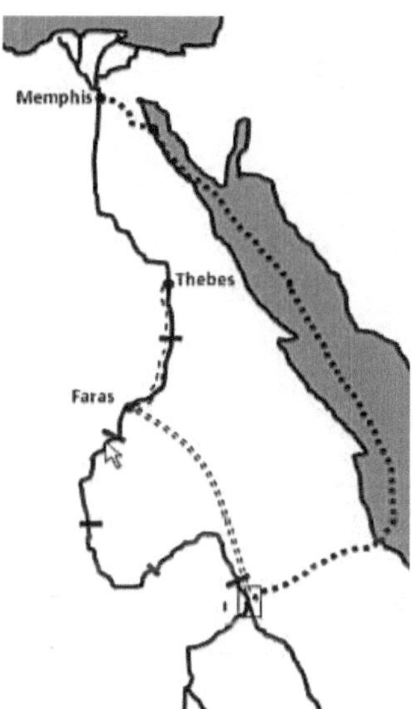

campaign that resolves the geographical confusion. Ten years after Thutmose I had pursued the Ethiopians beyond the 4th cataract, they regrouped beyond the 5th cataract and orchestrated a sophisticated two-pronged revenge attack against Egypt - a naval strike against Memphis via the Red Sea as a diversion, while their main forces prepared to advance from their southern stronghold. Josephus' account becomes more strategically coherent when considering the role of naval operations along the Red Sea. The Ethiopians likely launched a sophisticated two-pronged attack: first sailing from their territory to Ain Sukhna (a key ancient Egyptian port on the Gulf of Suez) using their impressive Nubian vessels—the same type of ships that Hatshepsut would later deploy in her famous Punt expedition, where Nubian maritime expertise was prominently featured. This naval force struck Memphis as a deliberate diversion, compelling Pharaoh to redirect his primary defensive forces northward. With Egypt's military attention fixed on Memphis, the main Ethiopian army prepared to advance from the south across their traditional border. This strategic situation explains why Pharaoh, desperately needing to counter this southern threat while his main army was occupied in the north, turned to Moses for leadership.

9 781764 162555